Twisted Lights

Twisted Lights

Susan M. Hoskins

Integrity Press, Ltd.
Fairway, KS

Published by
Integrity Press, Ltd.
P.O. Box 8277
Prairie Village, KS 66208

Printed in the United States of America

Second printing of *Twisted Lights* December 1997

Editor: Roderick Townley
Cover design and layout: Smart Graphics
Production management and marketing: Paul Temme
Publicity: Diana Trott, Holistic Marketing Cooperative

Library of Congress Cataloging-in-Publication Data
Hoskins, Susan M.
            Twisted Lights
1. fiction
catalog card number 97-072394
ISBN 0-9656581-0-4

To Our Readers:

We honor the sacred place within each of us that
is the true source of inspiration. With gratitude
and purpose, we present *Twisted Lights.*

Integrity Press, Ltd.

D e d i c a t i o n

To Kathleen, for revealing my scars.
To Philip, for loving them.

I dedicate *Twisted Lights* to the memory of my father,
Joseph A. Hoskins.
His spirit and love, his integrity and compassion
will remain forever in my heart.

Acknowledgments

I would like to acknowledge and thank a woman who is my faithful friend and spiritual mentor. Without her wisdom and guidance, the realization of my dream would not have been possible. Thank you, Rayna Horner, for your tremendous contribution to my growth and my work.

I would like to thank my family for their love and support through a most challenging period of my life. Thank you for your belief in my ability to achieve my goals. To my daughter, Danaria, you have been my inspiration to become more and do more than I ever thought possible.

To my dear friends, thank you for viewing me with eyes that did not waver. Thank you for helping me hold a vision. That which was conceived in spirit has now, with your help, become reality. I am most grateful.

Integrity Press, Ltd. has been blessed with a tremendous team of creative people. I am honored to know and to have worked with Diana Trott, Chris Smart and Paul Temme. I am most grateful to my gifted editor, Roderick Townley, for his talent, suggestions and encouragement. Thank you for challenging me to reach deeper within myself to set a higher standard and to aspire to reach that place . . . just beyond my grasp.

Susan M. Hoskins

In addition to being an intrigue novel, *Twisted Lights* is a story about personal transformation. It is a story about the healing of the mind, body, and spirit. *Twisted Lights* speaks to the spark of heroism contained within all of us. There are no throwaway people. Everyone has the potential to be more than what they are.

Susan M. Hoskins

PART I

Paul Owens finished his third cocktail just as the plane made its final approach into Kansas City. His flight from Pittsburgh had been uneventful but he was anxious for United 799 to land. Grabbing his suitbag and his carry-on, he quickly deplaned.

Owens was edgy. A lean, lanky man in his late forties, he had sandy blond, slightly graying hair, brown eyes and a pleasant smile. But today his palms were sweating and his eyes sparkled behind the gold wire-rim frames.

Walking the short distance from the plane to the gate area, his eyes quickly scanned the faces of those waiting for deplaning passengers. Towards the rear, above the crowd, he saw the placard. In big bold letters was the name OWENS. Waving, he acknowledged that he was indeed the man sought.

"Mr. Owens? Good evening. My name is Thomas. I'll be your driver this evening. May I carry your bags?"

Paul smiled at the handsome black man dressed impeccably in a three-piece pin-stripe suit.

"Any other luggage, sir?"

It was then that Paul Owens smiled a most mischievous grin.

"I'll only be staying the night, Thomas. This is everything I'll need."

"Right this way, sir. Please follow me. Did you have a pleasant flight?"

Seeing the white limousine, Paul Owens felt his pulse race. How he yearned for these layovers in Kansas City! This was his third such excursion in recent months. Somehow these trips were the only diversion which gave his life pleasure.

The chauffeur opened the rear door to the limo. Paul's knees buckled slightly as he stepped inside. Collapsing into the plush leather seat, he dared to glance up. It was then Paul saw the vision he had waited weeks to see again. It was not a dream. She was real.

With some difficulty, he found his voice. "Hello, Sabrina."

The magnificent blonde leaned forward and kissed him with luscious full lips that stirred him like no other woman he had tasted.

"You look beautiful," he said. Like a smitten schoolboy, Owens glanced at his mistress—or so he liked to imagine her—with unrestrained admiration. "It's so good to see you again."

Relishing the adoration, Sabrina sat back in the limousine, facing Paul as the driver sped away. Her low husky voice was like silk to his ears.

"I've missed you, Paul. I'm glad you're here. I have a wonderful evening planned for us."

Paul Owens was a self-made, independent businessman who defined the meaning of control. Except in Sabrina's presence. This woman had the ability to set his soul on fire.

He guessed her to be about twenty-eight, although she spoke very little about herself. She was not from Kansas City, that much he knew. She was working her way through school. Or so she said. He didn't like thinking about that. He preferred to imagine that she was his alone. Yet he didn't even know her last name.

She stood nearly six feet tall and her platinum hair was long and straight. She had baby blue eyes and high cheekbones. She'd been a lingerie model until she'd found this, an even more lucrative profession. He didn't want to dwell on the particulars of her profession. Not now.

She leaned forward. She wore a sheer, low cut, cream silk blouse. No bra. Her surgically perfected, voluptuous breasts were partially exposed. Her nipples stood firm and hard, enticing him. His imagination started running wild. She wore a short black leather skirt, revealing her garter belt and sheer black hose. Her long, slender legs drew his lustful glance. She wasn't wearing panties.

Seeing him squirm, she smiled. "Here, darling. I've made you a pitcher of martinis stirred with olives just the way you like it."

Handing him a martini, her free hand caressed his inner thigh. Paul was immediately aroused. He wanted her now. Here in the limo. But that would never do. He had reserved her for the night. He had to make it last.

"It's perfect," he said, sipping the martini.

Once again Sabrina leaned towards him, running her fingers through his hair. It was cold outside, late November. Yet inside the limousine, Paul Owens was sweating.

"Relax, darling. We have a long ride."

Owens loosened his tie as he thoughtfully sipped his martini. He tried to imagine what it would be like having Sabrina waiting at home every night. He had no wife, no children, no family at all really. A workaholic trying to build an empire, he had little time for friends. This was not a night to think about business. This was a night of indulgence. A night to fulfill all the fantasies he denied himself.

As her tapered fingers traced the outline of her creamy throat, Owens willed the limo faster through traffic. He could barely wait to get to the hotel. Twenty-four uninterrupted hours of anything he desired. Anything he could imagine.

In less than half an hour, it would all begin. Accepting a second martini, he attempted to relax and endure the ride from the airport to the Plaza. It reminded him of sexual bondage. First the pain and then the pleasure. Sabrina's perfume filled the limousine. His mind was reeling.

"Look, Paul. We're coming into the Plaza. I wish you could be here next week. They turn on the Plaza lights Thanksgiving night. It's beautiful. You'd love it."

Owens stared at Sabrina but his eyes just wouldn't focus. He had to back off the martinis. It wouldn't do to be drunk tonight. He couldn't bear to miss a single moment with her.

"Here we are, Paul. I've checked us into the hotel already. Thomas will bring your bags up later. You won't need a thing for what I have in mind."

Thomas pulled the limo into the driveway of the posh Michelangelo Hotel. Rather than stopping at the main lobby, he pulled the car around to a side entrance.

"Come, darling. The suite is ready."

Thomas assisted his passengers from the rear door. Sabrina took Paul by the arm and led him away. In a hushed voice, Sabrina gave final instructions to the driver.

"I'll call down when we're ready."

Alone on the elevator, Paul Owens took the lovely Sabrina in his arms. His kiss was too short. The elevator door opened. Sabrina led him down the softly lit hallway to the room at the far end of the east corridor. Using the electronic card, she opened the door to Room 413, the magnificent suite her service always reserved for this purpose.

The Michelangelo was perhaps the finest hotel in Kansas City. Overlooking the Country Club Plaza, the visitor had a panoramic view of the lovely shops and horsedrawn carriages below. The suite comprised a huge sitting room and master bedroom furnished with eighteenth-century English antiques. A spacious bath adjoined the bedroom.

"Everything is ready, Paul. Follow me."

Allowing himself to be led, Paul followed Sabrina into the huge living room. He seemed unsteady on his feet. His eyes would not quite focus.

"I want you to go into the bathroom and change into the robe. You'll find everything you need. But first, darling, may I have the money?"

Paul fumbled in his pocket for the packet of money and waited as she counted twenty hundred-dollar bills. To most men, two thousand dollars for one night of sex would seem absurd. To Paul, the pleasure he'd found with Sabrina was worth every cent. Besides, for one sum, the limousine, hotel and room service were included.

She smiled, placed the envelope on the small coffee table by the sofa, and led her client into the bedroom.

"Hurry, darling. Get ready. I can't wait for our night to begin. The champagne is chilled. I'll pour us a glass."

Teasingly, she took him in her arms and allowed her tongue to play with his. Waves of exquisite pleasure shot through his body.

"Go change, Paul. I'll get our glasses."

Sabrina waited until the door to the bathroom had closed. Then she dialed downstairs. When the familiar voice answered, she said, "Tell Thomas we're nearly ready. Give me ten minutes."

Paul felt better when he came out of the bathroom. He was naked under the hotel's robe of navy blue. Sabrina gently guided him towards the bed.

"Unbutton your blouse," he told her. "I want to see your breasts."

Doing as he commanded, Sabrina allowed the creamy silk blouse to fall to the floor.

"Oh God," he moaned. "You're so beautiful. I want you now."

"Let's not rush, Paul. Let me get our champagne."

She returned in a moment with two chilled glasses. With slightly quivering hands he accepted his.

"To time standing still," she said as they clinked their glasses.

"Naked," he slurred. "I want you naked."

Sabrina slowly unbuttoned her skirt. "Drink up, darling. Tell me where you want me to begin."

Paul couldn't answer. He just stared with vacant, glassy eyes. He didn't realize he was on the floor. He didn't hear the knock at the door. He didn't notice Sabrina dress quickly then answer it. He didn't hear the voices. He didn't see the four men gathered in the living room. The first man he would have recognized as Thomas. The other three were strangers. One man, the shorter of the two, was Iranian. The older man carried a doctor's black bag. The final one, Sabrina's boss, carried an ice chest and a heavy leather bag.

"Is he ready?" the doctor inquired.

"Yes," Sabrina answered.

"Where's the money?" the one known as Nathan demanded.

Sabrina handed him the envelope. He counted the money carefully, then smiled and handed her half. This was nearly twice the amount she usually made.

"Good work, Sabrina. Enjoy your bonus. Now go."

Wistfully, she glanced back to the bedroom and the man she had come to rather like. She started to ask what would happen but Nathan silenced her with a killer glance.

This was the third time this had happened, with a client she knew and liked. She wished she could stop it. She couldn't. Better not to ask. The one named Nathan was her ruthless pimp. Thomas, the driver, was a former cop.

Sabrina told herself she had a job to do. She did it well. She knew she would never see Paul Owens again. What happened to him after tonight, she didn't know and didn't want to know.

The four men waited until she had departed. It was the Iranian who said, "The plane is waiting. Let's proceed."

Thomas unzipped the cumbersome leather bag and got the supplies they required. Towels, a rubber sheet, a zipped body bag. The two men rearranged the furniture in the living room to give the doctor the space he required. Only when the rubber mat and towels were in place, did they bring in Paul, alive but unconscious. He had been primed with laced martinis but the potent final drug had been carefully placed in the champagne. He would feel no pain. But he had been denied his final pleasure.

Placing him face down on the rubber sheet, the three men stood quietly, respectfully, to the rear as the doctor knelt down over the body. Not one of the three men wanted to be physically involved. The mere sight of what was to come caused them to gag. It was the small Iranian man who waited most anxiously.

Opening his black leather bag, the middle-aged Caucasian doctor picked out the tools he would need. First he donned sterile gloves. Then, taking his sharpest scalpel, he made a single precise incision. He was careful not to splatter unnecessary blood. Using retractors, he pulled back flesh and bone to get to the area he wanted. With crude metal staples he deftly clamped off arteries, then soaked up the pool of blood inside the chest cavity with sponges. Only when he located the precious organs, did he smile.

Short and bald, William Scofield at fifty-four was not very pleasing to the eye. He was, however, a skilled surgeon who could separate himself quite easily from the job he had to do. Deep inside he enjoyed the drama. Pausing a moment over his patient, he turned to the anxious men behind him. Locking eyes with the small pensive Iranian, he permitted himself a smirk. In this one brief moment, it was as if he were God, solely responsible for the commodity he had created.

"Will you look at this!" he exclaimed gleefully. "Two of the most beautiful kidneys I've ever seen!"

c   h   a   p   t   e   r   *2*

Solomon Bucy waited patiently for the private jet to taxi to its
hangar. He was dressed in the uniform of a lawyer, in a three-piece
Hart Shaeffner and Marx suit and wing-tip shoes. He was a
paunchy middle-aged man with thinning black hair. His thick
neck, double chin and flabby lips made him a ludicrous sight, particularly with the reading glasses that perched precariously on his
most prominent feature. No matter how tailored his vest nor
strong his suspenders, his gut still protruded, betraying the
lifestyle he had chosen for himself.

At the age of forty-eight, he was a tenacious attorney who had
once had an honorable reputation. Having worked for one man
too long, he was now, like his client, a man feared and shunned by
his peers. His client was Michael Clay, whose private jet came to
a stop a short distance from where the attorney was standing.
Clearing his throat, Solomon wiped his glasses clean as he waited
for his client to disembark. He was nervous. Solomon hadn't seen
Michael Clay since he'd left Velours in June for six months of rehabilitation at the Craig Hospital in Denver, a facility specializing in
upper spinal cord injuries. After so long communicating only by
phone, Solomon had no idea what to expect or what to say.

How do you tell a man like Michael Clay how sorry you are for
his loss? And just which loss would you be addressing? It took a
few minutes for Clay to be off-loaded from the jet. Solomon slowly
approached but Clay barely acknowledged his presence. Bucy

waited until the lift to the waiting van was lowered and Michael, with assistance, was wheeled on board. Only when Clay's chair had been strapped in place was Bucy summoned to join Michael Clay, his driver, Max, and the man who would become Clay's closest associate, his personal care attendant, Tony Baxter.

Solomon attempted small talk as the van pulled away from the airfield onto the main road, but his attempts were rebuffed. Bucy chose not to be offended. It was Michael Clay who had requested the meeting. When it suited Clay, their business would commence. In the meantime, he tried not to stare at the man who had once been the dynamic, power-driven broker he had known. There was no sparkle left in Michael's eyes nor lilt to his once resonant voice. Michael Clay, who once made men tremble in his presence, was now completely dependent on personal care attendants for every bodily need.

It was a dismal afternoon in the town of Velours, nestled in the rolling hills of bluegrass Kentucky. The sky was dark and dirty. It was chilly but not cold enough to snow. Instead a light mist had begun to fall. It was the week before Christmas, yet it was clear from Michael's demeanor that he felt no holiday cheer as the van sped into town. Crippled by a spinal cord injury, as a result of the collapse of the Maggie Hall Casino in April, Michael Clay had dreamed of returning home all during the endless days he spent in rehab, watching summer turn into fall and fall into winter outside the tiny window of his room.

Today, at last, he was free. Yet the day held no joy for Michael Clay. As the sole heir of the most powerful family in Velours, Michael had grown up knowing only wealth and power. Unlike his father, Martin, who had retained a measure of ethics, to Michael power was an insatiable addiction, and corruption merely a means to his end. The indulged boy had grown into manhood playing people like pawns in a chess game. And until that fateful night in April, when the casino collapsed and his father was killed, he had been invincible. Now his life lay in ruins just like Maggie Hall.

Crushed under the weight of the fallen balcony, Clay had sustained a serious spinal injury at vertebrae C-3 and C-4. The injury was not complete; his spinal cord was damaged but not severed.

He had only limited movement in his arms, none in his legs, and none in his fingers or hands. He had no control of his bladder or bowels. Finally after weeks of rehabilitation he could breathe without a ventilator, but he was susceptible to pneumonia, bladder and colon infections, and a score of other maladies. He could do nothing for himself but talk, maneuver his electric wheelchair using his arm to guide a joystick, and, perhaps most importantly, think.

His thoughts were often his only companion, particularly during the hours of midnight to dawn.

Nearing their turn, the driver cocked his head slightly and queried, "Home, sir?"

There was loathing in the very word. Michael Clay had no real home, not anymore, not without his wife, Kathleen, and their son, Daniel. Even his own widowed mother, Margaret, had fled Velours after the Maggie Hall disaster. Because of Michael's involvement, her husband was dead, her name disgraced. All she retained was her own personal fortune. With no regret, nor thoughts of her crippled son, she moved away, leaving Michael to fend for himself.

Thinking he'd not been heard, Max repeated his question.

"Are we going straight home, Mr. Clay?"

"No, Max, not just yet. Take me to Maggie Hall."

Incredulous, Solomon Bucy glanced at Michael. Without thinking he repeated, "Maggie Hall?"

Michael's cold eyes dismissed further comment. As best he could without the ability to move his head, he allowed his glance to roam the manicured streets of his city. Block after block of rambling Victorian mansions were aglow with holiday decorations. Yet his focus was not upon Christmas. He had a purpose that kept him alive and kept him going. It was not to walk or to reclaim his vitality. These were goals which were far beyond his reach. No, having lost everything worth having, there was only one thing which was truly important. That was revenge against his wife for taking their son and deserting him. Revenge was the single driving force that kept breath flowing in his feeble body. It was his reason for waking in the morning and the lullaby that rocked him to sleep at night.

At the age of thirty-six, Michael Clay had been a handsome

man with a well-toned physique. After months in the hospital, his robust body had withered, giving him the look of a frail, much older man. Glancing at his reflection in the driver's mirror, Michael was relieved that at least his face looked familiar. His angular features were still rigidly defined. His hard, determined jaw set the stage for his pinched lips and angry mouth. His salt and pepper hair had grayed since the accident, giving him the distinguished look of a gentleman.

The van came to a halt atop a hill overlooking the Ohio River. Before them lay the ruins of Maggie Hall. Sickened by the sight of what had once been a magnificent hotel and casino, Max glanced away. Tony stared with fascination. Solomon fixed his gaze upon his client who without the ability to turn his head could only glance with peripheral vision.

It was rumored that Clay had ordered the hotel and casino destroyed after the collapse of the casino walkways, fearful that his involvement in the disaster would be revealed. During construction, Clay, as president of the development company in charge of the project, had authorized the substitution of inferior bolts for the tensile grade steel the engineer had ordered. It was simply a matter of economics. The inferior bolts were available. The tensile grade steel had to be ordered. In order to complete the project and open the casino on time, the inferior bolts had been installed. The inspector had been bribed and a few thousand dollars saved. Yes, merely to open the casino on schedule, a hundred people lay dead, and scores more maimed. Now all that was left of Maggie Hall were the charred remains of its shell and the pile of debris left behind.

Clay's eyes remained fixed but his mind flashed back to the gala. In gruesome, vivid detail, he saw them all once again. Fifteen hundred people, dressed in their finest regalia, laughing, drinking, having a great time gambling....

First he had heard it—the crack—like the popping explosion of a fireworks display. Then he had seen it. He had been trapped on the main floor underneath the suspended walkway. Surrounded by a crowd of people likewise unable to move, Michael had watched helplessly as the walkway ruptured, suspending people midair, then vomiting its guts to the floor below.

The screams . . . even now he could hear the screams of those on or below the balcony's surface as, for many like Michael, life as they had known it came to a crushing end.

Michael Clay could stand the scene in his mind no longer. "Tony, go for a walk with Max. I want a few words in private with my attorney."

Clay remained silent until both his attendant and driver departed. Then he asked, "Just how *bad* are things, Solomon?"

Bucy shook his head sadly. "The situation is much worse than we first expected. There is a criminal investigation under way and a huge class action suit has been filed against your development company on behalf of the victims and their families. If it can be proved that you knowingly approved the substitution of the inferior bolts which caused the balcony to collapse . . . or that you bribed inspectors to falsify reports . . . your insurance company will wash their hands of all liability. In other words, Michael, the plaintiffs will come after *you* personally. In anticipation of this, your personal assets as well as those of the company have already been frozen. I'm afraid it doesn't look good."

Michael permitted himself the luxury of a small smile. "I wonder how much it really matters. Between the hospital here in Velours and my stay at Craig, my insurance coverage is nearly exhausted. Do you have any idea how much my care will cost per year? Knowing the court system, I'll have my assets spent before anyone can touch them!"

Clay laughed but it was not a pleasant sound. Bucy felt queasy. There was something about Clay's demeanor that disturbed him.

"Where's my wife?"

Solomon's mouth grew dry as he sought to avert his client's gaze. He didn't want to answer the question. Kathleen Callihan Clay had suffered enough. She deserved whatever solace she might have found. While his father had been killed and Michael crippled, Kathleen had been brutally disfigured in the Maggie Hall disaster. It was while she was still trying to cope with the shock of her disfigurement that a news anchor by the name of Sydney Lawrence discovered and revealed Michael's involvement in the disaster. With Sydney's help, Kathleen fled Velours with her son and little more than the clothes on her back, leaving her husband paralyzed, unable to stop her. For the past seven months she'd remained in hiding, dreading the day he'd be well enough to try to find her.

"I'll only ask you one more time, Solomon. Where is my wife?"

"Let it be, Michael. You have enough trouble."

Clay's eyes narrowed. For a few seconds, it seemed difficult for him to breathe. There was a cold edge to his voice when he finally spoke. "She took my son. I want him back."

Sighing, Bucy relented. "Kathleen is hiding in Boston, that's all I know. She's being exceedingly careful. Her face is a mess, Michael. She'll need major reconstructive surgery. I can only assume that she'll remain in Boston until the surgery is completed."

"I don't give a damn about her face!" Clay countered. "She betrayed me, Solomon. She left me and took my son!"

Bucy stalled. He liked Kathleen. Perhaps better than anyone else, he understood why she had abandoned Michael Clay. Throughout their years—nearly fifteen in all—of marital hell, Clay had brutalized Kathleen, physically and emotionally. He robbed her of her spirit. He kept her his virtual slave. He tried to convince her that she was nothing without him and he beat her down to the point that she nearly believed him. Yet he failed to conquer her completely. Deep within, Kathleen harbored a secret strength, and in a way the collapse of Maggie Hall helped her to release it. Although she was mangled, she didn't succumb. Instead she rose to claim what was hers. Her life. It seemed worth the risk.

In losing her beauty, Kathleen Callihan Clay lost everything she thought mattered. With the help of Sydney Lawrence she fled Velours with her son at the only time in his life Michael was powerless to stop her. For once, she treated him as she'd been treated. This was part of what he couldn't forgive. But only part.

Solomon Bucy admired Kathleen, but seeing the determined resolve in Clay's eyes, he realized that his loyalty must remain with the man who paid his fee.

"Perhaps I know someone with the time and expertise to track her down." Bucy's hesitation was laced with emotion. "A man . . . willing to do . . . whatever he's told."

For the first time during their brief meeting, Michael Clay truly smiled, causing Solomon Bucy to chill.

"Get him," Clay decreed.

For months, Michael Clay had thought of little but his wife during the sleepless hours between midnight and six. Yet again he imagined his campaign of revenge. How he would do it or where, he didn't know. But somehow, revenge would be his. He didn't dare say it aloud, but uppermost in his mind was the thought, "You'll suffer, Kathleen. That I promise."

Susan M. Hoskins

Solomon Bucy parked his Cadillac as close to the building as he could. Ralph Noland's neighborhood made him uneasy, here in The Bottoms on the city's east side. After activating the security system on his car, Solomon glanced hastily down the block. Seeing no one, he hurried into the decrepit building. In the hallway, he pulled a crisp, new, linen handkerchief from his breast pocket and wiped his hands. Just being here made him feel dirty.

Puffing, he climbed the three flights to his brother-in-law's apartment. He hadn't bothered to call. He knew he would find Ralph at home. Now he could only hope that he would find him sober. He rapped on the door sharply, then waited. When there was no reply, he turned the knob and stepped inside. The television was blaring. Ralph didn't hear his name being called.

"For God's sake!" Bucy shouted. "Turn down the noise!"

"Is that you, Sol? Come on in, man." Noland fumbled for a remote to switch off the TV. "Can I get you a beer?"

Glancing around the messy apartment, the attorney shook his head.

"You're a pig, Ralph. How can you live like this?"

Bucy searched the living room for a place to sit, some place not littered with clothes or beer bottles, or cluttered with papers. Finding none, he chose to stand.

Ralph struggled to his feet.

"I'm sorry, man," he stammered. "I wasn't expecting company. Here, take my chair. I'll get you a beer."

"Don't bother," Bucy murmured. Ralph ignored him.

Heading into the kitchen, he opened the refrigerator and grabbed two cans of Coors.

"To what do I owe the pleasure of this visit?" he asked, staggering to Solomon's side.

"Sit down!" Bucy ordered. "I've got something important to tell you."

"Yes, sir," Ralph collapsed on the couch. "Whatever the hell you say!"

His tone softening just a bit as he sat down in the armchair across from Noland, Solomon asked, "How are you, Ralph?"

"I'm fine, man. It's good to be home."

"Did they treat you okay at the mental health center?"

"They treated me like crap, Sol. I'm nothing but a stinking veteran no one wants to bother with. But what do you expect? Nobody cares if vets live or die. Either way, we're nothing but a goddamn problem."

Solomon sipped his beer slowly while he studied his brother-in-law. Ralph was not well, that was plain to see. He'd been a strong, muscular man. But the last few months had taken their toll. Now he was consumed with self-pity and sinking fast. His rugged, worn features made him look older than his thirty-nine years, and his melancholy blue eyes were puffy.

"I thought you were going to stop drinking," Bucy chastised gently. "You gave Lois your word."

"My word don't mean nothing, Sol. You should know that by now."

"Your sister cares about you, Ralph. You promised her you'd do better."

Sighing deeply, the younger man glanced away. "How is Lois?" he asked finally. "I meant to come see her this week."

"She's fine," Solomon replied tightly. "It's you we're worried about."

"I'm okay, really I am. Tell Lois I'm fine, Sol. Don't tell her I've been drinking."

Bucy looked away as Noland began to weep. Finally he felt compelled to console the man.

"I'm sorry you lost your job, Ralph. You were a fine police officer. You deserved better."

"I was a damn good officer! It's not fair what they did to me, Sol. It's just not right!"

Solomon Bucy had to agree. Married to Ralph's sister for twenty-two years, he'd known Noland for over two decades. Ralph Noland was born the younger of two children to Fred and Pauline Noland in Pryor, Oklahoma. Fred was a hard-drinking, three-pack-a-day smoker who worked for a local construction company when he was sober enough to hold a hammer. Pauline, a devout Catholic, was a homemaker. The family got along well in the community. But neighbors didn't know what occurred behind a locked front door. Fred was an abusive man who tormented his young son for never quite measuring up to his standards. Pauline, even while clutching her rosary, turned a blind eye to the abuse. Lois was safe from harm. She was a girl. Nothing much was expected of her.

Ralph hated his father for the constant torment, but he loathed his mother as well for allowing the beatings to go unchallenged. He graduated from Pryor High School in May of 1966 and was drafted the following June. Glad to leave home, he received his basic training at Ft. Polk, Louisiana. Ralph Noland was a physically fit, muscular kid who'd played varsity football. He stood about 6´1″ and weighed a hefty 225 lbs. Unlike most of his peers, he liked the challenge and the discipline he discovered in the Army. Most of all, he liked the opportunity to escape Pryor, Oklahoma, leaving an abusive father and an inept mother behind.

Very quickly, he demonstrated his skill with a rifle. He learned demolition, night escape and evasion tactics. He was enticed by the lure of Special Forces and a mission that would grant him extra pay and status. The assignment seemed straightforward. He, together with ten other guys, would be air dropped by helicopter behind enemy lines, to observe and report troop movement and create havoc when so ordered.

What his commander failed to tell Ralph was that the men would be scattered in different directions for weeks at a time, leaving Ralph alone in the jungle with only a shortwave radio and his supplies. The only voice Ralph heard was that of his commander, sporadically by radio when needed. He spent his time alone, observing the brutality of the North Vietnamese against the South. Villages were plundered, old men murdered, women raped, children slaughtered for sport or enslaved for labor. Ralph could do nothing but watch and report. He had no one to talk to; no one to share his fears. A young boy grew to manhood in the sweltering heat and humidity of the Vietnamese jungle. His body finished maturing; his mind remained fixed upon the horrors that he witnessed but couldn't share.

Vietnam was never declared a war. It was a police action. Ralph's assignment was never sanctioned. No one, not his family, not his friends, knew where he was. He wore no identification. It was part of the deal that earned him extra pay. If he had been killed, no one would have acknowledged his death. He would have been, like numerous others, just one more soldier forever missing in action.

Ralph was seemingly one of the lucky ones. After a year, he was sent back to the States to finish his time as an MP at Ft. Bragg, North Carolina. Ralph thought he'd be welcomed home as some kind of hero. He was wrong. Upon discharge from the Army, he discovered that a soldier who had served in Vietnam was a man despised. He had trouble finding a job. He drifted from place to place until he came to Velours to be near his sister, Lois, now married to Solomon Bucy.

Through his brother-in-law's connections, Ralph secured a position with the Kentucky State Police. He used his training and his experience in Vietnam to become an outstanding trooper. He was selected to become a bomb technician, strategically located between Louisville and Lexington. For a time, Ralph Noland was happy; but on April 9, 1987, his reasonably content world came crashing to an abrupt halt. The night Maggie Hall collapsed every available law enforcement officer—state and local, on-duty and off-duty—were dispatched to assist with the rescue.

With little training and no warning, Ralph Noland found himself part of the rescue team. He thought he'd be prepared to deal with the carnage after what he witnessed in Vietnam. But the sight of so much blood and gore brought back too many repressed memories of the "police action" he thought he'd forgotten.

Stoically, he tried to follow orders, wading through blood and pulling victims from the wreckage. He tried to match bodies that were no longer whole—scattered pieces of flesh, dismembered limbs, shattered skulls with vacant eyes.

In the end, the trauma proved too much. The flashbacks from Vietnam came back. And new nightmares began of a disaster he could never forget.

"They threw me off the force, Sol! They told me to file for disability. Thanks to that prick, the guy who *calls* himself a psychiatrist, I'll never work as a cop again."

"You're talking about Gerald Bradley and you're right, Ralph. He treated you unfairly. But there's nothing we can do about that." For the first time in a long while, Solomon Bucy felt a measure of sorrow. "You were a fine officer, Ralph. That's a fact."

"What am I going to do?" Noland cried, sobering more than he realized. "What in the hell am I going to do?"

"Listen to me, Ralph," Bucy said firmly. "Listen to me carefully! There's a man I want you to meet tomorrow morning when you're feeling better. He may have a job for you. It's a damn good opportunity, so don't blow it!"

Ralph Noland said nothing. Reaching for a cigarette, he examined the traces of nicotine staining his hands.

"You want to work again, don't you, Ralph?"

Tears filled his eyes. He nodded. "I'm useless unless I'm working. I'm good at what I'm trained to do. You know that, Sol."

"Yes," Bucy agreed gently, "I know. But you'll have to prove yourself again. The man I want you to see demands the best. He'll pay big bucks if you do the job right."

At the prospect of a job, Noland's eyes brightened. Thinking his life was over, he had given up hope. He wanted to work. All he needed was a chance.

"What do I have to do?"

"First, you've got to quit the booze. Not just for now, but for good. The man won't tolerate a drunk."

"What else?"

"Clean up, Ralph. I'll help you. We'll pick out some clothes. You can spend the night with Lois and me. You've got to be at your best in the morning. The man requires total loyalty."

Dragging on his cigarette, Noland nodded.

"One more thing," Bucy added. "Don't light a cigarette in his presence. He's a fanatic about smoking. Play his game. Dance to his tune. Whatever he says, you do it. Keep your mouth shut. Ask no questions. Don't repeat what you hear."

His curiosity aroused, Ralph Noland snuffed out his cigarette and leaned forward.

"Who's the man? What's the job?"

c　h　a　p　t　e　r　4

Michael Clay's first morning back proved difficult. Making the transition from the rehabilitation hospital to home was arduous. Providing adequate care required meticulous planning and trained execution. Everything took time. Patience was a virtue Michael would have to develop.

He'd been awakened at seven. His catheter was changed and a suppository given. After being fed a light breakfast, he was bathed and dressed. His personal physician arrived at eight-thirty for a brief exam and to check on the nurses he had ordered for the first few weeks of Michael's home care. A physical therapist stopped by to schedule sessions for the coming week.

The mansion had been renovated to accommodate his disability. A ramp was added to the main entrance outside and the doorways of all the interior rooms widened to oblige his wheelchair. An elevator was installed to give him access to the second story of the mansion. Even though all the accommodations had been completed satisfactorily, the Clay mansion didn't feel like home.

Michael came downstairs shortly before eleven. He dismissed Tony. He wanted a few quiet moments alone in the library to collect his thoughts. There was a roaring fire blazing in the hearth. Soft classical music graced the room. But Michael Clay found no solace in those amenities. After six months of grueling rehabilitation, he'd returned to his mansion. But without his family—his wife, son, mother and father—he had no home. And without the use of his body, his life at the moment had little meaning.

Promptly at eleven o'clock, Henry, the butler, showed Solomon Bucy and his brother-in-law into the library. Strapped securely in his wheelchair, Clay waited until the butler departed. His chair was locked and planted a few feet from the divan where he ordered the two men to sit.

Ralph Noland was a composite of contradictions. He was ordinary yet somehow different. Nothing was wrong but something was definitely not right. His hair was neatly combed and he wore a freshly pressed, coordinated suit and tie. Yet the sleeves of his jacket and pants were much too short, telling Clay immediately that his clothes had been borrowed.

There was more. So much more. Nothing could mask the puffy bleariness of his eyes, or the slight quiver to his hands, belying the drinking problem Ralph sought to hide. Yes, underneath Noland's shaky exterior, Clay detected a seething, boiling rage. And for his purposes, this was good. This was very good indeed.

Wilting under the intensity of Michael Clay's scrutiny, Ralph Noland yearned for a drink or at the very least a cigarette, neither of which he would receive here. Nervously he glanced away, focusing instead on the lavish furnishings of Clay's private study.

"You may be excused, Solomon. Wait in the foyer. I'll call you when I'm ready."

Reluctantly Bucy came to his feet. "Whatever you say, Michael." Turning to leave, Solomon caught Ralph for an instant in his peripheral vision. He said nothing but his message was abundantly clear. "This is it, you bastard! Don't screw up!"

Noland glanced away nervously.

Clay initiated the interview only after the door to the study had closed. "Tell me about yourself, Ralph."

Noland cautiously responded. "What would you like to know?"

"Who are you? What do you want?"

"I want a job," Noland stated humbly. "A chance, Mr. Clay. Just a goddamn chance!"

"Solomon said you'd been an officer with the Kentucky State Police. What went wrong?"

"It's like this, Mr. Clay. The night of the Maggie Hall disaster I was forced to see and do things that weren't human. I did my job, though, just like I was told. When it was over, I couldn't sleep. When I was awake, I just kept seeing the whole thing over and over again."

Ashamed, Noland paused.

"Go on," Clay encouraged. "Tell me what happened."

"I reported for work but I just couldn't function. I started drinking pretty heavy. I wasn't the only guy who had trouble, but I'm the one they singled out. My supervisor forced me into the hospital for an evaluation. They assigned me a shrink. I tried to explain what happened. He wouldn't listen. It was just like when I came home from 'Nam. Nobody wanted to know what it was like, so I just gave up."

Noland's cheeks flushed crimson. "The psychiatrist told my boss I was uncooperative and had me fired. He said I didn't have the ego strength to cope with Vietnam and now this disaster." Inhaling sharply, Noland continued. "It's true that this disaster brought back many ugly memories of the past. But the psychiatrist was wrong. He wasn't there. He doesn't know what it was like that night at Maggie Hall."

Ralph's eyes lingered on Michael's helpless body. With respect he said, "You and me were there. We know what it was like."

Clay nodded, encouraging Ralph to proceed.

"Things will never be the same. I miss my job. I miss my life." Feeling a kinship with the powerful man who sat before him, Ralph asked, "What do you miss the most, Mr. Clay?"

Michael Clay could have responded with a list of losses. Oddly, one thing in particular came to mind.

"I miss ribs, barbecue ribs. That was my favorite food as a kid. You can't eat barbecue ribs without your hands. And they don't taste the same cut up and fed to you on a fork. Isn't that something, Ralph? I miss barbecue ribs."

A sense of melancholy filled the library. Clay didn't desire to remain in silence for long. His eyes narrowed and his voice lacked warmth when he continued. "I know what Maggie Hall was like for me, Ralph. The experience must have been very different for you."

Oblivious to Clay's aloofness, Noland's anger began to surface. "It was hell! There were parts of bodies everywhere! The place reeked of blood. The smell . . . the smell reminded me of 'Nam."

"How long were you in Vietnam?"

"I served a year. I was a good soldier who never questioned orders. I did what I was told. I was a good cop, too. Now thanks to the bastard who calls himself a shrink, I'm finished."

Clay's attention perked at the mention yet again of the psychiatrist.

"Who was the doctor?" he questioned.

Hatred echoing in his voice, Noland spat, "Bradley . . . Gerald Bradley! That son-of-a-bitch wasn't there. If Gerald Bradley had seen what I did, I wonder how well he would have coped!"

Almost imperceptibly, Michael Clay smiled.

"What experience do you have?"

"What . . . experience . . . do you want?"

"What did you do in Vietnam? What have you done since?"

"In 'Nam, I was in Special Forces. I worked behind enemy lines doing reconnaissance and demolition. When I got home, I drifted around for a while until I landed a job with the Kentucky State Police. I became a bomb technician."

"With your experience, I trust you're well versed in surveillance."

Ralph nodded in agreement.

"What if you had a stakeout that required weeks, even months? Could you handle the boredom?"

"Not a problem, sir. I'm used to following orders."

Cocking his head, Clay scrutinized the desperate man. The silence was brutal. Noland began to sweat. Finally, Clay edged his chair closer.

"Have you ever killed a man, Ralph?"

Caught off-guard, Noland swallowed hard. Images of Vietnam filled his mind. Remembering the feel of his knife in another man's belly, Ralph Noland nodded.

Changing the subject abruptly, Clay asked, "Are you married?"

"No," Ralph answered quietly. "I've never had much luck with women."

Michael's voice softened. "My wife left me after I was paralyzed in the disaster. She took my son. I haven't seen them since."

Identifying with Clay, Ralph's thoughts turned to his own mother. He could still feel her betrayal.

Clay paused, then almost as an afterthought he asked, "Could you kill a woman if you had to?"

"If I had to," Noland declared. "I would!"

Without a smile, Michael abruptly concluded the interview. "It was nice meeting you, Ralph. Thank you for coming."

Sensing that his audience was over, Noland cried out, "I want a job! Please, Mr. Clay, just give me a chance! You won't be disappointed. You're the commander. I'm the soldier. Whatever vermin you want destroyed, I'll get rid of."

Ignoring the fervor in Noland's voice, Michael Clay terminated their meeting. "That will be all."

Dejected, Ralph Noland stood. He was being dismissed. He had lost again. His best just wasn't good enough. Little did he know he had the job. Like a broken, beaten dog, he was perfect.

■

After lunch and a brief rest, Michael was returned to the library to await his last appointment of the day. Promptly at two o'clock, he heard the doorbell, and then heavy footsteps as two men crossed the marble hallway to the library. The butler announced the visitor's arrival in a clear voice, "Dr. Bradley to see you, sir."

It was with great effort that Michael maneuvered the joystick on the right side of his electric wheelchair, allowing him to turn slightly and face his visitor.

"Would you like tea or coffee, Dr. Bradley?" Henry inquired.

"That won't be necessary," Clay replied curtly. "Our guest will not be staying long."

After the butler departed, Gerald Bradley, a man of slight build in his early fifties, greeted Michael Clay warmly. With a full mane of thick, white hair, his colleagues dubbed him the silver fox, not only for the color of his hair, but because of his unorthodox tactics as a psychiatrist.

"How nice to see you, Michael."

"It's been a long time, Gerald. Sit down."

"How are you feeling, Michael?" said Bradley, sitting on the divan. "Your physician tells me that you are progressing nicely."

Michael's left eye began to twitch. "I'm a quadriplegic with little hope of recovery. My wife has left me and my son is gone.

I'm being sued for millions and I'm under criminal investigation. If that is doing well, Gerald, then believe me I am superb!"

Loathing the pity he saw in Bradley's eyes, Michael Clay sought to change the subject. "And your wife, how is she?"

"Bernice is fine," the debonair physician replied. "She and the girls are out of town until late tomorrow evening. And frankly, Michael, I'm enjoying the peace."

"The 'piece'?" Clay bantered. "What's her name?"

Chuckling at their chauvinistic joke, the psychiatrist let down his guard.

"You wouldn't know her, Michael. She's not in your league. She has the IQ of an ant, but she's a hell of a good screw!"

Michael's gray eyes narrowed. "Another one of your patients, I presume?"

Bradley was astute enough not to answer, but neither did he blush or feel ashamed. Thinking himself superior to the frigid woman he had married, he felt no remorse bringing another to her bed.

Michael got to the point. "I trust you brought the tape."

Bradley snapped open the briefcase beside him. "I would have delivered it to you sooner," he replied. "But with the trauma of your injury, followed by the months of rehabilitation, it never seemed the right time."

Annoyed with Bradley's dribble, Clay snapped, "My wife's dark secret, what is it?"

Gerald Bradley glanced first to the tape and then to Michael before responding. "Are you really sure you want to know? As I indicated the day Maggie Hall collapsed, Kathleen's revelation may prove to be quite a shock...."

Born the eldest of three girls on a dirt farm outside of Velours, Kathleen Callihan grew up knowing only poverty and deprivation. She had graduated high school but college was beyond her grasp. She understood that to escape her dreary existence, she had to marry well. So shortly after her eighteenth birthday, Kathleen left home and moved to Velours. There, working as a waitress in a small cafe on the outskirts of town, she met Michael Clay.

Opposite ends of the pole of life, Michael and Kathleen were attracted to one another by a force more powerful than reason. Despite the objections of Michael's parents, a few months after they met, Kathleen Callihan indeed married well.

Having it all did not come cheap, and few if any knew the price Kathleen had to pay. Her heritage was thought unworthy of the Clays. Giving birth to Michael's heir gave her a measure of status but she was never welcomed into the family as an equal. Moreover, Michael had an unquenchable thirst for women. He made no secret of his many affairs. Only once did Kathleen try to get even. That mistake caused her nothing but heartache. She tried to bury her guilt deep inside, but every day she was forced to face the truth. She lived in constant terror that Michael would discover her sin. The burden finally became too great to carry alone. Hence, only hours before the collapse of Maggie Hall, she purged her soul. She shared her transgression with the only man she knew to trust—Velour's most respected psychiatrist—the good Dr. Gerald Bradley. She had no way of knowing that he would secretly tape their session.

Bradley leaned forward attempting to make Michael, like all his patients, feel more at ease. He spoke in the well-modulated voice he had practiced years to develop.

"Several years ago, your wife had an affair. It didn't last all that long . . . a few weeks . . . a few months . . . just long enough . . ." Bradley paused for effect. He shook his head then cleared his throat as if he were hesitant to proceed, ". . . to produce a child."

"That's not possible. You're mistaken."

Bradley was accustomed to dealing with people in denial. "Listen to me, Michael. Daniel is not your son."

The twitching of Michael's left eye intensified; otherwise, his stoic face betrayed no emotion. "Prove it."

"Remember your wife had problems getting pregnant? She saw a fertility specialist. The tests proved inconclusive. Her physician suggested it might be your problem."

Michael's features paled.

"He suggested that you be tested for a low sperm count. You refused. Then suddenly Kathleen got pregnant."

Bradley paused. Clay did not respond. Satisfied that he'd made his point, Bradley said, "I'm so sorry, Michael. Is there anything I can do to help? Perhaps if we talk . . ."

Clay struggled to control his rage. "Save it for your patients, Bradley. Our business is concluded. Leave the tape on the table, then get out of my sight!"

The psychiatrist stood, smoothing the lines of his cashmere jacket. An offensive odor emanated from Michael's chair. It was apparent that he had no control of his bowels. Gerald Bradley wrinkled his nose in disgust. Eyeing the tape a final time, he had to ask, "Are the procedures we discussed to be followed?"

With eyes of molten steel, Clay replied, "You'll find the money wired into your account in the morning."

Taking his cue, the psychiatrist turned to leave. Another day. Another dollar. He had a job to do. He did it well. For twenty-five thousand dollars, he had gained Kathleen's confidence then sold her out. It was simply a matter of economics.

Alone again, Michael glared at the tape. A sense of profound loss consumed him. He recalled an earlier time in his marriage. He'd dismissed the notion of a low sperm count as absurd. He was too much of a man. Instead he feared his promiscuity might lead to illegitimate claims against his estate. Therefore after Daniel's birth, in order to ensure his son's legacy, he'd undergone an irreversible vasectomy. Now there could never be a true Clay seed to carry on the family name. Bursting with rage, he yearned to strike out, but Kathleen Clay was nowhere to be found. And Daniel—the precious child who was not his son—was, in truth, the only human being besides Kathleen that he had ever loved.

The image of Gerald Bradley burned angrily in the recesses of his mind. The psychiatrist knew too many secrets. He was the only human being besides Kathleen who knew that Daniel was not his son. Suddenly Clay recalled the conversation that had occurred earlier today with Ralph Noland.

"Whatever vermin you want destroyed I'll get rid of!"

Clamping his eyes tightly shut, he cried out, "Tony, come here at once!"

Hearing the anger in his voice, Michael's personal care assistant ran into the library. "What is it, Mr. Clay?"

Clay struggled to steady himself. "I've had an accident that needs to be cleaned. Then call Solomon Bucy! Tell him to get Ralph Noland. The commander has his first assignment. Vermin are lurking in the shadows! The enemy must be destroyed!"

■

Slumped in his car parked across the dimly lit street, Ralph Noland stalked his prey. During the past two hours, under the cover of night, the ex-cop had determined several things. The alarm system on the house was not activated. The man and the woman were alone. There were no barking dogs to alert them.

Shortly before midnight, he had glimpsed the couple through the filmy curtains of the bedroom window, their naked flesh molded together in a passionate embrace. Thinking of Gerald Bradley stroking his whore, Ralph Noland grinned.

"Enjoy it, you bastard. Enjoy!"

Ralph waited patiently until the bedroom light went off and he thought his victims were asleep. Donning plastic gloves, he retrieved the only items he would need for the job—a penlight, a small knife and a gun. Creeping to the rear of the house, he deftly jimmied the lock with his knife. In less than a minute, the back door was open. Using his pin light for direction, he tiptoed soundlessly up the back stairs. He quickly located the master suite. There in the lavish king-size bed, curled in the rapture of each other's arms, he found the lovers asleep.

Stealing closer, adrenaline shooting through his veins, the pounding of his own heart was the only sound Ralph could hear. His eyes came to rest upon the woman. She was blond and voluptuous. Ralph guessed her to be about thirty. Her left thigh was thrust casually over her lover's leg, her head cocked to the right.

In his hand, Noland carried a Beretta Model 84, 380 caliber, fitted with a custom designed silencer to prevent any noise. He questioned which one to shoot first. If the woman woke suddenly she might panic and scream. It would be best if he killed her at once. Yet despite what he had told the commander, it was killing the woman that bothered him most.

Conjuring up images of his own mother, he pulled the trigger.

Hearing the puff of the silencer, Bradley stirred but did not wake. Noland edged closer. With great fascination, he examined the penis of the man who had robbed him, in essence, of his own manhood. Seeing Bradley's small, limp dick, Ralph nearly laughed aloud. For all his arrogance, Gerald Bradley was not nearly the great stud he pretended to be. Carefully he placed the cold steel of his Beretta against his enemy's testicles and pressed hard.

Bradley awoke with a start. His eyes focused slowly first on the figure at the end of the bed and then on the woman beside him. Man. Gun. Blood. Instinctively, he tried to back away, up and out of the bed. There was nowhere to go. He panicked, losing control of his bladder. Ralph Noland smiled. With perverse twisted pleasure, he pulled the trigger. In horror, Bradley shrieked in agony. Instinctively, he tried to stop the gush of blood flowing from the gaping hole of his genitals.

Sauntering to the side of the bed, Ralph knelt down. Driving the gun into the psychiatrist's cheek, Noland forced Bradley's glazed eyes to his. His hot mouth pressed against Bradley's ear, Ralph spoke in the very language the psychiatrist flaunted.

"It seems that you've experienced a terrible tragedy, Gerald. Is your ego strength intact? Can you cope?"

Realizing his death was imminent, the psychiatrist began sobbing. "Don't shoot!" he pleaded, gasping for air. "I'll do anything you want! Please, in the name of God, don't shoot!"

Noland glanced at his watch then stood.

"I'd really like to stay and discuss your feelings, Dr. Bradley. But unfortunately, your time is up."

Savoring each second of perverse pleasure, Ralph carefully steadied the revolver between the psychiatrist's horrified eyes. He then fired a single precise shot.

Moving away from the bed, he surveyed the damage. The bed was now soaked in blood, and the walls splattered with pieces of flesh. His mind flashed back to the night Maggie Hall collapsed. He recalled a similar horror, but this time, it was different. *He* was in control.

Noland left the lovers as they were. It would be awhile before the bodies were discovered. Hurrying down the stairs, Ralph cautiously peeked outside. The neighborhood was quiet. No one's sleep had been disturbed.

He waited until he reached his car and started the engine to hide his gun and remove his gloves. Driving home, he thought about his future. From now on, he would report directly to his brother-in-law, Solomon Bucy. Never again would he meet with the commander. His money waiting, his first job complete, Ralph would leave for Boston in the morning for his next assignment.

As he parked his car and stepped outside, he inhaled the brisk Kentucky night air and smiled. For the first time since the disaster, Ralph Noland had a purpose and a reason for being.

"The commander will be pleased. The enemy has been defeated, the vermin destroyed."

Susan M. Hoskins

It was a picture-perfect Christmas Eve in Velours, Kentucky. Shortly after dusk, a gentle snow had begun to fall, creating the illusion that soon St. Nick himself would come to call. It was the kind of Christmas the brokenhearted people of Velours never thought they would enjoy again. The collapse of Maggie Hall in April had permanently scarred this quiet peaceful community. No one who lived here had escaped the pain. Everyone knew someone profoundly affected by the disaster, from the victims to the rescue personnel.

On this Christmas Eve, there was not a man, woman or child who dared ask for a secret wish. Those whose loved ones had survived the collapse of Maggie Hall understood they had been granted their Christmas gifts for a lifetime. For the unfortunate others, there was no gift the good Lord could deliver that would repair their broken hearts.

In a lovely old Victorian house on a quiet street, a man and woman settled in to savor their first Christmas together. They had met shortly after the collapse of Maggie Hall. Sydney Lawrence was the lead news anchor covering the disaster. Sam Ellis had been the doctor in charge of the rescue operation. Their meeting was a blessing rising from the ashes of the disaster.

Sam would always cherish the first impression Sydney made. At thirty-two, she was a tall, fiery redhead with disposition to match. She had a firm handshake and her deep-set, hazel eyes never wavered when she spoke. Her voice was low and husky but, trained to speak before an audience, her words were concise and clear. She was a no-nonsense woman with an unforced laugh and flair.

Sprawled on a fur rug in front of the fireplace, Sam and Sydney Ellis nestled close sipping their wine and relishing their first holiday together. They were dressed in short matching robes of emerald silk. Sydney studied the dancing flames, her skin lit by their glow. Sam, his own robe carelessly drawn at the waist, pensively sipped his wine, an ever-so-slight frown creasing his brow. It was the glimmer of sadness in his eyes that caught Sydney's attention. This should be a time of joy and happiness, the grace period in life that only newlyweds are blessed to know.

Stealing an unnoticed moment, Sydney studied her husband. After three months of marriage, their lives had a semblance of order and routine. Yet lately, Sam seemed a bit distant and remote.

"Sam," she whispered. "What's wrong?"

"Nothing's wrong, Sydney. I was just thinking about Kathleen. It's Christmas Eve. I wonder how's she doing?"

"I talked with her yesterday," Sydney replied. "She seems okay."

"It must be lonely for her in Boston with no family or friends. At least she has her son."

Sydney cocked a mischievous grin. "She's not completely without family, Sam. You'll never guess who's come forward to help her. Michael's mother, Margaret Ruthingford Clay."

"But I thought she despised Kathleen."

"Disasters have a way of bringing people together. Both women lost everything they thought mattered. Now they find themselves alone with nothing to sustain them but their common love for Daniel. He's Margaret's only grandson."

Pleased by the news, Sam smiled. At forty, he was a lumbering bear of a fellow who looked more like a football player than a skilled surgeon. He had chestnut, curly hair and intense burnt-almond eyes, etched with character lines. When he was happy, the tiny brush marks disappeared and his entire demeanor brightened. When he was troubled, as he seemed tonight, every line in his face deepened. Belying his size and stature, Sam Ellis had a sweet, sensitive soul. His sense of compassion was his most alluring quality. At the same time, it was his greatest weakness. Oftentimes his empathy made him vulnerable to the suffering of his patients.

Sam opened his strong arms to Sydney and she came. Stroking her shoulder-length gleaming hair, the color of autumn fire, Sam realized that since meeting this spirited woman eight years his junior—with the razor-sharp mind of a reporter and a tumultuous temper to match—his life had never been richer. Despite having so much, there was still something missing.

Her deep-set, hazel eyes searching his, Sydney repeated, "Sam, what's wrong? Are you still upset about Gerald Bradley?"

"No," Ellis replied slowly. "That's not it. His murder was a shock but the more I learn about him, the more I realize that he was a man with an evil, dark side. I'm sure the police will find whoever did it."

"Then what is it?"

"There's nothing really wrong, sweetheart. I'm restless, that's all. So much has happened this past year. The disaster . . . finding you . . . ."

"I hope they're not one in the same," she teased, attempting to lighten his mood.

"I'm bored, Sydney. I need a change. Frankly, I think you do too."

Sydney said nothing, but a part of her yearned to agree.

"When I came to Velours five years ago, the hospital was nothing more than a small, adequate community facility. With time and hard work, we've become an outstanding Regional One Trauma Center." Sam paused. Then in a voice barely above a whisper, he confided, "Now there's nothing left for me to accomplish."

As her mood began to sink along with Sam's, Sydney's temper flared. It was Christmas Eve, after all, their first Christmas together. It was a time of peace and joy, of presents, and of prayers. It was not a time to be despondent.

"We've had this conversation before, Sam, many times in fact. We both agreed to wait a year before making any major decision. We need time to adjust to our marriage."

Tracing the outline of her creamy throat, Sam had no choice but to smile.

"I think we've adjusted quite well, Mrs. Ellis."

"So we have, Sam, but we still need time."

"No," he argued firmly. "We need a change." Sydney turned away from the fire and swallowed her wine, allowing it to warm her. Sam was right and she knew it. Her career was also at a standstill. As anchor for VKTV news, Sydney Lawrence had climbed the local ladder as high as she could go. Yet she had forged a comfortable life here in Velours. Within her own realm, she was a celebrity. To start over was more frightening than she cared to admit.

"All right, Sam," she said slowly, her wary eyes level with his. "This is not another idle conversation about the futility of your life or mine. You've something definite on your mind. Out with it!"

Sheepishly, Sam was forced to agree.

"A friend of mind called last week. You've heard me talk about Richard Baldwin. We went through medical school together."

"Yes," Sydney nodded. "I recognize the name."

"For the past several years, Richard has been the Chief of Staff at St. Vincent's Hospital in Kansas City."

Thinking of the Kansas prairie and the "cow town" in Missouri, Sydney smirked arrogantly. "Kansas City? You must be joking! What could this possibly have to do with us?"

Ignoring her tone, Sam plunged ahead. "Baldwin has resigned his position to move to Stanford. It seems that the medical school there made him an offer he couldn't refuse."

Dreading to hear the inevitable, Sydney hesitated to ask, "And so?"

"And so," Sam continued quickly, his voice tinged with excitement. "Richard recommended me for the job. St. Vincent's wants to fly us to Kansas City for an interview and a look."

"When?" Sydney questioned.

Nervously, Sam extracted two tickets from the pocket of his robe. Displaying them before her, he grinned, "New Year's."

Sydney stared at her husband aghast. "You arranged this behind my back?"

Sam glanced away.

"Oh dear God, Sam! Kansas City, of all places! Why there?"

Smugly, as if armed with a secret knowledge few people possessed, Sam replied, "Kansas City is one of the most beautiful cities

I've ever seen. It's a great place to raise a family. You have to be open-minded. Give it a try, Sydney. I think this could be a great opportunity for us."

"For you perhaps, Sam. But what about me? Have you given any thought to what a career change at this time would mean to me?"

"I've looked into that already, sweetheart. Kansas City has three television stations with major network affiliations. Richard called the station managers at all three. They'd seen your coverage of the Maggie Hall disaster and admired your work. Each of them has requested an interview. So you see, Sydney, this might be just the change you need. With exposure in a large metropolitan market, who knows what the future might hold!"

Struggling to be fair and look at her options carefully, Sydney brooded silently. The clock in the hallway chimed ten. Soon Christmas would be over, followed shortly by the closure of another year. Perhaps Sam was right. Perhaps a change was in order. And yet, Sydney thought she had finally found a home.

Turning to face Sam, Sydney caught the flicker of hope in her husband's eyes. Sam—dear, sweet, gentle Sam. The lumbering giant of a man who asked for so little. Sam had made life too easy for Sydney. All she had to do was bask in the warm loving embrace of his big heart. Now it was Sam who needed the change. Perhaps in a few years, it would be she. To deny him this opportunity was ultimately to deny herself.

After several minutes of agonizing, Sydney reluctantly concluded, "I don't like the way you went about this. Marriage is not about secrets. I'll agree to go to Kansas City for a visit, but only on one condition."

"What's that?"

"If we don't like it, we'll come home."

Nodding, Sam rose and cast a log upon the waning fire. Finally a spark took hold, and the embers flared.

He returned to Sydney's side. He hated confrontation with the one person he loved above all others. He kissed her lips. Her frown melted. Playfully he loosened the belt at her waist. Her robe fell open, revealing the matching teddy that she wore beneath.

With some trepidation, his gaze sought hers. The fire in her eyes had tempered. What he saw instead invited him to proceed. He slid the loosened robe from her shoulders. He toyed with the straps of her silk teddy. Carefully, he inched the garment downwards, until her breasts stood naked, firm, and ready. He caressed her nipples teasingly, first one and then the other. Her body responded hungrily to his touch.

With a fling of her wrist, Sydney loosened Sam's robe. Then she traced the letters *I love you* upon the curly brown hair of his chest. He found her mouth once again. This time her lips parted, inviting his tongue to enter. He laid her carefully back against the fur rug. Lovingly, seductively, his lips traveled down her body inch by inch.

Silhouetted in front of the dancing flames, Sam and Sydney relinquished their individual needs and aspirations as they merged to become one being. In those fleeting moments when they experienced the total joy of their union, Sydney realized that her fears of leaving Velours were groundless. Home was not a place. Home was the feeling she shared with Sam.

■

As the airplane began its descent, Sam reached over and gently caressed his wife's hand. "How are you feeling?"

"Nervous, Sam. Aren't you?"

Sam Ellis drained the last of his cocktail. "Of course I'm nervous, honey. I'm excited too! Do you have any idea how much I appreciate your making this trip with me?"

Sydney gazed out the tiny window as the plane banked sharply to the left. It was dark, the night before New Year's Eve. In the distance, she could see the lights of the city beckoning.

"There's an aspect of our move we haven't discussed, Sydney. Now may not be the most opportune time, but we can't avoid the topic forever."

Sydney noticed Sam's tone and gave him her full attention.

"I want a child, Sydney. I've waited a long time to start a family."

Exasperated by the reminder of a subject she sought to avoid, Sydney had to choose her words carefully.

"I've told you how I feel, Sam. The timing's not right, particularly if we both make a career change now. Someday, when we're more settled, we can talk about children. Not now, Sam! Please?"

"But when, Sydney? I'm not getting any younger. When will the time ever be right?"

Casting her glance once again to the window, Sydney wondered. It was not that she disliked children. Rather she was a modern career woman who had recently married. She had no desire to further complicate her life with a child who would claim her time and devotion.

"What you're asking is unfair, Sam. Starting a family would change your career goals very little, but it would devastate mine. Think about what having a baby means to a woman. I'd be the one to carry the child and give birth. Then I'd have to be the primary caretaker. Don't you see, Sam? I'm not ready to make that kind of commitment. Maybe someday. But not now. I love what we have together. Let's take our time and enjoy it."

"Perhaps you're right," Sam conceded softly. "But remember, life can't always be planned. I love you, Sydney. I'd like to grow old knowing we've left a part of our love behind."

The sound of the pilot's voice mercifully ended their discussion.

"Ladies and gentlemen, this is the captain. If you will direct your attention to the right side of the aircraft, you'll be able to see the world-renowned Country Club Plaza."

The Ellises glanced out the window. Gone were the white lights of the neon city. In their place were 156,000 brightly colored bulbs adorning 14 square blocks of the shops and businesses known as the Plaza.

"Look!" Sydney exclaimed. "It's like a Norman Rockwell Christmas postcard."

"So it is," Sam mused. "Kansas City will be good for us, Sydney. Wait and see!"

The dining room of the Michelangelo was filled for New Year's Eve. Sam and Sydney shared a cozy window table, high atop the revolving restaurant overlooking the Plaza. To the north, perched atop rolling bluffs, the skyline of downtown loomed majestically. Sam and Sydney focused only on the Plaza, as they savored the brightly colored lights, the snow-capped shops, and horse-drawn carriages below. Toasting the past, the Ellises prepared to bring in the first full year they would enjoy together.

"What time is it?" Sydney inquired.

"It's after eleven. We haven't long to wait."

"Tell me more about the hospital, Sam. You seemed so pleased when you returned."

His eyes bright with excitement, Sam described his first visit to St. Vincent's.

"It's a beautiful facility, Sydney. It was built eight years ago and has a bed capacity of over four hundred. The surgery department is top-notch, and the pediatric unit is impressive. The emergency room seems solid. The hospital operates on a healthy budget."

"Go on," Sydney encouraged, declining dessert and waving the waiter away.

"One aspect of the hospital that I'm really excited about is the Organ Transplant Program."

Sydney's interest perked. "Is St. Vincent's doing organ transplants?"

"The hospital is in the process of being accredited."

"Aren't transplants risky and expensive?"

"The technology has come a long way, Sydney. Insurance companies have now recognized the need for organ transplants. Many major medical policies will cover transplants. So if you have insurance, getting an organ is not that difficult. Truthfully, a lot of money can now be made, both for the surgeons and for the hospitals. St. Vincent's realizes that by being the first hospital in Kansas City to be approved, they will be on the cutting edge."

"Do you mean to tell me that in a city this size no other private hospital is doing transplants? I was told the population is well over a million."

"You're right, Sydney. Kansas City has been slow to get started. Omaha is the closest place doing transplants, and it's a city only about half as big as this one. St. Vincent's application will be the first to be approved locally. That approval is expected before the end of this coming year. So you see, Sydney, performing organ transplants should prove to be extremely lucrative for this small, private institution. We ... they ... will be able to attract top surgeons."

Sam's slip did not go undetected. He was hooked on the place. He already considered himself a member of the staff.

"In the meantime," Sam continued, "St. Vincent's houses the regional office of the Organ Procurement Program."

"What does that mean, Sam?"

"In 1984, Al Gore sponsored a bill in the Senate to assure the equitable distribution of viable organs. Prior to that, since organs are such a rare commodity, only the favored few were granted their chance at life. With the passage of the bill, a federal program was created to assure that every patient has an equal chance for consideration. Now when a need arises, the patient's name and medical profile are entered into the federal computer system. After an organ becomes available, each patient in this pool is matched by the computer against the donor organ's characteristics. Then the computer prints out a list of suitable matches ranked in order of need and compatibility. It's that simple."

"Sounds fascinating."

"The country is divided into eleven regions. Kansas City is located in Region Eight. The office of the Regional Director of the Organ Procurement Program is at St. Vincent's."

"What's he like?"

Sam's expression changed as he thought about the strange enigma of a character he had met this afternoon.

"The Director's name is Farhad Rajid. He's a man of Persian descent. He's quite bright, but he seems a little odd. There's something about him ... I can't put my finger on it ... that makes me uncomfortable. Maybe it's a cultural thing."

Having thought enough about Farhad Rajid, Sam was anxious to steer the conversation onto another topic. Reaching across the table, Sam tenderly brushed his wife's hand.

"Have I told you tonight how much I love you?" he whispered.

"No," Sydney replied. "Tell me now."

"I love you, Sydney Lawrence Ellis. You're everything I've ever wanted, and a whole lot more than I bargained for!"

Gazing out the window to the slowly revolving city below, the tantalizing excitement of the Plaza waned, replaced now by the tranquillity of quieter neighborhoods to the west. The scene reminded Sydney of an exclusive area she had visited earlier today.

"I like the city, Sam. At least what I've seen so far. Michelle Johns, the realtor St. Vincent's provided, took me to a lovely area not far from here called Mission Hills. You wouldn't believe the magnificent architecture. Some of the estates were huge. And the parks and fountains! I thought Kentucky was famous for grass and trees!"

Taking but a quick breath, Sydney continued in a rush.

"My favorite street was Verona Circle. There were beautiful homes of all designs, shapes and sizes. One in particular was a mansion. It belongs to an Iranian named Ali Hassan. He owns an exclusive oriental rug store on the Plaza."

"Hassan," Ellis murmured. "It seems like I've heard that name before."

"Next-door to this monstrous structure was a simple, white Colonial for sale. Michelle didn't have the listing but she obtained a key. The house has three bedrooms, four baths, a huge living room, dining room, kitchen . . ."

"Good heavens, Sydney! It sounds mammoth!"

"Well it is . . . but it isn't, Sam. And it's reasonably priced. You have to see it for yourself. Tomorrow, please?"

With a glint in his dancing brown eyes, Sam signaled the waiter.

"Champagne," he requested. "Dom Perignon."

Sam threw a quizzical glance to Sydney. Searching her intelligent, hazel eyes, he waited until the corners of her lips curled mischievously and she nodded. Then as the waiter scurried to fill their order, the Ellises watched the south side of the city slowly rotate into view. In the near distance was Loose Park. Located halfway between Mission Hills and St. Vincent's Hospital, the park would be a great place to meet and talk. To walk or simply to be.

"What time is it?" Sam asked.

"Fifteen minutes before the hour," the waiter replied, popping the cork on the champagne.

Waiting until they were alone, Sam proceeded cautiously.

"What do you think?" he asked, his gaze level with Sydney's.

Taking time to reflect, as the hospital to the east came into view, Sydney smiled. "Six months," she responded finally.

"Six months?" Sam repeated, confused.

"Tell St. Vincent's that they can have you the first of June."

Reaching into his inner pocket, Sam extracted a thin, rectangular box, wrapped in silver and white.

"This is for you," he offered rather shyly.

"But why?" Sydney retorted. "Christmas is over."

Thinking of the woman who constantly amazed him, he quipped, "With you, my dear, Christmas is never over. Unwrap it. It's nothing fancy, you'll see."

Deftly tearing the paper, Sydney lifted the lid of the box. Underneath the tissue was an unusual necklace. Attached to a gold chain was a clear crystal sphere. Sydney peered closer. Inside the circle was a tiny seed.

"Do you know what that is?"

Sydney was slow to answer.

"Did you ever hear the parable of the mustard seed?"

"It has something to do with faith," she recalled.

"That's right," Sam answered. "The story I learned in Sunday school was that if you had the faith of a mustard seed you could move mountains."

Sydney glanced first to the necklace and then to Sam. "What are you trying to tell me?"

"I'm asking you to trust me."

Sydney felt a sudden chill. For some reason, this simple gift and Sam's request touched her to the core. Her eyes filled with tears when she said, "I love you, Sam." From the bottom of her heart she meant it.

Rising to stand behind her, he fastened the necklace around her delicate throat. Bending to kiss her neck, Sam noticed the Plaza as it slowly returned to view. Coming full circle, the bright lights once more caught their fancy as the clock in the tower struck twelve. Taking her hand, he helped Sydney to her feet.

Embracing her, he said, "Happy New Year, my love."

Reaching for her glass of champagne, Sydney toasted her husband. "To a new year!" she declared. "And faith in a new beginning!"

Susan M. Hoskins

6

It was a rainy Friday afternoon in late May. The streets of Washington were congested. In anticipation of the three-day Memorial Day weekend, many people were leaving work early. It was a different scene at FBI headquarters. The air conditioning had been turned down for the weekend and the building was stuffy. Special Agent, Joe Morrison, was perspiring as much from impatience as the heat.

At forty-three, Joe Morrison had unruly, caramel-colored hair and dancing cobalt-blue eyes. He was an attractive, if not a particularly handsome, man. Patience was not his strong suit and his boss, John Taylor, was late for their five o'clock meeting.

Finding himself alone in his boss's office, Joe settled into the chair across from John's desk and reached in his pocket for a cigarette. Taylor kept an ashtray on his desk just for Joe. Morrison didn't give a damn that the federal building had just adopted a designated area smoking policy. He figured that wherever he wanted a cigarette was a designated area.

Morrison checked his watch. It was already 5:15. His impatience had little to do with the time. He had no plans for the weekend. He was bored. He yearned for a new and different assignment. After a decade with the FBI, he felt stagnant. He'd voiced his concerns to Taylor. The Deputy Director agreed to see what he could do. He'd called Joe shortly after three o'clock. He was planning a weekend away with his family; but mindful of Joe's restlessness, he'd scheduled a briefing at four o'clock with the head of Counterterrorism. Joe had never been assigned to this unit. He was intrigued.

Glancing around the sparsely furnished office, he wondered, "How many times have I sat in this chair during the past few years?" Morrison couldn't answer his own question. Enough times to feel comfortable. He slouched in his chair, threw his feet up on the desk, and waited for his next assignment.

Morrison eyed his cigarette but, as was his custom, didn't light it immediately. He just rolled it back and forth between his thumb and index finger. The ritual had a history. Alone, with time on his hands, he began to reminisce.

Joseph Eugene Morrison was born at Hope Memorial Hospital in Chicago on September 14, 1953. His dad, Frank Morrison, had been a Chicago city cop. His mother, Anna Marie, was a homemaker. Frank was a widower and retired now, still living in the same modest house where Joe and his sisters were raised. Joe admired his dad. That's why he'd chosen to follow in his dad's big footsteps.

Morrison graduated from the University of Illinois with a degree in criminal justice. Then, after a brief stint at the police academy, he'd joined the Chicago Police Department.

Joe's glance remained fixed upon his cigarette. Rolling it back and forth in between his thumb and finger, he'd already flattened the butt. He smiled, remembering the man and his ritual.

After putting in his time on the beat, he'd been paired with a crusty old detective by the name of Vincent DeSalvo. He would never forget the first time he met his partner. He got in the unmarked squad car. There sat a man of slender build with jet black, oily hair, brown eyes and a weathered olive complexion. DeSalvo wasted no time getting the rules straight.

"There are four things you need to know. First, you can call me Vincent, DeSalvo or partner. Upon occasion I may let you call me a son-of-a-bitch. But never *Vinnie*."

"Second, I drive, not you. I like my coffee strong and black and hamburgers with lots of onions. And I'll smoke wherever and whenever I want. Third, keep your mouth shut and learn."

Vincent paused while he took a large swig of muddy coffee.

Then he turned to Morrison with eyes that were dead serious. "If you got a brain in your head, I can teach you to stay alive. If you don't, we'll bury you and I'll have to break in a new partner." Vincent DeSalvo started the car. With a measure of disgust, he mumbled, "And I hate like hell breaking in new partners!"

As they pulled away from the curb, Morrison thought to ask, "What's the fourth thing you wanted to tell me?"

"That will come later," DeSalvo replied.

Finally lighting his cigarette, Morrison remembered when he learned the fourth and most important thing his partner had to teach him. It was a few days later. They had a murder suspect in custody. Vincent stopped Joe just before entering the interrogation room.

"Son, do nothing but sit there and observe everything I say and do."

The interrogation lasted two hours. Afterwards, Vincent took his rookie partner into an empty office. The older man seemed amused. His young partner was sweating. "So tell me what you observed."

"What's the deal with the cigarette, Vincent? Why didn't you light the damn thing? You just kept rolling it between your fingers alternately looking at the suspect and the wall. I'd never seen you do that before. You were driving me and the perp nuts."

"Yeah, you're right. What else?"

"You didn't ask as many questions as I thought you would. You just sat there staring at the guy and playing with your cigarette. He kept asking for a smoke. You'd change the subject then throw him a question. You refused to give him a cigarette until you had your answers. You're a piece of work, DeSalvo."

"Keep your mouth shut, Joe, and let people reveal themselves. Sooner or later they always do. Ask a question, then sit back and listen. Play with them and they'll go nuts. They'll reveal themselves in time. The most important thing I got to teach you is not to listen to your head."

"What?" Morrison asked, confused.

"Listen to your gut, Joe, not your head. People are never what they appear. Everybody tells a good story. Your mind wants to believe a logical explanation. Your head will let you down. Your gut will never lie."

Heaving a sigh, Joe grabbed the lighter from his shirt pocket and finally lit his cigarette. Inhaling a deep drag, he saluted his former partner. "To you, Vincent!"

Studying the cloud of smoke hovering above his head, he muttered, "I hate this damn office. Ventilation's lousy."

Beneath the surface of his words was a measure of respect. He'd come a long way from the working-class neighborhood of his youth and the beat he patrolled as a cop. He'd learned his lessons with DeSalvo. Lessons that proved to be invaluable. The move from the Chicago Police Department to the FBI had saved his sanity. But he didn't dare dwell upon those reasons for long. The memories were far too painful.

Hearing footsteps in the hallway, he dismissed any reminders of his wife and son. He stood when John Taylor approached. He didn't recognize the two men who followed.

"Joe, I'd like you to meet Roger Brennan. He's in charge of the Counterterrorism Unit. And this is George Massoud."

Joe snuffed out his cigarette, then shook hands with the two men.

"Make yourselves comfortable, gentlemen."

Brennan and Massoud took seats on either side of Morrison. John Taylor assumed the chair behind his desk. Joe said nothing as he studied the group. Taylor was a haggard man in his late fifties, given to wearing rumpled white shirts with paisley ties. Roger Brennan created an entirely different image. Joe noticed his shoes immediately. Unlike his boss's, Brennan's were gleaming black and polished to a high gloss. Brennan's slightly graying hair was parted precisely to the left. He had small narrow eyes and a tight angular jaw. Joe guessed him to be slightly younger than Taylor.

He'd seen both types of agents in the FBI. Neither of them seemed particularly interesting anymore. They were too predictable. It was the unassuming man seated to his left that Joe found most intriguing. George Massoud was in his early thirties. He had closely cropped, chestnut hair, light brown skin and intelligent ebony eyes. He was a man of slight build. Of all of them, he seemed the most uncomfortable.

John Taylor began. "Roger has an assignment we think you might find interesting. Technically it comes under the auspices of his unit. But the assignment is a little odd. He wants a seasoned agent in charge."

Morrison smirked. If nothing else, he was seasoned.

Brennan directed his question to Joe. "Are you familiar with the Counterterrorism Unit?"

"Only superficially."

"Our investigations differ from white collar or organized crime. We have the authority to investigate individuals prior to any crime having been committed. We operate under the William Smith guidelines adopted in 1983, which state that to prevent crimes, we can initiate investigations in advance of criminal conduct. A terrorist investigation may be initiated whenever the circumstances indicate that two or more people are engaged in an enterprise for the purpose of furthering political or social goals wholly or in part through activities that involve force or violence and a violation of U.S. criminal laws. In other words, the Smith guidelines make it clear that the FBI does not have to wait for blood to be spilled before it can investigate a terrorist group. Follow?"

John Taylor interjected, "The FBI is authorized to open a preliminary inquiry when it receives information which requires further scrutiny. In any given year, the FBI engages in about two dozen domestic terrorism investigations. Since the Smith guidelines were adopted, nearly two-thirds of these investigations were opened before a crime had been committed."

"Okay," Joe countered. "You've perked my interest."

"How good is your knowledge of the Middle East?"

Morrison's blank expression was answer enough.

"George Massoud is our expert in Middle Eastern culture. George, give Joe a brief history lesson."

Massoud's voice was softer than the others. He spoke slowly but intelligently.

"During the Shah's reign in Iran, the Savak was the secret police force that created terror throughout the region. They were anonymous faces in the crowd, but let someone speak ill of the Shah or his policies and that man or woman would disappear only to experience unspeakable acts of torture, imprisonment and death. They controlled the masses using fear as the weapon of choice. When Khomeini came to power, the Shah's elite, including Savak generals, fled Iran with great sums of money. Most of them settled in London or other major cities in Europe. A few came to the United States."

Brennan added, "We've received information that a terrorist training camp located near Dubai is being funded by an organization called the New Savak. The purpose of the camp is to arm and train a new breed of terrorists whose acts are violent and random. Their objective is to create havoc and ultimately to control oil production in the Middle East. They are more dangerous than terrorists of the past because their targets are far less specific. Their strikes are more dangerous because they're random and chaotic."

"While this is very interesting," Joe countered, "What does this have to do with me?"

"Somehow, the New Savak is raising enough money to arm and fund a terrorist camp, perhaps more than one. To raise that kind of money they have to be involved in something big and something illegal. We're talking millions of dollars. That's where you fit in."

"How?"

"We think the leader of the New Savak is living in Kansas City. We need help to crack this group. My men are involved with other investigations. We'd like you to lead a team to discover where the money's coming from and how the hell they're financing their organization."

Morrison leaned back in his chair. Instinctively, he pulled a Marlboro from his pocket, but he didn't light it. He contemplated the assignment while he rolled the cigarette in between his thumb and index finger. It was clear he was intrigued.

Brennan continued. "We have a potentially dangerous situation on our hands. We have a Middle Eastern group headquartered here in the United States purchasing arms and training terrorists. They've come into this country claiming political asylum. They enjoy the full privileges of a democracy. They fund their illegal activities with American dollars. If history serves us, they will eventually use their arms and men against American interests here and overseas. We have the authority to try to stop them."

Morrison glanced briefly at his boss. Then locking eyes with Roger Brennan, he asked, "What do you want me to do?"

"I want you to leave for Kansas City early next week. George will go with you."

Focusing on Massoud, he asked, "Where do you fit in the scheme of things?"

"I was born in the United States but my parents are from Saudi Arabia. My father is a successful businessman but my family has experienced a great deal of prejudice. People of Arab descent are feared and misunderstood. We're not all terrorists."

"George has a master's degree from Harvard. He'll educate you in matters of culture. You can teach him the ropes. You need the information he can provide. He needs the experience of working under an agent of your caliber and reputation. When you get to Kansas City, you can pick the rest of your team and set up surveillance. You'll have ninety days before you'll require further authorization from headquarters. It is hoped that during the next three months, you can crack their organization. If they're breaking any laws, we can bust them. That's it. That's the deal."

For the first time during the meeting, Joe Morrison truly smiled. He'd heard enough. "Pack your bag, George. We'll leave for Kansas City on Monday. You don't have any plans for the weekend, do you?"

Morrison exited Taylor's office first. In the hallway he took the younger man aside. In a voice the others couldn't hear, he said, "You seem like a bright kid but let's get some things straight. First, I like my coffee strong and black. Second, I'll smoke wherever and whenever I want. Third . . . . "

Susan M. Hoskins

It was a lovely warm morning on the first of June in Kansas City. Having arrived the night before, the Ellises rose early, taking breakfast on the balcony of their suite overlooking the Country Club Plaza.

The intervening months had passed quickly for Sam and Sydney upon their return to Velours. It had been a stressful time as they sold their home, packed their belongings and resigned their jobs. It had been painful as well, as they bid good-bye to their friends and a way of life they had enjoyed. Leaving Velours, they vowed not to look back as they let go of a past that had grown too comfortable.

Sipping their coffee in the soft morning sun, they decided Kansas City was even more beautiful in the lush renewal of late spring than it had been during the dreary slumber of winter. They had a lot to do on their first full day back in town. Right after breakfast, they'd meet their realtor, Michelle Johns, at the title company to close on their new home. Then Sam would go directly to St. Vincent's Hospital and assume his duties as Chief of Staff, leaving Sydney to take possession of the house.

Shortly before eleven, Sydney found herself captive in the realtor's Honda Accord. She was anxious to get on with the move. Michelle, on the other hand, seemed intent on showing her every attraction the city had to offer. Michelle slowly eased her Honda through Mission Hills before turning on Verona Circle. There in the center of the cul-de-sac stood Hassan's mansion, seeming even more intimidating than Sydney had remembered.

"Are you ready?" Michelle asked, parking the car.

Sydney gazed at the white Colonial. "I hope it's as lovely as I remember."

The realtor smiled knowingly. "It is."

Sydney opened the car door and started up the brick pathway. Halfway to the house, she stopped as a shadow across the way caught her notice. Shielding her eyes against the bright morning sun, she glimpsed the figure of a small child peering from an upstairs window at the mansion. As quickly as it appeared, the fleeting image vanished.

"What's wrong?" asked Michelle.

Sydney shrugged. "Nothing."

With a flourish, the realtor unlocked the door and handed the keys to the new owner.

"After you, Mrs. Ellis. Welcome home."

Catching her breath, Sydney stepped through the door into the marble hallway. Without furniture, the living and dining rooms seemed huge. Light, airy, lush, plenty of windows—just as she remembered. Tomorrow the furniture would be delivered. Today the space was all theirs.

"What shall we see first?" Johns asked.

"The kitchen," Sydney replied brightly. "Next to the bedroom, it's Sam's favorite place."

A huge, state-of-the-art kitchen had been designed for someone who loved haute cuisine. Unfortunately, while Sydney loved the pleasures of a gourmet meal, she had no skill in cooking. Still she loved the center island, the Jenn-Air cooktops, the cherry cabinets and double ovens. The fixtures were all brass and the hearth room was fitted with a fireplace against the outer wall.

Glancing from the huge bay window to the patio, she beckoned Michelle to follow. Unlocking the patio door, she stepped outside. For a moment she stood in silence, planning the garden. Then, unwittingly, her eyes traveled next-door.

Bordered on all sides by a heavy metal gate, her neighbor's yard seemed immense. Despite the fact Hassan had a child, she saw no toys, no swing, absolutely nothing of play or pleasure. Suddenly at the back door a man in a dark suit appeared. He was large and stocky. Strapped to his shoulder, he cradled a large semi-automatic weapon. Sydney shivered.

"Are you cold?" Michelle asked.

At the sight of the man with the gun, Sydney faltered. "Tell me," she said. "Why the armed guard?"

Michelle hesitated. "Ali Hassan is overly protective of his daughter. He worries constantly about her safety because he's away on business a great deal of the time."

"Tell me more about him," Sydney continued.

The nervous woman hastily ushered Sydney back inside. Only after securing the sliding glass door did she reply.

"No one knows Ali Hassan well. He's a private man, Sydney, who keeps very much to himself. He's lived in Kansas City a number of years. He's rarely seen in social circles although he contributes periodically to worthwhile projects. Sorry, that's about all I know. Say, let's have a look at the rest of your home."

As the two women toured the empty house, Sydney visualized her furniture in place.

"Shall we go upstairs?" Michelle asked.

Climbing the winding staircase, Sydney suddenly asked, "What's the child like?"

"Lydia? She's quite pretty but rather delicate. She suffers from a heart condition."

"Does she go to school?"

"Off and on," Michelle replied, sighing. She hesitated. "Lydia attends a private school near the Plaza. She's in my nephew's class. She's had a hard time being accepted. Hassan permits her no friends. The guards you see around the house accompany the child to school."

"How awful!" Sydney exclaimed.

Michelle opened the door to the master suite. Sydney followed. It was huge, with a fireplace and a cozy sitting area. Just off the bedroom was a dressing room with a large vanity that Sydney especially liked. As she stood in her dressing room, her eyes were drawn to a third-floor window across the way. The curtains parted and there stood the child. Alone, dressed in blue.

Sydney waved. Then, tentatively so did the girl. Suddenly she turned around. The man standing behind her pulled the drapes shut. As quickly as she had appeared, the child named Lydia was gone.

Sydney felt compelled to continue. "Where is Lydia's mother?"

"My understanding is that she died a number of years ago."

"How?"

"I have no idea."

Beckoning Sydney away from the window, Michelle tried to explain.

"Ali Hassan appears to be the head of the local Iranian community. You'll see quite a few cars parked here night after night. You'll be perfectly safe living next-door to him. With the number of guards Hassan employs, you'll never have to worry about crime. Ali Hassan will not bother you. Probably he won't even acknowledge your existence."

Sydney tried to get Michelle to elaborate but she declined. Sydney returned her gaze to the empty window, then finally turned away and returned to the bedroom.

■

More than a week passed before she met the child. It was a Saturday early in June. Due at their welcoming party at seven, Sam showered while Sydney fussed at her dressing table. Tonight everything had to be perfect, for Sam's sake and for her own.

A formal dinner had been planned in their honor. Sam would wear his tuxedo, Sydney a smashing gown of silver lamé. Wrapped in a light robe, Sydney carefully applied her makeup and sipped a glass of Chardonnay. She was brushing her hair when she felt a slight chill run through her. Setting her brush aside, she glanced outside. There in the same high window stood the girl. Several times during the past week, their eyes had connected only for a few seconds. After each encounter, Sydney was left troubled, yet somehow, yearning for the next.

Lydia smiled and gestured vigorously. Sydney was puzzled. Was she waving or pointing to something below? Again the child signaled. Then the curtains closed abruptly and she disappeared.

Reaching for her glass, Sydney went over and poked her head in the bathroom. Sam's shower was steamy, and the mirrors fogged.

"Sam," she called above the shower's hum. "I'm going downstairs. Can I refresh your drink?"

"Please, honey," he answered, peeking from behind the curtain, his hair lathered with shampoo. "My glass is on the dresser."

Sydney hurried down the stairs. What was Lydia trying to say? Turning on the light in the kitchen, she waited, anticipating something, not knowing what. Then she heard the sound—a light rap at the patio door.

The young girl smiled shyly when Sydney turned on the patio light and opened the door.

"Hello. My name is Lydia. What's yours?"

"Sydney," she replied. "Would you like to come in?"

Her expression clouding, Lydia glanced furtively behind her.

"Okay," she answered. "But I can only stay a few minutes."

Allowing Lydia to enter, Sydney took advantage of the unexpected encounter to study the child carefully. Lydia was a slight girl of perhaps twelve, with a complexion of olive satin. She had long, raven hair and huge ebony eyes. With an exquisite face framed in curls, Lydia was more beautiful than Sydney had imagined. But there was a sadness about her.

"I can only stay a moment," Lydia warned. "No one knows I'm gone."

Sydney found herself at a loss for words. "I'm glad you're here," she said at last. "I've been hoping to meet you."

An eerie feeling engulfed Sydney. This sweet girl seemed vaguely familiar yet somehow strange . . . as though she knew her, although they had never met.

"You're very pretty," Lydia offered. "I like your hair. It's golden red." Tentatively she revealed the hand she hid behind her back. In it was a tightly curled red rose. "This is for you from me."

Smiling, Sydney took the flower from the girl's small tapered fingers.

"Thank you," she whispered. "The rose is lovely."

"I'm glad you've moved in here. Look for me at the window. I'll come over whenever I can."

"Please do," Sydney replied quickly. "Tell your father I welcome you anytime."

A horrified frown creased Lydia's face. "Oh no!" she cried. "Father must never know! He wouldn't approve!"

Fearing Lydia would bolt and run, Sydney assured her, "All right then. We'll keep it our secret."

Backing towards the door, the wisp of a girl stammered, "I must go now before my father's men discover that I'm gone."

Turning abruptly, the beautiful child fled. Watching her disappear into the shadows, Sydney shivered. Was it the father that made her uneasy, or was it the child? Lydia's face had left its indelible mark . . . sad ebony eyes and a smile that warmed her heart.

■

At seven o'clock, the limousine arrived. Sydney straightened her husband's tie before Sam led her down the brick pathway to the street. Only once at the car did she look back. The heavy draperies at Lydia's window remained shut.

Settling into the rear seat, Sam grasped his wife's hand. With a chuckle, he drew a handkerchief from his pocket and caressed her moistened palms.

"You seem nervous tonight, honey. Anything wrong?"

"Nothing's wrong, Sam. I want the party to go well, that's all."

"It will, Sydney. There's nothing to worry about."

Sydney averted her eyes. Although they had been married for nearly a year, there was one aspect of her personality that she had failed to share with him.

"I have a secret, Sam. You might as well know it. I hate cocktail parties. I'm no good at making small talk with strangers. I get nervous. My hands perspire and I'm all thumbs."

"I don't understand . . . "

"I know what you're going to say," she interrupted. "How can I relate to thousands of people every night and fall apart on a one-to-one?"

"Precisely."

"It's simple really. Projecting through a camera lens, I'm protected. No one gets close to the real me."

It was a short ride to the Carriage Club near the Plaza where the party was to be held. A command performance, Sam's staff would be there, from the Director of Finance to the heads of every department.

"Who's important, Sam? Is there anyone in particular you'd like me to meet?"

A mischievous smile creased his lips as he nodded. "There's one man, Sydney, who's especially interesting. I hope he'll be there tonight. He's a surgeon so he may be on call."

As the limousine came to a halt at the main entrance of the club, a uniformed doorman stepped forward and greeted them.

"Go directly through the main hall, sir, to the private dining room on the right."

Clutching Sam's arm, Sydney took a deep breath as she entered the crowded room. All eyes turned to stare. Genuinely smiling, Sam proudly introduced his wife. Sydney shook hands with his colleagues—doctors and their spouses, members of the Board of Directors and the Administrators. Chatting nervously, her palms once again began to sweat.

Sam took Sydney by the arm and gently urged her forward. "There's the man I want you to meet."

Standing alone three steps above the main floor was a man who appeared to be about forty. Sydney paused, studying the stranger from a distance. He was not particularly handsome. He was a gangly man of average height with wavy, mahogany-colored hair and a strong jawline. She was curious about his eyes. They seemed compelling yet masked behind the dark-framed glasses he wore. She couldn't tell if they were brown or green. He looked intelligent, but awkward as he fiddled with the collar scratching his neck.

"Sydney, this is Philip Wentworth. He's the surgeon I was telling you about. Philip, may I present my wife, Sydney."

Blushing slightly, Sydney clasped the doctor's hand. His smile softened. He didn't seem offended by the dampness of her grip.

"How nice to meet you, Sydney," he began. "Your glass is empty. May I get you a drink?"

"Please," she answered. "White wine."

In a moment he returned with a single glass for her.

"Nothing for you?"

"I'm on call," he explained.

Sam saw one of the directors signaling to him, and excused himself.

Nodding, Philip watched the big man walk away.

"Your husband has a tremendous reputation. He'll be a great asset to our staff."

Philip was still holding the wine glass. He held it out to Sydney; but reaching with clammy hands, she fumbled the glass and it fell to the floor, shattering.

Sydney gasped. Philip met her horrified gaze with a grin. "How clumsy of me!" he drawled. "You'd think a plastic surgeon would have a steadier grip!"

With a cocked eyebrow, Sydney repeated, "A plastic surgeon?"

Tugging at his collar, Philip led her away from the mess as a waiter scurried to clean it up. "You seem to hate these affairs as much as I do."

"Oh yes," Sydney agreed. "I can't stand them!"

Pulling a crisp handkerchief from his pocket, he offered it to Sydney.

"Use this. It might help."

Gratefully, Sydney wiped her palms.

"Keep it," he said. "It may be a long night."

Sydney edged a bit closer. "May I share a secret? It's a trick I learned working under hot lights. Powder your neck before you dress in a tuxedo. That way, if you perspire, your starched shirt won't itch."

"It is indeed nice to meet you, Sydney Ellis. You're a breath of fresh air. I already sense we have more in common than we know."

"I look forward to seeing you again, Philip. You might make these command performances bearable."

It was past midnight before the party ended. Kicking her shoes off in the back of the limousine, Sydney huddled close to Sam, his bow tie askew, his jacket abandoned.

"It was a lovely party, Sam. I had a good time."

"Did you, Sydney?" he asked hopefully. "Did you really?"

"I especially enjoyed meeting the surgeon. The *plastic surgeon*!"

Sam smiled knowingly. More than a year had passed since they'd befriended a woman by the name of Kathleen Clay who had been horribly maimed in the Maggie Hall disaster. With Sydney's help, she had fled her husband and sought refuge in Boston with her son.

"I like Philip," Sydney confided. "What do you know about him?"

"He has a great reputation as a plastic surgeon."

"Do you think he could help Kathleen?"

Sam's tone was serious. "If anyone can . . . . "

"Why don't I call her, Sam? We could arrange a consultation."

"I'll speak with him in the morning."

Throwing her head back against the seat, Sydney sighed. "I've got to get back to work. Tonight proved that once and for all."

Even though it was dark in the limousine, Sydney sensed that Sam's body had tensed and his expression hardened. Sydney feared it was disappointment that he felt.

"I love being your wife," she assured him quickly. "But I need more."

"More?" he asked.

"I need to achieve my own career goals. I have to get back to television and do what I'm trained to do. I miss working, Sam. I can't be happy just standing in your shadow."

Sam caressed Sydney's hand before bringing her fingers to his lips for a gentle kiss.

"I understand, honey. I'll do whatever I can to support you."

The chauffeur signaled his turn onto Verona Circle. As the limousine slowed, the activity at the Hassan mansion caught Sam's eye.

"Look, honey. We're not the only ones attending a party tonight."

Sam counted twenty cars parked along the street but Sydney's thoughts were focused elsewhere. Her eyes sought a child's face in an upstairs bedroom window. The room was dark, the window empty.

Susan M. Hoskins

Entering Terminal A, Ralph checked the clock. The shuttle had taken longer than he expected but he still had more than enough time to beat the flight. As he walked purposefully towards the gate, he spotted a lounge. Pausing at the doorway, he counted five people sitting at the bar. Yearning for a drink, he checked his watch once again. Biting his lower lip, he turned and hurried away. This was not the place. Now was definitely not the time.

He'd been instructed to fly ahead to Kansas City in order to meet Kathleen Clay's flight. She'd scheduled an impromptu trip to Kansas City. He wasn't quite sure why. He'd had Kathleen and her son under surveillance for six months. In return for a substantial monthly check, he reported directly to Solomon Bucy, never Michael Clay.

Before reaching the gate, Ralph picked up a black coffee and a *Kansas City Star*. Dressed casually in brown pants and a lightweight tan shirt, he meshed well with other people killing time until the next flight. Taking a seat just outside the gate, he buried his nose in the paper.

■

Speeding to meet Kathleen's flight, Sam Ellis circled the drive into the airport. Parking his Jeep Wagoneer in the nearest lot, he ran inside the terminal and scanned the screen. Eastern Flight 247 was on time.

Shoving his paper into his bag, Ralph Noland stood. Blending into the crowd, he hovered towards the rear. Kathleen was not the first to deplane, so he was forced to wait, studying each of the passengers carefully. When she finally emerged, the small delicate woman was difficult to spot in the crush of people. Her face was partially veiled with a thin, black netting.

"Kathleen," Sam called. "Over here!"

Glancing up, she smiled as the lumbering bear of a man threw open his arms and hugged her warmly.

"It's good to see you, Sam. You look well."

"So do you, Kathleen. Welcome. Sydney and I have missed you."

Ralph Noland studied the tall, broad-shouldered man carefully, noting his clothes and build. She had called him *Sam*. Who was Sam?

"Do you have much luggage?" Ellis inquired.

"I checked only one small bag. I'll be here just overnight."

Noland inched his way towards them as they walked slowly towards the baggage claim area.

"Let's wait over here, Kathleen, out of the way."

His eyes never wavering, Noland followed. Reaching for a pair of dark glasses, he slowly edged closer, careful to remain obscured by the crowd.

"You look marvelous, my friend. What a change!"

Dressed beautifully in a black Chanel suit with matching hat, the veiled lady smiled sadly.

"Hats are wonderful, Sam. They hide a multitude of flaws. But underneath the veil, I'm still the same."

Ellis patted her arm tenderly. "Philip Wentworth can fix all that, Kathleen. You've come to the right place."

Claiming her bag, they departed quickly. Just outside the terminal, Noland hailed a cab.

"See that Jeep Wagoneer?" he inquired.

The cab driver nodded.

"Don't let it out of your sight!"

■

Sitting behind his gleaming mahogany desk, Dr. Philip Wentworth allowed himself a few minutes to unwind. It had been a brutal day—back-to-back surgeries in the morning, followed by a dozen patients in the afternoon. The office, though, had been emptied shortly after four o'clock in preparation for his final appointment of the day.

It was just as well that he had been kept too busy to dwell upon the significance of this particular day, the anniversary of his mother's disappearance. Taking a moment to study Kathleen Clay's file, he plowed through the data from the accident in Velours, to her most recent hospital stay in Boston. He felt comfortable rummaging through the familiar medical jargon, but when he read her personal history, his heart again grew heavy. The coincidence was startling.

Kathleen Clay, born December 8, was thirty-three years old. Sadly, he recalled his mother's birthday. It was the same, and the age she had been when Philip last saw her. Shaken, he abandoned his desk and walked to the window, gazing absently at the quiet street outside.

So many years had passed. Still he remembered the horror of that day as if it had been yesterday. He had been a happy twelve-year-old then, living in the Middle East with his American father, an oil executive, and his Iranian mother, a professor at the University of Tehran. On this particular day in June, young Philip took no notice of the strange men lurking outside the building as he strolled from school to his mother's office.

"Mother!" Philip called out, "wait until I tell you what happened at school!"

He was a gawky adolescent but he still welcomed his mother's embrace. She held him a bit longer than she intended. He felt the power of her emotion even then. When they parted, he searched her troubled eyes wondering why he felt so strange.

With black, luminous hair and deep sable eyes, Sophia Wentworth was a beautiful woman, petite and delicate looking. And her mind was brilliant. Educated in Europe, she was employed as a university teacher. That feat alone was quite rare for an Iranian woman.

Sophia loved her students and encouraged their free thinking and uncensored speech. She permitted political discussions in her classroom about the struggle for civil rights in Iran. It was this that brought her notoriety as a professor and filled her classroom with eager students. It was this behavior that her colleagues feared. No one was allowed to criticize the Shah or his regime.

Tousling Philip's auburn hair, Sophia gazed fondly into her son's emerald eyes and smiled.

"What a handsome boy you are, Philip. What a wonderful man you shall become."

Sophia Wentworth suddenly looked up at the sound of soldier's boots outside in the hallway. Four men entered her office. Silently three stood at attention as their leader stepped forward. He was a man of stocky build around thirty with a swarthy, pitted complexion. What distinguished him from the others was the glaring red scar on his right cheek.

There was no emotion in his voice when he said, "Sophia Wentworth?"

"Yes," she replied, her voice cracking. Clutching Philip's shoulder, she stood. She glanced around for a means of escape, but instantly realized there was none. With as steady a gaze as her pounding heart would allow, she faced the man directly.

"What do you want?" she asked, yet deep inside she knew.

"Come with us," he directed.

Sophia knew her fate was sealed. Her thoughts were only of her son.

"Please let the boy go. He's done nothing."

Sophia searched the man's eyes for compassion, finding none. Instead, with a snap of his fingers, the men surrounded the mother and her son and led them down the hall. The corridor remained quiet except for the echo of heavy boots.

There were tears running down her cheeks as Sophia descended the steps of the building towards the waiting truck. She kept her head erect but her eyes darted in all directions. Groups of students watched silently. They could do nothing, but their presence did not go unnoticed. The Savak guarded their anonymity and secrecy. They murdered and tortured in private. They would not want to create a scene.

Sophia drew Philip closer. She was flanked on either side—

but a few paces behind—by two of the soldiers. The leader of the group and the other brought up the rear. She was doomed but she glimpsed a risky chance for Philip.

Firmly, she whispered, "Live, then so will I." Then she shoved him as forcefully as she could and shouted. "Run, Philip! Run!"

Instinctively the boy obeyed his mother. He darted in front of the soldier to the right, past a small group of students, to the cluster of buildings off to the side. The soldiers halted. Their eyes sought their commander's. With a shake of his head, he directed them not to follow the boy. Instead he shoved Sophia into the waiting truck.

Gasping for air, Philip hid in the shadow of one of the buildings. He dared not scream as he watched the truck slowly pull away. He never saw his mother again. He ran home begging his father to find her. It was useless. Realizing his son was in danger, his father fled with him from Iran. No one spoke about it openly, but Philip heard the hushed whispers of people who talked about the anguish inflicted by the Savak. His sleep was haunted by nightmares imagining his mother's torture and death.

Arriving in the States, Philip was sent to live with his aunt and her husband, a well-respected physician in the Midwest. At first his father tried to find his mother. He beseeched the American government to intercede, but there was nothing anyone could do. Oil was a precious commodity. Maintaining a relationship with Iran was critical. The fate of a single woman was not. He died a broken man.

Throughout the years, Philip clung to the memory of his mother for strength and guidance. She'd been a wise woman who encouraged her son's brilliance and achievement. He dedicated his life to her memory.

Philip turned from the window and went back to his desk. Kathleen's file lay open before him. This was his next challenge. It was, after all, his mission. Glancing but a moment to his hands, with the long tapered fingers of a surgeon, Dr. Philip Wentworth reminded himself of the truth. The boy had been helpless to save his mother, but the plastic surgeon had found a way to heal the wounds of others.

■

Kathleen sat alone in the empty waiting room. She battled a familiar demon—the fear that the doctor would say there was nothing that could be done. She didn't hear Philip approach. Neither did he make his presence immediately known. Collecting his own thoughts, he studied her for a moment then softly called her name.

"Mrs. Clay?"

Kathleen slowly rose from the chair, steeling herself to meet the one doctor who might just be able to help her. A sense of calmness engulfed her. She'd experienced the feeling before when she'd taken her son and left her husband, the sense that somehow she was safe and doing the right thing.

"My office is the first door on the right," said Philip, taking a deep breath.

Seeing Kathleen unnerved him. Yes, it was the anniversary of his mother's death. And yes, while this woman shared her same birthday, he was carrying his grief too far. The delicate woman walking slowly down the hall was a patient, not the haunting ghost of his murdered mother.

Running his fingers through his thick hair, he followed Kathleen into his office.

"Sit down, Mrs. Clay."

Philip assumed the chair a safe distance behind his desk. He opened Kathleen's file but he could not take his eyes from her face.

"Why are you here?" he asked simply.

Slowly Kathleen raised her veiled glance to his.

"I want to live," she whispered.

A vise tightened around Philip's heart. "Live," his mother had whispered, "then so will I."

"Live?" he asked, his voice raspy. "What does that mean?"

More powerfully than he would have imagined, she replied, "I want to be whole once again." Briefly, she fingered the light black netting shielding her face. "Behind a veil there is no life, only a shadow of existence. Please, Dr. Wentworth, can you help me?"

"The procedure you would require is not an easy one. Do you have any idea what would be involved?"

"The doctors in Boston were vague."

"Facial reconstruction is a painful, arduous process. You would require two, possibly three surgeries, with several months in between to heal."

"What would you have to do?"

Philip's voice was kind and his manner a bit more thoughtful when he replied. It was always difficult to explain complicated surgical procedures in simple terms. He did his best.

"I've studied your file. The severity of your injuries is quite apparent. But I believe I can help you. The majority of your bones were crushed on the right side of your face. First, I would need to rebuild and reconstruct the entire area from the bones just below your eye clear to and including your jawline in order to correct the marked depression. This would be the most difficult part of the process. You have a great deal of damaged tissue along with the splintered and crushed bones. I'm not sure this could be corrected all at one time."

Kathleen remained silent but she hung on Philip's every word.

"After this has been completed and you have healed properly, I would eradicate the scars from the initial suturing. As I indicated earlier, this is a very delicate procedure and would require a lengthy hospital stay. You would be a virtual recluse for months."

Philip lowered his voice. "Even after all of this, there's no guarantee that surgery would be a complete success. You may never look as you did before. Do you understand?"

Kathleen nodded.

"Are you willing to take that risk?"

Kathleen's lips quivered. "What do I have to lose?" she asked simply.

Philip hesitated. "I spoke with Sam Ellis about your situation. He's making arrangements for you to remain here for your convalescence if we choose to go forward. I understand that you're married and in the process of divorce. Correct?"

Kathleen nodded.

"The reconstruction of your face will cost several hundred thousand dollars. Who will assume the financial burden?"

"My husband's mother is a wealthy woman. She's offered to pay all expenses."

The catch in Kathleen's voice did not go unnoticed, but Philip did not feel it was his place to comment. Instead he said, "Does your husband know you're here?"

"My husband is a vindictive man. I've lived in seclusion with my son in Boston since I left him. My whereabouts must be kept secret."

"What about your son?" Wentworth prodded. "Who would care for him during your absence?"

"He'll remain in Boston with his grandmother." Suddenly Kathleen grew anxious. "Please, Dr. Wentworth. You never answered my question. Can you help me?"

"Let me examine you. Then we'll decide."

With trembling hands, Kathleen removed her veiled hat and waited for the doctor to begin.

Almost ashamed, Kathleen kept her gaze averted as Philip slowly approached her. Bending slightly, he cupped her chin and gently lifted her face towards his. His grip was sure, his manner tender. Despite her anguish, Kathleen softened to his touch and that sense of calmness came over her again.

As he turned her slightly to the right, he could see that the left side of her face was flawlessly perfect. Her porcelain complexion was like that of a delicate cameo set against the backdrop of her shoulder length, honey blond hair. The sapphire blue of her uninjured eye was deep and compelling, yet the pain he saw there touched his heart.

Very slowly, he rotated her face to the left so the right side came sharply into focus. As he did, the magnificent woman faded from view. A horribly disfigured replica took her place. Hit by a large piece of flying steel, Kathleen had been gashed from the upper corner of her hairline, across her right eye, clear to the bridge of her nose. The laceration was deep, requiring initially over two hundred sutures to close. He could see that the cornea of her eye had been cut as well, but luckily, not as severely.

Philip gingerly fingered what had once been the right side of her face. Crushed, the fractured bones had splintered, causing a pronounced depression to that side of her face. This would be the greatest obstacle to restoring Kathleen to wholeness. Studying the wound carefully, Philip appeared almost aloof.

Slowly he forced her eyes back to his and for the first time they truly connected. She looked for the same horror and disgust she saw elsewhere. Instead in Philip's eyes, she found compassion. He searched for weakness. In Kathleen he found only strength. In that moment of connection they realized that they were embarking on a journey together. The journey through their scars would be a painful one.

Susan M. Hoskins

The call caught Sydney completely off-guard. The gruff voice on the phone introduced himself as Jacob Kahn, the station manager of KMKC. He kept the conversation brief. Would Sydney come to the station first thing Monday morning for a chat?

This is exactly where she found herself promptly at nine o'clock on Monday morning. She was dressed smartly in a conservative navy blue suit. She had no idea what to expect as she walked into the station carrying a small briefcase with her résumé and references in hand.

A fully equipped facility in a large metropolitan market, KMKC seemed, on first inspection, vastly superior to stations she had known in the past. Yet there was something familiar about the first person she encountered. No matter how big or small the market, television stations always chose the same look to greet the public. This young receptionist was under twenty-five, blonde and perfectly groomed. Sydney smiled.

The receptionist smiled back. "Good morning. How may I help you?"

"I'm Sydney Lawrence. I have an appointment with Mr. Kahn at nine o'clock."

"Oh yes, Ms. Lawrence. You're expected. Please have a seat. Someone will be with you shortly."

Settling into a plush, comfortable chair in the lobby, Sydney waited with growing anticipation. Nervously, she toyed with the mustard seed necklace Sam had given her New Year's Eve. It was coming to symbolize her new beginnings. She wondered what this new adventure might hold in store. She was kept in suspense but a few minutes. A short fellow bounded through the door calling her name.

Seeing the wiry man approach, Sydney's spirits sagged. He was scrawny with a hawkish nose and glasses that were much too large for his pinched face.

Sydney smiled only when he uttered his name.

"I'm Stephen Cranfield, the Director of Personnel. Normally, I would be the one to conduct the initial interview, but Mr. Kahn insists on seeing you himself. Come with me."

Following him into the newsroom, Sydney felt her pulse beat in rhythm to the machines and bustle of reporters formulating their stories. As always when a stranger approached, they stopped for a moment to stare. Not particularly impressed, they resumed their duties quickly. Deadlines mattered. Another pretty face was of little consequence.

To the left of the newsroom was the studio marked with a sign *No Admittance*. To the right was the office labeled *Jacob Kahn*.

"Go right in, Ms. Lawrence. He's waiting. Try not to be apprehensive. He's not quite as gruff as he appears."

Neither reassured nor intimidated, Sydney stepped through the door without knocking.

"Come right in, little lady!" the hearty fellow roared, rising halfway to his feet. "I'm Jacob Kahn. Most folks call me Jake. Have a seat."

Sydney complied. As unobtrusively as possible she scanned his sparsely decorated office. Her gaze came to rest upon the numerous plaques on the wall, his Commendations of Merit. As her wary eyes slowly returned to the man himself, she struggled to form a distinct impression.

Jacob Kahn would never be termed handsome. He was short and bald with a definite middle-age paunch. What little combed-over hair he had was disheveled. His closely set eyes were so small that Sydney couldn't even tell their true color behind the gold-rimmed glasses. She guessed him to be in his early sixties. He looked like a cross between Humpty Dumpty and Lou Grant.

Masking her confusion, Sydney returned her gaze to the boss.

"I'm tired of pretty faces who expect big money to put on a show. I grew up covering a beat where raw guts counted more than hard bodies and capped teeth. To this day, backbone and integrity mean a hell of a lot more to me than credentials." Kahn paused, seemingly to savor his cigar. "From what I can tell, little lady, you've got both!"

Leaning forward he continued, "I know you want the anchor's chair. However, my lead man still has a year to go on his contract. He's an airhead but the viewers love him. I've got something much bigger in mind for you."

Grabbing a stack of files from behind his desk, Jake Kahn thrust them before her.

"Here . . . in here . . . are the real stories! I need someone with enough grit and guts to find them."

Sydney started to comment but he silenced her.

"Kansas City is a good place, a damned good city, I might add! But we have crime. Did you know there's at least one homicide reported every other day here? And scandals? Like anywhere else, we've got an ugly side. Patting his secret files, he nodded. "We bury our garbage deep, that's the difference."

Gazing wistfully to the plaques on his wall, he paused, remembering another time, a different way.

"Times have changed, Sydney, that I know. But damn it! The truth is still the truth! And even if it's ugly, the people have a right to know. I'm no fool, Ms. Lawrence. You've got the talent to command a key position anywhere in town. But I've watched your tapes and from what I can tell you're hungry to report the *real* news. Don't you see? Anchors come and go. You're someone who could make a difference."

"I'm flattered, Mr. Kahn, but . . . "

"Don't be flattered, hear me out! Become the reporter I used to be, and the reporter I know you are. Find the story beneath the facade. Then present it truthfully. Commit yourself to me for a year. If you still want the anchor's chair after that, it's yours. No questions asked."

Letting pretense go by the wayside, Sydney retorted, "You're demanding a hell of a lot! What are you willing to pay?"

"No bullshit!" he laughed. "I like that. I'll start you off in the low nineties. Produce what I think you can and I'll raise you to six figures by the end of the year."

Paling, Sydney drew a deep breath. Her title might be investigative reporter but her salary would be commensurate with the top anchors in town.

"When do you need an answer?"

"Forty-eight hours or less."

"And censorship?" Sydney inquired. "Who would be in charge?"

"I'm the only censor you'd need to worry about. You'd answer to no one but me. I'll be your harshest critic, but I'm the man who can keep the wolves at bay."

Sydney sat back in her chair, buying a little time. Kahn's offer sounded intriguing, but it was different from anything she had ever tried. She glanced at the mustard seed necklace and thought, "Plant your faith—like a mustard seed—wisely. Watch it grow."

"I can give you my answer in four seconds. Hand me those files, Mr. Kahn. You and I have a deal."

"Well I'll be damned!" he bellowed, reaching in his desk drawer for a bottle of J & B Scotch and two glasses. Pouring her a straight shot, he grinned. "Drink up, little lady! This calls for a celebration!"

Swallowing hard, Sydney grimaced as the shot of Scotch burnt all the way down. Setting her empty glass upon the table, she fingered her necklace. "Looks like you've just been planted, little seed." Then she smiled at her new boss. A throwback to a time when journalists were not afraid, Jake Kahn had set her free. Theirs would not be a partnership made in heaven, but over Scotch and a stinking cigar.

■

Sydney hurried into the station early the next morning, well before nine o'clock. Taking only enough time to pick up her press pass, she barged into her new boss's office without knocking, her notebook and files in hand.

Jake Kahn took no notice. He was reading something that profoundly disturbed him. Absently, he reached for the large cherry Danish sitting atop his desk. Sydney cleared her throat in order to make her presence known.

Startled, he sputtered, "What the hell? Damn it, Sydney! Our meeting isn't until nine o'clock. Can't you let a man eat his breakfast in peace?"

Undaunted, Sydney took a seat opposite him. Kahn quickly dabbed his chin with a napkin but a significant portion of the jelly remained.

"You're not eating a very nutritious breakfast, Mr. Kahn."

He ignored her and quickly inhaled another bite.

"I understand we're covering a medical fair today. Perhaps you'd better get your cholesterol checked."

Disgusted, Kahn wrapped the remainder of his Danish in a napkin and set the gooey mess aside.

"Mind your own damn business, little lady! I deserve what meager pleasures I can find."

"You seem upset, Jake. What's wrong?"

The station manager's troubled glance returned to his papers. He liked Sydney Lawrence. He was happy she'd come aboard KMKC, but he had no history with the woman. She'd have to prove herself before he entrusted her with a story of this magnitude.

Jacob Kahn was perhaps the most respected newsman in Kansas City. He had enemies to be sure. More importantly, he had friends. Well-placed friends in high places. One of the best contacts he had was Tom Andrews, the Chief of Police.

During recent months, pieces of dismembered bodies had been found floating in the Missouri River. Hands with no fingers. Skulls with no teeth. The police were puzzled. They had no clues. There were no missing persons reports to link victims with murdered John Does. Chief Andrews had confided in Jake, asking for help in containing publicity. No one wanted to terrorize a city with the rumors of a serial killer on a rampage. Not until they had more facts. In return for sitting on the story, Chief Andrews would keep Jake informed so that when an arrest was made, KMKC would be the first station to break the story.

Jake had a hunch. Whoever was behind the macabre murders

had something definite in mind. These were not random hits. Somebody knew what he was doing. Hands with no fingers. Skulls with no teeth. *No means of identification.* There was something even more sinister than murder involved in this. One day he might enlist Sydney's help in the story. Not now. He had to be sure she was the reporter he hoped she was. In the meantime, he marked time. There would be more bodies. There would be more clues.

So instead of being truthful, he ignored her concern. "Why are you here?" he barked. "What do you have on your mind?"

"It was you who called the meeting, sir. It was my understanding you wanted to discuss my first assignment."

"So I did," Kahn muttered. "Did you study the file I sent home with you yesterday?"

"On the Winds?" she queried. "Yes, sir."

"What do you think?"

"I think it stinks."

"My feelings exactly," Kahn agreed. "Unfortunately, you and I are in the minority. The city fathers have thrown their wholehearted support behind the project with no regard for the people it hurts."

Kahn paused only long enough to monitor Sydney's reaction. "With your help, I'd like to burst their little bubble."

Her eyes brightening, Sydney grabbed a pen and pad.

"Where do we start?" she questioned.

"At the top," he countered slowly. "And at the bottom."

Seeing the confusion on Sydney's face, Kahn grinned.

"The Winds is a three-phased multimillion-dollar condominium, office and shopping complex, located just east of the Plaza."

"Yes," Sydney acknowledged. "I've seen it."

"The mastermind behind the Winds is a fellow named Gary Atwell. He's a horse's ass, but he's got clout and brains. He comes from a distinguished Kansas City family and he married money. He's slick as owl shit so watch your step. Gary Atwell is motivated by only one thing. That's greed. His vocabulary doesn't include words like compassion . . . only money and derivatives of power. He thrives on publicity. Let him think you're simply doing a story on the progress of construction. Sucker him in. Ask the right questions, then nail the bastard. I think you know what I mean."

"Yes, Jake. I think I do." Sydney paused. "What did you mean start at the top and at the bottom?"

Jake opened his desk drawer. Rifling through some loose papers, he extracted a name and handed it to Sydney.

"Gary Atwell will paint a lovely picture of the Winds and its eventual benefit to the community. This man will tell you quite another story."

Glancing at the note, Sydney questioned, "Charles Cole? Who is he?"

"Charles Cole is one of the forgotten ones, displaced in the name of progress. He lost his job when the restaurant he worked at was torn down to begin construction. Soon he'll lose his home as well. Kansas City is a caring city, Sydney. But like most metropolitan areas, our unemployment rate is high. Quite frankly, despite what the city fathers would have you believe, many folks here are prejudiced as hell. So to put it simply, despite his qualifications, there is no work for Charles Cole. In addition, he has a seriously ill child who may require a liver transplant. He's a black man with no job, no insurance, and soon no home. What kind of chance does he have? Pay him a visit, Sydney. Talk to him. Meet his family. Decide which version of progress you wish to pursue. Understood?"

Gathering her papers, Sydney stood.

"I suppose you'd like me to get started right away?"

Glancing at the remainder of his cherry Danish, Jake quipped, "The sooner the better! Perhaps then I can eat my breakfast in peace!"

■

Jake had a camera crew on standby at the station. First he wanted Sydney to scope the story. Alone in her car on this sticky summer's day, with a map as her only guide, Sydney traveled the side streets of Kansas City. From now on, life would not be simple. No two days would be alike. Her title would be *Special Investigative Reporter* doing topics of interest on the six o'clock news. From time to time, she might substitute for the current anchors. Mainly, her job was to dig . . . .

Beside her was the first of Kahn's puzzling files. Fingering the folder, she was anxious to begin. Driving slowly to the northeast, she came to an ugly ghetto, only blocks from the Plaza. Sydney was reminded of places she had visited in Mexico where people dwelt in hovels in the shadows of the finest resorts. Weaving her way through the littered streets, men with lifeless eyes watched her pass. Sydney wondered what life must be like for them.

She located the street, East 39th. And the building, Number 616. She parked her car but did not immediately go in. Peering over her shoulder, she had an eerie feeling she was being watched. Clutching her purse, she locked the car and walked briskly into the building.

Stepping over broken beer bottles, she started up the rickety stairs towards the Cole apartment. It was hot, unbearably hot in the building. The stench of garbage rotting in the hallway was overpowering. Sydney suddenly felt faint. Pausing to catch her breath on the landing, she felt a light fluttering sensation across her foot. She glanced down. Horrified, she started to scream but the poor rat looked nearly as frightened as she was. Gasping, she ran down the hall to the shabby apartment on the west end.

Sydney knocked sharply on the door of Apartment 301. When no one answered, she took a deep breath and tried again.

Finally she heard a soft, timid voice: "Go away."

Sydney spoke gently. "My name is Sydney Lawrence. May I speak to you please?"

"My mama don't allow strangers!" the child declared emphatically.

"I don't mean any harm. I just want a few minutes of your time."

Sydney waited, expecting a reply. Only silence filled the air. Discouraged, she decided to leave, vowing to return another time. As she turned to walk away, she heard the faint rattle of a chain.

A girl's frightened eyes were barely visible through the crack. "What do you want?"

"I'd like to talk with your parents. Are they home?"

"No," the little girl answered. "Not right now."

"Do you think I could wait for them?"

The little girl became suddenly frightened. "Are you from Division?"

"Division?" Sydney repeated, not comprehending.

"The Division of Family Services. Mama doesn't leave me alone very often. Today she had to work. Mama says we have to be careful. The social workers might try to take me away if they find me here alone."

Fumbling in her purse for her credentials, Sydney smiled. "I'm not from Division, honey. I'm a news reporter. See, here's my identification." Sydney held her press card in front of the cracked door, hoping the child could see it.

"We don't get too many white folks in this neighborhood," the little girl stated maturely. "What do you want?"

"I'm researching a story for a television report. I think your parents could help me. Do you think I might wait inside?"

Maybe it was the sincerity in Sydney's voice that made the difference. Or perhaps, it was simply the intriguing color of her burnished, copper hair. For whatever the reason, against the child's better judgment, she opened the door for a closer look.

"I guess it's okay if you come in."

Stepping through the door, Sydney tried to mask her revulsion as she glanced around the child's squalid surroundings. With no air conditioning and only a single fan, the tiny apartment was stifling. The bare light bulbs, peeling paint and exposed wires were more than a little disturbing. But as shabby as it was, the apartment was immaculately clean, and that amazed her.

Sydney took a seat on the tattered couch with the exposed springs. "Mama's due home in a few minutes. Once in a while she cleans houses but only if I'm feeling okay."

Engaging her tiny hostess politely, Sydney asked, "What's your name?"

"Tanya," the youngster replied. "Tanya Cole."

Sydney smiled as she observed the delicate child carefully. Tanya Cole was thin and obviously sickly. She had lovely, inquisitive eyes, but they were puffy and tinted with a jaundiced cast.

"How old are you?" Sydney inquired.

"Seven," Tanya answered.

Sydney was surprised. Although the child was dressed in patched jeans and a torn blouse, she appeared clean and well cared for and much older than seven.

"You look hot," Tanya observed. "Would you like a glass of water? We don't have much else."

Nodding, Sydney rose. "Let me get it."

Shrugging, Tanya followed.

"The glasses are in the cabinet above the sink."

Opening the cupboard above her head, Sydney reached for a glass. When she did, the shelf moved. In a sea of swirling black motion, the roaches scattered.

Aghast, Sydney backed away from the cabinet. Wheeling around sharply, she confronted not Tanya but another far more imposing figure. Regally, the woman stepped forward, her hand coming to rest protectively upon the child's bony shoulder.

"Who are you?" she demanded. "What do you want with us?"

Stunned, Sydney said nothing.

"State your business, Miss, or leave."

Sydney struggled to find her voice. "My name is Sydney Lawrence. I'm an investigative reporter with KMKC."

"What do you want with us?" the woman repeated.

"We're doing a story on the people displaced by the Winds project. I was hoping you might be of help."

Abruptly the woman nodded, indicating Sydney to follow.

"Now that you're here, have a seat. Go to your room, Tanya. It's time to rest."

The mother's gaze trailed her child as she disappeared into another room. Mrs. Cole was a tall, willowy woman. She had evenly spaced, nearly flawless features and creamy, mocha brown skin. Sydney imagined she might at one time have been a model because of her high cheekbones and classic nose. Sydney was surprised. It was obvious the woman with the seriously ill child had suffered greatly. She had expected her eyes to be dull and cold. Yet behind her regal carriage, her eyes were warm and full of compassion.

Those same lovely eyes glanced back to the kitchen where the cabinet door remained ajar. "We've begged the landlord to spray. He refuses."

She returned her sorrowful gaze to Sydney.

"May I call you by your first name?" Sydney inquired.

"Yes, my name is Belva."

"I understand that Tanya has a rare liver ailment."

"A rare *fatal* disease," Belva added. The resignation in her voice was all too clear.

"You've been told that a liver transplant is her only hope?"

Belva Cole grimaced. "Look around, Miss Lawrence. Here we have no hope."

"Can't something be done?" Sydney persisted.

Belva Cole wove her long, slender fingers tightly together in her lap. Fighting back tears, she turned away.

"There's nothing more we can do. We've taken our child to every hospital in town. All the doctors agree. A transplant is her only chance. Do you know what that involves?"

Sydney shook her head.

"To be put on the list you have to have money, lots of money. We don't have insurance and my husband is too proud to take welfare."

"Charles is your husband's name. Right?"

"Yes," she answered. "He's a good man and a hard worker. We're different, though. That's a fact. My parents made me finish high school. Charles got his education on the street."

Sydney reached into her purse for a pad and pen.

"My husband got in trouble when he was a boy. The judge ordered him into the Army. He fooled everybody because he decided to make something out of himself. He did well. He got special training in electronics. When he came home, he thought he'd have no trouble finding a good job. He was wrong. We managed, though. He worked as a fry cook in a restaurant. I had to quit my job at the Ford plant when Tanya was born. The baby was sick all the time. Finally, Charles lost his job when the project was begun and they tore the restaurant down. Now he does odd jobs whenever he can find the work. It takes every penny we have just to pay rent and put food on the table." Hopelessly, she glanced around their tiny apartment. "Soon they'll demolish our home as well."

"You spoke about the project. Do you mean the Winds?"

The mere name seemed to leave a bitter taste upon her lips. Sydney knew that this was the opportunity she sought to pursue the subject of the Winds, but somehow there seemed a much more immediate concern.

"Tanya's transplant," she ventured. "What would it cost?"

Sighing as if answering the question required more energy than she had to give, Belva replied quietly. "What difference does it make? It costs more money than we'll ever see. Every penny we've ever had has gone for Tanya's care. Without insurance, most doctors won't treat our baby without cash."

"Surely in a city this size, there must be someone who can help."

Trapping Sydney in the snare of her despondent eyes, Belva Cole answered. "No one cares."

Thinking of Jake Kahn, KMKC, and the resources she now had at her command, the feisty, fiery-haired reporter stared at her pen and pad. Rolling up her sleeves, she settled in to await Charles Cole's return. In the meantime, she had a story to write about a family shattered in the name of progress and a lovely little girl with a life-threatening disease who desperately needed help. It was then she dared to look Belva Cole squarely in the eye and state the very words the desperate mother needed to hear.

"I care, Belva. And I intend to prove it! I can have a crew here in a few minutes. Would you be willing to say into a camera what you just told me?"

After spending the afternoon with Charles, Belva and Tanya Cole, Sydney scheduled an on-camera interview with Gary Atwell, the developer of the Winds. Situated just north of the plush Country Club Plaza, Atwell's office was not hard to find. In fact, the luxurious building was less than a mile from Charles Cole's apartment. Sydney was struck by the irony of a city where poverty and deprivation dwelt only blocks from opulence and splendor.

Taking up the entire top floor of the most exclusive office building on Main Street, the glassed high-rise offered a panoramic view of the city.

Atwell's receptionist eyed the news team warily. "Mr. Atwell is expecting you. His office is the third door on the left."

Light, airy, plush—no expense had been spared on Atwell's office, nor by the looks of him, on the man himself. In his late fifties, Gary Atwell had silvery gray hair and a trim, well-toned physique. He was expensively dressed in a custom-tailored Italian suit with Gucci loafers. With a strong determined jawline and a perfectly shaped, patrician nose, his closely set eyes seemed cold and calculating. They were neither blue nor a true shade of gray, but rather a disturbing, unsettling color somewhere in between.

Accustomed to being interviewed, Atwell said, "How would you like to proceed?"

"Why don't we make this as comfortable as possible. I'd like to shoot this segment with you sitting behind your desk. Okay?"

Still smiling, Atwell complied. While the crew set up, he evaluated the news reporter, boldly eyeing her head to toe. "You're not from Kansas City, are you?"

"No," she replied, surprised by the question.

Refusing to elaborate, he nodded. "I thought not."

When the crew was ready, Sydney said, "I have a number of questions to ask you about the Winds. I'd like you to answer each one thoroughly. We'll edit the tape later to fit the segment. Okay?"

Atwell smoothed his hair and straightened his tie.

Holding a small microphone she began. "What can you tell me about the Winds, Mr. Atwell?"

"Where do I begin? The Winds project is a three-phased multi-million-dollar condominium, office and shopping complex located just east of the Plaza."

Atwell paused, eyeing Sydney smugly. "The first stage of construction is a high-rise office building due to be completed by the end of this current year."

"I understand that initially your project ran into difficulty with residents concerned with the effect a complex this size would have on the Plaza."

"Yes, unfortunately, that's true. You'll always find the bleeding hearts, Miss Lawrence. Uneducated, shortsighted people who are only willing to view things from their own limited perspective."

"Limited perspective?" Sydney repeated, as her mind wandered to Charles Cole and his roach-infested apartment. His perspective, thanks to Gary Atwell and the Winds project, was now limited to issues of basic survival.

"Do you have any idea how much business we will bring to Kansas City as a result of this development? We're talking millions, Miss Lawrence, hundreds of millions of dollars pumping life into the city's economy. We'll attract the kind of people not afraid to make things happen."

Having met the kind of people Atwell was describing, Sydney's expression cooled.

"Money, economics and prosperity . . . that's what we're discussing. If the price we have to pay is a sacrifice of some of the old ways, well then in my mind, the end more than justifies the means."

"And the people, Mr. Atwell. What about them?"

"The people?" he repeated, not understanding at all.

"The people who lost their homes and jobs as a result of this project."

Not liking the tack of their conversation, Atwell changed direction.

"Have you seen the complex for yourself, Miss Lawrence?"

"From a distance driving by."

"Well then, if you have the time, I'd like to broaden your horizons. Let's take a ride to the site."

Agreeing, Sydney terminated this portion of the interview. She, with her crew, followed Atwell's gleaming new white Mercedes to the Plaza. Sitting in the front seat of the station's van, she jotted notes, planning her strategy. Gary Atwell came to halt in front of the Winds, a massive complex under construction covering nearly a square mile. No small undertaking, the Winds would cost several hundred million dollars before the last of the three phases was completed. Sydney wondered how to champion the cause of a few unfortunate souls against such a mammoth undertaking.

It was a pleasant, breezy day in late June. The crew took a few minutes to film background shots before proceeding with Sydney's interview.

On camera she said, "How many people are now employed in the construction of the Winds?"

"Hundreds," he replied. "Maybe more."

"How many people have you displaced in the name of the project? Hundreds, maybe more?"

"I don't understand," Atwell replied curtly.

"How many people lost their jobs when you tore down their businesses and homes to start construction? What figures have you kept on them?"

"That's not my job, Miss Lawrence."

"What's being done for the forgotten ones, Mr. Atwell? Has your company helped them to find work or relocated them to better housing?"

Gripping the steering wheel tightly, Atwell stammered, "We've done what we could . . ."

"How many of these people have you employed in the construction of the project?"

A twinge of pain shot through Atwell's tightly clenched jaw. Grimacing, he spoke deliberately. "Most ghetto people are uneducated and not trained for the work we do."

"And if they were?"

"They'd be given a fair chance like everyone else."

"What if I knew one man among many," she continued carefully, "who'd been displaced by your project and likewise was still in need of a job? Would you be willing to consider him for employment?"

Atwell's reply was cool but correct. "By all means, if you know such a man, have him call my office."

Thinking he had handled the troublesome reporter cleverly, Atwell relaxed. Let the poor bastard apply for a job just like everyone else. Whether he was ultimately hired or not was of little or no concern. Unfortunately, Gary Atwell had grossly underestimated his opponent.

Sydney terminated this portion of the interview, then she turned to Atwell, frowning. "Oh dear," she mused aloud. "I don't think we have the time."

"The time?" he repeated.

"It's already Wednesday. I plan to air my story by the end of the week. Perhaps you'd like to meet the man before I piece together the story. Or perhaps . . . you'd rather go back on camera and tell the viewers you declined."

Grinding his pearly white teeth, Gary Atwell faced Sydney Lawrence squarely. His cheeks were crimson when he haughtily inquired, "Do I detect a threat?"

Offering the developer her most alluring smile, Sydney merely stated, "Charles Cole lives just a short distance from here. If we leave now, we might just find him at home. I'm sure he's just the kind of man your company would love to hire."

"No doubt," Atwell sniped, "you could direct me."

The slight arch of her eyebrow and the self-satisfied curve of her mouth stated the obvious.

■

With great reluctance, Gary Atwell followed the KMKC van to the squalid building. When Sydney approached, he opened his mouth to speak but he could not find the appropriate words. Instead, he glanced around the neighborhood. Men lurking in the shadows were watching him with dull, hostile eyes. Gary Atwell was afraid. He hated the ghetto and all its inhabitants because deep within its crevices were pieces of humanity he could not control.

Sydney asked her crew to remain in the truck. Charles Cole was a man of dignity. She thought he deserved a private meeting with Atwell. Later, if an arrangement was made for employment, she would conduct an interview with both men on camera.

"Shall we go inside?" she inquired.

"Of course," Atwell stammered. "If you think it's safe."

Sydney eyed the entrepreneur with contempt.

"No one will bother you, Mr. Atwell."

Atwell followed her into the building. After touching the door, he grimaced as he examined his hands. No one knew they were coming. No one had cleaned to impress them.

Determined to do her story, Sydney tried to control her temper, not for her sake but for the Coles. After all, Atwell did have the power and resources to help this family.

Turning, Sydney started up the stairs but she was forced to dodge a piece of falling plaster.

"Watch your step," she instructed. "The wood on the stairs is rotten."

She knocked lightly on the door of Apartment 301, then waited for Tanya to answer. Instead it was Belva, looking tired and wan, who responded.

"Sydney, it's good to see you. Come in."

"Belva, I'd like you to meet Gary Atwell. He wants to speak with Charles if he's home."

"Of course," Belva answered. "Follow me."

Taking but a few steps, Sydney halted. There on the worn, tattered couch lay Tanya. Her color was jaundiced, her stomach distended, her eyes glassy and unfocused.

"My baby's worse, Sydney. Much worse. I don't know how much longer we can wait."

Leaving Atwell behind, Sydney hurried to the couch and knelt down beside the listless child. Stroking Tanya's forehead, she soothed, "Hi, honey."

"Sydney," Tanya whispered. "Is that you?"

"Yes, darling. Your mama tells me you're not feeling well today."

"I'm glad you're here. Hold my hand."

Sydney took her fragile hand and kissed it gently. "I feel so helpless, Tanya. I wish there was something I could do."

Tanya's voice grew raspy. "Help my mama," she whispered. "She's so scared."

Tucking the covers protectively around the child, Sydney stood as Atwell lowered his glance in embarrassed silence. Ignoring him, Sydney linked arms with Belva and followed her into the kitchen.

"Where's Charles?" she inquired.

"I'll get him, Sydney."

Belva turned to leave but something about Atwell caused her to halt. She glanced at him for only a moment—to have stared longer would have been thought rude—but Sydney could see the scorn hidden in her eyes.

"Sit down, Mr. Atwell," she directed.

Charles emerged a few minutes later, his swollen eyes red from too little sleep and too much worry. He was a gaunt man with an intelligent face who was clean and neatly dressed.

Standing, Sydney said, "Charles, I have someone I would like you to meet."

Atwell rose halfway to his feet.

"Charles Cole, Gary Atwell."

Politely, Charles extended his hand. Atwell hesitated a moment before shaking hands.

"Mr. Atwell owns Atwell Development, the company responsible for the Winds."

Charles's chiseled features hardened noticeably. Out of respect for Sydney, he held his tongue.

"I understand you're out of work and need a job," Atwell said pleasantly. "My company would like to help."

"Your company didn't give a damn when they tore down the restaurant where I worked. Why would you want to help me now?"

Atwell turned to Sydney. She chose to let him dangle all alone.

"We need good men like you who are not afraid to work. Sydney tells me you've had experience."

His eyes narrowing but his spine still erect, Charles repeated, "Experience? Yes, Mr. Atwell, I've had plenty of experience in the Army, at work and in life. What kind of ...experience ...do you want?"

"We need construction workers, electricians and carpenters."

"I can do it all and I can do it well. I'm not afraid to work. I've never been a man to take something for nothing."

Charles's unrelenting gaze would not let Gary Atwell be. Despite his prejudice, Atwell admired what he saw. In Cole he found a man who was not afraid of power nor intimidated by money.

"Do you have a union card?" Atwell asked.

"You can't get a card without a job and you can't get a union job without a card. So no, sir, there you have it."

"The construction company we use hires only union workers. We can get you a card but it'll take time."

"Time, sir, is what I don't have." Glancing over his shoulder, Charles lowered his voice. "My baby's sick and I can't help her. I need to work. I'm a man. I want to feel like a man again by providing for my family. I want a job."

Sydney leaned forward causing Atwell to turn.

"Isn't there something else Charles could do in the meantime? A job that wouldn't require a union card?"

Gary Atwell leaned back in the rickety chair and pondered. Buying time, he glanced from one to the other. If he so chose, he now had a way out. No card, no job. No job, no card. Yet despite himself, he liked the kind of man he found Charles Cole to be. He knew in his gut that he would not regret giving this man and his family a break. In addition, there was the matter of the reporter. Sydney Lawrence was much too cunning. She'd never accept the lame excuse he had tried. No matter what he did, she would air her story. How did he want to be portrayed? A thought crossed his mind.

"Well there might be one thing," he offered slowly. "We do need a security guard for the project. Atwell Development could hire you instead of the construction company. That way you wouldn't need a union card. The job would require you being on the premises nights and weekends. Would you be willing to leave your family for that long?"

Helplessly, Charles's spirits plummeted. To abandon Tanya and Belva at this time would be unthinkable.

"No sir," he answered. "I couldn't do it."

Tracking every word of their conversation like balls being volleyed at a tennis match, Sydney had remained astutely silent. Finally she had to intervene.

"But would he have to? Couldn't a trailer be provided for his family on site? That way he could be on call at all times. Think about it, Mr. Atwell. Not only would you be the one to finally give this man a job, but your company would provide him with a decent home as well." Sydney's piercing hazel eyes sparkled with intent. "I like the slant," she drawled deliberately so he could not mistake her meaning. "I like it a lot."

Atwell started to protest but Charles stopped him.

"I don't want charity, Mr. Atwell. I want to work. If you give me a chance, I won't let you down. That I promise."

Feigning resignation, the developer acquiesced. "All right! All right! I know a good man when I meet him. The job is yours, Cole. I'll put you on the payroll at once. How soon can you start?"

"I can start immediately."

Charles Cole came to his feet. Warmly, he extended his hand for a shake. This time Gary Atwell shook the man's hand with no hesitation.

Pivoting, Atwell confronted Sydney directly. It was in a level, even voice that he said, "I'm giving this man a chance because he's got guts and I like him. And not for any other reason!"

"All he needed was a chance, Mr. Atwell. The rest is up to him."

"Belva, come here, honey!" Charles shouted. "I've finally got some good news!"

His wife appeared in the doorway but she was devoid of any joy. Her face was streaked with tears and her lips quivered.

"My baby!" she cried. "My baby!"

Fleeing the kitchen, Charles rushed to his daughter's side. Dropping to his knees beside the pale, lifeless child, he cried, "Tanya!"

It was in a weak, frightened voice that she whispered, "Papa."

Trying to calm the tears that flowed in uneven patterns down Belva's cheeks, Sydney exclaimed, "I'll call an ambulance!" No sooner had she uttered the words, she realized there was no phone. "Where's the nearest phone, Charles?" she asked helplessly.

Pushing past her, Atwell barked, "There's no time! We'll take her to the hospital in my car! It'll be faster!"

A man who relished being in charge, Atwell scooped the fragile child up and fled the apartment. Cradling the tiny girl protectively in his arms, he bolted down the stairs. His mind was racing as he planned the route he would take out of the ghetto. At the curb, he thrust Tanya back into her father's trembling arms while he fumbled for his keys and unlocked his car.

Charles tried desperately to remain calm for Tanya's sake and for Belva's. But his guts were churning and an odor of fear oozed from his pores. Climbing into the front seat, he held his baby tightly while Sydney, after shouting for her crew to follow, joined Belva in the rear. Atwell started his engine, turned on his flashers, and quickly sped away.

"Where should I take her?" he shouted.

Sydney leaned forward for a better look. "Isn't St. Vincent's the closest hospital? My husband is the Chief of Staff."

Atwell punched the mobile emergency number into his cellular phone. His voice was shaky but still in control when the dispatcher answered.

"This is Gary Atwell. I'm driving a white Mercedes, license number JOA41919. I'm located at 45th," he paused and scanned the street for a sign. "45th and Harrison! I need a police escort to St. Vincent's Hospital. I have a critically ill child and I need assistance. Repeat, this is urgent! I need help!"

Breaking the connection, Atwell handed the phone back to Sydney. "Alert the hospital!" he commanded.

Sydney quickly dialed the number she had already memorized.

Cutting the operator short, she cried, "Put me through to Dr. Sam Ellis! I'm his wife and this is an emergency! Hurry, please!"

In less than a minute, he answered.

"Sam, I'm on route to the hospital with the Cole child. Remember, I told you all about her last night. She's the little girl with the liver disease. She's taken a turn for the worse"

Sam interrogated her briefly. In response to his final question she answered, "I'd guess it'll take us about five to eight minutes to get to you. Wait! I hear sirens! The police escort is here! Get ready for us! We'll be there shortly, Sam!"

Belva cast her eyes to Sydney. She said nothing, but the anguish in her eyes broke Sydney's heart. This was the day they had dreaded.

Whimpering in her father's arms, Tanya pleaded. "Don't let me die, Daddy! Don't let me die!"

His hands clenched tightly around the wheel, Gary Atwell tried to ignore the child's tears. Gunning the engine, he sped faster, cursing the police to hurry. Power, force, speed—this was what Gary Atwell knew and the only part of himself he had to give.

Minutes later, they screeched to a halt outside the emergency room door. True to his word, Sam was waiting with a full staff to assist.

"They're here!" he shouted. "Stretcher, stat!"

Sam ran to the car and threw open the door. Taking the child from her father, he placed Tanya safely on the gurney and wheeled her swiftly into the hospital.

Charles, Belva and Sydney immediately followed. With his

Mercedes still idling, only Gary Atwell remained behind. Shaken, alone in his car, he mopped the sweat dripping from his furrowed brow. The stress, the tension, the adrenaline had taken their toll.

Backing his car out of the drive, he straightened his tie and glanced for a moment into the mirror. Smoothing his hair, he took a deep breath. It was time to return to his world. He had already tarried far too long. Retrieving his phone, he dialed his secretary as a most interesting idea crossed his mind. Sydney Lawrence had accused him of being a man with no compassion, head of a company with no heart. The cool smile slowly returned to his face.

"Helen, alert the Public Relations Department for an immediate press release concerning one Charles Cole."

A job, a home, perhaps even a small donation—Atwell Development could play this tragedy to the hilt.

He liked the sound of his own headline. *"Atwell Development Refuses to Abandon the Forgotten Ones!"*

His mind once again separated from his heart, Gary Atwell returned to his office and the only part of himself he knew well.

■

Sam emerged from the emergency room thirty minutes later looking worn. His handsome face was etched with worry. Despite his years of training, he was not particularly skilled in masking his emotions, especially where children were concerned. His greatest asset, his compassion, was in this instance, his most pronounced weakness. Sam took a chair in the waiting room beside Sydney, across from Charles and Belva Cole. The lounge was nearly empty, yet he drew the group inward to maintain the privacy of their conversation.

"How is she?" Charles stammered. "Is my baby . . . ?"

"She's stabilized for now, but your daughter is critically ill."

Charles lowered his head, trying to mask the terror that welled up in his eyes as tears.

"Her liver is failing rapidly. We're doing an extensive work-up now. So far, her kidneys are still functioning, but they could deteriorate at any time."

"What can be done, Sam?" Sydney implored.

"Tanya suffers from a condition called Biliary Artresia. Her bile ducts have failed to develop normally, preventing bile from being drained from her liver."

Trapping Sydney in the intimacy of his sorrowful gaze, Sam shook his head helplessly. "The disease is much too advanced. We're powerless to do more than maintain her. Her condition will deteriorate by the hour. What she needs to survive ... we just can't provide."

"A liver?" Sydney asked, already knowing the answer.

"A liver transplant," Sam confirmed. "It's her only hope."

Belva buried her head in Charles's embrace, weeping openly. But Sydney refused to accept the hopelessness of the situation.

"Damn it, Sam! There must be something we can do! What would it take to obtain a liver?"

Taking a deep breath, Dr. Sam Ellis tried to buy a few seconds of the precious commodity that was so scarce. Time.

"What would it take?" he repeated. "Time, money and a suitable donor, none of which we have here. I'm not an expert on organ transplants, Sydney, but they cost thousands of dollars. Besides, St. Vincent's is not accredited to do the procedure and Tanya is too critical to be moved."

Her eyes glistened with determination. "Well then, who *is* the expert?"

"The Regional Director of Organ Procurement," Sam answered. "Farhad Rajid."

Rising, Sydney proclaimed, "I want to see him, Sam. It's a long shot but I have an idea. Could you arrange a meeting immediately?"

Wearily, Sam likewise rose to his feet. At this point, any action seemed better than no action at all. But unlike Sydney, the realistic physician could see no miracle lurking in the bottom of the magician's hat.

■

Within minutes, Sydney found herself in the waiting room of Farhad Rajid's office. Preoccupied with the child's immediate condition, Sam remained by Tanya's side.

Sydney peered at Farhad Rajid through the open doorway.

The Director of Organ Procurement was a small, fastidiously groomed, darkly handsome man who seemed consumed by the paperwork upon his desk.

Finally in his own time, he pushed the papers aside and called her in. As she entered, they locked eyes briefly. It was Farhad Rajid who glanced away, and Sydney felt a queasiness from somewhere deep within.

He gestured for her to take a seat, as he resumed his own chair. "How may I help you?"

"I appreciate you taking the time to see me, Mr. Rajid. I want to ask you a few questions about organ transplants. One case in particular."

"The Cole child," he responded coolly. "Correct?"

"Yes," Sydney retorted. "Are you familiar with the case?"

"Only what your husband has told me."

Sydney plunged ahead. "Tell me how the system works."

Rajid's manner seemed aloof and to Sydney disturbingly condescending. Turning, he sought to familiarize her with a rather large, complicated piece of equipment.

"It's really quite simple," he explained. "Through the computer, St. Vincent's Hospital is tied into UNOS, the United Network for Organ Sharing located in Richmond, Virginia. When we discover a need, such as the Cole child, we input the necessary patient data."

"What data?" Sydney interrupted.

"The clinical diagnosis, condition status, and age of the patient, as well as blood and tissue type. For a liver transplant, the only requirements are that the donor and recipient be approximately the same size and of compatible blood types. A specialist from UNOS takes this information and matches it to potential donors. Once a match is made within our general location, the patient is flown to the nearest hospital doing transplants and the operation takes place.

"Why solely within the general location?"

"The reason should be obvious," Rajid answered curtly. "Time is a critical factor. Once a donor is found, the organ is harvested and placed on ice. But depending upon which organs are involved, they can only be kept viable between four and twenty-four hours, some a little longer."

Perhaps it was the futility of the situation coupled with a reporter's sixth sense, but there was something about Farhad Rajid Sydney did not like.

Leaning forward, she forced his cunning eyes to hers. "How much money would it take for Tanya Cole to be considered?"

The slight curve to Rajid's lips seemed almost malicious. "Since the family has no insurance, they would need at least a hundred thousand dollars to be put on the list for consideration. This would cover the preliminary cost of the operation should a suitable donor be found in time. In addition, many facilities require up to three hundred thousand as a reserve in case something goes wrong."

Undaunted by the staggering amount of money required, Sydney pondered her next question.

"Suppose we could raise the money? How quickly could you locate a suitable donor?"

Farhad Rajid's answer seemed devoid of human emotion. "Currently there are 2,765 candidates . . . all with a legitimate need . . . on the list awaiting a liver. What makes you think this little girl deserves priority?"

"Jake, I'd like you to meet my husband, Sam Ellis. Sam, this is my boss, Jake Kahn."

The two men shook hands briefly.

"Please have a seat," Sam directed. Kahn lowered his bulky frame into the leather chair across from Sam's desk.

"Thanks for coming over on such short notice, Jake," said Sydney. "I've got a breaking story that can't wait."

"You sounded pretty anxious on the phone, Sydney. Fill me in."

"I spent yesterday afternoon with the Cole family. Then today, I interviewed Gary Atwell. As you predicted, I learned a whole lot more than I anticipated."

The station manager of KMKC permitted himself the pleasure of only a slight smirk. "I thought you might, little lady. What have you got?"

"The Cole child is very ill. She took a turn for the worse today. She's here now in critical condition."

"Go on."

Sam broke in. "Tanya Cole desperately needs a liver transplant. She won't survive long unless a suitable donor can be found. Since the Cole family has no insurance, we can't even begin the search for a liver until we have the necessary funds secured. It may seem unfair but that's the way the system works. No insurance, no money, no chance."

"Charles Cole doesn't have that kind of money," Sydney

continued. "Nor does he have the ability to raise it. That's where we come in."

"How?" asked Kahn, dreading the direction the conversation was taking.

"I'd like to run their story on the six o'clock news and broadcast an appeal for immediate donations. If this city has the heart you claim it does, Jake, it's possible that we could raise the money in time."

"How much are we talking about?" Kahn asked.

Sydney took a deep breath. "For Tanya to even be *considered* for a liver transplant, we have to raise a hundred thousand dollars. That's only the beginning. Before any surgery takes place, we'd need a reserve just in case anything goes wrong."

"How much time do we have?"

Remaining silent, Sam and Sydney locked worried eyes.

"Weeks, days," Kahn prodded. "How long?"

Shifting his gaze to Kahn, Sam replied, "A few days. Probably no more."

"So what you're asking," Kahn deduced, "is impossible." Shifting his bulky frame uncomfortably in the straight-back chair, Kahn forced Sydney's attention to follow.

"Set your emotions aside, Sydney. Track this thing logically with me. Even if I give the go-ahead to do the story, chances are we can't raise the money in time."

"No," she argued, "but ... "

Kahn dismissed her protest. "The key to your success with KMKC is your acceptance by the community and your long-range appeal. That's why it's crucial your first story be well-timed, appropriate and thought provoking. If we rush into this, no matter how worthy the cause, and we fail, how will it look? Nobody wants to donate money only to have it wasted."

Sydney flushed. "We're talking about a human life, Jake! This child will die without a liver transplant. How can we sit idly by and do nothing? I don't give a damn who broadcasts the story. If you think it's too risky for me, give it to your anchor. All I know is that without our help there is no hope for Tanya Cole. Aren't you the same man who told me he was tired of playing it safe?"

Exhaling sharply, Jake glanced first to Sydney and then to Sam. Finally he returned his gaze to Sydney. "I don't like it, Sydney. You're putting yourself on the line for a hopeless cause. Believe me, it's not an auspicious way to begin. But I admire your guts. More importantly, I can't deny this child her only chance."

Glancing at his watch, he shook his head. "We don't have much time but we already have a crew here. I'll alert the station."

Turning to Sam, he reached for the phone. "I'd like to meet the child and her parents. Then with your permission, Dr. Ellis, we'll broadcast the story from here."

■

6:00 pm

"Good evening, ladies and gentlemen, this is Jim Stevens with KMKC. We begin tonight's broadcast with a heartbreaking saga taking place right now at St. Vincent's Hospital. Earlier today, a seven-year-old child was admitted in critical condition. Tanya Cole suffers from a rare liver disease called Biliary Artresia. She will die within days without a liver transplant. For more on this story we switch to the Intensive Care Unit at St. Vincent's Hospital, and the newest member of the KMKC news team, Special Investigative Reporter Sydney Lawrence. Sydney?"

Taking a deep breath, Sydney waited for the director's cue. Smiling nervously, she faced the Kansas City audience for the first time.

"Thank you, Jim. The story of Tanya Cole is not a pretty one. Since birth, Tanya has suffered from a complicated medical condition which prevents her from living the kind of life most of us take for granted. But life, as fragile as it is, will elude Tanya Cole for good unless a suitable liver can be found.

"Unfortunately, our current medical system cannot provide the surgery she needs without your help. Without insurance or the money to pay for their daughter's operation, her parents, Charles and Belva Cole, are powerless to save her. I'd like you to follow me now into the Intensive Care Unit to meet Tanya and her parents. The staff, together with the machines you hear in the background, can maintain this child for a while. How long? No one can say.

"In order to be eligible for the federal computer list of suitable donors," Sydney continued, "the Coles must secure the funds to cover the cost of the operation. Without an initial deposit of a hundred thousand dollars, Tanya cannot even be considered for an organ or for life. After that, she'll require a reserve of at least another hundred thousand dollars before the transplant can take place.

"In 1984, the Senate passed a bill to insure the equitable distribution of organs. The system, however, is far from fair. Without insurance or a substantial sum of money, children like Tanya have no chance. In Tanya's case, the cost of her survival begins with a hundred thousand dollars."

Sydney paused for effect. Then taking a deep breath, she turned her pleading eyes a final time toward the camera.

"We need your help and your generous support to grant Tanya Cole her last chance at life. There is no guarantee that our efforts will be successful or in time. A miracle is this child's only hope.

"At the end of this segment, a phone number will be flashed on your screen. Operators at KMKC are standing by to take your pledge tonight. Country Club Bank has established a trust account in the name of Tanya Cole to accept your donations. We'll meet Tanya Cole now, and I think afterwards you'll agree that this is a child who deserves to live. This is a child who needs a miracle now!"

■

Jake Kahn waited in the studio for the cameras to dim and the anchor to leave his chair.

"Get Sydney Lawrence on the line!" he barked.

Nodding to his camera crew, he displayed little emotion as he waited for Sydney to answer. Pacing the studio, with the cordless phone cradled to his ear, he maintained a reserved smile but deep in his eyes there was a measure of satisfaction.

"That was a good piece, little lady. Now all we can do is wait and see."

Still cradling the phone, he exited the studio. The newsroom was quiet. Today's stories for now had been completed.

"Next time you're on," he continued, "we'll have to give the viewers a more thorough introduction to Sydney Lawrence, Special Investigative Reporter. For now you came across well."

His mind racing ahead to the next broadcast, Kahn sauntered down the hall. To his right, a phone light began blinking. First one and then another. In rapid succession a third, fourth and fifth. Halting abruptly, he stared as everyone in the newsroom scrambled to answer their phones.

"Jake!" Sydney exclaimed. "What's wrong?"

Again her boss ignored her. He was too engrossed in another dilemma. The nervous staccato pitch of his assistant's voice pierced his eardrum.

"We've got people calling in from all over town wanting to donate, Mr. Kahn, and only three operators standing by. What do you want us to do? The switchboard can't keep up!"

"Call in reinforcements! Round up everybody not currently on assignment!"

"Jake!" Sydney shouted. "What's going on?"

Retrieving a pencil from behind his ear, Jake Kahn grinned, content with himself and the newest member of his KMKC team.

"Can't talk to you now, Sydney. I'm needed on the phone!"

Susan M. Hoskins

9:00 am

Sydney paced outside the Intensive Care Unit as she had for the better part of an hour. It was Thursday, June 30. Finally Sam appeared.

Anxiously, she grabbed his arm. "How's Tanya?"

"Not good." Taking her hand, Ellis led his wife away from the unit. "How do we stand?" he asked.

"We're close, Sam, but still short. At last count, eighty-five thousand dollars had been pledged."

"The clock is running out, Sydney. Being close just isn't there."

Deflated, Sydney gave her husband a quick hug and hurried out. Sam was right, of course. Pledges were one thing, cash in hand quite another.

■

11:35 am

Sydney returned to the station but her thoughts remained with the Coles. Unfortunately there was little she could do for them. Tanya's fate now lay in the hands of the people of Kansas City.

She had checked with the bank twice in the last hour, confirming the figures she had relayed to Sam. The phone lines had calmed significantly since the flood of last night. Sporadically a pledge or two dwindled in. The viewers had responded to the emotion of her broadcast, but Tanya's plight had dimmed with the new dawn.

Staring blankly at the script before her, Sydney tried to plot her next move. Kahn had okayed a follow-up broadcast from St. Vincent's tonight. Perhaps a few thousand more could be raised then. If Tanya had not worsened significantly. If another's story had not become even more compelling today. If . . . if . . . if.

The phone on her desk blinked, signaling yet another call. Composing herself, she put her troubled thoughts aside as she calmly answered, "Sydney Lawrence."

"Good morning, Ms. Lawrence. That was a good piece you did last night."

She recognized the voice and involuntarily flinched. "What can I do for you, Mr. Atwell?"

"How's the Cole child?"

Sydney sighed wearily. "She's holding her own. Just barely."

"How much have you raised?" Atwell asked bluntly.

"Eighty-five thousand. Perhaps by now a little more."

The pause on the other end of the phone was profound.

"Despite what you may think, Ms. Lawrence," said Atwell, "my company is one of compassion. We'd like to help."

"How?" Sydney said warily.

"With a donation and a challenge."

"A challenge?" Sydney repeated.

"To start, my company will pledge the remaining money needed to begin the search for a donor liver."

Atwell paused. Sydney was startled and pleased by the donation. Tanya could now be registered with UNOS and the search for a donor liver begun.

"But our efforts will be wasted," Atwell continued, "unless we raise the necessary funds for the operation. Am I not correct, Ms. Lawrence? Isn't this what you broadcast last night?"

Taking a deep breath, Sydney agreed. "Yes, Mr. Atwell. We would have to raise at least another hundred thousand dollars before any surgery can take place."

"All right then. What if I have a way to raise the whole damn amount? What would you say to that?"

"Go on."

"Atwell Development will put up a sizable sum of money and challenge other Kansas City corporations to do the same. I think that you'll find the spirit of *competition* thrives here, perhaps even more than compassion. No one in the corporate world wants to be outdone, particularly in matters, shall we say, so close to the heart."

Wary of the tone of his voice, Sydney shot back, "Where were you and your sense of compassion before this began, Mr. Atwell? When did you start giving a damn about people like the Coles?"

Atwell measured his words carefully. "You're playing hardball with me, Ms. Lawrence. Are you quite sure you're in a position to do so? It seems to me that you can't afford to lose."

Sydney's jaw tightened to the point of pain. He was right and she knew it. Her personal feelings about Gary Atwell and the Winds project were irrelevant. Tanya Cole's life was at stake.

"Assuming we accept your donation and the corporate challenge, what would you expect in return?"

"My company only wants to be of help. You should realize that by now, Ms. Lawrence."

Sydney resisted arguing with him. The truth was, Atwell's scheme might just work if they could pull it off in time.

"I'll go you one better, Mr. Atwell. It's nearly noon. Get your own Public Relations Department involved. You put out the challenge and see how quickly we can get results. I go on the air in six hours. Give me a real story to report. Give me the money in hand."

■

Sam Ellis barged into Farhad Rajid's office. "We've got the money! Now get me a liver!"

Sydney had done it. She had pulled off the impossible. Just minutes ago, broadcasting live from the lobby of St. Vincent's, she had accepted checks from Atwell Development and several other major Kansas City corporations. They had raised nearly a quarter of a million dollars! One miracle had been achieved. Obtaining the second miracle, the precious liver, might be even more difficult.

"Sir, what you ask is impossible!" objected Rajid. "I'll input the data immediately but it will take time even to process the child's application. She'll be given a high priority, of course, because of her critical condition. But there's no telling when a suitable donor can be located. Time, sir, these things take time."

Sam had no patience with the Director of Organ Procurement. Using his status and his stature, he towered above Rajid's desk. He spoke sharply.

"I have every reason to believe that it can be done. If this were your child or mine, we'd do everything possible to get priority. Don't tell me there's no way around the system. I'm cynical enough to know that if you want something badly enough it can be had. In conjunction with this, you posed a question to my wife yesterday that I found offensive."

Taken aback, Rajid countered. "Oh really, sir? What was that?"

"You asked her, *'What makes you think this child deserves priority?'* Well I'll go you one better, Rajid. What makes you presume she doesn't? If this were the daughter of someone important, every string in the book would be pulled. Right or wrong, fair or not, I want you to put forth the same effort for Tanya Cole. Do you understand?"

Farhad Rajid paled. He understood more than Sam Ellis could possibly imagine. His face was stoic and his voice calm but inside his guts were churning when he replied. "Give me a few hours, Dr. Ellis. Let me see what I can do."

The Regional Director of Organ Procurement waited until the door to his office had closed and he was certain Sam Ellis was gone. Then wiping the dampness from his brow, he tried to think what to do. He had a network in place around the country. He needed an organ. He needed it quickly. Finally he decided upon his contact in Texas, Region 4. He had proved himself to be trustworthy and resourceful.

Rajid was relieved when a familiar voice answered.

"I have a serious problem. I need a liver. I need it badly. Search the computer for a match. If you find one, my request gets top priority. If you don't find a match, do whatever it takes to obtain one. Pay any price. Just get me the organ!"

Rajid relayed the data his contact would need to complete the search. He paused as he was asked a most important question.

"Twenty-four hours. That's all we have. I repeat. Do whatever it takes to get the liver in time. Just be careful. Every step we make will be monitored."

Rajid's hands were trembling as he cradled the receiver. His operation to this point had been flawless. Americans he had found to be such trusting fools. In a society based upon free enterprise, no one had thought to market the very commodities— so valuable yet so limited—that a desperate individual would pay any price to obtain.

Friday, July 1
5:00 am

The ringing of the phone seemed at first hazy and distant. He caught it on the fourth ring. Glancing at the clock, Sam realized it was not yet dawn.

"Dr. Ellis, I apologize for disturbing you. This is Farhad Rajid."

"Yes, Farhad. What is it?"

"I've located a possible donor. Could you meet me in my office as soon as possible?"

"Certainly," Ellis snapped awake. "I'll be there in forty-five minutes."

Hearing the name *Farhad* Sydney too came awake.

"What is it, Sam? What's happening?"

Sam turned to his wife. "That was Farhad Rajid. He may have found a donor."

Sydney threw off the covers.

"Go back to sleep, honey. I'll call you from the hospital."

"No, Sam," she argued. "I'd like to come with you."

"Let's hurry, then."

On his way to the bathroom, Sam paused. Turning to Sydney with a quizzical look, he had to state a troubling thought.

"What is he doing in his office so early? I wonder if he stayed at the hospital all night? Perhaps he's more compassionate than I realized."

It was not compassion on his face that Sydney saw as she trailed her husband into Rajid's office. Seeing her, his expression clearly changed. Was it anxiety she saw or was it scorn?

Sam quickly began the meeting. "Tell me what you have."

Clearing his throat, the Director of Organ Procurement replied. "I've located a possible donor in Texas. The child was in an automobile accident and suffered a severe head injury. He's still alive but he's in extremely critical condition. There's virtually no brain activity. He's being maintained on life support."

"Is it a suitable match?"

Rajid nodded. "We have a Caucasian child, nine years old, but small for his age with O-positive blood. For our purposes, the organs would be compatible."

Exhaling sharply, Sam queried, "What do we do now? Has consent been obtained?"

"Consent will be no problem, sir. The family has been made aware of our situation. That is why the child is still being maintained on life support. We must act quickly. Time, as you know, is a critical factor."

Sydney said nothing. Rather as a trained journalist, she sat back and simply observed.

"Where is the child now?" she asked finally.

"He's about two hundred miles from Houston, which would be the nearest city doing transplants. Shall we prepare the Cole child now for transport?"

Sam's answer was immediate. "She's much too critical to be moved. The surgery must take place here."

For the first time during their early morning encounter, Rajid displayed true emotion.

"What you ask is impossible, Dr. Ellis! St. Vincent's is not accredited to do the procedure."

"What would it take?" Sam retorted.

"I would need emergency authorization from Washington. I'm afraid it would be highly irregular...."

"Do it!" Sam ordered. "Now to the next problem. Is there anyone within the area qualified to do the procedure?"

"Not that I'm aware of, sir."

"I located a guy I went to medical school with in Houston. His name is Miguel Alvarez. He's available and standing by with his whole team."

Farhad Rajid broke out in a sweat. The situation was rapidly deteriorating. Little did the doctor and his nosy wife know what it had taken to buy this particular organ. It had cost the New Savak over three hundred thousand dollars to broker the deal. Rajid had been here all night arranging the details. Once the liver had been purchased, he thought his subterfuge would be finished. Apparently, it was only beginning.

The plan was to be a simple one. Once the organ had been harvested, it would be rushed *by Farhad's own team* to the nearest hospital performing transplants. A legitimate team of transplant surgeons would complete the procedure, strictly by the book, never knowing the organ had been illegally purchased. How simple it all would have been.

Now they were asking him to alert Washington and invite even more scrutiny. Time. He needed time to think. His mind began racing. A bizarre twist caught his fancy.

"Please, Dr. and Mrs. Ellis, have a seat. We must talk."

Surprised, Sydney and Sam complied.

"Dr. Ellis, you asked me yesterday to pull strings. This, at your request, I have done. I insisted that Tanya Cole be given undo priority. To do this, I had to circumvent the system. UNOS was established to see that EVERY patient had an equal chance for life. By securing Tanya Cole a liver, I may have denied an equally worthy child of life."

Hearing this, both Sam and Sydney paled. They had never thought of the situation in these terms. Seeing their discomfort, Rajid pushed on.

"Likewise, I led my superiors to believe that the child had a better chance for survival than in fact she really does. If we suddenly pull strings to have the surgery take place here because she's too critical to be moved, my actions will come under even more scrutiny. I'm willing to do what you ask, at great risk to my own reputation, but only if you understand the consequences."

"I'm not sure I understand anything," Sam warily countered. "We have a desperately ill child. We now have a suitable organ. We have to do the procedure here. Tanya Cole simply can't be moved."

In a level voice, Rajid responded.

"St. Vincent's Hospital is due to receive accreditation to perform transplants by the end of the year. Dare we risk this approval in order to save one little girl?"

Sam weighed the considerations carefully. He had a hospital's reputation to think of versus the life of Tanya Cole. It was a tremendously difficult decision to make. Yet in truth, there really was no choice.

"Get me emergency approval. I insist that we do it legally and by the book. Under those conditions, I'm willing to assume the risk." Farhad Rajid nodded. His ploy was rapidly becoming a plan.

"It will take a few hours to secure approval, Dr. Ellis, but I believe it can be done. Let me request that the donor be maintained on life support for as long as possible. You must understand, however, that if the boy's system shuts down, all of his organs will be useless. We must act quickly."

"I'll contact Dr. Alvarez immediately. What then?"

Now it was Sydney's turn for Rajid's scrutiny.

"You managed to secure a great deal of corporate involvement in raising the money for this child. Would it be possible now to obtain the use of a private jet?"

Sydney hesitated. Thinking of Gary Atwell and his connections, she nodded yes.

Farhad Rajid tried to calm his queasy stomach. He was treading in treacherous waters.

"Mrs. Ellis, I must ask that you refrain from making the details of this transplant public. Proceed with the jet quietly. If your husband can secure the team of surgeons, I will arrange for the harvested organ to be flown to Houston. We can then transport both the team and the organ here. The operation can take place quietly."

"It's not as simple as all that," said Sydney. "It is because of the people of Kansas City that any of this is possible. They deserve to know the outcome of their effort."

"I understand. Broadcast only that a donor has been found and the transplant will take place here. That is all they need to know for now."

Sam's eyes narrowed. "Something about this doesn't feel right."

Farhad Rajid inwardly smiled. "The decision of course is yours, Dr. Ellis. It was my understanding that you desired a miracle for this child. Well sir, you can have your miracle, but not without a price."

■

3:30 pm

The hours dragged slowly for Tanya's parents. Yet time was passing far too quickly for the child. Her condition continued to deteriorate. Soon she would be beyond the point where a transplant could save her.

For the fourth time today, Sam found himself in Farhad Rajid's office. They had accomplished a great deal in a short time. Sydney had arranged for a corporate jet. It would be landing in Houston momentarily. Sam had spoken with Dr. Miguel Alvarez. He had agreed to perform the surgery. His team was assembled and waiting. As far as Sam knew, there was only one obstacle remaining. Rajid quickly relieved his mind.

"I have good news," Rajid announced. "I have secured the necessary approval from Washington. Surgery can take place here. I've given the go-ahead for the procurement to take place. The donor child has been taken into surgery. The harvesting will take approximately an hour. Then the procurement team will leave by private plane. They will meet Alvarez and the corporate jet at the Houston airport at six o'clock."

Sam smiled broadly. "Good work, Farhad. I'll have a press release prepared immediately."

■

6:00 pm

Broadcasting yet again from the hospital corridor, Sydney— together with a city—watched as Dr. Sam Ellis, Chief of Staff, issued a statement.

"A liver has been successfully harvested from a brain-dead

child in Texas. A team of transplant surgeons led by Dr. Miguel Alvarez of Houston will be departing by private jet shortly. The flight from Houston will take an hour and fifty-seven minutes. St. Vincent's will dispatch Life Flight to retrieve both the organ and the team of surgeons when they arrive at KCI. The transplant will take place immediately thereafter."

■

7:05 pm

A small tense group gathered in Sam's office. Belva Cole sat quietly praying, her eyes etched with worry and swollen from tears. Charles nervously paced the floor while Sydney and Jake Kahn counted minutes in edgy silence. It was Ellis who took the call as the others gathered anxiously around his desk.

"Both the transport team and the surgeons have now landed at KCI. Life Flight is loading now. They should arrive in approximately fifteen minutes."

Charles gripped Sam's arm as the Chief of Staff started to leave. "Please, Dr. Ellis. Could we see Tanya?"

"I'm afraid not. She's being prepped for surgery now."

"Please," the desperate father pleaded. "It may be the last time."

The pain in Charles Cole's eyes was unbearable.

"All right, Charles. I'll take you and Belva to the holding area. You may see Tanya but only for a few minutes."

The grateful father clutched Sam tightly. Holding back his own emotion, Sam gave Charles a warm embrace.

"It's going to be okay. Wait and see. We're about to see a miracle. I feel it."

Saturday, July 2

2:58 am

Sam was completely drained. He ripped the sterile mask from his face and the gown from his aching body. He had to compose himself quickly. He had to find the Coles. Seeing him enter the surgical waiting room, Belva cried, "Oh dear God! Is it over?"

"Yes," Sam answered. "It's finally over."

Choking on the word, Charles stammered, "Tanya?"

Sam gripped Charles by the shoulder. "Tanya is holding her own for now."

Collapsing in the chair, the surgeon mopped his furrowed brow.

"The operation went well. The team of surgeons were brilliant. It was a privilege to assist Dr. Alvarez and to observe his work. Your daughter is a fighter, Charles. She beat both the clock and the odds. But believe me, our struggle is far from over."

Sydney reached for Sam's hand, encouraging him to continue.

"So far, the liver is functioning. But the next few hours will be critical."

"Can we see her?" Belva pleaded.

"No," Sam responded firmly. "Not now. She'll be in recovery for several hours, then we'll move her to an isolation room in Intensive Care. It'll be much later today before she's alert. We'll keep you posted. It's going to be a long haul. Try to get some rest."

Sam drew Sydney closer as he whispered, "I'm going to check on Tanya. Are you going home?"

Glancing briefly at the Coles and knowing the lonely vigil they faced, she shook her head no. "I'm due at the station early to prepare a follow-up story for tonight. For now, I'll stay here."

■

Buffing the deserted corridor, the janitor was careful to be thorough. It was only his third day of work. He hesitated at the entrance of the waiting room, just outside ICU. Three people asleep in their chairs caught his notice. He wondered what the hell to do! He had a schedule to meet and this room to clean before the nurses changed shifts at seven.

Shrugging, he walked to the far side of the room. He decided to begin by making coffee. Feeling another presence, he wheeled around, confronted by a tall, imposing figure in the doorway. He recognized the man immediately as a doctor. That was not what disturbed him. The man looked familiar, too familiar. Yet Ralph was new to the city. He'd met very few people. He had secured a cheap apartment just blocks from the hospital and kept strictly to himself. No, this was a man he recognized from the past. But for the life of him he could not put a name with the face.

"Don't let me disturb you," the doctor said. "Carry on."

Sam meandered over to the family and spoke quietly as he gently nudged the sleeping man. "Wake up, Charles."

At the sound of Sam's voice, Charles immediately roused. "Tanya," he stammered. "Tanya?"

"She's fine," Sam assured him. "She's resting comfortably. Her vital signs remain stable."

"What time is it?" Sydney inquired, wiping the sleep from her own eyes.

"Six-thirty," he replied.

Drawing a chair into their circle, Ellis rested. "It'll probably be late this afternoon before Tanya is fully alert. She's fine for now. Everything looks good. So there's no need for you to hang around here. Why don't you go home and get some rest? I'll call you if there's any change."

"No," Charles answered firmly. "We're staying right here!"

Sam started to argue but Sydney intervened. "They don't have a phone, Sam. There's no way you could contact them quickly."

"I see. Then at least let me find a room where you can get some rest. Have you eaten?"

The Coles shook their heads.

"I insist you let me order you breakfast. Look, this is going to be a long, hard pull. You'll be no good to Tanya if you don't take care of yourselves."

Sydney stood and embraced her husband briefly. "Let me walk you to the door. You look tired, Sam. Why don't you go home and get some rest?"

The Chief of Staff shook his head. "I can't. I've got a staff meeting later this morning and appointments all afternoon. I think I'll go down to the cafeteria after I find them an empty room. Would you like to join me?"

"No," Sydney replied. "I haven't time."

The aroma of freshly brewed coffee filled the air.

"The coffee smells good, honey. Don't you want some?"

"No, I've got to go," Sam answered, brushing her cheek lightly. Glancing back to the Coles, he whispered, "I'll call you if there's any change."

Stretching, Sydney struggled to overcome the fatigue. Unfortunately like Sam, she too had a full day planned. Retreating from the bathroom he had just cleaned, the janitor did not see her approach. And with her eyes focused on the coffeepot, Sydney failed to notice him. When they collided both of them turned, startled.

"Excuse me, ma'am," he exclaimed. "I didn't see you!"

The janitor locked eyes with the woman. He recognized her face immediately and started to panic.

Studying the stranger dressed in a uniform of drab blue, Sydney wondered why he was so upset. "It's okay, really," she assured him. "I wasn't watching where I was going."

Too stunned to move, Ralph Noland remained where he was. Remembering Sydney Lawrence from her days as a television reporter in Velours, he feared his deception would be exposed. She had interviewed him on camera shortly after the Maggie Hall disaster, before he had been hospitalized, and his career ended.

Noland had been one of the key people involved in the rescue, and Sydney Lawrence had been interested in his reactions. She had treated him kindly and with respect—like a valued soldier who had completed a mission. He remembered every detail of her face and manner. Did she likewise remember him?

"Goddamn you, Solomon!" he cursed silently. "Why didn't you warn me she of all people was here?"

Feeling sorry for the man who seemed so upset by their encounter, Sydney turned and poured herself a fresh cup of coffee. Turning back, she was surprised to find him still staring. She smiled, trying to put the poor man at ease.

"Did you make the coffee?" she asked.

Casting his eyes to the floor, he nodded.

"It's good. Thank you."

As he started past her, she added brightly, "Have a good day."

■

After a shower in the doctor's lounge and breakfast in the cafeteria, Sam Ellis felt like a human being again. Even after all his years in practice, it still amazed him how a simple thing like hot soapy water and a bit of food could transform a doctor from a robot into a person again. Returning to his office shortly before nine o'clock, he scanned the paperwork on his desk in preparation for his staff meeting at ten.

His secretary, Elizabeth Wright, rapped sharply on the door.

"Dr. Ellis, there's a woman here to see you. She says she's expected."

Sam glanced up from his desk surprised. "I didn't think I had any appointments this morning. Are you sure she wants to see me?"

"Yes, quite sure. Her name is Kathleen Stein."

Sam continued to draw a blank as he repeated the name. Finally he exclaimed, "Stein! Oh dear God, yes! Show her in!"

Rising, Sam straightened his tie then threw open his arms to greet Kathleen Clay, still veiled, but now going by the alias of Stein.

"Kathleen, forgive me! I was so exhausted from last night, I completely forgot you were coming."

Kathleen set her suitcase beside Sam's desk. Nervously, she scanned the office belonging to the Chief of Staff, hating this hospital as she had all the others.

Sensing her anxiety, Sam said, "Everything will be okay, Kathleen. You've made the right decision."

Kathleen handed an envelope to Sam. Inside was a check for $100,000 written on the account of Margaret Clay.

"My mother-in-law has offered to pay all my medical expenses. You'll find a deposit in the envelope and a notarized letter of intent." Sadly she added, "Margaret never liked me. She made my life miserable while I was married to Michael. I think she feels guilty. But who am I to judge her for trying to make amends?"

Kathleen's eyes were penetrating. "I'm keenly aware that my being here puts you and your staff at risk. I appreciate more than I can ever say the lengths to which you have gone to protect me so that I can have this surgery. If Dr. Wentworth succeeds, you'll be giving me back my life, Sam."

"Then let's get started. May I show you to your room, *Mrs. Stein?*"

"I suppose." Her voice lacked enthusiasm.

Retrieving her suitcase, Sam escorted Kathleen to the elevator. In silence, they rode to the sixth floor, a small private wing of St. Vincent's. Kathleen's face remained passive as they traveled the short distance to her room. The veiled lady was not particularly impressed with this facility. It might be newer than some but it was basically like all the others. When Sam opened the door to Room 605, she smiled. It was then she truly saw something different.

A large, spacious suite awaited her. It was decorated beautifully in soothing shades of light pink and muted yellow. Kathleen was reminded of a first-class hotel, not a hospital.

Walking to the window just beyond the settee, Sam threw open the drapes. "You've got a northern exposure. That's my favorite view. Look, Kathleen, you can see the Plaza."

Wistfully, Kathleen joined her friend at the window, very briefly touching his arm.

"The room is lovely, Sam. Thank you."

"There's nothing too good for Kathleen Stein."

Kathleen slowly returned to the bed. Fingering the softly

colored chintz spread, she smiled. No one would suspect it was a hospital bed. Only the controls overhead gave away the fact that this was still a hospital, not a hotel.

Hoisting her suitcase onto the bed, Kathleen tried to buoy her spirits.

"Would you like to see a recent picture of my son, Sam? He's grown so much since we left Velours you won't recognize him."

She handed him the photograph.

Sam couldn't help smiling at the captivating image. The little boy, with devilish blue eyes, had light brown hair and a mischievous grin. His two front teeth were missing. "How old is he now?" he asked, returning the picture.

"Seven," she replied. Her eyes remained fixed upon the boy's face as if wishing could make him suddenly appear. "I already miss him."

Sam took Kathleen gently by the elbow and guided her back towards the settee.

"Sit with me a moment," he urged softly. "We need to talk."

The delicate woman complied, still clutching the photograph.

Sam searched for the right words. "After what you've told me about Michael, you must understand that your safety is my primary concern." Sam forced Kathleen's eyes to his. It was paramount that she understand. "That's why we've arranged this room and the alias. But I can't protect you without your help."

"I don't understand what you mean, Sam."

"Daniel might be recognized by his picture. The photograph would be safer with me. I'll lock it away. And identification. Have you brought anything with the name Clay?"

Reluctantly, Kathleen nodded. "My driver's license and a credit card."

"Please give them to me, Kathleen, so I can lock them away. I'll get you anything you need while you're here."

Retrieving her purse, she located the cards Sam wanted.

"But the photograph, Sam! Don't make me give up my picture! I'll hide it. I promise. This picture is all I have to remind me of Daniel. I don't know when I'll see him again. I can't even call him at Margaret's. Don't you understand? This picture is my only connection."

Tears filled her eyes.

"Promise me you'll keep the picture hidden," said Sam, relenting.

Clutching the photograph, Kathleen agreed.

Somehow hating to leave her, Ellis said, "I'm afraid I have to go, Kathleen. I have a meeting at ten but I'll be back this afternoon. Take your time getting settled. No one will disturb you. Dr. Wentworth will be in to see you later."

"Thank you, Sam," she whispered.

"Will you be okay?"

Her eyes were devoid of sparkle and her voice was flat. "Yes, I'll be fine."

Kathleen's gaze followed him to the door and remained there long after it had shut. She stared at the picture burning the image of her son deep in her heart. Then she tucked the photograph away in the table beside the bed and returned to the window. Lost in the view, she thought about her life, herself. Born Kathleen Callihan, she had been Kathleen Clay longer than she could remember.

Glancing out the window to the street below, she marveled at the people going about their business. Men, women, children, all with their lives and identities intact. As she fingered the depression that was once her face, she realized that her heart and her soul had been crushed as well. It would take more than rearranging bones and suturing skin to heal her wounds. She posed a question that she dared not dwell upon for long.

"I'm Kathleen Stein for now. But who will I be when this is over?"

Susan M. Hoskins

It was well past noon before Philip Wentworth could break free to greet his newest patient. Stopping at the nurses' station on the sixth floor, he requested her chart. He noted that only the preliminary admitting work had been completed.

"How's she doing?"

"She seems depressed," the nurse replied. "I suppose that's only natural."

Nodding, Dr. Wentworth turned towards Kathleen's room. A bouquet of flowers caught his eye.

"What's this?" he asked.

"Mrs. Lowry was dismissed this morning. She had so many other arrangements to take home, she left this one behind."

Philip hesitated, studying the bouquet. Smiling, he plucked a single pink rose.

He peeked inside the slightly cracked door. "May I come in?"

"Of course," Kathleen answered.

Hiding the flower behind his back, Philip cautiously approached. She was sitting on the love seat by the window allowing the soft reflection of the sun to light her hair. Dressed comfortably in a gown and robe of palest blue, she looked more fragile and somehow sadder than he had remembered.

Observing her lovely but sterile surroundings, he understood. There was nothing here but empty fabric. Nothing of Kathleen to call home. And for the next several months this hospital room would indeed be her home.

As he extracted the delicate bud from behind his back, he said almost shyly, "This is for you."

Her eyes brightened a little. "The rose is lovely, Dr. Wentworth. Thank you."

He sat on the window ledge beside her. "Please call me Philip. I'll call you Kathleen. During the next several months, we should come to know each other very well."

Their eyes connected as they realized the truth of his simple words. It was in that moment that they grew awkward with one another.

"Have you had a chance to get settled?" he said finally.

"Yes," she replied. "What few things I brought have been put away."

"Sam told me about your situation. I promise you that we will do everything we can to protect you."

Saying nothing, Kathleen glanced away.

Philip's voice took on a firmer, more professional demeanor. "Your situation is more difficult than most. I'll need your complete cooperation to make it work."

Kathleen's hand touched her face. "Because of this?" she asked.

Philip edged closer.

"No, not at all," he said. "Believe me, I've repaired worse. Usually my patients return home with their families between surgeries to convalesce, Kathleen. Having that support makes it easier."

Once again, a look of despondency returned to her face. "It's true. I have no one."

"You have Sam and Sydney," he offered quickly. Then softly he added, "And you have me."

He paused to adjust his glasses. "The flower," he stammered. "We must do something with the rose."

He searched in vain for a vase. Finding none, he walked into the bathroom in hopes of obtaining at least a glass.

Kathleen remained seated but her eyes followed Philip's every step. When he disappeared from view, she caught his reflection in the mirror above the dresser near the bed.

He was a composite of contradictions. She thought him handsome but she didn't know why. There was nothing remarkable about his features. He had an aura of strength that she found appealing. It was the kind of strength that spoke of courage not brutality. And his hands, the sure steady hands of a surgeon, that fingered the rose as delicately as they might a fragile piece of human tissue.

He returned to Kathleen's room and placed the flower near the bed, rotating the bud so it could be nourished fully in the light to unfold slowly in its own way, in its own time.

He returned to the settee and sat down opposite Kathleen. She reached out and lightly touched his arm.

"I need a friend. Thank you, Philip."

With a slight catch to his voice, Philip asked a seemingly trivial question. "Do you have any hobbies?"

Kathleen paused to reflect a moment. "No."

"There must be something you like to do."

"I used to enjoy painting. But that was so long ago, Philip."

"Why so long ago?" he asked.

Rising, she turned her back on Philip and stood by the open window. The light was too bright for her sensitive eyes. She was forced to return her gaze to the doctor.

"How do I make you understand? You seem to be a strong man, yet you're so different from my husband. I was married to an abusive monster who had to be in complete control. I was permitted no friends, no talents. Not even my son was my own. I was simply a convenience for Michael Clay. That's where I lost my identity the first time."

"The first time?" Philip pursued.

Leaning forward, she turned slightly to the right so he could understand her past. Then slowly she rotated her face back to the left. She needed desperately for him to understand that which she had been, and that which she was now. She was split, two halves of the same unfinished whole.

It was then Kathleen posed the question that she could not answer. "Philip, who will I be when this is over?"

Cupping her chin, Philip drew her troubled eyes back to his. "Perhaps together, Kathleen, we can discover who you really are."

Something about Philip's words struck a chord. She feared

that the journey to find herself might be more painful than the surgery she was about to face.

"I must be going," he said suddenly. "I'll be back to see you later tonight or in the morning."

Kathleen nodded. The hours ahead would be difficult to fill.

"We have a wonderful Occupational Therapy Department," said Philip. "Perhaps you'd like to spend some time downstairs painting."

At the thought of exposing her scarred face, Kathleen cried, "No! I couldn't!"

"I have an idea," he offered brightly. "Let me order the supplies you need and have them brought here. Then you could paint or draw to your heart's content and there would be no one to bother you, or to judge you."

For the first time Kathleen smiled.

"I would really like that, Philip."

"I'll order an easel, pencils and some paints. If you think of anything else, just let me know."

Dr. Philip Wentworth shut the door gently behind him as he left. This time Kathleen's eyes did not follow. Lost in her own world, she found solace once more near the window. She glanced outside, her eyes shielded with sunglasses. It was not the view that captured her thoughts, nor dreams of painting, her fancy. Again and again, she repeated Philip's words, seeking to comprehend their meaning.

"Perhaps together we can discover who you really are."

It was nearly seven-thirty before Sydney got home that evening. Her body ached for rest, but sleep eluded her. Sitting alone in the dimly lit kitchen with a cup of herbal tea, she waited for Sam to return. Tanya's crisis had eased for now. Sydney and Sam had done everything they could for the child. Only time would tell if the transplant would save her life or if her body would reject the precious organ.

By sheer will, they had obtained the unobtainable, the precious liver, Tanya's chance for life. Yet now in the darkness, Sydney was left to ponder the ramifications of her actions.

Farhad Rajid's words continued to haunt her.

"Currently there are 2,765 candidates . . . all with a legitimate need . . . on the list awaiting a liver."

"What makes you think this little girl deserves priority?"

"By securing Tanya Cole a liver, I may have denied an equally worthy child of life."

At last report, Tanya remained critical but stable, isolated in the Intensive Care Unit. She was alert and her liver was functioning. Yes, thanks in large part to Sydney Lawrence, Tanya Cole was alive. But whose child had died? The Cole family would remain forever grateful for Sydney's strong will in raising the necessary money. Yet Sydney would always wonder what parents were weeping at their child's grave because she, Sydney Lawrence Ellis, had dared to play God?

Lost in thought, Sydney failed at first to hear the tentative knock at the patio door. Finally the sound penetrated her mind. She arose and cracked the back door. There, to her delight, was the smiling face of her little neighbor.

"Lydia! What a surprise! Come in."

Lydia Hassan was dressed primly in a short-sleeved, white blouse and blue denim skirt.

"I saw your story about the little girl. I want you to have this for her." Shyly, Lydia handed Sydney her piggy bank. "I've been saving for a new bike but this is more important. Last time I counted, I had nearly twenty dollars."

Touched, Sydney caressed the child's hand. "Thank you, Lydia," was all she could say.

"How is she tonight?"

"She's holding her own for now."

A sad look clouded the child's delicate features as she followed Sydney to the kitchen table.

Taking the chair right next to Sydney, she spoke quietly.

"It's lonely being sick. Maybe when she's better I could be her friend."

Sydney started to respond that perhaps it could be arranged. But the pain she saw in Lydia's eyes caused her to change direction.

"Lydia," she prodded gently. "Are you sick?"

The beautiful young girl with raven curls did not immediately respond.

"My father says I am," she answered finally.

"I don't understand."

"I have spells."

"Spells?" Sydney questioned. "What do you mean?"

"I have a weak heart. I get tired easily."

Sydney scooted her chair closer, urging Lydia to continue.

"We were living in London when I got sick. No one knew what was wrong. I kept fainting all the time. My father took me to many doctors. They said I had strep throat that went into rheumatic fever. I have to be careful. My heart has a weak valve."

"So you're not allowed to go to school?"

"I had a spell earlier this year. Now my father says I must stay home. I have a tutor. Oh Sydney! It gets so lonely! I wish he'd let me go back to school."

"Do you still see your friends?"

"I have no friends," she stated much too maturely. "My father says that's much too dangerous."

"Dangerous? Dangerous for whom, Lydia?"

Before she could respond, a loud angry voice startled them. "What is the meaning of this?"

Terrified, they turned around. Sydney had failed to secure the patio door. There stood the very man of whom they spoke, Ali Hassan.

"What is the meaning of this?" he demanded.

"Fa . . . father!" the child stammered.

Sydney jumped to her feet. Ali Hassan merely waved her away, as he would dismiss one of his servants.

"You don't belong here, Lydia. Go home."

Sydney's temper flared. She was a woman used to being treated with respect. This man's behavior was an outrage.

"I beg your pardon, Mr. Hassan. But Lydia is always welcome here."

Ignoring Sydney still, Hassan, his own voice suddenly bellowed, "Go home, Lydia!"

With tears spilling down her cheeks, the child fled. Ali Hassan started to follow but Sydney stopped him.

"I insist upon a word with you, Mr. Hassan!"

Hassan turned to her. "What do you want?"

Sydney paused, then forcing herself to be gracious, she walked towards Hassan with her hand outstretched.

"I don't believe we've been formally introduced. My name is Sydney Lawrence. We've only recently moved into the neighborhood."

Ali Hassan did the unthinkable. He ignored Sydney's hand, and stood mute and unmoving. Gamely, Sydney forged ahead.

"Your daughter is a delightful girl. She's welcome in our home anytime."

Ali Hassan's face remained rigid, his eyes cold. "We're private people. We keep to ourselves."

"I respect that," Sydney acknowledged, "but . . . "

"I bid you good night," the Iranian stated firmly, abruptly turning on his heel.

Hassan slammed the back door, ending further conversation. She was a woman, after all. That fact alone made her unworthy of his attention. In his homeland, Muslim women knew their place. They would never have attempted to address him so boldly.

Ali Hassan despised the country which had made him wealthy. He viewed the United States as weak and the culture decadent. It was the brazen behavior of American women that he despised perhaps the most.

Shaken, Sydney sat back down at the kitchen table. Her hands trembled. What had begun as anger now festered into rage. She yearned for the warmth of a cup of tea but when she raised the cup to her lips she found it had cooled. She let it be. A tear trickled down her cheek.

At thirty-two, Sydney Lawrence thought she had her life in order. With a husband who adored her, and a career she now found challenging, she had no room for anything or anyone else. Yet first Tanya, and now more than ever Lydia, invaded a part of Sydney's heart that she tried to protect. Tonight, the price of caring seemed too high.

She had told Sam she wanted no children. Yet these particular children affected her in a way that was most disturbing. She felt suddenly vulnerable. If she dared to surrender to the feelings that stirred inside her, she might get hurt. Both children could be wrenched away in a heartbeat—one by fate, the other by a father's whim.

■

Slamming the ornate mahogany door, Hassan summoned his major-domo.

"Mansur!" he bellowed. "Come quickly!"

Hurrying from the kitchen, the older man appeared in the hall-way. He was noticeably out of breath.

"Yes, sir. What is it?"

"Where is my daughter?"

"Lydia is in her room, sir. I'm afraid she's crying."

Glancing up the winding staircase, Hassan started towards her, but the tone of Mansur's voice stopped him.

"Sir, if we might speak, in the library away from the others."

Closing the door, Hassan waited for his servant to begin.

"I'm worried, sir. I think I'm being followed. I have no proof. It's only a sense."

"Trust your instincts and be careful," Hassan warned. "We've too much at stake to permit anything to go wrong."

"I'll tell the men to keep a tight watch."

"Do that," Hassan ordered.

"You have several messages, sir," Mansur continued. "You'll find them on your desk."

"Anything important?"

"Yes," the major-domo replied. "Two messages seem particularly important. Your brother needs to speak with you at once. There's a problem. And Sanchez called. He asks that you return his call immediately."

Ali Hassan nodded.

"Shall I see to your dinner, sir?"

Still annoyed by the encounter next-door, Hassan shook his head.

"You must watch Lydia more carefully, Mansur."

Dismissing his major-domo, Hassan sat down at his desk. Lydia's tears would have to wait. Using his secure phone line, he dialed his brother's private number.

Their conversation was brief. What troubled Hassan was not the recent situation, which his brother had handled with his usual cunning and connections. It was the involvement of other people that bothered him. For the second time tonight, he heard the name he was rapidly coming to loathe. It was the name of the woman, Sydney Lawrence, and his brother's disclosure of her profession. His problems were rapidly mounting.

He dialed a second number. Then the familiar voice of Sanchez.

"Is the shipment ready?" Hassan asked.

"Yes," Sanchez replied. "We can have it here by the end of next week."

"Very good. Tell your boss to get ready. We will have need of an even greater shipment soon."

Hassan considered his next words carefully.

"We must be diligent, my friend. I do not wish the shipment of arms to enter the United States. Rather, we will use the airstrip just outside Mexico City. See that the arms arrive late at night. My people will meet your plane there. After we inventory the supply and unload, you will be paid. We will fly the arms to Dubai from there. In the future, keep the calls here to a minimum. Do not call me by name. Understood?"

Impatiently, Hassan drummed his fingers on the desk as he listened to the man's concern on the other end.

"No," he tried to assure him. "Nothing's amiss here. Proceed as usual, just be cautious."

Troubled, Hassan replaced the receiver and stood. There was a problem upstairs he could no longer ignore. Wearily, he climbed the stairs to the third floor. The guard stationed in front of Lydia's room saluted.

"Leave," he commanded. "Return in ten minutes."

The guard nodded and left.

Cracking the door, Hassan found Lydia on the bed but a long way from asleep. Her head was buried in a pillow. Her muffled sobs saddened him.

"What is this, my precious one?" He sat on the edge of her bed. "Lydia, we must talk."

Clutching her pillow tightly, Lydia refused to turn.

"There, there," Hassan soothed as he tried to quiet her tears.

"Oh, Papa," she cried, taking her head out from the pillow, "I like Sydney so much. Please don't forbid me to see her!"

His jaw twitched at the mention yet again of the troublesome woman's name.

"Please, Papa, please! Listen to me!"

Hassan searched for the right words to tell his child no. Inviting a relationship with a television reporter was much too dangerous for his operation. How could he make his precious one understand?

Born in Iran where hierarchy is paramount, Ali Hassan was used to giving orders. He was a man who expected to be obeyed. In truth, most everyone feared him. Lydia Hassan was his daughter. According to Islamic law, she was his property. Yet she was the only person on earth who could penetrate his veneer.

This situation was troubling, and he had to resolve it quickly. Brushing the ringlets from her dampened forehead, he sought for the moment to be gentle, not mean. But as he opened his mouth to break the news to her kindly, another thought crossed his mind. To forbid Lydia any contact with the neighbors might arouse suspicion. That at all costs he must avoid. Perhaps there was another way.

He spoke softly. "All right, child. Listen carefully. If I permit you to visit Sydney, you must do exactly as I say. Do you understand?"

Quieting her tears, she nodded.

"Sydney and her husband are very important people like your daddy. We must respect their privacy as we would expect them to respect ours. You may visit them occasionally, but only very briefly. You must obey my wishes. Otherwise, I'll have no choice but to confine you here. Do you understand?"

"Yes, Papa, yes!" Lydia answered hastily. "Thank you!"

"Now go to sleep, child. An upset like this is not good for your heart."

Tucking the covers around her, Hassan stood.

"A kiss, Papa?" she begged, her arms outstretched.

Awkwardly, Hassan lowered his bulky frame over his child's delicate body. Brushing his thick lips upon Lydia's forehead, Ali Hassan quickly departed. He did not smile; neither did he feel relieved. He now had two concerns: first, his daughter's well-being; second, his mission. At all costs he had to protect his very dangerous but lucrative operation. Now there was a threat to it. Her name was Sydney Lawrence. She was a news reporter and she lived next-door.

PART II

Five men gathered in a small, brightly lit conference room inside the federal building in Kansas City. Joe Morrison was there with his boss, John Taylor, and Roger Brennan, who had just come in on the red-eye flight from Washington. Special Agent in Charge of the Kansas City field office, Bill Hoffman, was present along with George Massoud.

As the group gathered, Morrison asked the secretary to bring coffee. He waited until she'd left before beginning. "Let's get started," he said when everyone was seated.

On the outside, Joe Morrison was cool and composed. Inside, he was a bundle of raw nerves. It was not that things were going badly, but they were progressing too slowly to suit his edgy temperament. He found the initial stages of an investigation boring.

"Let's discuss what we have so far. We've set up surveillance around Hassan's business and house. George and I have been tailing the man himself."

Morrison focused on Bill Hoffman. He supervised the local agents assisting Joe with the investigation.

"The subject in question owns a small business on the Plaza known as *Hassan's,*" said Hoffman. "It appears to be a respectable enterprise dealing with the sale of imported Oriental rugs. Traffic into the store is light to moderate during the week, heavier on weekends."

"Have you observed anything unusual during those hours?" Taylor inquired.

"Not really," responded Hoffman. "The local clientele is primarily upper middle class. A female agent posed as a customer. She's shopped the store a number of times. She reports that other customers like the quality of Hassan's rugs and thought his prices at least competitive if not a bargain. We checked with the Better Business Bureau and no complaints have been filed during the last three years. We've informally questioned other store owners on the Plaza. They're satisfied he runs a decent operation."

John Taylor set his coffee down and leaned forward, resting his elbows upon the worn, slick table. "You said that his clientele was mainly local. What about his employees?"

"Well now, that's a different story," said Hoffman. "Everyone who works for Hassan is Persian. People think nothing of it since it's assumed they'd be more qualified to handle imported rugs."

Joe reached into his pocket for a cigarette, which he didn't light. Fingering it, he said, "Access into the store is limited."

"The main entrance faces the street," continued Hoffman. "The door at the rear opens into the alley. It's used for employee and delivery access."

"Have you seen anyone besides employees or delivery people using the rear door?" asked Brennan.

"Periodically throughout the week, we've seen other men enter and exit through the rear. The times of day vary as do their length of stay. Usually they come in groups of two, never more than five."

"Iranians?" Taylor inquired.

Hoffman nodded. "Nicely dressed. You know, the professional type in a suit and tie."

"Tell John and Roger about the house," said Morrison.

"Hassan owns a mansion on Verona Circle in Mission Hills. He lives there with his daughter, Lydia, and a number of Iranian servants. He has an unusually large staff, even for a house that size. There's one guy in particular who seems more in charge than the others. He's a short, older Iranian named Mansur. He orders everyone around, including the guards, and reports only to Hassan himself. I've been keeping a pretty tight watch on him, but so far I've turned up nothing."

"The guards," Joe repeated. "Tell the rest of them about the guards."

"It's real weird. We're not talking a bodyguard or two. Rather, Hassan has men stationed throughout the house and an armed guard posted at all times in front of his bedroom and that of his daughter. No one gets in the house without their approval. Even the child is not allowed outside without one or sometimes two guards present."

Joe finally lit his cigarette and savored the first puff.

"So tell me, gentlemen," he mused. "What does a rug dealer have to fear . . . or hide . . . that his house is armed like a fortress?"

John Taylor leaned back in his chair wondering the same thing. Focusing on the head of the Kansas City Bureau, Bill Hoffman, he posed a question.

"Bill, what can you tell me about Ali Hassan?"

Hoffman opened a rather thin file. "We don't know much. We can't even be sure Ali Hassan is the man's real name. This is probably our own government's fault. The Shah, as you well know, commanded a great deal of sympathy in the States. At the time of his overthrow, many of his top advisors sought refuge here. Our government helped change their identities so they could avoid persecution by Khomeini's followers. The profile we have states that Hassan's wife and son were killed during the revolution. He fled Iran with his daughter, Lydia. He lived in London before coming to the States, then moved to Kansas City five years ago. He capitalized his business heavily and has been thriving ever since. He keeps a low profile in the community except for his Iran connections.

Hoffman started to close the file then stopped.

"One more thing. Hassan is thought to have a brother residing somewhere in the States. Who he is or what he's doing we need help in determining."

Nodding, Roger Brennan jotted a note to check with his people in Counterterrorism for more information on Hassan's family and their possible whereabouts.

Meanwhile, Joe studied the smoke swirling softly above his head. "George, you've observed something unusual regarding Hassan's strong Iranian following. Fill John and Roger in."

"Well it's strange," said George, "but two or three times a week, Hassan hosts a gathering of sometimes twenty to fifty people. Wives are present, and from all appearances it's strictly a social affair. But always before the evening ends, the men retire into another room to discuss business, leaving the ladies alone in the living room."

Roger Brennan shrugged. "What's so unusual about that? Often in Middle Eastern cultures, the men adjourn to separate quarters for cigars and to discuss business, much as we used to in times gone by."

"But, sir," George countered, the chords in his neck beginning to pulsate, "never before have I seen two armed guards posted in front of the door to keep the ladies out. What kind of business would require that kind of secrecy?"

Massoud glanced to Brennan for an explanation. There was none. He continued.

"There's a large segment of Iranians living here in Kansas City and throughout the Midwest. Our records indicate that some ten thousand Persians reside in this region alone. And it's no secret that Ali Hassan is their unofficial leader."

Growing impatient, Taylor asked, "So what's the purpose for these gatherings?"

"That sir, we've not been able to determine."

"Well let's find out, damn it! It seems obvious that this is crucial. Let's step up surveillance."

Taylor shifted his focus to Hoffman.

"Do you have enough available agents for twenty-four-hour surveillance?"

Hoffman nodded.

Morrison seemed lost in thought. "There's something I can't quite figure out," he said finally. "Bill said that Hassan does a respectable business, right? Nothing out of the ordinary. Yet he maintains a mansion and servants in Mission Hills. Where in the hell does he get the money? Rugs cost a chunk but give me a break!"

"Let me address the subject of Iranian wealth," George said. "I was raised in the United States. Being Arabic, I met a number of Iranian students while getting my undergraduate degree. I got to know them pretty well. Their profile was the same."

George paused, taking a sip of coffee before he continued. "It's hard to imagine the amount of wealth the Shah amassed from the sale of oil. During this time, a new class of people emerged. They were called the *petro-bourgeoise*. They were the favored ones. Promotion into this class was based solely on the Shah's favor. As sons of the Shah's elite, these kids were given the opportunity to study in the United States. Many of them came to colleges in the Midwest and married local girls so they could remain in this country. All of them had money to spend, believe me. When the Shah's regime started to crumble, a great deal of wealth was smuggled out of Iran through the Shah's advisers and their families. It doesn't surprise me that Hassan has money. And because of our government's sympathy for the Shah, no one thought to question people like him and their unbelievable wealth."

"You have a point," Roger Brennan acknowledged. "But there's a hell of a lot more here than meets the eye. And frankly, gentlemen, we don't have much time. Our intelligence reports that activity at terrorist training camps in the Middle East is accelerating. We're concerned that more random strikes are planned against American interests overseas as well as here in the States. If Hassan is funding terrorist training camps and supplying their arms, we've got to crack his organization and determine where the money is coming from. It takes millions to arm and train terrorists. We've got to find the source."

Joe Morrison's face brightened. "It sounds to me like it's time to step up our operation. Are you authorizing a tap?"

Roger Brennan immediately responded. "Get the court order. Let's proceed."

"How difficult would it be to bug the business and home?"

George Massoud was frowning. "I don't think that the business would be any problem. We could go in right after the night cleaning crew. The mansion is a different story. It's guarded twenty-four hours a day. No one gets in without Hassan's permission."

"George is right," Hoffman stated.

"Why don't we start with the phones first?" Brennan said. "Let's not risk a mistake now."

John Taylor had remained quiet. His eyes were fixed on Joe

Morrison. He knew the man too well. Morrison neither liked nor respected regulations.

"I want you to go strictly by the book, Joe. Tap the phones but you know the Supreme Court ruling as well as I do. We're listening strictly for an arms deal connection somehow linked to Hassan. If there's any other conversation get off the line. Understood?"

Taylor waited impatiently for Joe's reply. Understood?" he repeated.

Joe had just about finished his cigarette. Rolling the butt in between his thumb and index finger, he grinned broadly, troubling his boss far more than any words he could have uttered.

When the door to the service elevator closed, Ralph Noland found himself alone. Pushing the button to the sixth floor, he smiled, pleased with himself.

"Dumb bastard," he mumbled. "What a guy will do for a piece of ass!"

It had been so simple really. He had made a buddy, a janitor working up on the top floor—the cream floor, the floor where only the "special" patients were treated. Many hospitals reserved a wing for this purpose. It was where the powerful and the wealthy could be guaranteed their privacy. Or like the president, protection. Working on the sixth floor of St. Vincent's was a piece of cake, not like the lower floors where Ralph had been assigned. Fred had come to Ralph this morning begging him to switch floors so he could be near his girlfriend, an aide working in the Pediatric Unit. With no hesitation and a big smile, Ralph agreed.

"They're probably banging in the closet right now," he muttered. ·For a moment, Ralph's thoughts wandered to that which he had done without. "We'll take care of business real soon," he promised himself.

Forcing his mind back to his primary task, he smiled. "If she's in this hospital, I'll find her up on six."

The elevator door opened. Ralph greeted the nurses on the morning shift.

"Good morning, ladies," he said pleasantly. "My name is Ralph Noland. I'll be working up here from now on."

"Oh?" one of the aides questioned. "What happened to Fred?"

Noland shrugged his shoulders. "He got reassigned downstairs. Is there anything special that you'd like me to do?"

Glancing up from her chart, the head nurse studied him briefly.

"As a matter of fact, there is. This nurses' station is a mess. Fred wasn't very thorough. Someone spilled a cup of coffee this morning. Nobody has had time to clean it up. Will you do it?"

"Certainly," he answered.

Whistling to himself, he located the supply closet and got what he needed. Mopping floors and cleaning toilets was not his idea of fun. He wished the commander would let him locate Kathleen and do the job. But the man had his own agenda. Taking his time, he began mopping the floor at the rear of the nurses' station and slowly worked his way towards the front. To the side, he spotted a chalkboard where each patient's name was written along with each admitting physician. He scanned the chart for the name he wanted. It wasn't there.

Near the bottom though, he spotted something queer. He hesitated then glanced around furtively. Busy with their own duties, the nurses paid him no heed. As he edged closer, his pulse started racing.

The patient's name was Kathleen Stein. The admitting physician was Philip Wentworth.

The phone rang. A nurse answered.

"We're swamped up here," she bellowed. "Don't you have anyone who could bring up the supplies? You know Wentworth. He'll have a hissy if we don't get them soon."

The nurse paused, listening to the excuses on the other end.

"Okay! Okay! I'll send someone down."

Disgusted, she slammed down the receiver and wheeled around angrily, but seeing the friendly janitor, her expression softened.

"Ralph," she called, remembering his name. "Do you have time to do me a favor?"

"Sure," he said, ambling forward. "What do you need?"

"Run down to Occupational Therapy and pick up the supplies for Kathleen Stein. I hate to ask but there's no one else."

Grinning, Noland set his mop aside. A short time later, he returned with paints, pencils and an easel.

"Got them," he winked. "I'd be glad to deliver them myself."

"Thanks, Ralph," the nurse answered. "It's Room 605."

Outside her door he paused, trying to compose himself and steady his breathing. It was important to play it cool. Fumbling for a free hand, he knocked but no one answered. Tentatively, he cracked the door. He glanced at the bed but found it empty.

Stepping inside, he halted as his eyes slowly scanned the room. The drapes were drawn. It was dark, making it difficult at first to see.

"Nice digs," he muttered to himself.

He failed to see her standing to the side of the window, hidden in the shadows.

"Mrs. Stein, are you here?"

"You frightened me," she stammered. "What do you want?"

Ralph took a few steps towards her.

"I'm sorry, ma'am. I knocked but I didn't hear you answer. I have the art supplies you wanted."

"Put them by the dresser," she commanded. "I'll look at them later."

Ralph knew that voice. It was music to his ears. For months in Boston he had stalked her, getting close enough to hear her talk, but never close enough to be seen. He set the supplies upon her dresser but the easel remained heavy in his arms.

Attempting to keep his voice as low and soft as possible, he queried, "Where would you like this?"

"Set it up near the window but not too close. I can't take the light."

Obeying, Ralph walked towards the settee. Taking his time, he placed the easel several feet from the picture window. Slowly he glanced in her direction but she kept her gaze averted. No matter, he reasoned. Her long, flowing, blond hair gave her away as did her delicate size and graceful stance.

Remembering Vietnam and the thrill of coming upon the enemy undetected from the rear, Ralph strained for a better look. Kathleen turned slightly, carefully keeping her scars in the shadow. She did not smile but her voice seemed kind.

"Thank you," she uttered softly.

Ralph found it difficult to speak. Never before had he gotten this close. Never had he ventured upon her uncovered by her precious veil. He searched for a reason to stay.

"So you're an artist, huh? I wish I could paint. Hell, I can't even draw a straight line!"

Kathleen did not respond. Anxiously, Noland scanned the room.

"Where are you going to sit when you paint, Mrs. Stein? Don't you need a stool or a straight chair?"

Without thinking, Kathleen turned and faced the janitor directly.

"Yes," she answered. "I suppose I will."

Ralph Noland choked on the words he was about to utter. He couldn't help but stare at her face, so magnificent on the left, so utterly maimed on the right. Even in the dim light, the travesty of her injury was all too clear.

Realizing his discomfort, Kathleen turned away, ashamed yet again to be seen.

There was a tremor in his husky voice when he spoke.

"I can get you what you need. A stool, a chair. You name it."

"A chair," she replied quietly. "Thank you."

Ralph turned to leave, but after only a few steps, he halted. Hopefully he glanced a final time in Kathleen's direction. Her back was to him. She did not stir.

"I'll come back later," he promised. "If there's anything else that you need, just ask."

Noland forced himself from her room. He was disquieted, not in the least in control. For months, he had stalked what he thought to be the enemy. Justifying his job, he placed her in the category of other women he had known, particularly his mother.

"Coldhearted bitches," he had called them. "All bitches. Never there for you when you're down."

But in that instant when Ralph saw Kathleen face to face, he glimpsed his own reflection in her scars, with all the pain and all the horror.

Kathleen knew upon awakening that she could put the inevitable off no longer. Dr. Wentworth had been right. The boredom of waiting was too depressing. Slipping on a robe of yellow silk, she forced her feet from the bed. She missed her son and, however desolate, she missed the life she had known before.

It was early, just past seven o'clock when she walked to the window and peered outside. Watching the people below engrossed in their own lives, Kathleen realized that she did not belong. Not here in the hospital and certainly not out in society. Floating in an abyss of self-pity, she turned toward the settee. There her easel waited along with the supplies Wentworth had ordered.

Glancing at her smooth, delicate hands, she wondered if she still possessed the gift. In school, they'd assured her she had great talent. During her marriage, she was convinced she had none.

Tentatively, she fingered her pencils and flipped the sketch book to the first page. Her glance traveled to the window where Philip's rose still stood, thirsting for sunlight, struggling to unfold.

It was only a simple pink rose, the kind one sees many times on a summer's day. Yet this rose, like every rose, was unique, if only Kathleen could capture its splendor on her page.

Just then, the clouds parted and a small stream of sunlight broke through. It was not enough to brighten the room, only enough to tantalize the rose. For a moment Kathleen sat watching the play of light and shadow on the petals. Intrigued, she closed her eyes and prayed, "God, let me see what you see." Centered, an eerie feeling of calmness engulfed her. Without thinking, she began sketching.

Kathleen became so engrossed in her work, she forgot about herself entirely. First one hour passed and then another. It was nearly noon before Philip made rounds. Kathleen did not hear him approach. She wasn't prepared for his touch upon her shoulder.

His gaze was fixed upon the sketched rose. "Beautiful, Kathleen. I sensed you had talent. I'm amazed at how much." His voice softened. "It's a pity you've kept your ability hidden for so long."

Kathleen set her pencil aside. Stretching, she sought to relieve the tension in her back.

"May I have the picture?" he asked. "Somehow it reminds me of you."

Kathleen looked startled that he would understand. She signed the name *Kathleen Stein* and handed him the page. Philip took Kathleen's hand and asked her to follow.

"Come," he said. "We need to talk."

Leading her to the small sofa, he took the chair beside her.

"I'm ready to operate as soon as you are, but we need to discuss the procedure. During this first surgery," he continued, "I will attempt to reconstruct the right side of your face. It is a delicate, tedious procedure as I rebuild your cheekbone and correct the damage. It should take about eight hours, and you'll require several weeks to heal."

From experience he hesitated, carefully considering his next words.

"You'll suffer a great deal of pain and discoloration, Kathleen. Believe me, there will be times you will wonder if it's worth it."

Hesitantly, Kathleen asked the only question that mattered.

"Will I look like I did before?"

Philip reached out and touched her hand, sending an unexpected shiver up her spine.

"After living through a tragedy like this, you are never the same."

Kathleen turned away, shadowing the right side of her face. It was as if she were trying to hide her disfigurement from Philip. He had seen her do this several times before. It was when he spoke to her like a friend rather than a physician that she turned away. At first, he had thought nothing of it. Now a troubling notion crossed his mind.

"Kathleen, have you studied yourself in the mirror? Have you come to know yourself the way you are?"

Kathleen's eyes widened. "Good God! No! I saw myself once when the bandages first came off. I never want to see myself like that again. I won't look at myself again until I'm whole."

Philip was shocked. He didn't claim to be a psychiatrist. Yet he was sensitive enough to know that the time had not yet come to operate.

Gently, he took her hand and forced her wary eyes to his.

"You have to see and accept yourself the way you are. I can't operate until you've made peace with your disfigurement."

"But why?" she asked.

"Kathleen, no matter how successful the surgery, I can never make you look exactly as you did before. I can repair the damage but the experience will have profoundly changed you. Unless you realize this, you'll always see yourself as maimed. Do you understand?"

Kathleen nodded slightly.

"I can fix the outer scars, Kathleen. You have to heal the scars inside."

"But how do I begin?" she cried.

"You begin where you are, right here. You have to know and accept yourself as you are before you can hope to change."

Abruptly, Philip stood. Walking to the easel, he grabbed a pencil. "Draw yourself, Kathleen. Exactly as you are today. When you see yourself truly the way I do, then I will know it's time to begin."

Philip Wentworth retrieved his picture. Without another word he left. Kathleen refused to go near the easel. For hours she sat by the window, trying to understand what he meant. Finally, when the sun began fading in the west, she returned to her chair and hastily sketched an image. It was a woman veiled in black.

Philip returned to make evening rounds. He looked at her picture but he did not smile. He left without saying a word.

■

Kathleen heard the familiar light rap at her door but chose to ignore it.

"Good morning, Mrs. Stein," came Ralph Noland's cheerful voice. "How are you today?"

"Fine," she mumbled. "Just fine."

Ralph sauntered over to her easel. There was nothing finished, only a basket heaping with crumbled pages.

Emptying the trash, he turned to Kathleen but she refused to meet his glance.

"Is there anything I can do for you?" he asked.

Silently, she shook her head no.

Every morning, Philip made rounds. Every evening, he came by to check her progress. Always his reply was the same.

"Keep working, Kathleen. I'm ready whenever you are."

Veiled ladies drawn in black. Women with only half a face. Round circles. No features. These were the images she drew on her sketch pad. These were the pages discarded in the trash.

Kathleen was particularly disturbed one morning when Philip made rounds.

"I don't know what you want! Tell me what to draw," she implored, "then I will!"

Philip started to leave. He paused when an object upon the dresser caught his notice. Thrusting a small hand mirror in her face, he said sharply, "Look at yourself, Kathleen!"

"No!" she cried, turning away. "I can't!"

Philip left Kathleen in tears. He wondered if he were not doing more harm than good.

"Damn it, Philip!" she cried. "You have to operate. I can't live like this any longer!"

Finally, the moment came when she could deny his request no longer. With trembling hands, she raised the hand mirror to her face. The pain was almost too much to bear as she studied what she had been versus what she was now. She brought the mirror even closer and forced herself to see and feel the gross depression that once had been a magnificent face.

"Oh God! Is this how I really look? Is this how you see me, Philip?"

Angrily, she grabbed her pencil and began sketching the outline of her own face. On the left she drew the once beautiful Kathleen Clay. The woman with the flawless complexion, sapphire eyes, the ravishing cameo that all men fancied but only one had possessed.

Clutching her pencil tightly, she began sketching the right side of her face slowly as her own tears began to fall. In great detail, she drew the crushed cheekbone, the caved depression, the damaged eye and the jagged scar that crossed from the hairline to the bridge of her nose. Staring at her image she began to see the truth.

Fingering the depression, she thought about the emptiness she felt inside. Her beautiful facade had been merely a shell. It was as if no one lived inside.

"I loved you, Michael, and allowed you to destroy me. God, will I ever be able to love again? Will I ever be whole?"

Kathleen drew her portrait, detailing the full horror of her disfigurement. She spared nothing. She denied nothing. It was graphic. It was grotesque. Gazing at her portrait, she shuddered.

Spent, finished, she threw her pencil aside and returned to the bed. Buzzing the desk, she waited for the nurse to answer.

"Tell Dr. Wentworth I want to see him now."

When he knocked, she did not answer. He stepped into the darkened room and waited.

"You wanted to see me, Kathleen?" he queried, his professional reserve intact.

Saying nothing, she merely gestured towards the easel.

Flipping on the light, he approached her sketch pad cautiously. There he stood speechless, studying her portrait. He turned to her and smiled.

"Yes, Kathleen. That's exactly how I see you. But only for now. I'm scheduling your surgery for the day after tomorrow."

Susan M. Hoskins

It was just past dawn. Dressed in scrubs but as yet unmasked, Dr. Wentworth waited impatiently in the hallway outside the OR, seeking to steady his mind in preparation for a most difficult surgery. The electronic door opened. Prepped for the procedure, Kathleen was wheeled inside, strapped on the gurney, wrapped snugly in blankets. The temperature in the OR was kept several degrees cooler than elsewhere in the hospital. Kathleen immediately felt a chill on her exposed face. Philip approached her. His manner seemed as impersonal as the sterile surroundings.

"Good morning, Kathleen. Are you ready?"

Biting her lower lip, she nodded. She yearned for the reassuring touch of Philip's hand. She was denied. Groggy from the sedative she had received upstairs, she struggled to master the fear that suddenly engulfed her. No surgery was totally without risk. Something could go wrong. What if her new face was not all she hoped? What if Philip could not repair the damage? What if in the end . . . she was still disfigured after all?

Philip, knowing the look of a patient's terror, had to react. Leaning over the gurney, he forced her wary eyes to his. He then took her trembling hand tenderly in his own.

A tear ran down her cheek. Tentatively he glanced up. Seeing no one watching, he did the unthinkable. He bent down and sweetly kissed her forehead.

"Don't worry. Everything will be okay, I promise. I'll be right here when you wake up."

Signaling the orderly to wheel her into the OR, Philip scrubbed while she was transferred from the gurney to the table. The anesthesiologist asked Kathleen to count backwards as he began his slow drip. Within minutes she was under. The rest of the surgical team surrounded the patient and waited for Wentworth's signal to begin.

Donning his gloves and mask, Philip accepted the scalpel and prepared to make his first incision. Placing it carefully on Kathleen's face, he made a precise deep cut. She, of course, felt no pain. But laying open her precious flesh, Philip did, in a secret place in his heart.

■

Jake Kahn's voice seemed unusually gruff when he saw Sydney cross in front of his door. "Grab a cup of coffee, little lady, and come in here! We need to talk! Bring me one too!"

Shaking her head, she wondered just what the hell was wrong now. Sydney quickly fixed herself and her boss a cup of coffee, then hurried into his office.

"Close the door, Sydney."

Something was definitely amiss. Taking a seat across from her boss, she waited for the ax to fall.

"How's the Cole child?"

Sydney sipped her coffee thoughtfully. At the mention of Tanya, her face brightened.

"She's doing fine, Jake. She's improving every day. So far, there's been no sign of rejection. We all know that could change."

Jake cleared his throat and glanced to the ceiling as if he were searching for the right words to say.

"You did a good job on the piece, Sydney. We logged several hundred calls here at the station. People liked your style and your sense of humanity. You're making a name for yourself around town."

Sydney smiled but it was neither a broad nor a particularly satisfied grin. As a reporter, she yearned for public approval. She was no different than an actress or a writer. Without public approval, her career meant nothing. Yet, Sydney harbored a secret she had not yet shared with her boss. Now seemed like the appropriate time.

Setting her empty cup back upon his desk, she spoke in a quiet, rather sad voice.

"There's something you should know about all of this, Jake. Something I'm not particularly proud of."

"Oh? What's that?"

"Sam and I used all our influence to get Tanya Cole her liver. We circumvented the system. We forced the Director of Organ Procurement to ignore UNOS policy and give Tanya top priority. What we did wasn't right. At least Tanya is alive."

Jake chuckled inwardly. Finally he had met a reporter with a conscience. Oh how Sydney Lawrence reminded him of himself, many years ago.

"You're being too hard on yourself, Sydney. The world operates on the premise of *who you know* not *what you know*. You and Sam did what you thought best to pull off the impossible. And why not? Tanya Cole is a poor, black kid. If you had not fought for her, who else would have? Trust me, if the governor's daughter had needed a liver, nothing would have stood in his way. No child would have taken priority over his. So what's the difference?"

"It's not that easy, Jake," Sydney replied. "Farhad Rajid said something that has haunted me ever since. He told me that by securing Tanya a liver, we may have denied another child life. How do I live with that? Who was I to play God?"

"Sydney, we all do what we must to save ourselves and those we love. It's that simple. We live in an imperfect world. Nobody promised that life would be fair. We play the cards we're dealt and make the best of it. Take comfort in the fact that Tanya Cole is alive. Let go of the rest. End of story. It's time to march on down the road."

It was indeed time to get on with things. Something was troubling Jake. She intuitively guessed that whatever it was would involve her.

"What's up, Jake?" she asked.

Kahn leaned back in his chair and observed Sydney quietly. In the short time Sydney had been employed by the station, he had come to respect her greatly. Never more so than this morning. It was time to trust her with perhaps the biggest story of both their careers.

"Before I begin, I must have your promise of complete confidentiality. What I am about to share with you must not be discussed with anyone. Not even with Sam. Do I have your word?"

"You have my word. Don't keep me in suspense. What is it, Jake?"

"As I told you during our initial interview, Sydney, Kansas City is a city with secrets and crime. We experience a murder here nearly every day. We've made national headlines with our own serial killer. I thought that was the worst. I was wrong. Several months ago, some very bizarre things began occurring. Pieces of bodies have been found floating in the Missouri River. Dismembered bodies. The police are bewildered."

Sydney leaned forward. "What do you mean *pieces of bodies?*"

"Trunks with no limbs. Arms, feet, hands."

Sydney paled.

"There's one fact, however, that makes this case even more twisted. The skulls have no teeth. The hands—no fingers. The feet—no toes. Get the picture?"

Sydney's answer was right on target.

"No means of identification."

"You got it, little lady. Someone has gone to a great deal of trouble to make sure the John Doe pieces cannot be identified. Most serial killers leave tracks. The profile is usually the same since they often want to get caught. The perpetrator . . . or perpetrators . . . know what the hell they're doing. The question is why?"

"My God, Jake! What a story! Why haven't we reported it?"

"The Chief of Police, Tom Andrews, is a personal friend of mine. We've worked together on many cases over the years. He involved me early on because the police are baffled. We both agreed that there was no need to alarm the city until we have more facts. That's why I'm telling you now."

Sydney was excited yet troubled. "What would you like me to do?"

"I'll assign you some low-profile stories to keep you in front of the camera. Put in your time. That's it. Use the rest of your day to investigate this story. We'll get you into Police Headquarters. I've arranged a meeting with Andrews and his top homicide detectives. You'll work closely with them. Luckily, you're a woman who is admired. They won't mind having you around. See what you can dig up. Broaden the scope of things. Check around the country for missing persons reports. See if you can discover any links to Kansas City. Let's see where all this leads us."

Sydney Lawrence was hooked.

Jake Kahn leaned forward.

"To tell you the truth, I'm worried, Sydney. I feel that knot in my gut that always means trouble. There's something more sordid going on here than we've ever seen before. We've got to find out what it is."

■

The delicate procedure required nine hours. It was past three o'clock before Philip left the OR. He was jubilant yet exhausted. The reconstructive process had gone well. Kathleen now had the beginnings of a new face. She would be in recovery for several hours. Philip desperately needed a break. After showering, his first stop was the cafeteria for some much needed coffee and a bite of lunch. Sam rose from his table when he saw his colleague enter. Going immediately to his side, he asked, "How's Kathleen?"

"Just fine, Sam. Surgery was tricky. There was even more damage than I had first detected. Luckily, there were no complications during the procedure. I'm cautiously optimistic that in time her face will heal nicely."

Sam clapped his colleague on the back.

"I told Sydney that there was no one better for the job. I'm relieved Kathleen's in your hands."

Too exhausted now even to reply, Philip merely nodded his thanks.

"Don't forget the party tonight," Ellis reminded.

"What party?" Wentworth inquired.

Sam shot Philip a quizzical glance.

"Dr. Meade's retirement party. My house. Seven-thirty."

"Oh dear God! I completely forgot!"

"It's a command performance, Philip. Don't be late."

21

Promptly at seven-thirty, the guests began arriving. Everyone was expected to attend, from staff physicians and their spouses to the heads of various departments. Dr. Meade had been a leading force in the hospital's founding. No senior staff member would dare miss this party.

Parked down the street, hidden in the darkness of the night, two men in an unmarked car noticed the party at the Ellis home. This was of little consequence to them. Their attention remained focused on the mansion next-door where a little girl watched from an upstairs bedroom window.

Sydney had agonized for days over the preparations. She had planned a splendid affair with richly catered food and drink. The house was lit by soft candlelight, and the aroma of fresh flowers graced every room. It was Sydney who greeted Philip at the front door of the Colonial home on Verona Circle.

"Philip, how nice to see you. Finally."

Returning her warm greeting, he said, "Forgive me for being late, Sydney. And I can only stay a few minutes. Kathleen had surgery earlier today. I don't want to leave her alone too long."

Sydney squeezed his hand and smiled. "I understand, Philip."

Then she spotted a man she needed to talk to across the room. Making her way through the crowd, she greeted him.

"May I get you a drink, Mr. Rajid?"

He seemed startled by her sudden presence. "No, thank you."

Rajid started to turn away but Sydney refused to budge. The Iranian was forced into conversation. "How is the Cole family?" he asked politely.

Sydney gave him a broad smile. "Tanya is progressing nicely. Sam expects her to be released from the hospital in a couple of weeks. Her body seems to be tolerating the new liver. So far, there's no sign of rejection."

Farhad Rajid smiled. Sydney thought she detected sincerity when he responded, "I'm glad."

Sydney's expression changed. "I've given a great deal of thought to our last conversation, Mr. Rajid. I'm very grateful that our efforts regarding Tanya were not in vain."

Rajid nodded. He understood. What Sydney didn't say— couldn't say—was that she felt horribly guilty. She still believed that she had stolen a liver from another child.

It was Sam who broke the spell. "Sydney, I have someone I would like you to meet."

Instinctively, she turned to greet her guest. Farhad Rajid remained immobile.

"This is Dr. William Scofield. He's a Senior Surgeon on staff and the Director of Emergency Services. And this is his lovely wife, Marsha."

Sydney smiled as her eyes moved from one to the other. William Scofield was a tanned, well-kept middle-aged man in his early fifties. His eyes were bleary. Sydney glanced at his glass. His drink was empty.

Scofield's speech was slurred when he said, "If you'll excuse me, I need a drink."

Taking a few steps backward, Farhad Rajid left the group without responding. Sam departed as well, leaving the two ladies alone. Marsha Scofield's gaze tracked Rajid across the room.

"What a strange little man," she murmured.

"How so?"

Marsha Scofield was a platinum-haired, petite woman who wore too much makeup. She had beady eyes and thick ruby lips. She was an active member of the hospital auxiliary and delighted in the thrill of a loose tongue. But more than her love of gossip, she relished the lifestyle her husband's profession afforded her. She turned to the wife of the Chief of Staff and smiled.

"I'm sorry, Sydney," she drawled. "It's really not my place to say."

■

At a social gathering of doctors, the sound of a beeper was as normal as the clinking of ice cubes in a glass. But there was nothing ordinary about the call William Scofield answered shortly after ten o'clock. Weaving slightly, the surgeon beckoned Farhad Rajid to a quiet corner of the living room.

"We've got a live one!" Scofield slurred, his eyes sparkling with intent. "She's a woman in her early thirties. She leaves a husband and two small children behind."

"What happened?" Rajid inquired.

"The usual," Scofield responded. "Massive head injuries in a car accident. Everything else remains intact."

Farhad Rajid permitted himself only the briefest of smiles as he calculated what each of her organs might be worth. It was then he studied his cohort.

"Are you drunk, Scofield? Go to the kitchen and ask for coffee. Sober up before you leave for the hospital. I'll go ahead to make the necessary preparations. You must be sharp, my friend. We can't afford any mistakes."

■

Draining his cup of coffee, Joe Morrison proclaimed, "I've got to piss!"

Opening the car door, he left George Massoud behind. It was a sticky July night, but the stars above were brilliant. Walking on the opposite side of the street, he crossed in front of Hassan's mansion. Everything was quiet. Morrison had determined that Hassan was at home with his daughter and staff of servants. Nothing to report.

Relieving himself in the bushes, he thought about the boring stakeouts, endless nights and too many cups of rancid coffee. Too many times pissing in the wind. Fishing a cigarette from his shirt pocket, he signaled Massoud that he was going to take a short walk. Inhaling a deep drag, he ambled past the mansion. The child was once again visible in an upstairs window.

Morrison found her behavior sad. "We don't have much of a life, do we kid?"

Her name was Lydia, that much he knew. She didn't attend school. She had a private tutor. She rarely left the house except for occasional visits with the lady next-door. She spent her nights roaming the upstairs hallway going from one large window to the next. Watching life from a distance.

Something about her disturbed him. His gut started rolling. He always carried Rolaids. He popped three. There was something familiar about the scene. Déjà-vu.

He turned away. He found his own life at the moment almost as mundane as hers. It was going to be another endlessly boring night. He rounded the curve of the cul-de-sac slowly, trying to find pleasure in a brief smoke.

Halfway between the two houses, he stopped. For the first time tonight he noticed the full moon. Morrison had no concerns about being observed. He was obscured by the dark shadows of one of the decorative gas lamps that graced the cul-de-sac. The party at the Ellises was still in full swing. Very few guests had left.

But now a man came out who seemed in a rush, his head lowered. Morrison had no idea why he found the man's movements curious. Perhaps it was the boredom, or perhaps it was his sixth sense. The man was alone. He had a purpose. Yet he slowed as he crossed in front of Hassan's mansion. Seeing the girl in the upstairs window, he halted. He glanced about. Seeing no one watching, he waved at the child. She leaned forward. Apparently recognizing the man, she smiled broadly and waved. Morrison found this more than a little odd. He had observed the girl to be extremely shy. She never interacted with strangers.

A large man Morrison recognized as one of Hassan's guards suddenly appeared behind the child at the bedroom window. The girl pointed towards the man standing in front of the house. The guard leaned forward too, perhaps for a closer look. Then he stood erect and saluted the stranger on the sidewalk.

Morrison had now ceased to be merely curious. He was intrigued. His gut was churning. The man on the sidewalk hurried to his car while the FBI agent followed from across the street. Luckily the man's car was parked under a street light. Morrison returned to his own vehicle with a memorized license number to call in.

Susan M. Hoskins

Alone in an isolated cubicle in the Emergency Room, a reasonably sober William Scofield peered down at the patient and feigned regret. The sound of the machines keeping her alive echoed in the background.

"What a pitiful shame!" he declared.

The charge nurse on duty had to agree.

"She leaves a husband and two small sons behind. It just doesn't seem fair."

"What happened?" Scofield inquired.

"Hit and run. Probably a drunk driver. The police are searching for him now."

"Where's her husband?"

"We've got him in a private conference room down the hall. Poor guy. He's distraught. Dr. Lipsky broke the news to him."

"Has he agreed to the harvesting?"

"Yes," the nurse replied. "The woman had already signed the back of her driver's license. Her husband won't stand in the way."

The doctor had to suppress a smile. "Okay, Nancy. That will be all. I'll make the necessary arrangements."

Waiting for the nurse to exit, William Scofield remained by the patient's bedside. Only when the nurse's footsteps faded, did he allow himself the pleasure of a grin. What he had suspected was now confirmed. And if all went well, it would be a very profitable night, a very profitable night indeed.

Farhad Rajid left the privacy of his office on the first floor to head to the Emergency Room one level below. In the space of thirty minutes, he had placed three calls. One was to his contact at UNOS. The second was to Mexico City. The third was to his team here. Everything stood ready. The harvesting could now proceed.

With short rapid steps, Rajid entered the ER. Huddled at the central desk, the staff remained quiet, looking perhaps a bit bored. It was nearly midnight. Activity in the Emergency Room had slowed.

No one paid Farhad Rajid any heed. He was a familiar figure in any drama with this kind of tragic ending. The Director of Organ Procurement needed no direction. He proceeded purposefully to the secluded trauma room off to the back and to the right. Pulling open the curtain, he entered. He was relieved to find his colleague alone. He was even more relieved to find him relatively sober.

Tiny beads of sweat dotted William Scofield's brow. Rajid wondered if it were the result of the booze or the excitement of the harvesting to come. Pulling the curtain securely behind him, he ventured to the bedside and peered down at the sleeping figure of what once had been quite a lovely young woman.

Her swollen head was swathed in bloody bandages. It was hard to get near her for the wires of the machines that sustained her. Drawing back the sheet, Scofield betrayed what little dignity the poor woman had left, as he invited Rajid for a closer look. The two men boldly examined her naked body as if it were a side of beef they were about to buy.

"She's young, healthy and strong. The heart's good and so are the kidneys. The liver looks to be viable."

"Is the work-up complete?"

"The preliminary studies are finished," Scofield answered. "Have a look for yourself."

Farhad Rajid examined the report carefully. He nodded and handed the chart back to the surgeon. He would fax the information to Mexico City to help the doctors determine the best matches.

"What do you want me to get?" Scofield inquired.

"I need the liver and both kidneys," Rajid replied.

"What about the heart?"

"There's no time to find a buyer."

Scofield was disappointed. A viable heart was worth more financially to him than anything else he might harvest. He understood the dilemma. The preservation time of livers was twelve to twenty-four hours. It was difficult enough to get them south of the border and transplanted in time. Kidneys were no problem. They stayed viable forty-eight to seventy-two hours. There were scores of patients waiting anxiously in a private hospital on the outskirts of Mexico City. Wealthy patients willing to pay any price.

Hearts were another matter. They had to be sold locally, certainly within the region. The demand was high. The price they commanded, unbelievable. They had a surgeon in St. Louis willing to perform the procedure. For a very hefty fee, of course. But this all had to be arranged in advance. Tonight there was no time. The heart would be wasted.

To these men, human organs did not represent life, only money. Farhad Rajid said it often and best: "Pounds of flesh. Pieces of gold."

■

William Scofield called in his two nurses and alerted the OR. Both women had gray hair. One was African American; the other, Caucasian. Both were overweight. Within an hour, everything was ready to proceed. Rachel Sinnes and Sally Cooper were good at their jobs. Forced into early retirement at sixty, they were not permitted to scrub for any other surgeon but William Scofield. It was thought—erroneously—that older surgical nurses could make mistakes. With dead patients it didn't matter. With live ones, the threat of lawsuits was too great.

William Scofield was different. He did more than tolerate their service, he valued them. He showed them great respect and generosity. That's why they would come to help with the harvesting at any time day or night, whenever Scofield called. The majority of nurses loathed this kind of duty. Most procurements took place, like this one, late at night. Neither of these ladies cared. They were grateful for the work. Most important for William Scofield, they were loyal . . . blindly loyal.

"Good evening, ladies!" Scofield called out heartily as he entered the OR to scrub.

"How good to see you, Dr. Scofield!"

While he scrubbed, the nurses made final preparations. William Scofield, they firmly believed, was a saint who walked on water. He seemed the epitome of a successful doctor. He and his wife lived in Hallbrook, a wealthy area south of the city. He was a civic leader. His wife commanded respect in society. People talked about his drinking problem and his fondness of gambling. These two nurses had never seen alcohol interfere with his ability as a surgeon. In the OR, he was a perfectionist. That's why these two ladies took such special care to make sure all the instruments were sterile and ready, and the containers precisely labeled. *Heart. Liver. Kidney-right. Kidney-left.*

When he was scrubbed, gowned and gloved, he assumed his place at the head of the table. Then like a maestro, he held out his hand to receive the scalpel and declared, "We shall begin."

He took a moment to appreciate the naked flesh of the young woman lying before him, sustained still on the machines that kept her organs viable. Shaking his head sadly, he sliced the body open vertically in a single, precise, yet rapid motion.

On the first shelf of his cart, he placed the containers of the organs deemed to be *good*. The second shelf was reserved for those thought to be of no use. It was he alone who made the determination. Rachel assisted with the surgery while Sally kept a detailed record as hospital policy demanded.

It was a good thing that William Scofield enjoyed theatrics. Oftentimes, depending upon what Rajid needed, he was forced to make up a story. Such was the case with the woman who lay before them. Thus, he began yet another tale.

"Damn!" he swore. "Look at all the blood! I think there's a tear in the major aorta. It appears that the spleen has ruptured. I'll lay you odds the liver is damaged as well."

Scofield deftly removed the liver. Then he placed the organ carefully in a labeled container and put it on the second shelf.

"Will you look at this? There was much more trauma to the body than we first suspected. Neither kidney looks good. Damn it to hell! What a waste!"

Dutifully, Sally charted each of the organs, the time of its extraction and the disposition of its usefulness. The second shelf—those containers worthy only of disposal—were filling rapidly.

William Scofield sought to console his nurses.

"Perhaps our efforts tonight will not totally be in vain. The corneas still look good."

Within an hour, the procedure was completed, the respirator silenced, and the dead woman crudely stitched back together. Scofield removed his bloodied gloves and accepted a new pair from Rachel. Turning his back on his nurses and the gory mess surrounding the table, he examined his precious organs.

"Just as I suspected. The liver is damaged and neither kidney is viable. The chart stands as dictated. I'll sign it."

Once the paperwork had been concluded, Scofield discarded his bloody scrubs. Then he bid his nurses a good night.

"It's late. Finish up, ladies, and go home. I'll run the organs down to the lab."

Gratefully, they nodded.

Their eyes never left William Scofield as they watched him wheel his precious cart through the electronic door.

"He doesn't have to do that," Sally acknowledged. "Yet he does. And my weary old legs appreciate it."

"There's no finer man alive," Rachel agreed. "Come on, girl. Let's get this mess cleaned up and go home."

William Scofield took the service elevator one floor down to the basement. The corridors were silent. The hospital was, for the most part, quiet. The doctor glanced quickly in both directions. His adrenaline was pumping. Every time he felt the rush. He had perfected his lie. He made a point to be correct and precise in all his legitimate affairs. He was a pillar of the community. He was a family man and a heavy contributor to his church. Except for his occasional bouts with booze, he was thought of as a fine, moral man.

The basement of the hospital contained three primary areas: the boiler room, the morgue and the lab. Adjacent to these areas was a service door used primarily for the transport of bodies from the morgue and the removal of toxic waste. Scofield rapped four times lightly on the door, then opened it.

Farhad Rajid did not disappoint him. A plain black van was backed up to the door. Rajid, with his men, all trusted Iranians, stood ready to receive and transport the precious cargo.

William Scofield handed the Director of Organ Procurement three containers.

"It's all here. The liver and both kidneys. Everything looks good."

"Well done!" Rajid exclaimed. "My broker has commanded top dollar."

"What's my cut?" the greedy surgeon inquired.

Farhad Rajid hesitated. He begrudged the bastard every dollar he paid him, but he needed him and others like him for the Cause.

"Your cut is twenty-five thousand dollars. Not bad for a single night's work."

Bidding Rajid a hasty adieu, Scofield quickly closed the door. He glanced in all directions. The corridors remained deserted, his secret safe.

Taking his time, Scofield continued on to the lab. He was greeted by a familiar technician.

"Hello, John."

"Hi, Dr. Scofield. Did you have a procurement tonight?"

"Not much of one, I'm afraid. All we could salvage were the corneas."

Scofield feigned regret as he glanced at what was left of his harvesting.

"Perhaps these will do some poor soul a measure of good. God knows they're needed."

Kathleen Clay was coming to understand the true definition of pain. It had been two months since her surgery. The agony caused by Philip's scalpel had abated. The sorrow in her heart remained.

It was early one morning when Kathleen made her way to the easel but creativity seemed to elude her. Fingering her pencils and paints, she waited for inspiration. Then she heard the door to her suite open and a familiar voice greet her.

In the weeks following her surgery, it had been Ralph who was her ever faithful visitor, stopping by every morning when he came on duty to bring her coffee and every evening before leaving. He didn't stay long, just a few short minutes. During her convalescence, he had inched his way into her heart. Every time she gazed into Ralph's eyes, Kathleen saw herself. And the hurt was almost too much to bear.

"Up and about already, Mrs. Stein?"

Kathleen merely smiled. "I was hoping to paint but nothing will come. How are you today, Ralph?"

"No complaints, ma'am." Pausing, Ralph glanced quickly around the room. "What can I do for you, Mrs. Stein? Run an errand?"

Kathleen's practiced smile slowly faded.

"Stay and visit with me a few minutes, Ralph. That's all I want. The time drags by so slowly."

Ralph edged a few steps closer.

"Your face is getting better every day. Dr. Wentworth sure knows his stuff."

Kathleen's hand tenderly touched her lightly bandaged cheek.

"Philip . . . Dr. Wentworth . . . says I'm doing real well. The swelling has gone down and he has lightened the dressing. The pain grows less every day. I still get funny tingling sensations. Dr. Wentworth says those are the nerves trying to heal."

Ralph watched her slowly move her head from side to side. Yes, she definitely had more mobility. And yes, he could tell the pain of healing seemed less. Yet the despondency he saw in her eyes was deepening every day.

"What's wrong, Mrs. Stein? You can tell me."

Kathleen turned away and focused upon the empty pages of her sketch pad. How could she tell this janitor that she felt hollow? How could she tell him that her new life seemed terrifying for she understood only misery? How could she tell him that she missed her son when no one must know he existed? And how could she tell him that her heart cried out for Philip when Dr. Wentworth was only a few floors away?

Reluctantly, she shared the only words she could muster.

"I'm tired, Ralph," she whispered. "Just tired."

Knowing she spoke a lie, Ralph inched even closer until she could feel his presence just behind her chair.

"Pain is a funny thing, Mrs. Stein. Sometimes no matter what you do, it won't go away."

Slowly, Kathleen turned around to face him.

"We all wear our scars, ma'am," he continued, "Some are just a little easier to see. That's the difference."

"What do you know about scars, Ralph?" she asked, not meaning it unkindly.

"I know too damn much," he replied softly.

He knew, but didn't say, that he hated the job he'd been assigned. He cursed Michael Clay every day he was forced to see Kathleen. Killing her was supposed to be easy. Like stalking prey. You don't befriend a deer before you shoot it. An assassin shouldn't have to know his victim. It makes doing the job much harder. But Ralph's feelings didn't matter to Michael Clay. He had his own time frame. He didn't want Kathleen killed until she had everything to lose.

"Your fine doctor can repair the scars on your face, but only you can fix the ones inside."

What Ralph didn't say was that his own scars ran too deep to heal.

Kathleen remained silent. Philip had spoken about inner healing before agreeing to perform her surgery. For the moment, Kathleen forgot her own torment as she focused upon another's. Under the intensity of her stare, Noland glanced away. He busied himself emptying the trash. Kathleen's eyes tracked his every move.

"What's happened to you, Ralph? Why are you so sad?"

He kept his back to her. He ceased working but he refused to turn around.

"I've seen too much, ma'am. Too much of life. You, you're young and still have a chance. Me, I got no chance at all."

Finally, Ralph turned back around and forced himself to confront Kathleen eye to eye.

"When I look at you, even now, I see a beautiful woman with a hell of a lot of life to live! But it doesn't matter what anybody else sees if you don't see that yourself."

Huge tears welled in Kathleen's eyes. She said nothing yet she knew Ralph Noland spoke the truth.

"You're a nice lady. That's a rare thing. See yourself for the woman you are. You'll never be beautiful again—even on the outside—unless you get to know yourself deep down."

Kathleen's sigh could be heard clear across the room. Ralph's words echoed Philip's yet again. From the skilled surgeon to the janitor, everyone saw Kathleen for who and what she was. Everyone, that is, but Kathleen.

Abruptly, Ralph turned away. He could face neither her nor himself a moment longer. He started to leave. She stopped him.

"Ralph!" she called. "Wait!"

He paused but didn't turn.

"Thank you," was all she could whisper.

Closing the door, the janitor started down the hallway. Just then he saw the auburn-haired reporter he had come to dread. She alone might recognize him from Velours and destroy his cover. Instinctively, he avoided her gaze as he rushed past her down the hall. Sydney turned and watched him leave as an eerie sensation engulfed her. Shrugging, she continued towards Kathleen's room.

Sydney found Kathleen in tears.

"What's wrong?" she cried. "Has the janitor upset you? Damn him! I'll report him immediately!"

Surprised, Kathleen ceased crying and glanced up bewildered.

"No, Sydney! No!" she entreated. "Ralph did nothing to upset me. Nothing, that is, but speak the truth."

Kathleen wiped her eyes, then spoke plainly from the heart.

"I know he seems a bit strange, Sydney, but Ralph Noland is my friend."

Sydney hated to leave Kathleen, but she had to. The assignment Jake had given her now occupied center stage in her life. She thought about little else.

Pieces of bodies floating in the river.

No means of identification.

Who had they been?

Why were they killed?

Sydney tried for the moment to focus on Kathleen. She made a mental note to tell Sam about the troublesome janitor. Yet would she remember? It was still very early in the day. She had a great deal to accomplish.

As she neared the elevator, she spotted a familiar figure at the nurses' station. His back was to her but she recognized Dr. Philip Wentworth.

"Good morning, Philip."

Philip slowly turned to greet her. He looked weary, but then so did she. It was the hazard of professional life.

"Sydney! How nice to see you!"

"And you, Philip. How are things?"

Sydney and Philip, both somewhat shy, exchanged casual pleasantries. Finally she broached the subject that concerned her.

"I'm worried about Kathleen. How do you think she's doing?"

"She's right on track, Sydney. Her face is healing nicely. I'm ready to do the final procedure next Monday. This will be a far simpler operation than the last. Kathleen should be healed completely and ready to go home within two months."

The look on Sydney's face caused him to pause.

"Is there something I should know?"

"I'm concerned about her. Kathleen seems depressed, lost even. Her only consistent link with the outside world is through a janitor. Forgive me for being a snob, Philip, but that's a scary thought."

Wentworth had to suppress a smile.

"I know I need to spend more time with Kathleen," Sydney continued. "Lately, I haven't even spent a long evening at home with Sam. We're both consumed by work."

Philip nodded. He didn't like what he was hearing. He kept his distance from Kathleen but it was not because he didn't care. It was because it felt safer.

"Would you talk to her, Philip? Let me know what Sam and I can do to help. She's come so far. Her confinement here will last another two months. I don't want her to fall apart now."

"I'll go see her. Thanks for your concern. I'll keep you posted through Sam."

It was with tentative steps that Philip approached Kathleen's room. He pretended to be studying her chart. The truth was he had her chart memorized. Every detail of Kathleen's face was etched into his memory—from the tiniest bone to mere fragments of tendons. He knew nothing else about her. This was his choice, not hers.

Kathleen Callihan Clay Stein terrified him. He didn't have a clue as to why. He rapped softly on her closed door.

"Good morning, Kathleen. How are you feeling?"

Her reply had not varied in days. She was fine . . . just fine. For a few minutes, the two went through their daily ritual with he as the doctor and she as the patient. After everything had been said about her face and the scheduling of her next procedure, Philip had exhausted his repertoire of comfortable chatter. Usually this was his cue to leave. Today was different. He forced his anxious feet to remain.

He searched her eyes for the despair Sydney had seen. He failed to see it. Yet neither did he notice how her face brightened the moment he entered the room. Kathleen waited. For what she didn't know. When Philip glanced at his watch, her spirits plummeted. He seemed bored and ready to leave. What he said instead surprised her.

"I have a few minutes before my next patient. Do you think we could talk? I'd like to get to know you better."

He guided Kathleen away from the bed to the sitting area near the window. Taking a deep breath, the shy doctor plunged ahead. "Tell me about yourself, Kathleen."

Attired in a comfortable pair of yellow silk pajamas, Kathleen sat cross-legged upon the sofa. She was amused at the sight of Philip struggling for conversation. She sensed she had control. She toyed with him just a bit.

"What would you like to know?"

Philip had no idea what he wanted to know. He registered only a blank stare. A thought crossed his mind and saved him.

"Tell me about a time in your life when you were happy, really happy. Yes, that's what I'd like to know."

A slow smile crossed her lips.

"I grew up really poor. We lived on a small, run-down farm in Kentucky. I was the eldest of three. My daddy was a sharecropper."

Philip liked the sound of her satiny voice. He liked the color of her golden hair lit by the sunshine of the open window. He liked the way her eyes softened as she threw her glance at him. He liked the gentle curve of her body underneath the yellow silk pajamas.

"What were your parents like?" he asked.

"Mama was pretty when she was young. She was only seventeen when she married. She worked the farm with daddy. She always looked tired and haggard. She was kind and good. My daddy was a different story."

Kathleen's eyes narrowed at the mention of her father.

"I suppose he did the best he could. But he drank a lot and he had a real mean streak. When he'd get drunk, we'd get the belt. All of us became his target. I wondered why Mama stayed with him. I guess she had nowhere else to go."

Philip didn't like the sadness he saw on Kathleen's face. He wanted her to remember something happier.

"So tell me about the best time in your life," he prodded.

Her response came quickly. "It was right after I graduated from high school and left home. I went to a small rural school back then. There were only twelve kids in my entire senior class. I couldn't wait to get out of there. Mama understood. She wanted a better life for me. She helped me leave. She saved up fifty dollars. Then she drove the old truck and took me to Velours. She knew a woman who had an extra room to rent. She dropped me there with my fifty dollars. I'll never forget what she told me. She told me to go out and live every minute to the fullest. She told me not to look back, only forward. She said she'd be all right knowing I was happy. I was to write her letters and tell her what I saw. She said she'd taste a bit of life through me."

A pain seared Philip's heart as he remembered the words his own dying mother had uttered. "Live, then so will I."

"I got a job as a waitress in a little diner on the outskirts of town. It was the first time in my life I felt free. I loved it. I loved everything about it."

Kathleen paused. She studied Philip's face. Could he understand what she meant?

"Do you remember what it was like being eighteen? Do you remember how fresh everything looked?"

"What do you mean?"

"My world had been limited to a shanty and a few acres of dirt. Suddenly I was meeting all kinds of people. I was earning my own keep. My whole life lay ahead of me and the possibilities seemed endless. Everybody liked me. The people in the diner became my family. Everybody cared how I was. Everything looked and tasted better. Like hamburgers and malts."

Kathleen uncrossed her legs and leaned towards Philip. The nearness of this woman in her yellow silk pajamas unsettled him, and he averted his eyes.

"Tony used to fry those burgers on a greasy open grill. Lots of onions and cheddar cheese. All the tastes blended together. He served it up on big fat fresh buns. Oh God, I haven't had a hamburger like that in years. And the malts? Chocolate, strawberry, vanilla. Philip, have you ever tasted *real* vanilla? Not the processed bottled stuff they have today. I'm talking about the kind our mothers used in baking cookies? Do you know what I mean?"

Philip sadly shook his head no. Kathleen didn't catch the meaning of his subtle gesture. Philip didn't allow himself those kind of memories about his mother. She had died much too violently when he was far too young.

"I can still remember the taste of that vanilla today. I might have another good hamburger someday but I know I'll never taste that vanilla again. And you know what? That makes me really sad."

Hearing her own rush of words, Kathleen grew suddenly embarrassed. "You must think I'm crazy rambling on like this."

Philip Wentworth did not think Kathleen crazy. He found her captivating. He loved the melodic lilt of her Southern drawl. All he wanted was for her to continue.

"How long did you work there?"

"About six months. Then I met Michael Clay. I don't want to talk about him. You know, Philip, after I married money, I discovered what fine dining was all about. You want to hear something funny? Nothing ever tasted as good to me again as those greasy hamburgers Tony used to make."

Philip said nothing. He just kind of stared at Kathleen in wonderment. She was so damned beautiful in those yellow silk pajamas. Finally the sound of her voice penetrated his secret thoughts.

"Philip, isn't that you being paged?"

Blushing, the doctor focused on the intercom above. It was indeed his page.

"I guess I'd better go."

Kathleen merely nodded.

"I'll see you later," he promised.

At the door, Philip cast a quick glance in her direction. Something about Kathleen Callihan Clay Stein bothered him. It was a strange sensation, one he hadn't felt in years. He couldn't tell quite yet if it made him happy or made him sad. Walking down the hall, he tried to erase her from his mind. But there she would remain to dwell for the day, so pretty in her yellow silk pajamas.

Susan M. Hoskins

chapter 25

"Hi baby!" Charles hailed, cracking the door to his daughter's room. "Today's the day. We're going home. Are you ready?"

Sitting up in bed, the pretty child smiled. "Yes, Papa. I'm ready. Where's Mama?"

"I'm right here," Belva answered, trailing Charles into the room. "My, don't you look pretty!"

"Sam and Sydney bought me a new dress. The nurses got me ready. Do you like my hair?"

Tanya was all dressed up with her hair braided in brightly colored ribbons. She looked like a child going to a birthday party. And in a very special way, each new day of life was just that.

"Papa has some good news. Tell her, Charles."

Hoisting himself up on her bed, Charles clasped his daughter's fragile hand. Stroking her tiny fingers, he too smiled.

"We're not going back to that horrible apartment. We've got a new home, Tanya."

Tanya glanced to her mother for confirmation.

"A new home?" she asked. "Where?"

"Papa got a job as a security guard for the Winds project. With it comes a trailer and a new truck. The trailer is real nice. You'll even have your own room. We'll be together right there at the project."

"Oh, Papa!" Tanya cried. Impulsively, she hugged her father's neck.

"From now on, we'll be clean and comfortable with plenty of good food to eat," Belva assured her. "No more rats and no more roaches."

Sydney watched the scene from the hallway. After the Coles had finished hugging, she motioned for Sam to follow her as she pushed a wheelchair into the room.

"Time to go," she announced.

Helping Tanya down from the bed, Charles shouted, "Let's go home!"

A few minutes later a very proud Sam Ellis wheeled Tanya into the lobby of St. Vincent's. A score of staff members had gathered for her send-off. The press was there as well. Sydney had arranged for a camera crew to capture this moment for the six o'clock broadcast. Astutely, Sydney stood back away from the glare of the cameras so she could report the story later from a seemingly objective viewpoint and not as a friend of the family. In reality, though, there was no distancing herself from this story.

"Charles," said Sydney after the celebration had been completed and Tanya was laden with presents, "why don't you go get the truck now? We'll wait here with Belva and Tanya."

"With pleasure!" said Cole, heading out the door.

Sydney came to stand beside her husband. Her eyes scanned the hospital lobby and came to rest finally on a man she had seen before.

He was not particularly tall, nor especially handsome. His behavior seemed odd. Rather than absently watching the people who meandered by, he studied each person carefully, with deep thought and intent.

"See that man over there, Sam? Do you know him? He looks familiar but I can't place him."

Sam glanced in the man's direction. There was nothing in particular that distinguished him from others that passed through the lobby of St. Vincent's on any given day.

"I don't know him, but I think I've seen him before. He probably has a friend or relative here. Hell, he might even be a member of my staff!"

Just then Charles returned, diverting Sam's attention. Sydney could not let it be. There was a queasiness inside she couldn't shake. It was not due to rancid coffee or eating greasy food on the run. She was a small-town girl who had been raised with straight-forward values. She had been taught that things were black or white. People's choices were good or bad. Behavior was right or wrong. Now the small-town girl found herself in the big city where things were not so clearly defined. People here were not always what they seemed. First, there was Farhad Rajid and then the pesky janitor. Now there was a stranger lurking in the lobby.

Sam might not understand, but something was amiss here at the hospital. She didn't know what. All she knew for sure was that her intuition never lied.

Susan M. Hoskins

c h a p t e r **26**

The first frost chilled the air that early October morning. Sydney was bundled in a heavy woolen sweater as she made her way to the station shortly before nine. She loved this time of year. It reminded her of the excitement of going back to school, new fall clothes, fires in the hearth, everything warm and cozy.

As had become her routine, Sydney fixed two cups of coffee, one for herself, the other for Jake Kahn, before entering her boss's office. Jake was in a foul mood this day. Sydney couldn't fathom why. There was something about his demeanor that caused her not to ask. She assumed her usual chair across from his desk and waited.

"Well, little lady, we haven't talked in a few days. What's the latest on the investigation? Has anything of use been discovered? Or am I wasting my best talent on a meaningless assignment?"

Jake glared at Sydney over his glasses, which perched on the tip of his nose. His cheeks were flushed as he waited for the answer. The look on his face made Sydney squirm. Something was rubbing him raw today. She dare not ask for she knew he was volatile. Breathing a deep sigh and thanking God above, she was relieved that at least she had something to report.

"Well I do have a little news, Jake. I'm not saying we have an answer, but at least some of our questions are falling into place. As you know, we've conducted a major search throughout the nation looking for missing *John Does*. We've come up with five men who have a possible link to Kansas City."

Jake took off his glasses and leaned forward. For the first time this morning, he stopped frowning.

"Go on."

"The five men who disappeared over the course of the past year were single or divorced with no children or strong family ties. They were independent businessmen who traveled frequently. They all had legitimate reasons for being absent for extended periods of time. You know the kind of guys who go to trade shows and conventions several times a year. None of them had a significant other, yet they were often secretive about their trips."

"You're intriguing me, Sydney. Is there more?"

"Well, here is where it gets interesting, Jake. The five were men of means. They all had private secretaries. Yet occasionally, they insisted upon making their own travel arrangements. Could it be they didn't want anyone to know where they were going or where they were stopping over? There was one guy in particular who caught my attention."

By this time, the station manager of KMKC had fixed his glasses back in place and retrieved a pad and pen. His grouchy mood had lifted. Sydney had produced more information than anyone else had obtained in months.

"This man is from Pittsburgh. His name is Paul Owens. He was a self-made man who owned a small manufacturing company. Mr. Owens left Pittsburgh supposedly for Chicago the week before Thanksgiving last year. He never made it back for turkey and dressing. He never made it back at all. No one has seen him or heard from him since.

"What really makes this bizarre is that we think he never went to Chicago at all. He was a creature of habit. In Chicago, he always stayed at the downtown Hyatt. There's no record he ever checked in. He was a well-known figure at the trade shows. There is not one soul who witnessed him there. So what do you make of it?"

"My blood is pumping, Sydney, but I don't want to get carried away. Maybe these guys were bored with their lives. Perhaps they just chose to disappear."

Now it was Sydney's turn to lean forward and cast her eyes upon those of her boss.

"Let's pretend you are a man of means, Jake. I know it's a vision you'd like to believe."

Kahn chuckled.

"You're middle-aged and bored. You're divorced. Your relationships are less than satisfying. You've succeeded in business but life holds no challenge. Perhaps you decide to start over. Disappear without a trace. Wouldn't you take at least a portion of your assets with you? Would you be so desperate you would leave *everything* behind? Not one of these men cleared out their accounts or cashed in their portfolios. They simply left town and never returned."

"You have a point there, Sydney. Most high-profile men would not settle for a tranquil life smelling flowers and sweeping streets. Anything else?"

"One more thing. I guess it's not unusual for a person to have a favorite airline. Yet I found it strange that all five of these guys liked to fly United. Now keep in mind that two of them came from Pittsburgh, two from Detroit and one from Cleveland. United flies to Kansas City from all three cities. Kansas City is oftentimes a stop-over city to other destinations. I may be stretching, but I have to wonder if it's merely a coincidence or something more."

"Okay, okay. You have my undivided attention. What do you think is going on? What's here in Kansas City that would be so captivating? There's gambling and prostitution. But what the hell! You can find that anywhere. *Who* or *what* is the attraction?"

"That's what I intend to find out. Would you like me to fly to any of these cities to interview acquaintances or business associates of the missing men? Or is that premature?"

Jake Kahn took a moment to contemplate.

"It's too soon, Sydney. We need more facts and a more concrete connection. I don't want to risk any of this leaking to the press. Keep digging. Most men are motivated by money or women. Check into local gambling and prostitution. Is there anything here that sets the city apart? Report back to me in a few days."

Sydney nodded. She started to rise but something stopped her.

"I need some guidance, Jake. I'm running out of legitimate things to investigate and report. I don't want to lose audience interest. Any suggestions for stories?"

Kahn nodded. He understood. Poor Sydney was pulling double

duty. An idea struck him as interesting. It had been seething under the surface for several weeks ever since Tanya Cole's transplant. He knew it to be a sensitive subject for his reporter. He decided to give it a shot anyway.

"October is Organ Donation Month. It would be appropriate for you to do a follow-up story on Tanya Cole. We had so much positive response from the transplant drama."

Kahn deliberately paused. He removed his glasses and cleaned them on the sleeve of his shirt before continuing. "There's an aspect of donation that troubles me. I'm wondering if you have thought about it as well."

"What's that, Jake?"

"In recent years, there has been so much publicity about the need for organs and organ donation. I know a great many people have already signed the back of their driver's license designating donation."

"I noticed that as well, Jake. When we moved here in June, and had to obtain a new license, there was a separate booth just for organ donation sign-up."

"Thousands of people die every day in this country from automobile accidents. With families willing to donate organs, why is there still such a shortage? Why do people die waiting on the list? Why don't you interview your favorite person to get his thoughts on the subject?"

"I suppose you mean Farhad Rajid. Thanks a lot. I'm not sure he'll even talk to me. Something about me really bothers him."

"It must be your good looks, Sydney. Pursue it. Perhaps it's not much of a story but maybe we can stretch it out for a few days. I'd like to air it next week. Let's see what you come up with. In the meantime, keep up the good work on the other. We're getting close. I can smell it."

chapter *27*

Sydney found herself troubled by her newest assignment. Jake's question could not be ignored. With the current level of awareness nationwide, why was there still such a discrepancy between the need for organs and the supply?

Sydney had a few questions of her own. Was the current system functioning? Was the allocation of organs fair? Sydney did not delude herself into thinking she could discover all the answers. She was merely looking for a fill-in story. Her primary focus would remain on the pieces of bodies found floating in the Missouri River.

Sydney immediately placed a phone call to Farhad Rajid. He seemed surprised and not pleased to hear from her. His voice lacked a certain enthusiasm. She told him about her plans to run a follow-up story on Tanya Cole in celebration of Organ Donation Month. She would like his expertise to be a part of that story. She wished to set up a meeting to talk about a television interview. It would be simple really. He could explain on camera just how the current system works. That's all.

Farhad Rajid had no choice but to agree to a brief meeting. This morning. Eleven o'clock. And so it was that Sydney found herself at St. Vincent's Hospital shortly before the appointed hour.

Approaching the waiting room of Rajid's office, Sydney noticed for the first time that the empty desk was occupied. Farhad had a secretary. She had never seen the woman before. Then she remembered what odd hours Farhad Rajid worked. The last time they had met was just before dawn when Tanya's donor had been found. It seemed strange to think of Rajid as a regular guy with straightforward hours and a secretary.

In her late fifties, the woman's hair was an unnatural shade of black, accentuating the lines around her mouth and eyes. In contrast to her pale skin, her nails were painted bright red.

"Good morning. I'm Sydney Lawrence. I have a meeting with Mr. Rajid at eleven."

The secretary stopped working and glanced up. Recognizing Sydney, she blushed. Rajid had departed just minutes earlier leaving her to handle the reporter.

"I'm afraid there has been a mix-up, Ms. Lawrence. When he set the appointment this morning, Mr. Rajid did not realize that he had a previously scheduled meeting outside of the office at eleven. We tried to phone you at the station. You'd already left. Mr. Rajid wonders if you might reschedule another time."

Sydney did not ask the questions now whizzing about in her mind. Did she so startle him with her unexpected phone call that he forgot an important meeting? Was he trying to dodge her?

Realizing that she would get nowhere with the nameless woman, she asked, "May I leave him a note?"

"Of course."

Sydney jotted some hasty words requesting a meeting for first thing in the morning. But rather than handing it to the secretary, she asked if she might leave it on Rajid's desk. The secretary hesitated. Mr. Rajid was a man who liked his privacy, yet the woman was no fool. Sydney Lawrence was not only a television reporter, she was the wife of the Chief of Staff.

"Go ahead."

Leaving Rajid's office, Sydney checked the time. She was not due at Police Headquarters until one. She decided to surprise Sam with an offer for an early lunch. While cafeteria food was not terribly exciting, being with her husband for a few unexpected minutes was.

It was shortly after twelve when Sam and Sydney finished a decent lunch of baked chicken, carrots and dressing. Sydney left Sam at his office and walked the short distance towards the lobby.

She was relaxed. For the time being, she was not thinking about Farhad Rajid or her work at Police Headquarters. She was simply letting her mind and eyes wander. That's why she spotted the man obscured by a large plant across the way. The same man she had noticed a few weeks before on the day Tanya Cole went home.

He was looking the other way and failed to see her. Standing back, she observed him carefully. Sam had thought he was either a visitor or perhaps an employee of the hospital. Sydney had the distinct impression he was neither.

For his part, Joe Morrison was bored. He had no clue that he was the focus of Sydney's scrutiny. It had been yet another endless, dead-end day. For the past few weeks, he had wandered the halls of the hospital—the lobby in particular—at odd times.

The night of the Ellises' party, he'd been given a clue, but as yet the pieces refused to mesh. Determining the identity of the man who knew Lydia Hassan had been easy. His name was Farhad Rajid. He maintained an office in the hospital. He was the Regional Director of Organ Procurement. Beyond his professional credentials, though, there was not much about the peculiar little man.

Farhad Rajid was a Persian with no traceable roots. He had emigrated to the United States fifteen years ago. As far as anyone in the Bureau could determine, he was insignificant. He had graduated from Penn State with a dual degree in business and economics. He was a diligent worker and an expert in his field.

Rajid had never married, neither did he have children. He lived in a modest apartment near the Plaza and rarely went out socially. Work seemed to be his only compulsion. He spent many hours at the hospital, odd hours. Then again Morrison had to remind himself that the procuring of organs was not a scheduled procedure. Farhad Rajid, like the surgeons, had to make the most of any given opportunity.

People found Farhad aloof and unfriendly. Unlike the majority of his heritage, he seemed to shun association with the Iranian community. All this made his recognition by the child seem even more puzzling. Joe made it his mission to dig and to observe, but so far he could find nothing on the man.

Morrison glanced absently towards the elevator. The door

opened and he saw a young girl leave with an older man. There was something vaguely familiar about the child. She was pale with huge dark eyes and coal black ringlets. His mind was racing as he tried to place her. Then he remembered the face he had seen peering from a bedroom window at Hassan's mansion the night of the party.

The child stopped suddenly. Breaking free from the grasp of the older man, she ran towards the front door of the hospital.

"Uncle!" she shouted happily to a man entering the lobby.

Frantically glancing about, Farhad Rajid scooped the girl up in his arms briefly then hastily set her down.

"Uncle," she had called him. "Uncle?"

Flustered, the older man Sydney knew to be the major-domo hurried to the child. Farhad whispered something in his ear. Mansur responded, nodding vigorously. Ushering the girl forward, they started to leave but Lydia turned back.

"Uncle, it's my birthday. Will you come to my party?"

Two people, as yet unnoticed, strained to hear Rajid's answer.

"I'll try, my pet. Run along now. I'm very busy."

Joe Morrison waited until the child was gone and Farhad had departed. "Bingo!" he exclaimed, grinning.

Sydney waited a few minutes, then she too left the hospital. She was more than just a little disturbed by the scene she had just witnessed. Farhad Rajid was Lydia's uncle. And the man in the lobby was ... definitely ... no employee.

■

Farhad Rajid returned to his office a troubled man. Never before had he encountered Lydia in such a public place. It was paramount to his mission that he not be linked to Hassan. Hassan's ghosts from the past haunted him. Rajid, on the other hand, had deliberately maintained a low profile and a clean slate. Younger than Ali by several years, Farhad had never been a member of the original Savak. Rather, he had emigrated to the United States to further his education. Rajid kept to himself and made no enemies. He did his job and did it well. Although he now served the New Savak as his brother did, Farhad worked quietly in the background amassing a sizable fortune ... organ by brokered organ.

Only a select few in the Iranian community knew his true identity. Even fewer understood the key role he played in the organization that trained and armed terrorists. While his brother, Ali Hassan, was the undisputed leader, Farhad Rajid was the financial wizard behind the New Savak.

Trying to console himself he murmured, "Stop, Rajid. Stop! The lobby was deserted. No one witnessed the child's outburst."

Lydia's words vexed him.

"It's my birthday, Uncle. Will you come to my party?"

Rajid knew his brother's schedule. Hassan was not due back in Kansas City until much later tonight. This party, like all of Lydia's birthday parties, would be no party. A part of Rajid yearned to be with his niece on her birthday, but he knew he could not risk the connection. Instead, a thought crossed his mind. He would send an arrangement of balloons, her favorite. That's what he could do.

He picked up the phone and dialed the florist, ordering a massive bouquet. He requested a late afternoon delivery. As he waited for the clerk to write down the information, he spied Sydney Lawrence's note. Just seeing her name upset him. Distracted, his mind was diverted to the troublesome reporter. It was then he uttered the wrong address.

Sydney returned home shortly before six o'clock. She was off for the evening, no stories to report. She looked forward to a brief respite alone. Sam had a Board meeting at the hospital and would not return until nearly ten o'clock. Lingering in the kitchen, Sydney fixed a cup of hot herbal tea as she sought to unwind. The doorbell startled her.

"I have a delivery, ma'am, for Lydia Hassan. Is she here?"

"I'm afraid you've made a mistake," Sydney explained. "The Hassans live next-door."

The delivery boy started to walk away. Sydney called after him.

"Wait. I'll take the arrangement to her myself. It's her birthday. I nearly forgot."

Tipping the boy generously, Sydney accepted the huge bouquet of balloons. She smiled. She had no time to buy a gift but at least she could wish Lydia a happy day. Walking next-door, though, she had an eerie feeling. The house was forbidding. Strangers obviously were not welcome. Refusing to be deterred, she marched to the front door. What could Hassan say? She only planned to stay a moment, just long enough to wish Lydia a happy birthday.

She rang the bell and waited. The arrangement of balloons was becoming cumbersome. There was a long delay. Then the front door opened a crack. Only eyes were visible. The head and face of the woman were covered.

Undaunted, Sydney volunteered an introduction. "Good evening. My name is Sydney Lawrence. I live next-door. May I speak to Lydia, please?"

Confused, the servant hesitated. Then she uttered a flurry of words in a language Sydney did not comprehend to a man who came to stand behind her. Slowly the door opened.

The woman was garbed in the chador of a Muslim woman, her clothing loose and black as the turban covering her head. Her face was only partially visible.

"You are Lydia's friend," she said in surprisingly good English.

Sydney took a step forward. At the mention of Lydia's name, the servant's wary eyes had softened.

"You may come in," she directed. "But please only for a moment. Her father is not at home. He permits no strangers."

Sydney followed the woman into the entryway, trying not to react to the sheer opulence of the mansion. It was apparent Hassan was a man of incredible wealth.

"Come with me," the shrouded woman entreated. "Lydia is in the dining room."

"I do hope I'm not disturbing Lydia's party."

"Party?" the woman queried. "We have no party here."

"I thought it was Lydia's birthday."

"It is," the Muslim woman explained. "We are her only party."

Sydney followed the timid, dark-eyed woman into a huge glimmering room of shining gold. The massive mahogany table which could seat thirty comfortably, spanned the breadth of the entire salon. At the far end of the table, all alone, sat Lydia.

"You have a guest, Lydia."

The girl glanced up. "Sydney!" she exclaimed.

Standing in the doorway of the kitchen, several other members of the household had gathered to observe the strange occurrence. The servant woman once again cried out in a sharp, shrill tongue causing the others to scurry. Only Mansur lingered behind, and two guards stationed by the windows.

Sydney addressed Mansur with courtesy. "I'll only be a moment. Would you kindly leave us alone?"

Reluctantly, and against his better judgment, the major-domo complied, ordering the servant woman to follow him. At the door, he glanced back first to Sydney and then to the guards. Issuing a curt command, he ordered the men to depart as well.

Sydney set the massive bouquet of balloons upon the table.

"These were delivered to our house by mistake. You must have a secret admirer."

Lydia smiled. She tore open the card attached to the bouquet. She seemed pleased when she whispered, "They are from my uncle."

Sydney yearned to pursue the identity of her uncle but she didn't want to jeopardize the precious time they had together. She would pursue the identity of Farhad Rajid sometime when Lydia was visiting her house and she could be guaranteed privacy.

Sydney's eyes came to rest upon a picture lying near Lydia's plate. It was a picture of an Iranian woman. She peered closer. Lydia's eyes followed.

"My mother is dead," she proclaimed.

"May I see the picture?" Sydney asked.

Lydia nodded and then said, "I don't remember my mother. She died when I was very young. I miss her, especially when Papa is not around."

Trying to keep her voice low, Sydney dared to ask, "Where is your father?"

"He's away on business," she replied. "He promised to come home tonight with presents for my birthday."

Sydney merely nodded but her heart ached for this wisp of a girl who seemed so sad and alone.

"How old are you today?" she asked.

"I'm twelve."

Sydney was surprised. Lydia's delicate size belied her age.

Sydney broached her next question carefully.

"Lydia, I saw you at the hospital today. Are you having another episode with your heart?"

"I'm tired all the time," she answered truthfully. "I usually see my doctor at his office or he comes to my house. He wanted to run some tests. That's why I was there."

Lydia paused and looked at Sydney quizzically. "I didn't see you there. Where were you?"

Sydney dodged the question. "I went to the hospital to have lunch with Sam."

Lydia's eyes sparkled. With a voice that was full of hope, she asked, "Would you like a piece of cake? I'll call Mansur to set a place."

"No," Sydney faltered. "I can't stay."

Crestfallen, the girl merely mumbled, "Oh, I see."

Instinctively, Sydney's hand rose to her throat. There was the mustard seed necklace Sam had given her on New Year's Eve. She remembered the night well. They had toasted their faith in a new beginning. Once again, her eyes fell upon the child. She felt such a strange bond with the little girl. Sydney had Sam's love. She needed no reminder. Lydia, sitting alone in this magnificent mansion, had nothing.

Sydney unfastened the gold mustard seed necklace. Silently she asked Sam to forgive her.

"I want you to have a very special present. Here, Lydia. This is for you."

Lydia's eyes widened in amazement.

"But isn't that the necklace . . . "

"Yes," Sydney answered, finishing the sentence for her. "This is the mustard seed necklace Sam gave me. But don't you see? That's what makes it so special. Sam gave it to me because he loves me. I'm giving it to you because . . . " Sydney stood and fastened the necklace around the child's delicate throat. "I love you. The seed represents a little piece of me to always be with you."

Neither Sydney nor Lydia heard the front door open. The servants had gathered in the kitchen to await the departure of their uninvited guest. No one expected Hassan until much later.

Expecting to find his daughter in the dining room, Hassan tiptoed towards the salon setting his briefcase quietly in the hallway. Not wanting her to be alone yet again this particular night, Hassan had flown home early. He had his presents tucked neatly in his case.

At the entrance of the dining room, he halted. The servants were nowhere in sight. Even the guards were not at their post. At first he was frightened for Lydia's safety. Then he saw his daughter with the woman he loathed. His fright turned to outrage. He opened his mouth to summon the staff but seeing Lydia embracing Sydney, he could not.

Fingering her necklace with tears streaming down her cheeks, Lydia cried, "I love you, Sydney! I wish you were my mother. Then I'd never be alone again."

Wordlessly, Hassan backed out of the dining room as his anger overtook his pain. Clenching his fist, he retrieved his briefcase. Then he fled the scene that sickened him.

Cut to the core, he left the mansion. He would not return until many hours later. Walking alone, he cried out in pain, "How dare you give your love to a stranger, Lydia! I am your father! You belong to me!"

Susan M. Hoskins

Hassan did not return to the mansion until long after Sydney's departure, long after Lydia was asleep. His presents remained locked in his briefcase. His pain remained buried in his heart. It was Mansur who greeted him at the door.

"Sir, we must talk."

Hassan led the way into the study. Taking a seat at his desk, he waited as the major-domo secured the door.

"Sit," Hassan ordered curtly. "Begin."

Mansur produced an envelope from his inner pocket. "This was delivered earlier tonight."

Tearing open the envelope, Ali Hassan studied the tersely coded message. His jaw tightened. The hard lines of his pitted face deepened. Committing the code to memory, he took a match and set the paper aflame in the fireplace to the rear of his desk, vigilantly watching until every shred of paper turned to ash.

"Our business is nearly concluded here," he declared.

"Just as I suspected," Mansur agreed. "Shall I alert the others?"

"Not yet. What I will tell you must remain in the strictest confidence. Is that clearly understood?"

"It is," Mansur promised. "Without question."

"The exile of our people is about to end. That which we have worked for so diligently shall come to pass. The New Savak is gathering strength. Strategic attacks are planned here and abroad beginning next year. But we need more weapons, at least one more shipment of arms. Then our mission here will be finished, and we will be free to join our comrades. You will begin to make preparations for our move, quietly, so as not to arouse suspicion. For now, go about your business as if nothing has changed."

Hassan waited until Mansur had departed and he was once again alone. Then and only then, did he smile, briefly though it was. Soon he would be in a position to return to the Middle East where he belonged. His work here would be rewarded in due measure. First, he must secure his final shipment of arms. He picked up the phone and dialed the memorized number. A man with a thick Mexican accent, groggy from sleep, answered.

Dispensing with formalities, Hassan began. "I need a shipment, five times the usual amount. I must have it delivered by the middle of November. Can you arrange it?"

There was no immediate response. Hassan waited in edgy silence while his contact pondered his request. "I believe we can comply. The terms have changed, however. What you are asking is risky and expensive. It will cost you more, much more."

"How much?"

"In addition to our regular fee, we will require a bonus of three million dollars in currency or raw, uncut diamonds. Your choice."

Hassan slammed his fist upon the desk. "What you ask is absurd! We will pay the same fee as before."

"No, my friend," the Mexican broker stated confidently. "If you want your arms, you will pay the price. Our needs too have changed. The fee is two million for the shipment and a three million-dollar bonus in either currency or diamonds. Take it or leave it."

At first, Ali Hassan remained silent. Then he said the words the broker knew he must. "It will be done."

Hassan replaced the receiver quietly. How could he raise such an absurd sum of money in a month? Rising heavily from his chair, he began pacing the study. Back and forth. Finally his eyes came to rest upon a photograph, one taken by a professional last year.

Pausing, he studied the winter scene. It was Christmastime on the Plaza after the magical lights had been switched on. A fresh snow had just fallen. It was a lovely picture designed to give the viewer a sense of tranquillity and peace. It did not have the desired effect on Ali Hassan. Rather his adrenaline started pumping and his pulse raced as a twisted idea caught his fancy.

Peering closely, Hassan was able to make out his shop halfway down the block. But it was not his own rug store that interested him. It was the other businesses. He immediately dismissed the department stores as useless. There were banks of course, two to be precise. But they were no good. Security would be impenetrable. There were fur stores, but furs were too cumbersome.

After allowing his eyes to roam block after block of the Plaza, they came to rest finally upon the store next-door to his own. It was a lovely store to be sure, the most exclusive and expensive jewelry store in town. Tripoli's had a fine reputation.

Hassan's attention shifted to take in the whole photograph, with brightly colored lights adorning the shops, boutiques and restaurants. One hundred and seventy-five thousand bulbs—red, green, orange, blue and yellow—that if stretched end to end would span sixty miles. In a month, on Thanksgiving night at precisely 8:00 pm, the switch would be thrown, illuminating the fourteen-square-block area known as the Plaza. There would be dignitaries and songs. The mayor would be present along with all the city officials. And of course throngs of people. Wasn't it 300,000 last year? Oh, it would be quite an event!

What would happen, he wondered, if the ceremony did not go off as planned? What if there were a catastrophe? Perhaps an explosion? All those poor people jammed into a square-mile radius. How would the police get through the crowd? How could rescue vehicles get to the injured?

Ali Hassan returned to his desk a happier man. He glanced at his watch. It was after midnight but he had a most important call to place to his brother. The New Savak now desperately needed the cash from every organ Rajid could broker. Damn the risk! They'd both be leaving the country soon. Tomorrow they must hold a meeting of the inner circle. The holidays were rapidly approaching. It was time to make Thanksgiving plans.

P A R T   I I I

Three men, each with his own concerns, waited in edgy silence for the fourth man to arrive. They had met secretly like this several times during recent weeks. The demand for organs had suddenly increased. The men were getting nervous. Nothing could take place without the doctor. Nathan lit a cigarette and paced the hotel suite. The driver, an ex-cop named Thomas, hovered in a corner of the living room. Farhad Rajid checked his watch. The time was twenty-seven minutes past eleven. William Scofield should have been here by now.

What was the delay? The three men had now done everything they could to prepare for the procedure. The client had been drugged. The furniture in the living room had been moved, the rubber sheet placed on the carpet. The victim was alive but unconscious, face down, naked, on the sheet. He felt no pain.

The woman had been dismissed. Her presence only made the others nervous. Nothing about the evening was going according to plan. Sabrina had telephoned her pimp once they had settled in the suite, shortly after eight o'clock. Plans had to be changed. The client had originally booked her for two nights, one day. The harvesting had been scheduled for tomorrow night. The man named Dan Davis informed her his plans had changed. He would be leaving first thing in the morning. He was not scheduled to return any time soon.

Nathan told her he was one they wanted. Too good a candidate to pass up. He was thirty-eight years old, black and husky. He had been a professional athlete, playing football for the Cleveland Browns. He had retired early. Bad knees.

Nathan fretted. Rajid was becoming increasingly more difficult. His greed was putting them all at great risk. Yet he paid so damn well!

Thomas knew what to do with the bodies, disposing them in pieces in the river, with no fingers, no teeth, no means of identification. He was an ex-cop after all. He'd worked homicide for over a decade. But he too was nervous. He was smart enough to know his luck was running out. He had the skill to outwit the police for a time. Sooner or later, though, he'd make a mistake. But damn! How he craved the money!

Both Rajid and Scofield had been located by nine o'clock. Rajid was found at the hospital, William Scofield at home. It was agreed that the harvesting would have to take place tonight. It was up to Sabrina to entertain her client until they arrived. She complied. At least this man had enjoyed a last hour of pleasure. Much to Sabrina's distaste. He was rough and demeaning, sadistic even in his sexual cravings.

More importantly, he failed to adore her. He paid for the company of prostitutes quite often. He expected a great deal in return. Unlike the others, she hadn't grown fond of Dan Davis. If anything, she'd be glad to be rid of him.

Nathan had begun to worry. He ran a high-dollar escort service. This aspect of his operation, while loathsome, brought him wealth beyond his greatest dreams. He had assured the Iranian that his people could be controlled; but the prostitute was becoming a problem. She knew too much. She had begun demanding more money to ensure her silence. Like the rest of them, she wanted her share.

Sabrina was his best whore. He'd hate to lose her. Nathan said nothing to the others but there was a chink in their armor. He could feel it. The six-foot blonde's days were numbered. He wondered how much her organs might be worth.

A light knock at the door startled them.

"Jesus Christ!" Thomas swore as Nathan let the doctor enter.

"Are you all right?" Rajid asked. "Where have you been?"

"We were having a dinner party," the doctor replied belligerently. "I had to get rid of our guests. Now let me have a look at what we've got."

William Scofield's eyes were red and glassy. Leaning over the prone body, he exclaimed, "He's beautiful! The best one yet! His kidneys should command top dollar!"

Like an artist examining a fine sculpture, Scofield permitted his eyes to roam up and down the man's gleaming flesh. He admired his rich ebony skin, his muscle tone, his sheer bulk. Oh God, he couldn't wait to begin. He folded his suit jacket and laid it aside. Then he threw off his tie and rolled up his sleeves. Methodically, he opened his black bag and pulled out his instruments and the crude metal staples he would use to clamp off bleeding arteries. Then he laid his scalpel, retractors and sponge upon a sterile cloth. The arrangement was less than ideal to prevent infection. But what the hell! In a few minutes it would make no difference to Dan Davis.

He went into the bathroom to begin his ritualistic scrub. When he returned, Farhad Rajid helped him into his sterile gloves. The ice chest stood ready. The car was waiting to transport the kidneys to the airport. Because of the lateness of the hour, a private jet had been booked to fly the precious cargo first to Houston, then on to Mexico City.

Farhad Rajid still marveled at the brilliance of his own scheme. No one ever questioned the origin of the ice chest marked *Human Organs*. If anything, people expedited its safe and speedy passage, from government officials to airline personnel. Everyone wanted to think they had played a small part in the saving of a human life.

William Scofield gently fingered his scalpel. Examining the body, he determined at what point to make his first cut. By now he had gotten quite adept at his work. He had learned to keep the blood splatter to a minimum, all within the confines of the black rubber sheet.

The others stood back in silence. They had grown accustomed to these gruesome scenes. They no longer felt it necessary to heave their guts each time a harvesting took place. None of them thought themselves as despicable as the doctor.

Within minutes, he was ready to harvest the first of the kidneys. The flesh had been cut, the skin retracted, the arteries clamped off with metal staples, and the blood soaked up with a sponge. He peered closer. Then with his exposed arm, he wiped his eyes and looked again. It was the booze. It had to be the booze that affected his vision. He couldn't believe what he was seeing.

"Holy Mother of God!" he swore.

■

Life had not been kind to Anna-Marie Lopez. She was a short, heavyset woman in her early forties, but looked twenty years older. Her breathing was labored as she stepped from the service elevator, her arms laden with clean white towels. Her back hurt. Her forehead was damp with perspiration as she waddled down the hall.

Poor Anna-Marie Lopez. What a dreary life she led! Her husband, Carlos, was disabled with a bad heart. The only solace he found was in cheap whiskey. Her daughter, Tina, was pregnant. She was only sixteen. No husband. No insurance. Soon a new baby.

While all of this was most disturbing, it was anxiety about her only son, José, that consumed her. He'd spent his eighteenth birthday in jail. He'd be there for Thanksgiving and Christmas as well. He'd been arrested for dealing drugs. Attorneys were expensive. Where would they get the money? Anna-Marie was the sole provider for the family. She was grateful for her job at the Michelangelo Hotel. That's why she worked long and difficult hours. She had no education, only strong hands and a husky body. And the determination not to let a bad life beat her.

The hotel was unusually busy that evening. Loretta, the night supervisor, took the call. A suite up on four needed clean towels. The husband and the wife were regular guests. They'd gone out for a late supper. Would Anna-Marie go in, tidy up their suite, and bring fresh towels?

"Sí," she had told her supervisor. "Of course."

Work was her salvation. She liked her job, particularly the night shift. She could take things at a much slower pace. However, a quiet night gave her more time to fret. She prayed to the Virgin Mary for guidance. She fingered her crucifix.

Approaching the end of the hall, her mind went blank. What was the suite number? Was it 415 or 413? She could call downstairs and ask Loretta, but that would make her look stupid. 413, she decided. That was it.

She would have knocked but her hands were full of towels. Besides she was sure now. It was Suite 413. The man and the woman were at dinner. She was free to unlock the door and go in.

Shifting the towels to her left hand, she fumbled with the electronic door card with her right. The green light flashed. The door opened easily.

Stepping into the living room, her mind at first did not register the horror. Seeing the three men standing in the far corner of the living room, she was startled. She uttered a pathetic little cry. Instinctively, she tried to back away. One of the men moved towards her.

Her glance fell to the floor.

To the wet rubber sheet.

A black man naked on the floor.

His back was cut open. He was drenched in blood. Another man hovered over him holding something in his hands that looked like a raw piece of meat.

It was then that the room started spinning. The ex-cop named Thomas was there to catch her. He looked to Rajid for instructions. The Iranian nodded. With a hard swift snap, he broke her neck.

For Anna-Marie Lopez, the hard life she had known came to a merciful end. For the others, her presence created yet another problem. The evening had not gone well, particularly for the Iranian and the doctor.

Although alarmed by this turn of events, William Scofield barely glanced at the maid. He left her fate to the others. Perhaps he'd have a look at her organs later. Right now he felt betrayed. The man had been a promising specimen. Glancing at the organ he held in his hand, he felt ill. This was no prize kidney. Rather it was diseased . . . shriveled . . . atrophied. Dan Davis's right kidney was dead. Had been for some time. The left kidney was little better. There would be no organs from this man to broker tonight.

30

The door opened and Philip Wentworth straightened his spine, bolstering himself to face her. There she was pacing the hallway, marking time. After weeks of seclusion she had come out of hiding. The boredom had become too oppressive. Besides, she had grown comfortable with herself now. As the time approached when she had to live life once again, she had come to know and accept her scars.

As she walked the corridor, she smiled at the nurses and other patients. She wore her hair today the way he liked it best—long, free flowing, natural.

There was something different about her. He had noticed it during the last several days. She exuded a confidence that Philip had not seen before. He was both pleased and disturbed. Deep down he feared he was losing her.

He picked up his stride and caught up with her. "Kathleen, we have to talk."

"Of course, Philip."

Without a word he guided her to her room and shut the door.

"You look troubled, Philip."

The doctor motioned for his patient to sit.

"You'll be leaving soon," he stated flatly.

"Yes," she replied lightly.

"Where will you go?" he asked. "What will you do?"

Kathleen turned somber. "I'll return to my son, of course."

"What then?" Philip prodded. "What will you do with the rest of your life?"

Quietly, almost imperceptibly, she whispered, "I don't have a clue."

"I'm worried about you, Kathleen. I know so little about you. In all these many weeks, we've barely talked."

"Oh?" she retorted, her sapphire eyes beginning to smolder. "And whose fault is that? I've been right here, Dr. Wentworth. Where have you been?"

Caught off guard, the doctor glanced away.

"I'm not blaming you," she offered a bit more gently. "You're a busy man. You have many other patients."

Even though Philip agreed, both of them knew Kathleen was letting him off the hook.

"What do you want to know about me, Philip? I'll tell you whatever I can."

"Remember that first day when we talked? You wondered just who you would be when the last of the bandages were removed. You've had four months to think about your life, Kathleen. What have you discovered about yourself?"

Kathleen rose from the small sofa. With an air of confidence, she walked to her easel. Clutching her precious sketches, she returned to Wentworth's side.

"Come and sit with me, Philip. I don't know what life will hold for me once I leave here. I'm not sure who I will be. But I have discovered who and what I have been."

Philip sat beside her on the sofa. Kathleen laid her sketch pad between them and flipped the pages until she found her first portrait. It was the woman Kathleen had been, the cameo, the empty shell. Philip studied her picture intently. He had not known her then but she looked exactly as he had imagined. Her classic features were perfectly aligned. Her gleaming blond hair fell softly around her shoulders. The color of her sapphire blue eyes was magnificent but her eyes seemed empty. She entitled her self-portrait *Plastic*.

"This was the woman I was. Married to Michael Clay, I barely existed. I didn't know life, Philip. I did what I was told. I was valued only for being beautiful."

Kathleen flipped the page. The beautiful woman was gone. A horribly scarred replica replaced her. Philip Wentworth needed no explanation. The inscription *Disfigured* said it all.

Veiled was the title of the third picture. Philip recognized the patient he had first encountered in his office. The left side of her face was flawless. The right side was concealed by a thin black veil.

Philip allowed his eyes to wander from the sketch to the artist.

"That seems so long ago, Kathleen. Has it really been only a few months?"

It was Philip who gently turned to the next page. The picture was of only half a woman. She was bandaged with vacant eyes.

"This is how I saw myself before surgery," Kathleen explained. "I felt raw and exposed. I was half a woman. I felt unworthy of anyone's love. If it hadn't been for my son, I wouldn't have given a damn if I lived or died."

Kathleen turned to the final page. Philip peered closer. Again only half a face was visible. The right side remained bandaged like before. But this time her eyes were filled with hope and for the first time a measure of life.

"Do you want to know something strange? It doesn't really matter what I look like when the final bandages are removed."

Confused, Philip queried, "What do you mean?"

Kathleen smiled that same bittersweet look Philip was coming to treasure.

"I know you've done your best, Philip. And for the first time in my life, I know I'll be okay. I'm working on my final picture now. It'll be finished when I am."

Philip leaned back against the cushions of the sofa watching Kathleen in amazement as she rose and put her drawings away.

"I had no idea you had made such progress, Kathleen. And all alone ... "

"That was how it had to be, Philip. At first I was lonely. And I was angry, particularly at you. Then I realized I had to do this by myself. The only way you heal is to go deep inside and find the pieces of yourself you left behind. I had hoped we'd get to know each other better."

Suddenly Philip's heart grew heavy and he experienced a wave of sadness he'd refused to feel in years. Stiffly, he came to his feet.

"I'm happy for you, Kathleen. I know now you'll be all right."

With slow steps, he started to leave. Aside from removing the bandages on Monday, his job was finished. Kathleen's voice stopped him before he could reach the door.

"What about you, Philip?"

"Me?" he questioned, pivoting to face her.

"You," she repeated. "Just who are you, Philip Wentworth? Why aren't you the man you could be?"

Philip's cheeks flushed. "I don't know what you mean."

"Everyone knows you're a great surgeon. I know you're a fake."

Too stunned to move, Wentworth stood immobile, his mouth agape.

"You fix everyone else's scars, Philip. Yet you refuse to look at your own. You're nothing but an empty shell like I was. God willing, you'll always be a great surgeon. But until you share your pain and your love, you'll never be much of a man."

Velours, Kentucky
Sunday, November 13

Michael Clay found himself alone waiting for Solomon Bucy.
It was a glorious morning in Velours, the sun bright and the
wind brisk, heralding early winter. From the window, Michael
studied the barren trees. Stripped of their leaves, they waited in
hibernation for spring. Clay smiled. He too was waiting. But
now he had a plan, one that would restore his wealth while still
granting him revenge.

Henry's voice intruded upon his pleasant thoughts. "Mr. Bucy
is here to see you, sir."

"Show him in. Then leave us alone."

The butler did as he was ordered, securing the door behind him.

"It's a lovely day, don't you agree, Solomon? Henry left coffee
on the tray unless you'd prefer something stronger."

"I need a brandy," Bucy answered gruffly.

He marched to the bar and poured himself a shot.

Using his arm to propel his joystick, Michael wheeled his chair
away from the window.

"You look terrible, Solomon. What's wrong?"

Taking a chair, Bucy gulped his brandy. "Things are bad,
Michael. You can expect to be indicted by the end of the year.
We'll need to assemble a hell of a defense team. On the civil side,

the class action suit against you is gaining momentum. I've asked for a continuance through the holidays, but I can't stall much longer. We'll have to start depositions shortly. The civil trial will begin in the spring."

Michael Clay merely nodded. "Is there anything else?" he asked.

"Isn't that enough? My God, Michael! Even if we can keep you out of prison, you stand to lose everything! If you're found to be liable in any way for the Maggie Hall disaster, you'll be ruined."

Clay showed little emotion. Seeing the befuddled look on his attorney's fleshy face, Michael said, "Don't fret, Solomon. It doesn't become you. I've survived a spinal cord injury and the loss of my wife and son. I plan to come out of this situation as well."

"Michael, you don't comprehend . . . "

Clay's eyes fell to a single sheet of stationery resting on his lap. "Do you see this, Solomon? This is the answer to my problems."

"It looks like a letter, Michael. Just a letter."

"Oh this is no ordinary letter, Solomon. This is from my mother. It seems that Margaret can't tolerate our separation any longer. Finally, after months of silence, she's resumed communication." Michael glanced at his mother's scrawl. "A mother's love is stronger than any scandal. Margaret's been lonely. She can't stand the pain of being without both her husband and her son."

His mouth twisted into a cold grin. "Well my father is dead but I'm very much alive. Mother has moved most of the family assets to banks in Switzerland. She says in her letter that she has one obligation to complete and then she'd like me to move abroad with her."

"Obligation?" Solomon repeated.

"Mother, of course, doesn't say but we know what her so-called obligation is. Ralph informed us that Mother is caring for Daniel during Kathleen's absence. Margaret feels some kind of obligation to my wife. She's paying for her surgery as well. It appears that once her debt to Kathleen is satisfied, she wishes to turn her attention to me. Generous, isn't she?"

"Michael, you can't be serious? You're going to be indicted shortly."

"Listen to yourself, Solomon. You're rattling on and on. Timing is everything. I still hold a valid passport. I can leave the country anytime I choose."

"Michael, be reasonable." Bucy's eyes lingered upon Michael's lifeless legs. "It would not be that easy for you to disappear."

"I have a plan, Solomon. A nearly flawless plan. There's only one thing standing in my way. Soon that too will be resolved."

Bucy hastily poured another brandy. Allowing the liquor to soothe his nerves, he asked, "What about Daniel?"

At the mention of Daniel, Michael's eyes hardened. He had loved the boy as only a father could, but Daniel was not his son. That was the flaw to his perfect plan. Should he ultimately reveal the truth to Margaret or bury the secret? Daniel was the one link to his mother that couldn't be broken. She would do anything for the grandson she thought to be hers. Despite his feelings of betrayal, Michael Clay had to consider his future. For now, Margaret need not know the truth about Daniel.

Dismissing troubling thoughts, he glanced around the study. "I'll miss my home," he said. "It's been in my family for generations. But with Mother and Daniel gone, it's only a house, an empty house at that. Yes, it's definitely time for a change. I'm ready to start a new life."

He shifted his focus to Bucy. "Time is a precious commodity, Solomon. There is a time to wait and a time to act. The time is now."

Clay maneuvered his joystick, turning his wheelchair towards the warmth of the fire. Solomon Bucy thought he had been dismissed. He started to leave. Michael's question startled him.

"How is Kathleen?"

"She's doing fine, Michael. Ralph says she'll be dismissed from the hospital in a few days."

"Was her surgery successful? Is she beautiful once again?"

"By all reports, her surgery appears to have been successful. She won't know for sure until the final bandages are removed."

"That's good," Clay murmured. "Real good. I want her to be healed."

Solomon Bucy was even more confused. First Michael talked about Kathleen's disappearance, and now he spoke about her healing. His client's mental status was of growing concern.

"Call Ralph today. Once the bandages are removed, Kathleen will think she has everything to live for. It is then I want her killed."

■

Ralph knocked softly on Kathleen's door. It was a quiet Sunday afternoon at the hospital. The Chiefs were playing at Arrowhead Stadium. Most everyone was either at the football game or glued to their television sets. Everyone, it seemed, but Kathleen and Ralph. Smelling the aroma of freshly brewed coffee, Kathleen smiled.

"Oh it's good to see you, Ralph. I was afraid it was your day off."

"No, ma'am. They changed my schedule. I'm working tonight, then I'm off for the next three days. I brought your coffee. It's hot and fresh just the way you like it."

Kathleen gratefully accepted the coffee in what had become their afternoon ritual. Then she offered Ralph a box of Russell Stover chocolates.

"Look what I got today. It's a present from Sam and Sydney. They're chocolate and caramel, my favorites. Take a handful, Ralph."

Smiling, Noland helped himself to several pieces.

"How's your day been, Ralph? You look tired."

"I'm fine."

Noland spoke a lie. He didn't feel fine at all.

Sitting near the window, Kathleen savored her coffee. "I don't know how you do it, Ralph, but you make the best cup of coffee around. I've been looking forward to this all afternoon."

Ralph shifted uncomfortably. For her part, Kathleen wished she could offer her friend a chair but hospital policy forbade that kind of familiarity between a janitor and a patient. She didn't want to jeopardize his job.

"I have some good news, Ralph. Dr. Wentworth is removing the bandages on Monday. I may be going home soon."

A frown shadowed Ralph's features but he managed to say, "That's good, ma'am. Real good."

Kathleen nodded.

"I'll miss you, Mrs. Stein," he stammered. "You're a nice lady."

Ralph's voice betrayed the quiver of fear he felt. He'd received the phone call he'd been dreading for weeks. He was to make the murder look like an accident with no possible link to Michael Clay. Unless Solomon Bucy could change Michael Clay's mind, the end was near, very near for Kathleen. Just as soon as the bandages were removed and she was whole and beautiful once again. The thought of it broke Ralph's heart.

"Where will you go, ma'am, once you leave here?"

Kathleen hesitated. For months she had kept her past a secret. But with Ralph, it was different. She felt safe.

"If I show you something, Ralph, you must promise to keep it confidential. My life depends upon your loyalty."

Faltering slightly, Ralph promised.

Kathleen retrieved the photograph she kept hidden in a drawer. She showed the picture to the man she thought to be her friend.

"I have a son living in Boston. His name is Daniel. I'll be returning to him."

Seeing the smiling face of the engaging boy, Ralph shuddered. "What will you do then, Mrs. Stein?"

Slowly, Kathleen rose from the chair and ambled to the window.

"My name is not Stein. It's Clay. I left my husband last year. I'm hoping that our divorce will be final soon. I've been in hiding with my son ever since. So in answer to your question, Ralph, I'll be searching for a safe place to live and start over. Someplace he can't find us!"

Kathleen gazed to the street below. Tentatively, he stepped towards her. Unlike most women he'd known, he found Kathleen to be a sweet and sensitive soul. He wondered why anyone would want to harm her. Something deep inside of him had to know.

"Your husband," he stammered. "What's he like?"

Kathleen's voice quivered. "He's a vicious man. I can feel his hatred. He'll never rest until he gets even with me for leaving and taking Daniel."

A bittersweet smile crossed her lips. Taking the picture back, she said, "I don't know why I'm telling you all this, Ralph. There are so few people I can trust. But I trust you. I'll miss you, Ralph. You, Sam and Sydney are the only friends I have."

Ralph had to glance away.

"When I was married to Michael, I had no friends. He wouldn't allow it. I thought that after I left him I'd finally be free. But I'm still in prison. Whom can I trust? How can I be sure they don't work for him?"

"Don't let your coffee get cold, Mrs. Stein."

"It's okay, Ralph. It's more important that we talk. I might not see you again. After the bandages are removed tomorrow, Dr. Wentworth plans to dismiss me."

"Are you afraid?" Ralph asked.

"I'm terrified," she replied. "But it's okay. No matter what, I know that I'm a better person than I was before. That's in large measure due to you, Ralph."

Slowly Ralph's troubled eyes met Kathleen's.

"I have to go," he said roughly, turning to leave.

"Wait, Ralph!" she pleaded, stepping closer. "May I have a hug before you go? I may not see you again."

Like a defeated child, he stood mute. Kathleen took him into her innocent embrace. Tentatively, his arms wrapped around her. Drinking in her scent and the fragile sincerity of her touch, he melted, damning God and Michael Clay for his fate. In that moment, his guard dropped.

It was Kathleen who finally pulled away. Stepping back, she gazed deeply into her friend's eyes. Suddenly she grew afraid. In his eyes, she saw something that was not love. She saw something akin to betrayal. Not wishing to believe what her intuition told her, she averted her eyes and said, "Take good care of yourself, Ralph. Thank you for being my friend."

The hospital seemed deserted this evening. An eerie stillness pervaded the corridors. The distant sound of televisions could be heard in the darkness of patient rooms. It was a typical Sunday night at St. Vincent's Hospital.

The sixth floor had been quiet—just the way Nurse O'Malley liked it. She was the skipper of the ship tonight. A cool-eyed woman in her sixties, she liked things predictable and in order. When the elevator door opened, she glanced up from her desk. There stood Philip Wentworth dressed casually in a sweater and wool slacks, with only a lightweight jacket to protect him from the chilling rain outside. Obviously he had too much to carry to be bothered with an umbrella.

"Good evening, Dr. Wentworth. It's rather late to be making rounds, isn't it?"

With a curious smirk, she stared at the small white sacks filling his arms.

"Do I smell onions?" she asked.

Wentworth ignored her. "How's Mrs. Stein?"

Mrs. O'Malley smiled. Philip Wentworth was one of her favorites. It amused her to see him squirm, particularly when he made reference to *Mrs. Stein*.

"She's fine, Dr. Wentworth, as always. I held her dinner tray as you requested. It looks like she won't go hungry."

Philip shifted uncomfortably. The greasy bags were becoming

rather cumbersome. He had to balance the food in one hand and keep the drinks upright in the other. Mrs. O'Malley chuckled. Philip Wentworth was not here making rounds. And Kathleen Stein was no ordinary patient.

"Have a nice dinner, Dr. Wentworth," O'Malley called after him, her eyes piercing his back.

Kathleen sat at the window. Wrapped in a blue fleece robe, she tried to see the Plaza, but the fog blocked her view. A lonely train whistle echoed in the distance. Pellets of sleet began tapping at her window.

She might be leaving the hospital as soon as tomorrow. The pain of her surgery would be forgotten; this chapter in her life, completed. She couldn't wait for that to happen. And yet, she felt sad, incredibly sad.

Her dinner tray had not yet come. Just as well. She felt too depressed to eat.

There was a light knock at the door. She ignored it. The knock grew more insistent.

"Come in," she said with a resigned sigh. She glanced back to the window. She waited for the nurse or technician to make herself known. No one did. But a strange smell permeated the room. Was it onions?

Kathleen glanced toward the door. All she could see was a hand and a white sack swinging back and forth, back and forth.

"Truce?" a familiar voice queried.

"Who's there?"

"Truce?" the male voice queried again.

"Truce," she said. "Now tell me who's there."

Shyly, Philip picked up the food he had set aside and stepped through the door.

"Is that you, Philip?" she asked, her heart pumping faster.

"It's me," he declared. "I wasn't sure I'd be welcome."

"What choice do I have?" she teased. "You're dripping wet. I suppose you'd better come in before you catch a chill."

Philip stepped into full view. The aroma filling the air was delightful.

"Whatever have you brought?" Kathleen inquired.

Philip carefully set his bags on the coffee table.

"It took me two days to research this project. I think I've used up my allowance of fat for the year. My mission was to find the best cheeseburgers in town. I think I've done just that. Mrs. Stein, may I introduce you to Chubby's?"

Kathleen watched in delight as Philip unwrapped each precious item. "For our main course, I have selected cheeseburgers with a special mustard and ketchup sauce. As you can see, the grilled onions have soaked the sesame buns."

"Oh God, Philip. It smells so good."

"I have two orders of greasy fries, one heaping order of onion rings and two thick strawberry malts. I'm afraid I couldn't locate pure vanilla. I'm quite aware that the bottled artificial stuff will not do. But I have found the best chocolate brownies in town."

"Take off your jacket. You're dripping!" Kathleen chided. "God, you'll catch pneumonia."

Philip's sneeze confirmed her fears. He searched for a place to hang his soaked jacket. Finding none, he cast it to the floor. "It's brutal outside," he said, rubbing his hands together. "Much nicer in here."

"Come," she said. "Sit by me. It's warm here by the window where the heat vents are."

Philip obeyed. Growing flushed in his presence, Kathleen shed her heavy fleece robe. There she sat cross-legged in her damned yellow silk pajamas.

"Oh God," Philip murmured. The sight of her disturbed him. Then he remembered something he had forgotten in the bag. He jumped up and retrieved a somewhat sagging red rose. "This is for you," he offered. "I'm afraid I left it a bit too long."

Kathleen smiled.

Presenting her with the flower, he dared to ask, "Peace?"

"Peace," Kathleen quickly replied. "I'm afraid I am the one who should apologize. I was much too harsh the other day."

"You were truthful."

Kathleen eyed him carefully. There was something different about her surgeon tonight. Perhaps it was the casualness of his slacks and sweater. The difference pleased her.

"You look nice, Philip. I've never seen you . . . . "

He finished the sentence for her. "Without the white coat. You've seen enough of the doctor in recent months. Since this is your last night here, Kathleen, I thought it was about time you got a look at the man."

The rose remained clutched in her hand, wilting before his eyes. He knew what to do.

"Don't get up. I know where the vase is."

Kathleen sank back into the cushions as she watched him fumble yet again with the vase and the rose. How reminiscent of her first day in the hospital, so many weeks ago.

His mission completed, he joined her on the couch. He felt awkward and shy once again in her presence. Kathleen saved him.

"Everything smells so good and I'm starved. Let's eat."

For the next few minutes, Kathleen and Philip lost themselves in the pure joy of their simple meal. When Kathleen could not eat another bite, and every food wrapper was empty, she sank back onto the couch and smiled. It was a smile Philip had never seen before. For the first time in many months, Kathleen was content.

"That was wonderful, Philip. Thank you."

Shyly, Philip reached for Kathleen's hand, and taking it firmly in his own, stroked it gently.

"We've wasted so much time."

"What do you mean?"

"You were right when you accused me of being a fake. I am. I have been for a very long time. I thought being a doctor was enough, but I was wrong. It's safe, though."

"Safe in what way?" Kathleen gently prodded.

"There are risks in my profession. If you carry enough insurance, you feel somewhat protected. There's no insurance you can buy to protect your heart from being hurt."

Cupping Philip's chin softly, Kathleen forced his face to hers.

"What are you trying to say?"

"You remind me so much of my mother. My mother was murdered when I was a boy. I know it's not your fault, but being with you brought back all the pain."

"Oh Philip," she whispered. "I had no idea."

"I try not to think about it. But it's time I tell you what happened. That is, if you want to hear."

Oh Kathleen wanted to hear every detail of Philip's past.

For an hour, she sat quietly, allowing Philip to journey at his own pace back in time. He spoke of his boyhood, growing up in the Middle East with an American father and an Iranian mother. In a voice barely above a whisper he talked about the last day he had spent with his mother. It was as if he were there as he recalled his joy seeing his mother at the university. How quickly his joy turned to terror at the sight of the Savak. In detail, he relived the horror of those last brief moments he spent with his mother.

"I'll never forget the face of their leader. He was a husky man with a pitted complexion. He had an ugly burn scar on his right cheek. I was terrified of him. His eyes were nothing but an abyss of hatred." Philip shivered.

Kathleen took his hand. As she listened to his heartbreak, she heard not the words of a man but the pain of a twelve-year-old boy, the pain he had never allowed to fester and heal.

"He shattered my life with the snap of his fingers. My mother was alive and then she was gone."

Tears clouded his eyes as he studied his own hand a moment, the hand he had trained to heal other people's wounds.

"How could I trust my feelings again, when in an instant the person I love could be wrenched away?"

He was choking on the emotions that had been buried so deep but now were breaking free.

"I loved her so much yet I could do nothing to save her. How could I ever allow myself to love like that again?"

"Look at me, Philip," she demanded gently. "I know better than anyone what you mean."

Philip's sorrowful eyes found hers. Then she took his hand and held it to her face.

"This was all I had. My face was the only thing that mattered. Then one night, in the course of a few seconds, what mattered most was taken away." She smiled in the bittersweet way Philip had come to know so well. "No matter how skilled my surgeon, I know I'll never be the same.

"But I'm alive, Philip. For the first time in years, I'm alive. In a lot of ways, I'm better. Like me, you can never recapture what you lost—your mother and your innocence—but you have to go on. You're too good a man to waste."

"I know," he whispered. "But how?"

"Look at your hands, Philip. Look what they've become. Realize what this experience has made you. You turned the horror of not being able to save your mother into a lifetime of work to heal other people's wounds and scars. Without that obsession, you would never have become the great surgeon you are. You might have been good but you never would have been great. Greatness only comes from pain."

Her words penetrated his heart. She was right. He knew it. He had never allowed himself or anyone else to journey through the pain far enough to see the good.

Drawing her to him, he whispered, "Oh Kathleen. Why have we wasted so much time?"

Falling naturally into Philip's arms, Kathleen savored his touch, his smell, his very essence. "We have tonight," she whispered.

Gently she removed his glasses and gazed deeply into the rich mix of sable and green. "You have beautiful eyes," she murmured. Then she playfully ran her fingers through his thick auburn hair. "Lovely hair."

Philip leaned forward. Their lips touched. His were smooth, hers warm. It was a brief brush at first. Then came the hunger. They devoured each other's lips, wanting to explore every ridge. Something forgotten stirred inside each of them. He drew her close, placing her hand upon his heart. Her own heart quickened in rhythm to his. Like a dance.

"Let's make the most of tonight," she whispered.

Philip stood, drawing Kathleen to him. As he gently removed her yellow silk top, he gazed at her fully. "You're beautiful," was all he could say.

Their lips had to meet again. Each kiss was complete but not enough, like dewdrops on a parched tongue. Then came the time when they wanted to be naked with each other—no more secrets, out of hiding, exposed. Melting completely into one another, they journeyed to their hearts where life resides. Feeling both the hunger and the satisfaction.

Obscured by the trees on Verona Circle, Joe Morrison studied Hassan's mansion. It was just past dawn when he and George Massoud began their watch. Setting down his coffee, Morrison fished in his pocket for a smoke.

Massoud could tell something was bothering Morrison. He was edgy and out of sorts. Hassan was out of town, and yet Joe insisted they maintain a tight vigil on the house. He was being too damn mysterious.

"What's eating you, Joe?"

"Nothing," Morrison replied.

"I've learned to read you pretty well in the past few months. I can sense you're onto something. What is it?"

Morrison lit his cigarette then paused. He stared at the window where he normally saw the little girl. It was empty. He dragged his cigarette before replying.

"It finally came to me why Lydia seemed familiar. I was on a kidnapping case once in Dallas. A little girl about seven. She was being held in an abandoned warehouse. I caught a glimpse of her in an upstairs window. I had a bad feeling then, but I was a rookie. I had no choice but to follow orders. When we stormed the house, the little girl got killed. I've always felt real bad about that."

Joe put a hand over his aching gut. "Have you ever gotten the feeling something was about to come down but you didn't know what? I keep telling you it's a feeling deep in your gut you can't explain. Know what I mean?"

"Yeah," Massoud agreed. "I suppose so."

Morrison returned his gaze to the mansion and the empty window.

"Well I've got that feeling today."

■

Sam left for the hospital around eight. Sydney was not due at the station until later. Reading her morning paper, she sipped her third cup of coffee. Her case had come to a standstill. There had been no new clues in days. As a result, she decided to slow her pace a bit until the tide turned. A knock at the patio door made her look up.

"Hi, Lydia. Aren't you working with your tutor today?"

"No," the girl replied quietly. "Not today."

Much to her father's dismay, Lydia's visits had increased in recent weeks. A strong bond was forming between the woman and child, stronger than either of them realized.

"Sit down, honey. Would you like me to make you a cup of tea?"

A cup of raspberry herbal tea was usually Lydia's favorite. This morning she declined. The girl was wan and obviously not well.

"What's wrong, Lydia?"

"I'm tired," she replied. "That's all."

Sydney scrutinized her young friend intently. Her complexion was normally a beautiful shade of olive, the texture of satin. Today her skin was so pale as to be nearly transparent. There were dark circles under her eyes.

"Does your father know you're here?"

"No," Lydia answered. "Papa is out of town."

Sydney had asked her real question in an indirect manner. What she really wanted to know was if Hassan had seen Lydia looking so feeble. Ascertaining the answer, she changed her tack.

"When was the last time you saw a doctor, Lydia?"

"I don't know," she replied listlessly. "Papa's been so busy."

"And Mansur. What does he say?"

"He says Papa is not to be bothered."

Abruptly, Sydney stood. Luckily, she had dressed early. She still had time to spare.

"Come with me, Lydia," she directed firmly. "I want to speak to Mansur."

Slowly, the child stood. When she did, her legs wobbled. She pitched forward, then everything went dark.

■

"Look, Joe! What the hell is going on?"

Morrison shifted his attention to the Colonial house next-door. There he saw the woman, Sydney Lawrence, running with Hassan's child in her arms. She hurried to the mansion.

It was Mansur, the trusted major-domo, who answered the door. He tried to take the child from Sydney's grasp, but she resisted. After some discussion, Mansur turned and summoned his men, then hurried from the house.

A limousine was parked in the circular driveway. Mansur took the seat beside the driver after two of the guards settled Sydney, cradling Lydia, in the rear. Four men jumped into a second car, a late model, dark blue Ford. Then both cars sped off.

Morrison watched as the procession sped past him. The windows of the limousine were blackened but he had the distinct impression his presence had not gone entirely unnoticed. Waiting a few seconds so as not to be blatantly obvious, he started the car and carefully followed the limousine and the Ford.

■

Hearing Sam's footsteps, Sydney turned to greet her husband. The child had been rushed into the Emergency Room. Sydney was required to wait outside. Acting in her father's behalf, Mansur refused to leave Lydia even for a moment. Two of Hassan's guards were posted at the rear entrance of the hospital. The other two remained in the waiting room. Using her connections, Sydney had found out what information she could.

"Lydia's in arrhythmia. Her heart has flipped into an irregular pattern. The cardiologist is with her now."

"Who is it?" Sam inquired.

"I believe his name is Carter, Neil Carter."

"That's good, Sydney. He's the finest cardiologist on staff. Where's Hassan?"

Sydney shrugged. "Mansur wouldn't tell me much, only that Hassan has been out of town for days. They are tracking him down now and expect to have him here by early afternoon."

Sam was relieved. By law, he was prohibited from doing anything more than stabilizing Lydia without her father's consent.

■

Alone in her room, Kathleen waited for Philip. He had said he'd be in around ten. It was now nearly eleven. She had finished her drawing by dawn. Then she'd packed what few belongings she'd brought with her. Sam had returned her identification. Her photograph of Daniel was now safely tucked away in her bag. She didn't have to worry about her bill. Margaret Clay intended to keep her promise. The account would be settled immediately. Once the bandages were removed, Kathleen would be free.

After she'd finished packing, she had bathed and dressed for what could be the most monumental day of her life. Since the Maggie Hall disaster, she had dreamed of the day she could walk once again in public, without her own shame and the pity of people who saw her pass by.

So much had happened these past few months. She was no longer the same person she'd been before. Yet the discovery of her new self was fragile and a little frightening. Shielded by the bandages and protected in the hospital, Kathleen had not yet faced the world.

Cracking the door, Philip said brightly, "Are you ready, Mrs. Stein?"

Taking a deep breath, Kathleen answered, "I've been ready for hours."

Philip approached the bed, wrapping Kathleen in the warmth of his embrace. "Last night was magic," he whispered. Cupping her chin, Philip forced her worried gaze to his. "Are you nervous?"

"I thought I'd be strong, but I'm terrified, Philip."

Philip kissed her lips lightly then brushed the hair away from her face.

"It'll be all right, Kathleen. I promise. I'll call my nurse and we'll begin."

"Wait," she said, slipping from the bed. "Before we get started, there's something I want you to see."

Kathleen retrieved her sketch and clutched it to her chest. She smiled tentatively.

"The woman I see, the woman I drew is the one you helped me to find. I want you to have this, Philip."

Slowly, Kathleen revealed her finished portrait. Philip took the picture in his hands, his eyes shining.

"Take off the bandages, Philip. I'm ready to see if what I sketched is what I really am."

Wentworth summoned his nurse and the instruments he'd need. Then, as Kathleen sat immobile on the bed, Philip deftly cut away the gauze and tape. Taking a deep breath, he stepped back and studied his finished work.

"That will be all," he told the nurse, dismissing her. She seemed surprised by his curt tone, but left without comment. Philip had not intended to be rude but he wanted to savor this moment alone with Kathleen.

"Look at your picture, Kathleen," he said with a tremor in his voice.

She obeyed.

"Now come with me."

Philip gripped her hand and led her to the mirror.

"Look at yourself. See what I see."

Slowly she lifted her gaze to meet her reflection. She stared transfixed as the image she had drawn came alive.

Her crushed cheekbone had been repaired and the depression to the right side of her face corrected. And all that remained of the gash from her hairline to the bridge of her nose was a faint scar, the same scar she had known and drawn in her portrait. Kathleen knew that there would always be a reminder of the horror she had experienced. Simple makeup would do much to hide the flaw. Even her eyes were different—as they were in the picture. The sapphire blue was more vibrant and alive. There was a depth to them that she had not known before.

Peering closer, Kathleen touched her face, turning slightly from side to side. She was different but in a way that was better. There were tiny lines etched around the corners of her eyes and mouth—they were lines of living and of experience. No, Kathleen was not the perfect cameo she had been before. She was a vibrant, feeling woman who had embraced life—the horror and the joy—and been marked by life in return.

"What do you think?" said Philip finally.

"I'm whole," she whispered. "I'm whole."

Sam poured Sydney a cup of coffee in a quiet corner of the waiting room.

"Lydia's stabilized," he reported. Then anxiously, he threw his glance to the clock. It was nearly noon.

"What's the latest on Hassan? Is he still expected soon?"

"Mansur tells me that Hassan is on his way. He should be here around one."

"It'll be a while before Lydia's condition is fully evaluated. Dr. Carter is with her now. There's nothing else either of us can do at the moment. Why don't you go on to work?"

Sydney shook her head. "I can't leave until I know Lydia is all right. I've already called Jake. He's not expecting me until later this afternoon."

"Look, Sydney, it'll do you no good to wait around the Emergency Room. You can't see Lydia and you certainly don't want to be here when Hassan arrives. Why don't we go out and have an early lunch on the Plaza? We both could use the break. I'll bring you back here afterwards."

Sydney hesitated. "I suppose you're right, Sam. But what if there's a change for the worse?"

"Honey, remember who you're with? I'm Chief of Staff and I come with a pager."

Sydney was tempted. Yet something told her to remain close by. She countered with a proposal that they grab a quick bite in the hospital cafeteria.

■

George Massoud set aside the newspaper that had shielded his face for hours. Luckily, with so many people in and out of Emergency, the waiting room had remained fairly crowded. Aside from the Iranian guards who stood watch, no one had paid him any notice. He watched Dr. Ellis and his wife depart, then slowly got to his feet. Stretching, he headed outside, where he found his boss, a cigarette dangling from his mouth, leaning against a tree.

"What's up?" said Morrison.

"Nothing much. The kid's conscious and stable. She has a heart condition. Hassan will be here soon."

"And the news lady? Where's she?"

"She and her husband are having lunch in the cafeteria. Apparently, he didn't think it was a good idea for her to be waiting around the Emergency Room when the big man arrives."

"Interesting," Morrison mumbled. "I wonder what that's all about?"

Massoud shrugged.

"How about if we switch places, boss? I've read the morning paper five times!"

"Not a chance," Morrison countered. "I might be recognized. I've encountered Sydney Lawrence too many times before. I have a better idea. You stay where you were. I'll mosey over to the main lobby. Check you later."

■

Dressed anonymously in jeans, a dark flannel shirt and tennis shoes, Ralph Noland entered the hospital through the basement entrance reserved for employees. The time was 12:25 pm. He scanned the hallway, then pushed open the door to the stairway. The sixth floor was a long climb so he took his time.

Arriving on six, he paused to catch his breath. Having worked up here for months, he knew the schedule. By now, the patients would have eaten and the staff would be taking their lunch breaks in shifts. That meant they were short covering the desk. No one would be wandering the halls.

He dared not think about the job he had to do. It had haunted him most of the night. He had misgivings. But more than anything, he had a mission. He focused his attention on two things: discovering Kathleen's plans upon dismissal and making her murder appear to be an accident. Nothing else mattered. The commander had spoken. The enemy must be destroyed.

He opened the door to the sixth floor a few inches. He glanced quickly to the right and left. The corridor was empty. A few feet away, across the hall, was Room 605. Just then, the door to Kathleen's room opened. Closing the door to the stairway quickly, Ralph tried to still his quickening heart. He heard voices he recognized.

"I'm so happy you decided to stay," Philip said. "I've finished making rounds, so I'm all yours for the rest of the day." Philip gently caressed Kathleen's hand as he spoke. "Thank you for giving me this one day."

"You made me an offer I couldn't refuse," replied Kathleen in a breezy voice. "Lunch on the Plaza, a tour of the city, then dinner at your house. I'm powerless to resist your charms, Dr. Wentworth. Anyway," she continued, "I've waited this long to see Daniel. One more day won't make that much difference. It's the only chance we'll have to be together for a while."

Ralph pressed his ear against the door as their voices trailed down the hallway. The last thing he heard was Philip saying, "Well you'll have to wait a few more minutes, lovely lady. The nurses have planned a going away surprise. It won't take long."

Ralph had to concoct a plan. Kathleen and Philip were leaving the hospital and going to lunch. Which way would they go? Ralph descended the stairs two at a time all the while trying to think.

"The doctor's parking lot. Where is it? Never before had the question arisen. He could kill her in the parking lot. Make it look like a robbery. But then, he'd have to hurt the doctor. He didn't think the commander would mind. "Yes," he cried. "That's it! The doctor's lot is in the front. If Wentworth is driving—and he must—they would leave by the front door.

Then a bizarre idea crossed his mind, one guaranteed to make the killing appear an accident. He'd read an article a few weeks ago about a crazed man shooting up a clinic. Perhaps there was a better way. Slowing his stride, he tried to master his frazzled nerves. He had time, he reasoned. They would be delayed at least a few minutes up on six eating cake and drinking punch, saying good-bye to the staff. Yes, Ralph Noland had plenty of time. Plenty of time to scope out the lobby and get into position.

The clock in the lobby struck one. Sam and Sydney heard the chimes as they left Sam's office and started down the administrative corridor. After a quick bite of lunch in the cafeteria, they had checked with Dr. Carter and seen Lydia briefly. She remained stable. They could do nothing more until her father arrived. Sydney decided to go on to the station. They were leaving the hospital now so Sam could drop her at home to pick up her car.

Joe Morrison noted the time. Taking a short break, he had stepped outside to smoke a cigarette. Feeling edgy, he didn't tarry. Crushing his cigarette out on the pavement, he stepped through the revolving door just as the clock chimed one.

Ralph Noland likewise was aware of time. Every minute or so he checked his watch. He was growing increasingly more agitated. Kathleen had not yet arrived. Every minute she delayed made him more anxious. The lobby was not crowded. Keeping his eyes averted and his back to the front door, Ralph remained obscured, not far from the elevators. Each time he heard the ring of the bell, he glanced to the doors that opened. She didn't appear. He didn't know how much longer he could wait before someone noticed him.

"Come on! Damn it! Come on!" he muttered to himself.

Joe Morrison sat down in a visitor's chair in the lobby. His eyes did not find Ralph Noland. Rather his attention was drawn to a familiar figure hurrying through the revolving door. With rapid authoritative steps, Ali Hassan crossed the lobby followed by two of his guards. Morrison's eyes never left the man. His stomach lurched yet again in that familiar, troubling sort of way.

The door to the elevator opened slowly.

"Look, Sam!" Sydney exclaimed as they entered the lobby and she saw Kathleen without her bandages for the first time. "Oh my God, Sam! Look at Kathleen! She's beautiful."

Halting, Sam and Sydney stared in wonder at her lovely face. The sound of her laughter filled the lobby. Hearing her voice, Ralph donned his ski mask and pulled out the revolver tucked in his pants.

With his right hand, Philip entwined Kathleen's. He carried her suitcase in his left. She nuzzled close as she murmured, "I'm so happy, Philip."

Philip Wentworth failed to hear her. Stepping out of the elevator, he froze. His skin crawled as he watched another man approach. Just then, the husky man with the pitted complexion and burn scar on his right cheek halted. Pivoting, he snapped his fingers, dismissing his two guards. Philip was hurled back in time, to that other place, to that other moment. Was it only last night he had allowed himself to remember the sound of the soldier's snap? The snap that killed his mother.

Ralph Noland, gun in hand, stepped forward. He prepared to fire randomly into the crowd but targeting only his victim. Then he saw Kathleen's face and he panicked. Innocently turning, Kathleen confronted the eyes that betrayed her, the eyes of her masked assassin. Ralph started to tremble as he raised the gun to fire.

Strangling on his suppressed rage, Philip cried out as he dropped Kathleen's hand and lunged forward. Startled by the abrupt unexpected motion, Ralph faltered. He fired his gun in haste.

Kathleen screamed. So did Sydney as Sam threw her to the floor out of the line of gunfire.

Philip fell at the feet of Ali Hassan.

Susan M. Hoskins

Ralph Noland fled down the stairway as screams of terror filled the lobby. Hassan immediately ordered his guards to follow. With guns drawn, they raced after him. Shaken, Hassan glanced to the fallen man. Then he walked away.

Philip tried to call out but no sound came.

Morrison jumped up, his revolver drawn. "Get back!" he shouted. "Move back for a doctor!"

Sam ran to Philip's side. Falling to her knees, Kathleen—her dress splattered with Philip's blood—knelt down beside him.

"Oh God! Philip! Oh no!"

The news of the shooting quickly spread throughout the hospital. Massoud abandoned the Emergency Room in search of his boss. "What in the hell happened?"

"No time to explain!" Morrison barked. "The gunman fled down the stairs with two of Hassan's guards after him. Call security. Have them block the exits!"

His brow was now dripping sweat as he shouldered his revolver and turned his attention towards the unconscious man. It was an ashen Sydney Lawrence he confronted. She'd been right all along. The man she'd seen repeatedly in the lobby was no visitor, no employee. Staring at his gun, she said, "Just who the hell are you?"

Pulling her roughly aside, he took out his identification.

"My name is Morrison. FBI. It's about time we talked, Sydney Lawrence."

■

Ripping the ski mask from his face, Ralph fled to the basement, his gun clutched tightly in his hand. Behind him, footsteps boomed. They were gaining on him.

Suddenly one of Hassan's guards threw himself full force against Ralph's body, sending him crashing into the basement door. A searing pain ripped through Noland's head.

A muscular arm grabbed him by the neck, snapping it back slightly in an agonizing vice. Feeling the barrel of a revolver against his back, he heard a man growl, "Drop the gun or you're dead!"

Ralph did what he was told. Thrusting the gun painfully against his spine, the guard forced Ralph forward as the other man threw open the door.

Once outside, they halted as the guards glanced in all directions. Seeing no one, they urged Ralph on.

■

Following Morrison's orders, George Massoud quickly notified security to call the police, close the floors and block the exits. Then he ran for the stairs where the suspect had fled. His gun cocked, he opened the door to the stairwell and started down. He hesitated briefly at the basement exit, then pushed open the door a crack and peered outside. No one was in sight. Clutching his gun, Massoud crept along the side of the building towards the Emergency Room entrance as an eerie stillness filled the air.

■

In a crouched stoop, Noland and his abductors darted in between the parked cars of the lot nearest the Emergency Room. They stopped behind a late model black Ford. One of the Iranians slammed Ralph's face against the car trunk. Blood started gushing from Ralph's shattered nose. With brutal efficiency, they bound his hands with a belt, then tied a handkerchief around his eyes.

Unlocking the trunk, they hurled the helpless man inside, then slammed the lid shut.

■

Sirens wailed in the distance as Massoud neared the entrance to the Emergency Room. He waited looking in all directions, but nothing moved, nothing happened. Then a car's engine roared to life nearby. Massoud aimed his gun as a black Ford sped past him. But recognizing the car as one of Hassan's, he held his fire. George Massoud was puzzled.

Where was the gunman? Had he escaped on foot? Why were the guards leaving in such a fury? Massoud shouldered his gun. Then he walked the parking lot. He noticed traces of fresh blood on the ground. Who was injured, the gunman or someone else? George Massoud now had more questions than he could answer. He dared not proceed without further orders.

■

"You'd better sit down, lady. We're going to be here awhile."

Trembling now, Sydney accepted the chair as Morrison slowly paced Sam's office.

"What do you know about the victim?" he inquired.

Sydney's voice quivered as she struggled to answer. "His name is Philip Wentworth. He's a plastic surgeon here on staff."

"What's his connection to Ali Hassan?"

Astonished, Sydney's eyes widened. "None that I know of," she answered truthfully. "Why do you ask?"

Morrison ignored her question. "Why would someone want to kill him?"

"I don't know. I wish to God I did."

"Who was the woman with him?"

"Her name is Kathleen . . . " Sydney halted in midsentence. "How can I be sure you are who you say?"

"Look lady, I don't have time to quibble. You want another look at my badge?"

Sydney shook her head. While not particularly fond of his

crude demeanor, she understood the breed. Joe Morrison was definitely a cop.

"Kathleen was one of his patients. Philip performed reconstructive surgery on her face. She's been at St. Vincent's for months. She's been using the name Stein."

"What's her real name?"

"Clay. Kathleen Clay."

"Why the alias?"

"She's been hiding from her husband, Michael Clay."

Before Morrison could continue his questioning, the door opened abruptly. Seeing Sam, Sydney jumped to her feet and into his arms. Morrison likewise stood.

"What's going on here?" Ellis demanded.

"My name is Morrison. FBI. I've been questioning your wife about the shooting."

"Why her?" Sam retorted. "There were plenty of other witnesses."

Morrison decided to play it straight.

"Look, folks, I'll level with you. What I say must remain in this room. Okay?"

The Ellises agreed. What choice did they have?

"We've had Ali Hassan under surveillance for months. Since you live next-door to him, we've been keeping an eye on you as well." Morrison directed his attention to Sydney. "Particularly in view of your relationship with his daughter."

"Look," Sam offered. "We'll help you in any way that we can. But you know more about Hassan than we do. We're not exactly his favorite people. Besides, what does this have to do with the shooting?"

"I don't know," said Morrison. "Maybe nothing."

Sam had heard enough. He had no more time to be distracted. Grasping Sydney by the shoulders, he forced her eyes to his. "I have to go now. I'll be back as soon as I can. Philip's still alive but he's critical. He's being prepped for surgery now."

"You?" she said.

"There's no one else available. The bullet is lodged just inches from the heart. He's lost a great deal of blood. I don't know if I can save him."

"How's Kathleen?"

"She's hysterical. We've sedated her. She's back in her room now. God, I feel horrible. Just when her life was beginning anew, she had to witness something like this."

"I think it's more complicated than that," Sydney whispered. "Didn't you see them holding hands? There's something very special between those two."

"Go to her, Sydney, as quickly as you can."

Ellis hurried out, just as George Massoud barged in.

"Joe, can we talk?"

Nodding, Morrison took the younger man aside.

"The gunman has disappeared. The police combed every inch of the hospital. Nothing."

"Did anyone get an ID?"

"Negative. None of the witnesses got a clear look at the guy. But there's more."

"Go on."

"The two Iranians who went after him left immediately. I got the license number and the make of the car. I found fresh blood in the parking lot. Do you want me to have the police pick them up?"

Morrison took a moment to think. "No," he said slowly. "Let's not be hasty. Step up surveillance around Hassan, the mansion, and the store. None of this makes any sense. I'm not even sure who the intended victim was. But if there's a connection, we'll damn well find it!"

chapter 36

Ralph had failed. That much he knew. The commander would be disappointed. All he had to do was squeeze the trigger. But when he confronted Kathleen face to face, he couldn't do it. Faltering for that split second had changed everything.

Now he was a prisoner, bound, gagged and in pain, in the trunk of a car.

"Steady," he told himself. "Keep calm. Panic and you're dead."

Silently counting seconds, Ralph calculated they had traveled approximately twelve minutes, pausing at three stoplights or signs, before coming to a halt.

When the trunk lid was finally opened, Ralph was jerked roughly from the car. Still blindfolded, he was shoved forward then forced down a short flight of steps. Someone knocked, and a door creaked open. Ralph was pushed inside.

■

Kathleen had been returned to her room, heavily sedated, a prisoner there once more. Her bloodstained clothes had been removed and she found herself once again dressed as a patient in a robe and gown. She laid her head in her arms and wept.

Saying very little, Sydney sat by her side. She occasionally stroked her hair and murmured any words of comfort she could find.

Finally as dusk gave way to darkness, the door opened and a

very weary surgeon entered. Quietly, Sam took the chair opposite the couch. Scooting it forward, he drew the three of them into a tight circle.

"Philip's alive and holding his own."

"Oh thank God!" Sydney cried. Kathleen wept yet again.

"I'm afraid the bullet did a great deal of damage. Luckily, no major organs are involved. Philip is not out of the woods yet. There's always the risk of infection. But with luck, he might make it."

Leaning forward, Sam took Kathleen's trembling hand in his own. "Are you okay?" he asked gently.

She nodded.

"Listen to me, Kathleen. The police want to question you, but I've bought us a little time. Let's talk about what happened."

Wiping her eyes, Kathleen tried to focus and find her voice.

"Everything happened so fast. Philip and I had planned to spend the day together. We were having a great time. Then he stopped walking suddenly. He was staring at someone. He seemed upset. I turned to see who he was staring at. I saw the masked man with the gun but it didn't register until he fired. Then Philip screamed and fell forward. That's all I remember."

Not wanting to further upset her, Sam proceeded cautiously.

"There's a guard posted outside your door. The police don't want you to leave. They haven't caught the man yet." He hesitated. "The police aren't sure that Philip was the intended victim."

Sydney's eyes registered shock. Kathleen remained passive, not comprehending.

"Well, I have to go."

"May I see him?" Kathleen implored.

Sam's voice was gentle. "He's in recovery, unconscious. You can see him later when he's moved to a private room. If you like, we'll put him here next-door to you."

"That would mean so much," said Kathleen.

"He'll need round-the-clock supervision," Sam continued, "but we can't protect him as well in the Intensive Care Unit. I've talked to the police. We're going to seal off the wing and move the other patients. From now on, only the regular staff, the police, you and Philip, and perhaps Sydney, will be allowed on this floor—at least until the gunman is apprehended. Okay?"

"But what about my son, Sam? Shouldn't I return to him?"

"Not just yet, Kathleen. Your place is here with Philip."

Sydney walked Sam to the door. "Surely you don't think Kathleen was the intended victim?" she whispered.

Sam silenced her with a gesture. "Philip has no known enemies. Kathleen has."

■

Name.

Rank.

Serial Number.

As a prisoner of war, this was all the information a soldier was required to give his captors. In Vietnam, Ralph had lived in terror. Not of death. That would have been a relief. Rather of this—being taken alive—a prisoner of war.

"My name is Ralph Noland, Spec 5, Serial Number RA56438197."

For hours in the damp, dimly lit basement, he had uttered only these three things in a rapid staccato pitch. Bound to a chair and still blindfolded, Ralph Noland focused on surviving. He was told that if he screamed or tried to make noise, he would be killed instantly.

From the sounds around him, he guessed he was being held in the lower floor of a business, most probably a store. Periodically he'd hear the jingling of a bell followed by voices coming from the floor above. Some, like his guards, were of foreign extraction. Others, customers perhaps, were American, primarily female.

If indeed he was being held in the basement of a public place, he was probably safe from torture as long as there were people above who might hear. What could happen at the close of the business day, Ralph Noland dared not think.

The two guards who had abducted him remained by his side, trying to extract more information. But to no avail. They had allowed him to use the toilet, but kept the blindfold in place, although it was soaked with the blood that had gushed from his nose. The bleeding had stopped, but a dull pain remained. He looked a sight, and they had laughed as he fumbled to relieve himself without the ability to see.

Finally the footsteps above faded. The sound of chatter ceased. It was then Ralph Noland began to sweat. Another hour passed. Then he heard a commotion near the rear entrance of the building, and the sound of footsteps approaching. There was more than one man. How many were there?

The footsteps stopped a few feet away, then one man alone approached.

"My name is Ralph Noland, Spec 5. Serial Number RA56438197."

The man's reply was harsh. "Yes, putrid soldier. I know who you are."

Noland raised his head as once more he uttered his name, rank and serial number. The sound of stinging flesh echoed through the basement as the man brutally slapped Ralph's face.

"Silence!" he bellowed. "You will speak only when I command! There are no rules of war to protect you here!"

With the snap of his fingers, Ali Hassan demanded a chair.

"Bring me the file," he ordered. One of his men hurried away, returning a minute later.

"Ralph Noland, Spec 5, you can make this as easy or as difficult as you choose. Either way, it makes no difference. I will pose my questions only once. Then you will answer. If you fail, my men will delight in making you talk. Do you understand, putrid soldier?"

Noland nodded weakly.

"Who ordered my assassination?"

"You?" Ralph stammered incredulously. "No, sir! It was not you!"

The sound of Hassan's laughter was chilling.

"You take me for a fool, Ralph Noland! Do not play games. Games I promise you will regret."

Ralph's voice came in a quivering rush.

"You don't understand, sir! I wasn't after you! I don't even know who you are!"

Hassan paused. The silence was terrifying.

"If that be true, what did you hope to gain from killing a doctor?"

"I wasn't after him either. The poor fool just got in the way."

Hassan leaned forward. The smell of his breath nauseated Ralph.

"Who sent you then and for what purpose?"

Desperately, Ralph tried to strike a deal. "If I level with you, will you let me go? I swear I wasn't after you. My commander wanted me to snuff out his old lady. Okay, now you know."

Ali Hassan scrutinized his captive. He knew Ralph Noland was telling the truth. No one who wanted Ali Hassan dead—and there were many—would have hired such an incompetent.

"Name, rank serial number. You Americans are such arrogant idiots. You gave my men the only information they needed. It took my network only minutes to gather everything there is to know about you, Ralph Noland. Not even your own CIA can boast as much."

The leader of the New Savak riffled through the pages of Ralph's file.

"You were born in Pryor, Oklahoma, the only son of Fred and Pauline Noland. You have a sister, Lois, who is married to a man named Solomon Bucy, living in Kentucky. You failed to distinguish yourself in service. You likewise washed out as a cop."

"That wasn't my fault," Ralph whispered.

"Ah yes," Hassan retorted. "So I see. It was a psychiatrist who ruined your career. Poor fellow. He seems to have met with an untimely death. No doubt that was your handiwork, Ralph Noland?"

"Who *are* you?" Noland gasped.

Abruptly, Hassan stood, casting his chair aside. He paced the floor, then wheeled about sharply. "Who is your commander, Ralph Noland?"

Quaking, Noland tried to remain silent.

"Tell me or die!" Hassan bellowed.

Ralph Noland answered with the name he was sworn to protect. "Michael Clay," he whispered.

Having now forced his prisoner to betray his commander, Hassan spoke in a quieter, kinder voice. He wanted Noland's loyalty—for whatever little it was worth.

"Your commander will be disappointed with your actions today."

"Kill me now," Ralph pleaded. "What difference does it make?"

Patting his prisoner's knee, he said, "No, soldier. Your file tells me you are too good a man to waste. If we allowed you to live, what would you do?"

"I would try to complete my mission," he answered quickly, feeling for the first time a measure of hope. "To a soldier, the mission is all that matters."

"If I gave you a second chance, what would you do for *me*?"

Defeated, Ralph answered, "I would do whatever you require."

Hassan returned his gaze to Noland's file.

"It states that you were a demolitions expert in the Army and a bomb technician with the Kentucky State Troopers. What exactly does that mean?"

"I can blow up anything, anywhere," Noland answered proudly.

Ali Hassan paused to ponder an intriguing idea. Then he walked slowly to the east side of the basement where a single wall stood between his store and the neighboring jeweler's. He placed his ear against the reinforced concrete directly in line with Tripoli's vault—the vault that contained the precious diamonds he so desperately needed.

"Could you blow a vault without damaging its contents?"

"Yes," Ralph answered. "I could."

"Could you arrange a separate charge to create a diversion?"

The prisoner nodded. Noland was reminded of his days in Vietnam when his only link to the outside world was the voice of a commander.

"Whatever you require I can do."

"What if, in the process, lives were lost and a great deal of property damaged? Could you follow orders without question?"

"Yes, Commander, yes!"

Hassan looked at his prisoner with a gleam of triumph in his eyes. Ralph Noland was exactly the kind of man he required. Moreover, Noland was expendable. Hassan's men, precious in number, were not. And even if Ralph Noland was caught after the disaster, he'd be ultimately linked to Michael Clay and not Ali Hassan. Noland did not and would not know his new commander's identity. He could not be trusted with the information. He'd proved that when he revealed Michael Clay's name.

"I have a mission for you, soldier. It takes precedence over everything else. If you succeed, you will live. If you fail, you will die the miserable failure everyone thinks you are. What do you say?"

"I can do it, Commander. Give me a chance."

So it was that Ralph Noland became a true prisoner in the undeclared war fought in the recesses of his own twisted mind.

P A R T   I V

Joe Morrison ordered a meeting with his top men at FBI head-quarters in Kansas City first thing the next morning. Bill Hoffman, chief of the local bureau, was there along with Richard Walker, Ned Powell and George Massoud. It had been a long night for everyone. Joe, in particular, was in no mood to play games.

"We all know why we're here," he began. "Let's get down to business. Walker, we'll start with you."

"As George reported yesterday, two of Hassan's men were seen leaving the hospital immediately after the shooting. I was in position near the alley directly behind Hassan's store doing routine surveillance. Two Iranian men parked their vehicle behind the store at approximately 1:40 pm. Unfortunately, from my vantage point I couldn't get a clear view of them actually entering through the basement door. In any event, the black Ford remained parked at the rear of Hassan's until three o'clock this morning. At that time the men left. Destination unknown. Following your orders, I pursued the vehicle but tried to remain out of sight. They circled the city for nearly an hour before I lost them on the interstate."

Joe looked disgusted. "So were they alone? Did you see anyone else?"

"They left the store carrying a large, cumbersome rug which they dumped, with some effort, in the trunk. They might have had somebody wrapped inside, they might not. I couldn't tell from my vantage point. You told us all to keep a low profile, Joe. What can I say?"

Morrison was weary. He'd been up all night trying to keep the local police in check while he followed his own agenda. He knew damn well the Iranians held the gunman. There was no other explanation that made sense. But he had kept this information from the police. He didn't want Hassan's place stormed and arrests made. An attempted assassination, serious though it was, did not warrant jeopardizing their entire operation, now that they were so close to cracking the case.

It was up to Morrison to discover the link between the gunman and Hassan. So far, his men were coming up short, much too short to suit his edgy temperament. His next words sounded more like a growl than a request. "Give us your report, Ned."

"Hassan tried to check his daughter out of the hospital after the shooting but Dr. Carter wouldn't allow it. The kid is much too serious to be moved. So Hassan had her put in a private room with a guard stationed at the door."

Morrison nodded.

"Hassan left the hospital around four o'clock," Ned continued. "He returned to his mansion where he remained for about three hours. He left about seven-thirty, but didn't go back to the hospital. Instead he was driven to his store on the Plaza. He went in through the basement and remained there nearly two hours."

Joe paced back and forth in front of the conference table. "Doesn't that strike you as odd? Here is a man who has a seriously ill child, yet he leaves her alone at the hospital and goes to his store which has closed for the day. What kind of business would be that pressing?"

Ned Powell had to agree. "What's more bizarre is that he never left the basement. No lights ever came on upstairs."

Morrison returned to the table and reached for his cup of coffee. It was cold. He directed his attention to George Massoud. "What did you find out about the victim?"

"Philip Wentworth was born in Iran. His father was an American oil executive. His mother was a teacher at the university. Philip witnessed her arrest at the hands of the Savak when he was twelve years old. She disappeared and was presumed executed."

"Knowing his connection with the Savak, I wonder what part

Hassan might have played in the mother's death? We have a lead here, George. Follow it through. Contact Roger Brennan. See if Counterterrorism can determine just where Hassan was at that time."

Bill Hoffman drummed his pencil sharply upon the table. "So why was he shot? Because he recognized Hassan? An Iranian hit would have been much more efficient, Joe. Besides, why did Hassan send his guards after the gunman? I'm not sure any of this is relevant."

"I'm not sure it isn't!" Joe countered.

"What about the woman?" Hoffman continued.

"She didn't see much. She's been hiding at St. Vincent's Hospital for the last several months healing from plastic surgery. She's been using the alias Stein. I've requested a thorough background check on her husband, Michael Clay."

Morrison glanced at his watch. "We should have it soon. Bill, your men handled the tap on Hassan's home and store. What have you got?"

"Nothing goes on at the store that's not strictly business," replied Hoffman. "Rug business, that is. It's the mansion that's got me really puzzled."

"How so?"

"Unfortunately, we couldn't gain access without risking discovery to place a bug. So we had to rely on the phone tap. We don't have a single voice recording of either Hassan or his majordomo, Mansur. Don't you find that strange? Surely at some point, he has to place or receive calls from his own residence. All we get is the Iranian staff and then nothing of significance."

An uncomfortable silence filled the room as Joe glared at each one of his men. "The bastard has a secure line. Trace it."

Hoffman agreed and then asked, "What about the neighbors?"

Morrison smiled. "They're clean and very cooperative. Particularly the news reporter. I made her an offer she couldn't refuse."

■

"You look ragged, Sydney. Did you sleep at all last night?"

Sydney shook her head. "When I wasn't on the air doing

updates from the hospital, I was sitting with Kathleen. It was horrible, Jake. I've never witnessed a shooting. You feel so helpless."

"Anything new on the doctor?"

Sydney's tired face brightened a little. "He's stable. That's all I know. The nurses told me that Sam did a hell of a job repairing the damage but the next 48 hours are critical."

"How's Kathleen holding up?"

"Of course we can't broadcast this, but Kathleen doesn't even realize that Philip may have taken the bullet meant for her. She'll remain at the hospital under protective custody until the gunman is apprehended."

On this particular morning it was Jake Kahn who fetched the coffee. Handing Sydney a cup he said, "You look like you could use this."

Smiling weakly, she agreed.

With an amused twinkle in his eye, Kahn had to ask, "What kind of a challenge have you brought me now?"

"It's more than a challenge, Jake. It's a deal."

"Go on," Kahn encouraged. "You've got my attention."

"I met with Joe Morrison for nearly an hour yesterday. He's the FBI agent who's had Hassan under surveillance for months. He couldn't get specific with details but the FBI has reason to believe that Hassan is funding a terrorist training camp in the Middle East through some type of illegal activity here in the States. He's close to cracking the case. In return for my cooperation, he'll give me the exclusive story when an arrest is made."

"What kind of cooperation does he want?" Kahn questioned skeptically.

"Since Hassan is my next-door neighbor, Morrison wants information and access to our home."

"What was the bizarre twist you mentioned on the phone?"

"I've been so busy for the last few weeks that I forgot to tell you about it before. Remember when you sent me to St. Vincent's to interview Farhad Rajid for Organ Donation Month in October? He failed to show up for our appointment. I saw Lydia at the hospital. She was there with Mansur, Hassan's major-domo. I think Rajid was trying to dodge me but Lydia saw him enter the hospital through the lobby. She ran into his arms and called him *Uncle*. We both know I can't stand the man, so my thoughts might be overly suspicious. But I wonder if he's involved in the Iranian plot? Whatever the hell the plot is!"

Jake Kahn glanced at his reporter with a mixture of admiration and concern. "I had no idea what I was getting into when I hired you. You don't have to dig for stories, Sydney. You're a magnet for trouble." Kahn shook his head amused. "I know your plate is full but I have an interesting proposition for you. It won't take much time, just one night. It's a public relations deal. How would you like to cover both the dedication of the Winds and the lighting ceremony Thanksgiving night?"

Now it was Sydney's turn to smirk. "I'm the last person Gary Atwell would want to do the honors."

Kahn smiled. "Quite the contrary, little lady. It was Atwell himself who requested you. He plans quite an affair. He's pulled all his civic strings. It seems his magnificent building will be lighted along with the rest of the Plaza at exactly 8:00 Thanksgiving night. Not only does he want you to cover the ceremony, he's already gotten approval for the very person to throw the switch and light the Plaza. Guess who?"

Sydney sighed wearily. She'd been forced to deal with too many assholes lately. "Knowing him, I have no idea."

"Little Tanya Cole. He wants to milk her recovery and his participation in her successful transplant for all it's worth. She's to be the star of the night."

Sydney's response was truthful. "Well his motives might be selfish, but I like his choice. After what the Coles have been through, Tanya deserves the honor. I can't think of a finer family to represent what's good about this city. Tell Atwell I'd be delighted to cover the lighting ceremony."

Kahn shifted his bulky frame back in his chair. Pretending to examine his glasses, he studied his reporter carefully. She was tired, damned tired. Yet they still had a bit of business to discuss before he sent her home. It had to do with a story they'd confidentially named. "Is there anything new on the *River Saga*?" he said, using their private code name for Sydney's secret assignment.

"Well, there have been no new pieces of bodies found in the river, if that's what you mean. The only floater recently was that poor woman they dredged up last week. You remember the story, Jake. She was a maid at the Michelangelo Hotel. Her son is in jail on drug charges and her sixteen-year-old daughter is pregnant. Her husband is disabled. With this kind of family life, the police thought it was a suicide at first. Forensics revealed she died of a broken neck rather than drowning."

Kahn's eyes narrowed. "Isn't that a bit strange?"

"It's conceivable that she snapped her neck jumping from the bridge into the icy water. They haven't closed the case yet. Since it's an unusually cold winter, the police don't think we'll find any more pieces of bodies until the spring thaw. What do you think?"

"You never know, Sydney. This story has been so damn twisted from the beginning that I have no idea what to expect."

Kahn paused to take a sip of coffee.

"Have you had a chance to research our *sin* factor?"

Sydney snickered. "You were right, Jake. Kansas City has its dark side and its share of sin. Gambling and prostitution are alive and well here. One thing shocks me, however."

"What's that?"

"I'm kind of a small-town girl. I presumed you'd find prostitution only downtown. Would you believe they arrested a hooker just a few days ago on the Plaza coming out of the Michelangelo Hotel? Gorgeous woman. Nearly six feet tall. Blond. Works for a high-dollar escort service. She didn't have any priors, so she made bail quickly. She'll be arraigned in a few days."

Kahn leaned forward intrigued. He'd caught something that Sydney in her fatigue had missed.

"Where did you say she was arrested?"

"The Michelangelo Hotel," Sydney repeated.

"Wasn't that the same hotel where the maid worked?"

"What about it?"

"We're grasping for straws right now, Sydney. Any coincidence, no matter how big or small, is worth our attention. I'll call Chief Andrews. Let's have the police pick our lady up for a little questioning. Do you remember her name?"

Sydney paused. "It was a pretty name. Sophisticated. Let me think." Sydney's mind was fuzzy. The night had been too long.

Then she remembered. "Sabrina, that's it. Sabrina." Sydney tried to think if she had ever heard a last name. "That's all I remember, Jake. But the lady was gorgeous. The boys in vice will remember every detail about her, I guarantee it."

"You go home now, little lady. You've got to get some rest. I'll handle this lead." Weakly, she tried to protest.

"No argument now. We'll talk again in the morning."

Sydney rose and left Kahn's office without another word. As quickly as the door shut, he placed a phone call to his friend Tom Andrews, the Chief of Police.

By the time their conversation ended ten minutes later, Jake Kahn had broken out in a clammy sweat. There would be no opportunity to question the lovely hooker by the name of Sabrina. Her body had been discovered behind a garbage dumpster in a seedy area downtown just after midnight. She'd been bludgeoned to death. It was only her fingerprints—so recently placed on file—that identified her.

Removing his glasses, Kahn took a moment to clean the specks of dirt clouding his vision. More than his vision was clouded. His mind was overloaded with jumbled thoughts about the story which for months had consumed him.

He picked up the phone and dialed 0.

"Hold my calls!" he barked. "I don't want to be disturbed."

He replaced his glasses and grabbed a yellow pad and pen. Thoughts made more sense when viewed objectively. One by one he bulleted the facts as he knew them. He reached for his cup of coffee, then decided he needed something stronger. Searching his bottom desk drawer, he extracted a bottle of Chivas, a Cuban cigar, and a big white ashtray.

Thursday, November 17
Day 1

The harsh shrill of the alarm woke Ralph just before six.
Rubbing the sleep from his eyes, Noland slowly got to his feet.
The countdown was beginning. He had seven days to complete
his mission. Parting the curtains slightly, he peered outside. He
saw no one but he knew the Iranians were there watching every
move he made. He had been removed from the basement, carried
out in a rug, and once again thrown into the trunk of a car. He
had been freed at his apartment. Now it was as if he were under
house arrest. He couldn't make a move without being watched.

It was fortunate for him that he was not due at the hospital
until today. He'd been granted three days off, prior to the shooting, in return for the overtime he had worked. This gave him time
to recover from the battering he had suffered at the hands of his
captors. Now it was time to face the world. He had a job to do.
It was time to make restitution for the mission he had botched.

Ralph dressed quickly in jeans, a warm shirt and heavy boots.
He was to meet his new commander's men in ten minutes in the
alleyway behind his apartment. There he would receive his orders
and the supplies he needed. Time was precious. One week was
all he had.

Shivering against the early morning chill, Ralph hurried to the alley. There he found an old beat-up Chevy truck with a camper top and two men standing watch. The taller one grunted and opened the camper.

Noland edged closer. The commander had come through with the blueprints of the buildings, two hundred pounds of explosives, a ladder, a tool pouch, some hardware and Teflon-coated wire. Ralph had all he needed to bring a city to its knees.

Fingering the latest plastic explosives now used in terrorist attacks, Ralph murmured his approval. He turned to the men. "Tell the commander I am ready."

The smaller of the two men handed Ralph a fake ID to clip to his shirt. It showed him to be an employee of Capital Electric. He said, "You are to proceed immediately to the Plaza. Begin with Hassan's and Tripoli's, then finish the block. Your work there will take no more than two days. After that you will receive your next assignment. Do you understand?"

"I understand."

The taller, stockier guard locked the truck then swiveled menacingly towards Ralph. Collaring him roughly, he snarled, "Never forget that you are being watched. One mistake and you're dead!"

Noland gasped for air. The guard released him then tossed him the keys to the truck. The commander had briefed him thoroughly on this phase of the operation. Ralph Noland knew what was required. He prayed to God he had the guts to follow through.

■

Ralph parked his truck in a covered garage a short distance from Hassan's. He had studied his blueprints carefully and he knew how to proceed. Jumping from the truck, he secured his tool pouch about his hips, then retrieved his ladder, donned his work gloves, and set out.

Stuffed in his pockets were the explosives he needed. He kept his eyes averted as he marched towards the block of shops housing Hassan's. It was just after eight in the morning. The shops weren't open, but the Plaza was far from deserted.

Noland's heartbeat quickened as he neared Hassan's. Once

more he scanned the street. Everything seemed normal. Carefully Ralph set his ladder in front of the store and began his slow climb to the ridge where the Christmas lights began. They were strung in perfect symmetry, one following another—red, blue, yellow and green in a line stretching from one store to the next throughout the block. Block after block, year after year, the sixty miles of colored bulbs turned the Plaza into a Christmas postcard . . . until now.

■

Ralph reported to St. Vincent's shortly before 3:00 pm. His presence, of course, had not been missed. Since he'd not gone near the hospital in days, he had no idea what to expect. Cops were everywhere. Most were trying to remain obscure, dressed in plain clothes. Having been a cop, Noland recognized them. Composing himself, he affixed his hospital identification to his shirt and went in through the rear employees' door. No one stopped him.

Noland took the service elevator to the sixth floor. Tentatively he smiled but the nurses were somber. He didn't know if he should try to make conversation or simply go about his job unnoticed. In truth, he had no idea if he had been recognized. He was in a terrible bind. To quit his job now might arouse unwanted suspicion. Besides, he still had his first mission to complete. But to return to the scene of the shooting was taking a very great risk.

Despite the danger, he was driven to see Kathleen. He had nearly killed her after all. He gathered his mop and supplies and started down the hall. Two uniformed policemen stood guard, one of them in front of Room 605, the other by the adjoining suite where Philip Wentworth drifted in and out of consciousness.

Ralph greeted the first of the two men. "Good afternoon!"

The policeman nodded, then looked closer. "What happened to you, bud?"

Ralph had forgotten what a sight he must be. His nose was broken. There were bruises underneath his eyes. He had tried to conceal his contusions with make-up but obviously he had failed. Had he just been caught by an alert policeman? He decided to go for broke.

"What else?" Ralph smirked. "I got in a fight over a broad. Geez, when will we ever learn?"

"You got a point," the policeman added.

"Yeah," Ralph continued. "Whiskey and broads make a bad combination."

Taking a deep breath, Ralph started into Kathleen's room.

"Hold it, mister. Let me see your identification."

Ralph unclipped his badge. The policeman examined it, then handed it back, shaking his head.

"Only doctors and nurses are allowed inside. Nothing's been said about a janitor."

Ralph's voice quivered. "Hey man, let me do my job. I only want to clean the rooms."

"I'll have to get an okay."

Ralph began to tremble. The last thing he needed was to draw attention to himself.

"Wait," he countered. "Is the lady still here? Mrs. Stein knows me. Ask her."

Reluctantly, the policeman cracked the door to 605. Tired and forlorn, Kathleen sat in shaded darkness near the window.

"Excuse me, ma'am. This guy says you know him."

Slowly Kathleen turned. At the sight of Ralph Noland, her bleary eyes widened, not because she recognized her assassin, or recalled the look of betrayal she'd seen in his eyes. No, for the first time in days, her sad eyes brightened because her trusted friend had returned.

c h a p t e r **39**

Friday, November 18
Day 2

For the third time in only a few minutes, Michael Clay glanced at the clock. To him, tardiness was unforgivable, and Solomon Bucy was late. He peered out the library window. Damn! How he hated Velours in this drab, bleak time of year.

He couldn't bear his existence here much longer. He'd suffered yet another bladder infection, a common malady for spinal cord injuries. He would remain forever confined to a wheelchair, scorned by everyone who used to flatter him. The threat of prison loomed and if the lawsuits prevailed, he'd be destitute as well. No, he would never let that happen. He'd commit suicide first.

He chided himself. It was time to put such thoughts aside. Better days were coming. His mother had called to say that the Swiss Alps could be magical this time of year. And if the cold proved troubling for Michael's condition, they could spend the winter in the Canary Islands.

"Mr. Bucy is here to see you, sir," the butler announced.

"Show him in, Henry."

Forgetting his annoyance, Michael maneuvered his wheelchair to face his attorney. His voice was nearly gleeful. "Was the hit a success?"

Taking a seat, Bucy reluctantly shook his head. "A doctor took the bullet for Kathleen."

"How in the name of God did that happen?" Clay cried. "I thought your brother-in-law was a crack shot."

"He is. Apparently, the doctor just got in the way. Ralph wants you to be assured that he escaped without being recognized. He'll try again as soon as he can. Security around the hospital is tight. He has to wait for the right moment."

"We don't have a lot of time, Solomon."

"What do you mean?"

"Thanksgiving is coming."

Solomon waited for more of an answer. "I don't understand," he said.

"Tell Noland that Thanksgiving is to be a day of celebration. I want my wife dead by the end of next week. I intend to spend Christmas with my mother and Daniel."

■

Yet another time, Sydney glanced outside at the window across the way. Lydia, of course, was not there. She remained at the hospital under guard. Sam updated her periodically but by order of Hassan, all visitors—particularly Sydney—were forbidden.

Sydney dressed and hurried downstairs. The limousine was nowhere in sight. She could only hope this meant that Hassan was not at home. Taking a chance, she crossed the lawn to the mansion, and rang the bell. The older woman she had encountered before appeared garbed in Muslim black.

"Could you tell me how Lydia is?" Sydney entreated.

"I'm afraid I don't know much," the woman whispered quickly. "She's still very ill but Mansur assures us that soon she will receive the best medical care available."

Sydney did not understand. Lydia's cardiologist, Neil Carter, was one of the top men in his field. Lydia was already receiving the best of medical care.

"What do you mean?" she asked.

The woman shook her head as if to warn her it was unsafe to say more.

"Is there someone who could give Lydia a message for me?"
The frightened woman glanced behind her.

"I'll try," she said.

"Tell Lydia that I love her. I'd be with her if I could."

The woman nodded. Sydney started to back away. With a quick gesture, the servant laid her hand on Sydney's arm.

"I can tell you this," she whispered. "They tell me that the child calls for you constantly."

Sydney returned home more disturbed than before. Over and over, she kept replaying the scene between the woman and herself. Soon Lydia would be receiving the best medical care available.

"What would that be?" Sydney wondered. "Where? And when?"

Returning home, she placed a phone call. After three rings, a gruff male voice finally answered.

"Joe, this is Sydney Lawrence. This may be nothing, but I heard something I think you'll find interesting."

At 11:25 pm a weary Ralph Noland clocked out of the hospital. He had spent much of the day climbing around buildings, then had put in a full shift at the hospital. He took a break only to bring Kathleen a fresh cup of coffee. This had become their evening ritual. Even with her, he was edgy.

Turning up his collar, he left the hospital through the rear entrance. It was late and the streets were deserted. Out of nowhere he heard footsteps. Before he could run, he was grabbed from behind. A gun was thrust painfully in his ribs.

"Do not scream!" a familiar voice warned. "Keep moving! Don't look back!"

Ralph Noland did exactly what he was told. He recognized the voice. He knew the footsteps. The rear door to a car opened. Ralph was pushed to the floor. Blindfolded once more, he was returned to the basement.

His body quivered. With what thoughts he could muster, he went over his assignment. He had done what the commander asked. Yet fear pervaded his whole being. Maybe both his time and his usefulness had run out.

Hearing the one he called the commander approach, Ralph's body tightened. A chair was brought forward for the commander. Ralph awaited his death sentence.

"You have done well, Ralph Noland. Perhaps you are a decent soldier after all."

Noland exhaled sharply. He could feel the dribble of urine staining his pants.

"The timers. Are they set?"

"Yes, sir. I connected the main explosives directly into the wiring of the lights. I set the shut-off switch. That way, if they test the lights before the ceremony, nothing will happen."

"Go on," the commander encouraged. "What then?"

"At 7:55 pm, Thursday night, the switches will be deactivated and the current free to flow. When the lights are thrown, the explosives will detonate. You'll have your diversion, Commander, just like I promised. And a hell of an explosion to boot!"

"That's very good. Very good, indeed. Now listen carefully. Tonight we will set a separate charge just a short distance from here. We have everything you need. Your blindfold will be removed in order to complete the task."

Ali Hassan paused. "You will not be permitted to look at me. And you must never repeat what you see or hear. Your life depends on it."

With a racing heart, Noland nodded. He understood. Hassan sat back in his chair.

"After that, I have one more assignment which you will begin tomorrow. But to accomplish this, you must be the demolition expert you claim to be."

There was something so sinister in the commander's voice that Ralph Noland felt a chill go through him.

"What I have in mind will make the first explosion seem like child's play."

Saturday, November 19
Day 3

"Belva, honey, don't wait supper for me tonight. I'll probably be late."

Gulping his coffee, Charles rose from the table and kissed his wife briefly. He paused in the doorway.

"It's going to be a long weekend, honey. The construction crews are working around the clock to finish the building in time for the dedication."

Smoothing the lines of his work jacket, Belva gave him a knowing look. "You don't fool me one bit, Charles Cole. You don't care how many hours they ask you to work. You love this job."

"It's become a part of me, Belva. I feel like the building belongs to me. Mr. Atwell gave me the chance I needed. I promised him I wouldn't be a disappointment."

"You have a good day, Charles. Tanya and I are going shopping for something special to wear Thanksgiving night. I still can't believe they've chosen our baby to be the star of the lighting ceremony."

"From what I hear, the party Mr. Atwell has planned is bigger than anything this city has ever seen. You buy something real pretty, Belva, for both of you. Thanksgiving is going to be a night for us all to remember."

■

Just after eight on Saturday morning Ralph drove through the quiet streets of the Plaza. It had been a long night. He had set the dynamite just as he'd been told between the basement of Hassan's store and the vault of the jewelry store next-door. The charge would be detonated separately from the explosives tied into the Plaza lights.

He traveled north on Main, then turned east on 47th. Up ahead he saw the posted sign. "Construction Entrance. Keep Out!"

Signaling a right turn, he steered the truck towards the rear of the building. Several other construction workers were already there. For his purposes this was good. He didn't want to stand out.

Glancing at the twenty-five-story skyscraper, he tried to imagine the scene he would be responsible for creating in less than a week. The Winds—like a cake taken out of the oven too soon—would collapse slowly from the center, the sides falling inward until there was nothing left but crumbled steel, shattered glass, and piles of debris.

Strapping his tool pouch around his hips and clipping the ID badge to his shirt, Noland locked the truck and headed towards the building. Just inside, he was stopped by a security guard.

"I've not seen you around here," Charles Cole began, peering closer to check his ID.

Keeping his voice as low and steady as possible, Ralph replied, "I'm a troubleshooter for Capital Electric. My boss sent me to check the wiring."

"Yeah, we were told to expect some new people this weekend. I guess you guys don't mind working overtime."

Ralph chuckled. "Hell no, man! I can use the money, especially this time of year."

Charles smiled. "I'm an apprentice electrician myself. I go to school on my days off. One of these days, I'll be trading in my security badge for a tool pouch."

"Have you done electrical work before?"

"Yeah, I went to school in the Army, but I couldn't find work when I got home."

A knowing look crossed Ralph's face.

"So you're a vet too? Did you serve in-country?"

"Two tours in the jungle. I still have nightmares."

Ralph shifted uncomfortably, remembering his own vivid dreams.

"The bastards treated us like shit when we came home," he said. "Nobody understands what it was like."

"You got *that* right, friend."

Ralph threw out his hand. "My name is Ralph Noland. What's yours?"

"Charles Cole." The security guard shook Ralph's hand firmly. "Do you know where you're going?"

"No," Ralph replied. "I could use your help. Where's the electrical room?"

"Come with me."

Cole led the way to the service elevator at the rear of the building. Together they rode to the basement. Ralph smiled. Things were going better than he'd planned.

"I understand the building is computerized."

"That's right," Charles answered. "Every system is tied into the mainframe on the first floor. The computer controls everything from the electrical to the heating and cooling systems. It's quite a fancy deal."

Noland had guessed he would have something like this to contend with, and dreaded the added complication. He forced a smile. "My boss wants me to make sure the lights are in order for Thursday night. How is the lighting ceremony supposed to work?"

"My understanding is that the building will go dark about 7:55 pm. At 8:00, the computer will activate the electrical system. The entire building will be lit up at the precise moment the Plaza lights are turned on. It'll be something to see."

Cole led the way down a narrow corridor. Fumbling with a big ring of keys, he unlocked the door to the electrical room.

"Here you go. Anything else you need?"

Ralph hesitated. It would be helpful if he could study the computer system, but he didn't want to arouse suspicion.

"Thanks for your trouble, man. I'll be seeing a lot of you this week. The boss wants me to check every piece of wiring in the building. You can't be too careful."

Charles Cole smiled. "Not with this building," he agreed, as he turned to go.

Alone with the massive task ahead, Ralph began to sweat. Basically, he'd wire the explosives the same way he'd done the lights on the Plaza. Connected through the wiring, the charges would have to be set on several of the floors above. A timed shut-off device would open the flow of current to the explosives only after the building was darkened at 7:55 Thursday night. Then at precisely 8:00, the building would blow.

Ralph was fairly confident he could wire the building without access to the computer, since the wires originated in the electrical room. He just had to discover at what juncture they were tied into the computer.

Noland realized just how careful he'd have to be. Clicking on his flashlight, he opened the main panel and began to study the wiring. Ralph Noland had no time to waste and no margin for error.

Sunday, November 20
Day 4

Philip's voice was so raspy that Kathleen didn't at first hear him. Then he said her name again.

"Philip!" she cried. "Oh, Philip!"

Impulsively, Kathleen reached out and grasped Philip's hand tightly. For the first time in days, he tried to ask what had happened.

"You were shot. Sam had to operate. He's promised me that you're going to be just fine."

"Who?" Philip croaked.

"The police don't know. The man got away. Nobody is even sure you were the target. It may have just been some crazy random hit."

Philip struggled to speak. "You?"

"Me? I'm fine. Really. The police want me to stay here so they can protect us both. There are guards posted outside."

For a moment Philip's concentration wandered as he tried to recall the moments just before he was shot, but his mind was too foggy.

Tears of relief sprang to Kathleen's eyes as she lifted his hand to her lips.

"Rest, darling."

"Time," he whispered. "Wasted."

"Hush, Philip," she soothed. "We're lucky. We've been given another chance."

Philip's words stabbed her heart. "Don't leave me."

Kathleen leaned across Philip's bed and forced his fearful eyes to hers.

"I'm staying right here until you're well. I love you, Philip Wentworth. I almost lost you. I don't intend to leave you now."

■

Ralph approached Kathleen's room cautiously. It was Sunday evening, later than usual. Carrying his customary cup of coffee, he tensed as he encountered a different policeman standing guard.

"Hello," he said tentatively. "My name's Noland. May I go in?"

"Hold it a second while I check the list. What did you say your name was?"

"Ralph Noland."

"Here it is. Go on in."

Once inside, he called Kathleen's name. The door to Philip's room was shut. He assumed she must be there. Setting the coffee on the table near her easel, he searched for a pencil to jot her a note.

"Sorry I missed you. Here's your coffee. I hear Dr. Wentworth is better."

Ralph had just signed his name when he heard the bathroom door open. Clad only in a robe, her hair wrapped in a towel, Kathleen froze when she saw the strange man in her room.

"Is that you, Ralph?" she gasped.

"Yes, ma'am," he replied. "I didn't mean to scare you."

"It's okay. Can you sit with me a minute, please?"

"Maybe for a moment."

Ralph took the chair nearest the sofa. Removing the towel, Kathleen shook her gleaming hair free. She looked fresh, alive and happy.

"Did you hear the good news?" she asked.

"Yes," Ralph replied. "Dr. Wentworth's better."

"He's much better. Sam says he's going to be just fine."

"And you?" Ralph had to ask. "How are you?"

"I'm fine now. Really I am."

Noland watched in silence as Kathleen savored her coffee.

"You spoil me, Ralph."

"I like spoiling you, ma'am. It's good to see you happy."

Cocking her head, Kathleen studied her friend carefully.

"You look tired, Ralph. What's wrong?"

Shifting uncomfortably, he replied, "Nothing's wrong. I've been working some long hours, that's all."

Suddenly chilling, Kathleen drew her robe tightly about her. There was something about Ralph's demeanor that disturbed her. But she pursued it no further.

Susan M. Hoskins

Monday, November 21
Day 5

Sydney was alone when she heard the doorbell ring. Sam had scheduled a meeting at the hospital and wouldn't be home for hours. Sydney hurried to the front door.

"Hi, Joe. Come in."

"Thanks for calling, Sydney. What's up?"

"I think you'd better see for yourself."

Sydney beckoned Joe Morrison to follow her upstairs to the bedroom.

"In here," she said, leading him into her dressing room.

"It all started right after we moved in. I'd be sitting here at my vanity. I'd glance up and Lydia would be standing there in the window."

Morrison's eyes followed Sydney's to the window across the way. The draperies were drawn tightly.

"We developed a secret ritual. Lydia would signal me from the window. I would go downstairs, then she would come over for a little visit. Since she's been ill, I've not been allowed to see her. I miss her."

"We followed up on your lead yesterday but I don't have much to report. As far as we know, Hassan has made no overt plans to take Lydia somewhere else. Didn't you tell me she was too sick to be moved?"

"Her heart is still in arrhythmia. Sam says that if the drugs don't work soon, they'll have to try more aggressive measures." Sydney returned her attention to the window. "I keep watching the window. I can't help it, even though I know she's not there." Not the least embarrassed at intruding upon Hassan's privacy, Sydney handed Morrison a pair of binoculars. "Call it a reporter's instinct or sheer nosiness. I wanted a better look."

Morrison focused on the upstairs window.

"Look down and to the left. See the open window? Do you see what I see?"

Morrison followed her lead to the exposed view.

"Crates," he muttered. "Packing crates."

"On the first floor and on the second. Could it be Hassan is moving?"

Morrison trained the binoculars on every window in his view.

"Have you seen any trucks or moving vans?"

"Early this morning," Sydney replied, "I saw two small trucks parked at the rear of the house. It looked like the guards were removing some computer equipment, file cabinets and other small items. But no moving vans and no furniture left the premises that I saw. But there's more . . . "

Morrison lowered the binoculars. "Go on," he said.

"I called the realtor who sold us the house. She checked the listings. Hassan's house is not up for sale. So where would he be going in such a hurry?"

Morrison looked around the room. It was more than big enough for Sam and Sydney, but it was going to get real crowded soon. Loosening his tie, he studied his new digs to determine where to set up his equipment. He also searched for an ashtray. He wondered if she would mind if he smoked.

Tuesday, November 22
Day 6

Jake and Sydney had grown comfortable with their morning routine. It was a time to catch up on the past day's events and plan for the day ahead.

Sipping his coffee, Jake studied his reporter with concern. She grew wearier every day. Soon even the skill of the station's make-up man would not be able to conceal for the camera the circles growing ever darker beneath her eyes.

"You look terrible," he stated.

"Thanks, Jake. You're great for a woman's ego."

Sydney took another sip of black coffee. She'd forsaken the cream. Rancid black coffee had become the main staple of her diet these days. "You're right, though. I am a mess. Sam and I had a slumber party with Joe Morrison and his boys last night. You can't imagine the fun!"

Kahn crinkled his eyebrows. "Slumber party?" he repeated.

"It seems our bedroom provides the best view of Hassan's mansion. Sam and I were relegated to the guest quarters. Morrison and his men have set up surveillance in our house, complete with camera and audio equipment. It's really quite something to see the FBI at work."

"Give me an update," Jake said.

"The servants are busy packing crates. I think Hassan is planning a hasty departure. Lord, how I worry about Lydia!"

"Anything new with her?"

Sydney shook her head. "No, she's still at St. Vincent's. They're trying to maintain her on drugs, but her heart has not reverted to a normal rhythm. Hassan refuses any other procedures."

"How long does Morrison plan to use your home?"

"I have no idea," Sydney sighed wearily. "Last night was the first night. It seemed like four days. I made sandwiches and coffee for the men. They kept pacing the house all night long. Believe me, Jake, having the FBI roaming your house is not conducive to either sleep or love."

Kahn smiled.

"I need to focus on work," Sydney continued. "Otherwise, I might figure out just how tired I really am. What's the latest on Thursday night?"

"I've been in meetings with Atwell and the Plaza Association for days. At first, Atwell insisted that you broadcast live from the Winds. I prevailed with a better idea. We can't keep our competitors from covering the actual lighting ceremony. However, we're the only ones authorized for both the pre-lighting show and the program afterward at the Winds. We'll set you up on a platform in the center of the Plaza and have a remote at the Winds. Beginning at 7:30, we'll switch back and forth between the party at the Winds and the festivities on the Plaza. The Mayor will speak. We'll feature some local high school Christmas carolers, the usual stuff."

Jake paused only long enough for another quick sip of muddy brew.

"About ten minutes before 8:00, we'll introduce Tanya Cole. The station will run some file video so viewers can relive the drama of her transplant. At 7:55, both the Plaza and the Winds will go dark. We'll fill in with camera shots of the crowd and carolers. The countdown will begin. Then at 8:00 sharp, Tanya will throw the switch and the lights will go on. At precisely the same moment, the computer at the Winds will light the building. It should be something to see."

"Sounds spectacular," Sydney assured him.

The ringing of Jake's phone interrupted them.

"Yeah?" he barked in his customary gruff style.

Immediately he tensed. "Put him through!" He held up a hand to signal Sydney to wait.

"What's up, Tom?" he said into the receiver.

Kahn remained silent for several seconds. Sydney didn't know who it was, but she guessed it might be Tom Andrews, the Chief of Police. The thick cords in her boss's neck began pulsating.

"We'll be right there!" declared Kahn, slamming down the receiver. "Come on, Sydney. Grab your coat!"

He paused at the doorway only long enough to say, "I hope you have a strong stomach!"

■

Jumping in his own car, Jake sped towards downtown. A body had been discovered by the Missouri River, a body Police Chief Andrews thought Jake and Sydney should see. They exited at Grand and took a secondary road to the edge of the river, not far from the Paseo Bridge. The roughly paved road had been blocked off with squad cars. Only Jake Kahn's car was waved through by Police Chief Andrews's order.

Jake parked and they jumped out. Sydney counted eight squad cars. Their lights remained flashing but their sirens were silent. An ambulance stood ready. The Medical Examiner's vehicle was there as well.

Puffing, Kahn urged Sydney forward down the sloping banks.

"Prepare yourself, Sydney. This isn't going to be pretty."

Right now, Sydney was concentrating on making it down the steep incline without falling. Slippery from the fallen leaves and crusted from the morning chill, every step was treacherous. Had she known what the day held in store, she would have worn running shoes, not heels and a tight skirt.

A small tense group circled the body, preventing Jake and Sydney from getting a good look. Tom Andrews immediately stepped forward. He was a contemporary of Kahn's. A big man with stark white hair, a thick torso, and a deep, resonant voice, he looked the part of the Chief.

Shaking hands with Sydney and Jake, he got to the point. "A body was discovered a couple of hours ago by one of the vagrants who camps under the bridge. He wandered down to the river bank this morning to take a piss. Our friend here was staring him in the face. We got the call about an hour ago. We thought it was just another jumper. But there's nothing routine about this one. Let me show you."

Sydney had never seen a cadaver pulled from the river before and she wasn't sure she wanted to.

"Jake, Sydney, I'd like you to meet our Medical Examiner, David Barton. David, show them what you've got."

A short wiry man with a pinched face and rimless glasses hovered over the body. He was wearing sterile gloves. The circle of officers parted and Jake and Sydney stepped forward for a first-hand look. Sydney shut her eyes tightly for a moment to steady herself, but then forced herself to open them again. She was a reporter. She couldn't afford the luxury of being ill.

Before them lay the partially decomposed remains of a human being. The stench was overpowering. The body was positioned face down with the head turned. Half of the face was exposed—what there was of it. The eyes were missing. The flesh had been eaten from the skull.

"Let me fill you in," said Barton in an impersonal voice. "We have a black male, dead for about ten days. Obviously he was murdered somewhere else and then dumped in the river."

Dr. Barton drew the others in closer. "This is what has me baffled. I've never seen anything quite like it before." He indicated an area of the lower back. "See this? It looks like the victim had some sort of surgical procedure. See the crude metal staples that were used to clamp off the arteries?"

Fascinated, Jake and Sydney peered into the cavity.

"You don't find this type of staple used routinely in the operating room. This method of clamping off arteries was used for expediency only. We're lucky that the temperature of the water preserved the organs."

"What do you mean?" Jake asked.

"Look, I'll need a full autopsy, but let me summarize what we have so far. This man had undergone a crude surgical procedure."

Dr. Barton paused. "This surgery did not take place under normal, sterile, operating room conditions. As you can see," he continued, "the left kidney is present. The right one is missing!"

Barton looked from one officer to the next. "I'm only a pathologist. You guys are the detectives. You tell me what it means!"

Susan M. Hoskins

c   h   a   p   t   e   r   **44**

Wednesday, November 23
Day 7
8:00 am

Sam had scheduled an hour alone in his office to catch up on overdue paperwork. He loved his position as Chief of Staff, but had to force himself to deal with the never-ending administrative details. He had just settled down to work when a sharp rap at the door startled him.

"I know you didn't want to be disturbed," his flushed secretary explained, "but there's an emergency on two."

"What kind of emergency, Elizabeth?"

"Ali Hassan has arrived with several of his men. He's trying to remove Lydia from the hospital."

"What?" Sam jumped to his feet. "That's impossible! Where's Dr. Carter?"

"The nurses had him paged immediately. He's not in the hospital. What do you want them to do?"

"Tell them I'm on my way and to stall. Call security. Have them meet me on two, stat! Call the local police for backup."

Sam started out the door but a thought stopped him.

"Call the Department of Social Services. Find out legally what we can do if Hassan tries to remove Lydia."

Sam raced up the stairway to the second floor and threw open the metal door to the Progressive Care Unit, commonly referred to as the Heart Unit. The room at the far end of the hallway was reserved for Lydia Hassan. A group of men in dark suits stood before it. Only a single woman dressed in white stood between them and the open doorway. Sam approached cautiously.

The nurse was a petite woman, a mere five feet tall, and young, no more than twenty-five. She had flaming red, curly hair and flashing eyes. And probably, Sam guessed, more guts than good sense. Confronted by Ali Hassan and four armed men, her voice quivered.

"What you ask is impossible, sir! Your daughter simply cannot be moved!"

Ali Hassan took a menacing step towards her. The young woman flinched.

In a soft, controlled voice Sam said, "What is the meaning of this?"

The guards wheeled around to confront Sam. The one in charge, their leader, took his time turning to face the Chief of Staff. The two were neighbors but they had never met. They had seen each other from a distance, of course, but neither wished to be involved with the other. Now it couldn't be helped.

"Go back to your duties, nurse," Sam stated calmly. "I'll handle this."

Taking her cue, Ellie Richardson immediately went to Lydia's side, closing the door behind her.

"I repeat," Sam said quietly. "What is the meaning of this?"

"I have come to take my daughter home," Hassan stated. "I will care for her there."

Sam had to work at keeping his own anger in check. "Your daughter is far too ill to be moved. As I'm sure Dr. Carter explained, Lydia's heart is in arrhythmia. She cannot be moved until the situation is corrected."

"I have made arrangements for a doctor to be with her at all times," Hassan countered. "She belongs with me."

Sam knew from conversations with Joe Morrison and Sydney that Hassan appeared to be making preparations for a hasty departure. This drastic step of trying to remove Lydia in her condition confirmed their suspicions. To move Lydia at this time . . . out of the hospital . . . more than likely out of the city . . . perhaps even out of the country . . . would put her life in great jeopardy.

Ellis heard footsteps behind him. He glanced back and determined that his security guards were now in place, but this proved to be of little comfort. Hassan's guards were heavily armed. Sam's security men were not.

Sam's voice remained calm and deliberate, giving no doubt he would do whatever necessary to back up his words. "This child will remain here under our care!"

"I am Lydia's father!" Hassan roared. "I make the decisions regarding my daughter! Not you!"

"Medically, you are mistaken, sir!" Sam countered evenly.

Sam heard the flurry of activity behind him and the hushed conversation between the security guards and the policemen who had been summoned for backup. He still had no idea what he could legally do. Yet it didn't matter. Lydia's life was at stake. He plunged ahead into uncharted waters. Let the courts decide later if he had been right or wrong. Dr. Ellis turned to the uniformed policemen who stood ready. He continued to speak in a low voice.

"I want this man and his men removed from my hospital. We're taking custody of this child now."

Sam faced Hassan a final time. "I will take good care of your daughter. You may visit Lydia under supervision. However, if you come back to my hospital with these men again, I'll have you arrested. Do you understand?"

Ali Hassan locked eyes with his most formidable opponent. He knew he had no choice but to comply. To do otherwise would jeopardize the mission which he held even more dear than his daughter. His eyes were filled with loathing when he spoke.

"My daughter must be protected!" he protested.

"Oh, she will be!" Sam assured him. "But with our men, Hassan. Not yours!"

At the same moment that Hassan was being escorted from St. Vincent's, another man was turning his truck into the construction entrance of the Winds. He was relieved. Today was the last day he would pose as a troubleshooter for an electrical company. He chuckled quietly to himself. He, Ralph Noland, eternal fuck-up, had accomplished something which no one thought he could. He had wired this magnificent twenty-five-story building to explode at precisely 8:00 Thursday night.

With the last of his powerful explosives tucked in his jacket, Noland marched towards the building. It still amazed him how easy his job had been. Only the security guard had questioned him. No one else had checked his identification or his reason for being there.

Speaking to no one, Ralph took the service elevator to the fourth floor. The architect had made his job easy by designing ornate, decorative columns. Noland had already hidden his explosives above them on the first and second floors. Today, he'd set the charges on floors four and six just to insure the building's total collapse. Then, for the first time in nearly a week, he could breathe.

He still had one troubling issue to settle—the matter of Kathleen. He decided not to distract his mind with thoughts about her now. He still had today and most of tomorrow to complete his primary assignment. Michael Clay had spoken. She was to be dead by the end of Thanksgiving Day.

It was well past two before Ralph finished the job. Clutching his ladder, he glanced around for the last time.

"You showed them! You showed them all! You did it!"

He wondered where he'd be tomorrow night at precisely 8:00 pm. Surely he could find a hill where he could park his truck and watch alone as a city was terrorized. By his hand, the hand of Ralph Noland.

Ralph took the service elevator to the first floor. He started to leave the building but the sight of the security guard stopped him. For a moment, Ralph Noland felt a twinge.

"Hey, man!" he yelled. "You got a minute?"

"Sure," Cole replied, smiling as he approached Noland with his hand outstretched. "Your name is Ralph, right?"

"Yeah," Noland replied. "You have a good memory."

"Are you finished with the job?" Cole asked.

"Everything is in good order," Noland assured him. "Are you all ready for Thursday?"

"I think so," Cole replied.

Ralph liked Cole. He was a mistreated veteran like himself. He didn't want Cole anywhere around the building when it exploded. Like Ralph, he'd suffered enough.

"They won't make you work Thanksgiving night, will they?"

Charles Cole was amused by the question.

"I take it you don't know Gary Atwell. Yeah, they got me working all right. But they done something real nice."

"What's that?"

"They chose my baby girl to throw the switch and light the Plaza. Can you imagine that? Tanya Cole, the star of the night."

Ralph felt his knees go weak.

"So you'll be at the Plaza, huh?" he asked.

"No," Charles replied. "I have to stay here. Atwell's having a big party for the dedication. It's my job to keep everything straight. I'll have to watch my baby on TV later. I hope she doesn't get scared. Can you imagine a quarter of a million people crammed into the Plaza just waiting for my little girl to throw the switch? Who would have ever thought that possible?"

Ralph fled the scene as quickly as he could. He made it to the side of his truck before he heaved his guts. The thought of Charles Cole being at the Winds while his little girl threw the switch on the Plaza struck him like a blow. In taking the job, Ralph had never put faces on the people who might be hurt. A horrible thought crossed his mind. Just where would the little girl be standing when she threw the switch to the lights? Would it be in front of one of the buildings he had wired?

Oh God! And all those people crammed into the few square blocks of the Plaza. Sure, the commander had told him some lives might be lost, but he had no idea so many people would be helplessly trapped when the Plaza blew up. He wasn't from Kansas City. He'd never even visited the city before. He had no idea what a tradition the lighting ceremony had become. He'd presumed most people would be at home eating turkey with their families, watching the explosion on TV.

With trembling hands, Ralph started the engine to the truck. He couldn't report for work. He was too ill. There was only one thing to do. It had been months since he'd had a drink. He had to get to a liquor store and fast. He had to forget. He didn't dare think about what he had done.

45

Thursday, November 24
Day 8
11:30 am

Thanksgiving began cold and dark. Sleet was forecast for the
afternoon, turning gradually to snow by early evening, just in time
to make the Plaza lighting ceremony a freezing nightmare.

Sydney Lawrence found herself alone in the kitchen making
her own holiday preparations. She was dressed appropriately for
her mood, in jeans and a tattered sweatshirt.

This was a Thanksgiving unlike any other she'd ever experienced. She'd grown up on a horse farm in Kentucky with her widowed father, Mack. There, the aroma of holiday cooking always filled
the kitchen of the brick ranch house. Friends and neighbors came
from miles around bringing casseroles and homemade pies. Today's
feast on Verona Circle would be vastly different. Sam had already
been called to the hospital. There was too much going on for him
to take a break. Sydney too would be working this holiday, covering
the dedication of the Winds and the Plaza lighting ceremony.

But food still had to be prepared. Joe Morrison and his men
were camped upstairs. Everybody needed to eat, probably in
shifts. In keeping with the day, she'd managed to stop by a neigh-

borhood deli for some turkey slices and fresh bread. Thanksgiving at the Ellis home would be sandwiches, coffee and fruit salad.

She'd called her father a short time ago hoping to buoy her spirits. The call had only made her feel worse. She couldn't tell Mack what was going on. She feigned a joy she didn't feel. She missed the simple life she'd known before. Her job, her relationships, her very life seemed much too complicated today.

"Hey, Sydney. What's up?" said a familiar voice.

"Hi, Joe. I made a pot of fresh coffee. Help yourself."

Mumbling his thanks, Morrison poured a steaming cup. He eyed the sandwiches. "Are those for us?"

"Who else?"

Joe smiled broadly as he bit into his turkey sandwich.

"This is great. Thanks a lot."

Sydney shook her head in wonderment. He seemed so happy with simple things.

Morrison remained on his feet pacing the kitchen. He'd been sitting too long. Finally he halted at the patio door. Pulling back the curtain slightly, he peered outside. The activity around Hassan's house had picked up dramatically, beginning last night.

"Not much of a holiday, is it?" Sydney queried.

Joe Morrison cast Sydney a quizzical glance. "They never are. I hate holidays."

"Really? How come?"

"I'm not much of a family man," he said quietly. Then he hesitated, averting his eyes. Clearing his throat, he spoke softly. "I was married once. My wife and son were killed in a car accident."

"Oh, Joe, I'm so sorry."

Joe's words came slowly. "It was my fault. Anna Marie had been bugging me to get the brakes on the car fixed. I was a Chicago cop then. I was working on a big case. I put it off."

Joe faltered. He never talked about his past. He wasn't sure why he was now. Something about Sydney made him want to.

"Anna Marie had just picked up the baby from her mother's. She was heading home when the brakes failed. She and Joe Jr. were killed instantly."

Joe wiped the corner of his eye on his shirt. "I've never forgiven myself for that."

Sydney sat in silence. She didn't know what to say.

"I joined the FBI a year later. I had to get out of Chicago. I've always hated holidays since then. Besides, something always goes wrong."

"What do you mean?"

"I'm a cynical son of a bitch, Sydney. Holidays mean that you have to get together with relatives you can't stand. You eat yourself sick. Someone always gets into a fight. If that doesn't happen, you get lured into a false sense of security. People want to believe they're part of the Norman Rockwell dream. That's when something always goes wrong."

Sydney unexpectedly shivered. Joe had put her own edgy feelings into words. While Sydney yearned for a good old-fashioned Thanksgiving, she knew it could not be. Joe was right. Something was about to go wrong. She'd been feeling it all day.

Morrison glanced outside again. "It's coming down today, Sydney. I can feel it."

Sydney joined Morrison at the door and, glancing over his shoulder, peered outside.

"How do you know, Joe?"

His reply seemed sarcastic at first. "What day is it, Sydney?"

Playing along, she replied, "Why, it's Thanksgiving, of course. It's the day we set aside to give thanks."

Morrison's eyes were hard and focused. "What about Hassan? Do you think that bastard is giving thanks for all his American blessings?" Joe paused. "I've been trying to figure out what he's up to. I've played a hundred scenarios in my head. Nothing makes sense. But my gut never lies."

■

Noon

In a much shabbier part of town, another man was spending the day drowning in his own morbid thoughts. There were no holiday aromas in his cramped apartment, only the stink of cigarettes and whiskey. He glanced at his Thanksgiving dinner—stale bread and old bologna. But it didn't matter to Ralph Noland.

Pouring another shot, he tried to reach that state of intoxication where no one else, nothing else, mattered. He'd been drinking for hours. No matter how hard he tried he just couldn't get there. He watched television, hoping for a diversion. Local news about the lighting ceremony. Thanksgiving parades with children. He switched off the set. He was in no mood to watch football.

With bleary eyes, Noland turned his focus to the kitchen table where his revolver lay. Tears filled his eyes. He ran his fingers through his thickly matted hair. Today was Thanksgiving. The day had finally arrived. It would not be a day for Noland to give thanks. It would be a day of murder.

■

The balance of the afternoon went no better than the morning. Sydney had busied herself around the house, but without Sam, the holiday hours dragged by. Sam had been gone several hours when Sydney suddenly grew concerned. What was keeping him? It was a holiday after all, meager though their plans were. Something must have happened at the hospital to detain him. What, she couldn't fathom. A phone call about two o'clock gave her the answer.

When Dr. Carter made rounds early Thanksgiving morning, he determined that Lydia's condition was deteriorating. The stress of her father's outburst yesterday had taken its toll. Since drugs had failed, he scheduled a procedure to shock her heart back into a normal rhythm. Time had become a critical factor.

As a result of Hassan's erratic behavior, Lydia had been declared a ward of the court. Sam Ellis had been granted full authority to make all medical decisions regarding her care. He'd agreed fully with his colleague that the procedure had to take place immediately even though there were risks. Sam decided to remain by Lydia's side. A strange but unique bond had begun to form between Sam and this little girl. It was shortly after five o'clock when Sydney received his call.

"It's over," said Sam, "and I'm relieved. Cardioversion is a routine procedure but there's always the risk that the heart could stop beating."

"Is Lydia okay?" Sydney asked.

"She's fine. It took two attempts, but her heart reverted into a normal rhythm. She's still in recovery. She's being monitored carefully."

"May I see her, Sam?" Sydney pleaded.

"Sure. Come on over. Be careful, it's begun sleeting outside. Come to the OR and have me paged."

Sydney had dressed in a smart royal blue Escada suit. She'd fixed her make-up in preparation for the evening's work. She didn't have much time. She was due at the Plaza to begin preparations for the seven o'clock broadcast. She hurried to the hospital and found Sam quickly. True to his word, he slipped her into the recovery room. Lydia was still groggy from the sedation. The Ellises didn't remain with the child long. She was pale and listless.

Leaning over the bed, she kissed Lydia's forehead and whispered, "I love you, darling. I'll be back to see you later."

Sam led Sydney out of recovery and down the hallway. Sydney couldn't stop crying. The sight of Lydia, abandoned and alone, tore her apart. She wanted to remain with the child but she couldn't. Legally, Lydia was no relation to her. Emotionally, the two were completely attached.

"Oh, Sam! What's going to happen to her? Her father is a monster. She might be a ward of the court for now, but for how long? And then what? Isn't there anything we can do?"

"No, Sydney. Nothing. Hassan will be given his day in court to prove he is a well-intentioned, caring father. If no abuse or neglect can be proved, she'll be returned to his care. There's nothing more I can do. I've overstepped my bounds already."

"Joe believes, as I do, that Hassan plans to leave the city soon. What if he tries to take Lydia with him?"

Sam Ellis had no answer. While a security guard had been stationed in front of Lydia's door, the hospital was not a fortress. Security could not protect the child from her father. It was only a matter of time before Hassan—one way or the other—would regain control of Lydia. Sam pulled a clean handkerchief from his pocket. He tried to dab the tears from his wife's face. It was pointless. Her make-up was ruined. Black streaks of mascara ran down her cheeks.

"Honey," he chided gently. "You look a mess. Why don't you go into the doctor's lounge and fix your face? Didn't you say you were due at the Plaza soon?"

She nodded.

"There's nothing more you can do for Lydia now. I'll hang around here until she's settled in for the night."

Cupping Sydney's chin, he added, "It's not much of a Thanksgiving, is it, honey?"

Sydney didn't know whether to laugh or cry.

"Come on, sweetheart. I'll show you where the doctor's lounge is. We're still pretty sexist here at St. Vincent's. The lounge is designed primarily for the comfort of our male surgeons, but there is a tiny ladies locker room just inside. No one will bother you there. Take all the time you need."

Following Sam's directions, Sydney located the ladies locker room inside the doctor's lounge. Sam had been right. The space set aside for females was small and antiquated. There was a single stall, a sink, a few lockers, and a rickety table with a chair in front of a mirror. Overhead was a dim light. Sydney had to chuckle. How could she repair her make-up to go in front of the cameras under these conditions?

It didn't matter, she decided. What she really needed was a few quiet minutes to gather her thoughts and quiet her emotions. She had been there only a short time when she heard the door to the doctor's lounge open, then footsteps. The sound of the two voices—two voices that she recognized instantly—shattered any hope she harbored for peace and quiet.

Very quictly, Sydney rose and moved stealthily towards the door separating the ladies locker room from the rest of the lounge. Suddenly the door opened. She froze against the wall. Farhad Rajid glanced around briefly but failed to see Sydney behind the door. Hassan and Rajid remained just outside the closed door to the ladies room. Although they kept their voices subdued, Sydney heard every word.

"What is the plan for tonight?" Hassan asked.

"The last harvesting will take place shortly," Farhad answered. "The hotel is packed, every room filled. While all the other fools are glued to their windows waiting for the lights to go on, we will take it all. The poor man is there already enjoying a last bit of fun before the end."

Ali Hassan snickered.

"I told Scofield to take everything this time," Rajid continued, "the kidneys, the liver, even the heart. I've secured a buyer already for the heart. The others will dispose of the remains quickly then leave town. This time they will not need to be so careful."

Sydney's entire being chilled. The image of the cadaver found on the river bank flooded her mind. And the floaters. Skulls with no teeth. Hands with no fingers. Suddenly everything made sense. She feared the sound of her trembling limbs could be heard banging against the wall. She willed her being into silence.

"What about the doctor?" Hassan queried.

"Scofield knows this is the end. He has been warned to proceed no further. He is aware that once we leave tonight, our operation shuts down. He would not be foolish enough to proceed on his own. He understands that all our contacts go with us. The man seems relieved. He's made enough money."

"And the others?"

"Everyone involved has been paid well. After tonight, they too will disappear. The agency will have many jobs to fill within the system. The organ sharing program will revert back to its original purpose. No one will ever be the wiser. No one will ever know how many organs were diverted or how much money we made."

"You have done well, Farhad. The New Savak is most grateful. There will be a special place for you within the organization."

Sydney felt ill. She dared not breathe. If she were discovered, hers would be the next body found in the river. She wondered for a moment how much her organs might be worth.

"Dear God!" she prayed. "Help me."

"Listen carefully, Farhad. My business will be concluded shortly after eight o'clock. We will meet at the airport and leave by nine. How long will the procurement take?"

"Not long, brother. I should have no problem meeting you at the plane. I'll have to take an alternate route out of the Plaza. From what you tell me, the roads will be jammed."

"What about Lydia?" Rajid inquired.

Sydney tensed.

For the first time during their conversation, Hassan's voice took on a genuine tone of sadness. He spoke quietly.

"Lydia will not go with us. She is too sick to travel."

"I'm so sorry," the child's uncle declared.

Sydney could hear Hassan's sigh. "It must be done. No single person is worth jeopardizing our operation. I will spend a little time with her now. I will deal with the loss of my daughter later."

"All right, then," Farhad said. "I must go now. The others are waiting. Until tonight . . . . "

The voices faded. Sydney heard the door to the doctor's lounge open and then the footsteps ceased. The only sound in the doctor's lounge was the sound of her own heart beating. Sydney's quivering legs gave way. She sank to her heels. She couldn't believe what she had heard. She replayed the entire conversation in her head. She had to be absolutely certain that what she thought she had heard was indeed the truth. But there was no time.

She forced her trembling wrist to her face. The time. What was the time? It was ten minutes past six. Grabbing onto the door, she forced herself to her feet. She had to tell somebody. But who? Who would believe her? Joe Morrison? Police Chief Andrews? What she had heard was more depraved than anything anybody had imagined.

What about Lydia? Should she warn Sam? No, she reminded herself. Lydia was not the priority. Hassan had said he would be leaving her here. She was safe.

Time. Time was running out. She had no time to linger trying to decide just what the hell to do. She had only one choice. She had to find the one man she trusted to make sense out of this horribly senseless mess. Yes, there was only one man who could decide what was best to do. That man was Jacob Kahn. But where in the hell was he?

6:20 pm

Ralph staggered from the kitchen towards the bedroom window of his apartment. He'd been drinking now for over twenty-four hours. No amount of whiskey could dull the morose feelings he harbored inside. He had tried to sleep but when he closed his eyes, he imagined the scene that in only a few hours he would create. Bodies would be scattered everywhere. Screams of terror would pierce the night. The smell of blood would permeate the air. It would be just like 'Nam. Just like Maggie Hall.

No, this time it would be different. A little girl named Tanya Cole would be found by the switch. She'd be all dressed up with ribbons in her hair, but her dress would be drenched in blood. Her father would be powerless to help her. The friendly Vietnam veteran Ralph had met would be trapped inside the Winds when the building exploded.

"No!" Ralph cried. "No!"

He tried to blot the horrible images from his mind but he couldn't. And there was nothing he could do to prevent the tragedy. He thought about calling the police with an anonymous tip, but he was afraid. He thought about running away. Approaching the window cautiously, he pulled the tattered curtain aside. The sleet of earlier this afternoon had turned to a fine misting snow. Even though it was dark outside, Ralph knew they were there, just waiting for him to leave the building.

The Iranians had been there all day lingering outside. They knew sooner or later he'd have to flee. The commander's men had come to kill him, plain and simple. Noland was sure of it. He knew too much. He'd done too much. He wouldn't be permitted to live or to complete his first mission. Time was running out for the people who now jammed the Plaza and for their executioner, Ralph Noland.

Ralph turned his back on the window and made his way back to the kitchen. He put down his whiskey glass. There was something much more important that he needed. Reaching with unsteady hands, he secured his revolver. It was loaded. He grabbed his jacket. He stuffed the silencer in his jacket pocket.

Ralph staggered around his apartment a final time. He found his billfold. He wouldn't take any clothes. No time. He wouldn't bother with the keys to the truck. The Iranians wouldn't let him near it. He had a better way.

Cautiously, Ralph cracked the door of his apartment and peered down both sides of the hallway. No one was there. Only the faint whimper of a baby crying could be heard in the distance. The enticing aroma of turkey and dressing wafted down the dimly lit corridor, reminding Ralph he had not eaten.

Carefully he inched his way down the two flights of stairs towards the main door. Gripping his revolver, he was ready for anything, or anybody.

He located what he sought a short distance from the main door. With the butt of his gun, he shattered the glass, then he pulled the lever. The piercing wail of the fire alarm shattered the eerie silence. He hid in the shadowed doorway of a quiet apartment. He presumed no one was home. Soon the police and fire-fighters would come. He imagined the Iranians fleeing in panic.

The sound of people screaming echoed all around as tenants fled their apartments with their children in tow and what meager possessions they could carry. He was sorry to spoil their dinners but it couldn't be helped. He merged with the crowd as they fought their way outside. Then he disappeared into the darkness.

His trembling hand gripped his gun. Let them try to kill him if they must. Ralph Noland, Vietnam veteran, had no intention of going down without a fight.

The brutal assault of the cold snowy air sobered him. He had to see Kathleen. He had to see her one more time. He had a mission to complete. He only lived a half mile from the hospital. He could make it there on foot.

■

It was an unlikely group that gathered in the station's remote van parked less than a block from the main stage set up on the Plaza. The snow was falling steadily now. The temperature had plummeted into the twenties but the weather did not stop the crowd from gathering. The Plaza, deserted this morning, had begun to fill up by late afternoon. Cars lined the streets. Helicopters hovered overhead. People stood everywhere, jockeying for position. This year, as in so many past years, the cold, the crowds, even the snow only added to the holiday spirit.

Chief Andrews was just finishing Thanksgiving dinner at his mother's apartment on the Plaza when the call came through. He left immediately.

It had taken awhile to track down Joe Morrison. He had followed Ali Hassan to the hospital. He hadn't seen Sydney. Otherwise, he would have known that his puzzle had been solved, not by his men or his efforts, but by a woman eavesdropping on a conversation through the thin wall of a bathroom door.

Shaken to the core, Sydney had stumbled out of the ladies room to the nearest phone. Her only thought had been to call Jake Kahn. Not just because he would know what to do but because her loyalty as a reporter was to her boss. Let him decide who got the case. She wanted her station to have the exclusive story. She had located Jake at home. He was a widower with no family in the city. He had no holiday festivities to attend. He had planned simply to come to where he found himself now. To the Plaza, to the van, to oversee Sydney's coverage of the dedication of the Winds and the lighting ceremony.

He couldn't believe what Sydney had overheard. Now finally

all his many facts jotted on a yellow pad made sense. Horrible, evil sense.

He had asked the engineer and the other television personnel to leave the van. Go get coffee. Check the cameras. Test the microphones. Have a smoke. Anything but hang around. He needed a few precious minutes alone with Sydney and the two men who had the power to take action quickly, before one more life was lost.

He had fixed Sydney a cup of coffee laced with a healthy shot of brandy. She had less than thirty minutes before she went on the air. She had to get a hold of herself. With the others, there was no time to waste on pleasantries. He sat both men down and explained the facts. Neither man at first could believe Sydney's story.

It was Joe who spoke first. "Sydney, let me get this straight. You heard Farhad Rajid tell Hassan that they were taking everything this time, the liver, the kidneys, even the heart. Are you absolutely sure they were talking about human organs?"

"Think about it, Joe!" Sydney countered sharply. "Farhad Rajid is the Regional Director of Organ Procurement. Of course they were talking about human organs!"

Chief Andrews leaned forward. The lines furrowing his brow deepened. "This man ... Rajid ... then told the other man that they would dispose of the remains but, because it was the last time, they didn't have to be so careful. Right?"

Sydney nodded.

Andrews turned to Kahn. "Are you thinking what I am, Jake? Skulls with no teeth. Hands with no fingers. No goddamn means of identification!"

Kahn interjected, "The black man found on the river bank with only one kidney! My God, Tom! This is worse than we imagined! We don't have a deranged serial killer. We have a group of businessmen who kill people for their organs! I've never heard anything like it!"

Sydney glanced at her watch. "We don't have much time. Rajid said that while the others were watching the Plaza lights, they'd be carving this poor guy to pieces. We've got to do something."

"Where do we begin?" Andrews mused. "Sydney, think about the conversation again. Are you sure they didn't name the hotel?"

Sydney paused, replaying yet again every detail of the conversation in her mind. "No," she replied evenly. "All they said was that while the others were watching the lights, they'd be taking the organs."

"Let's think about this," Kahn said. "How many hotels are there on the Plaza?"

Joe remained silent. He'd never noticed.

"Four," Chief Andrews replied.

"That's right," Kahn responded. "Which ones would be sold out for the view?"

"Only two," the Police Chief replied. "The Ritz and the Michelangelo. I could send cars to both of them."

Joe Morrison bristled. "We can't converge on the hotel with a fleet of squad cars. To make a case, we have to catch them in the act. This matter should have been turned over to the FBI long ago!"

Andrews's voice rose with anger, "Finding bodies in the Missouri River is not that unusual. Maybe you should have had the courtesy to inform me of *your* investigation. Perhaps we would have discovered the link sooner."

"Well the FBI has jurisdiction now."

Jake Kahn interceded. "Gentlemen, we don't have time to argue. Jurisdiction is irrelevant. When I air the story, I guarantee that both the FBI and local police get full credit. For God's sake! This is bigger than all of us! Can't you work together?"

Two men stared at one another for a moment with competitive contempt. Kahn's words made sense. The time was 7:05 pm. Sydney would go on air in twenty-five minutes to begin her preliminary coverage. In less than an hour, the light switch would be thrown. One more man would be dead. There was no time to bicker. Besides, they still had an important matter to resolve. Which hotel was the one?

"I've got a hunch, but it's only a hunch where to go," Kahn said. "It's got to be the Michelangelo."

"Why?" Andrews inquired.

"Remember the hooker? Remember the maid? Neither one was from the Ritz. They both were connected to the Michelangelo. I don't think there's time to converge on both places. Besides,

Joe's right. To make the case, you have to catch them in the act. I suggest we focus on the Michelangelo."

"Okay," Andrews conceded. "We'll begin with the Michelangelo. But what floor? What room? We can't do a room by room search. It would take too much time. And it might alert the bastards that we're on to them."

Joe Morrison paused. He fingered his cigarette.

There was a sharp rap on the door. "Sydney! You're on in twenty minutes. Let's get situated."

"Shit!" she muttered. Turning to Kahn, she said, "How do I look?"

"Terrible," he replied. "But it can't be helped. You've done your job, little lady. Now go out and give the performance of your life. Pretend nothing's wrong. We'll handle the rest."

Sydney turned to Morrison. "Find the poor guy, Joe. Whoever he is, find him in time!"

Sydney exited the van and prepared to take her place on the covered platform. Tanya Cole was waiting for her, all dressed up in a green velvet dress with white ribbons in her hair.

"We've got to vacate the van," Kahn ordered. "The boys have to get to work. It wouldn't do not to go on the air as scheduled."

Everyone rose. Morrison turned to Chief Andrews.

"Come with me. Call for back-up but have them stay out of the way. I'll bring two guys and you bring two. Let's go to the Michelangelo. I've got a plan!"

"Philip, you've been edgy all afternoon. What's the matter?"

It was true. Philip Wentworth had been nervous and irritable for the past several hours.

"Please tell me," Kathleen pleaded.

Wentworth shot yet another glance towards the closed door of his room before uttering a reply. Then he looked back to the dinner tray before him.

"It's this crap," he said finally, pushing his Jell-O aside. "What kind of Thanksgiving dessert is this?"

Kathleen smiled with relief. "Having you alive and well enough to eat makes this the best Thanksgiving of all."

Philip's eyes seemed a bit mischievous when he replied, "Well since you put it that way . . . "

At last, Philip heard the knock at the door he had been expecting. He was not the least bit surprised when his favorite nurse, Mrs. O'Malley, appeared carrying a small brown paper bag.

"Good evening, Dr. Wentworth. I believe this is for you."

"I'm happy to see you, O'Malley. Did you find everything in order?"

"I did indeed," she replied. "You have a lovely home, Dr. Wentworth. Your plants, however, were in desperate need of watering. I did that straightaway."

"It's been awhile since I've been home, Mrs. O'Malley. I thank you for taking care of things. May I have the bag, please?"

Mrs. O'Malley placed the bag and Philip's house keys on the table and turned to leave. She smiled at her two favorite people. She yearned to laugh aloud. Kathleen had the look of a quizzical schoolgirl. Philip Wentworth looked plain scared. She left shaking her head in amusement.

"Thank you for your trouble, Mrs. O'Malley. You'll be the first to know how it turns out."

Waiting until they were alone, Philip turned his full attention to Kathleen.

"Please sit with me, here on the bed."

"What are you up to, Philip?" Kathleen inquired curiously.

Philip pretended to ignore her. He only wished he could grab her hand and drop to his knees. That was not yet possible. Instead, he fumbled in the bag for the small rectangular box. Trying to keep the box hidden under the folds of his sheets, he took Kathleen's hand and gently caressed her fingers.

"You cracked the shell around my heart, Kathleen. That's something no one else has ever done. It took a bullet for me to realize how precious you and life really are."

Nervously, Philip let go of his lady's hand and retrieved the jewelry box. He struggled to open the lid but his hands were shaking so violently now that he nearly dropped the precious contents.

"I love you, Kathleen. But I need time."

"Time?" she questioned. "Time for what?"

"A lifetime to show you how much."

Reaching for her hand, Philip displayed a very simple diamond ring. There were tears in his eyes when he spoke.

"This was my mother's ring. When I lost her, I thought I'd never be able to love again. You've taught me love, Kathleen. My mother told me to live and then so would she. You opened up my heart and gave me life. I know she'd want you to have this." Taking a deep breath, he prepared to ask the big one. "When your divorce is final and the time is right, will you marry me, Kathleen Callihan Clay Stein?"

For a moment, Kathleen was speechless. She remembered one of their first conversations so many months ago. It was then she had asked another important question. "I'm Kathleen Stein for now. But who will I be when this is over?"

Now she knew. Without a doubt. She, with courage, had revealed her scars. Philip through love had healed them. In truth they were married now. A ceremony of words didn't matter. Their souls had already and forever bonded. And so, with tears of joy, she gave him the only answer her heart would allow. And that of course was yes.

■

The streets were treacherous from a crusty mix of ice and snow. Ralph fell several times as he trudged his way the half mile towards the hospital. Somehow he managed to keep moving forward, all the while glancing behind him. Waiting for pain. Waiting for death. But he remained unhurt. The brutal north wind chilled him. Huge snowflakes fell upon Ralph's uncovered head, hands, and face. He was grateful for the bitter cold. His senses, dulled from the alcohol, had sharpened. But Ralph's deranged mind couldn't think.

Ralph's life was in shambles. He had to get out of town, but he had no money. He had to kill Kathleen to collect from the commander. Noland had only one chance to escape. He had to see Kathleen one more time. Ralph didn't know if he had the guts to shoot her even though it was his only way out.

The hospital had taken on a holiday air. Families, having finished their own dinners, had journeyed to visit those less fortunate. Ralph had no trouble blending in with the people who roamed the hallways. He concealed his revolver. He knew he reeked of whiskey but this couldn't be helped. He took the passenger elevator up to the sixth floor. He had neither the time nor the inclination to change into the uniform of a janitor. He had a mission. A mission he had to execute quickly.

The elevator door opened. Ralph held his breath. The nurses would surely recognize him. Ralph didn't want any trouble. He didn't want anybody else to get hurt. His hand rested atop his revolver, hidden in the top fold of his pants.

Strangely, the nurses' station was empty. Ralph was puzzled. Had there been an emergency which commanded their attention?

Was it Dr. Wentworth or Kathleen? There were only two patients on this floor. Slowly, Ralph edged down the corridor towards their rooms. A single uniformed policeman remained stationed in front of Kathleen's door, but a crowd, including a second policeman, gathered around Philip's.

"Oh shit!" Ralph swore. An emergency with Philip Wentworth could complicate his plans. He approached the first policeman cautiously.

"What's up?" he dared to ask.

The policeman whose name was Bob Wiley stared at him quizzically. Ralph hastened to explain his appearance.

"I'm the janitor. You know me, man. I'm the guy who brings you coffee."

"Oh yeah," the cop responded. "You look different."

"I'm not working tonight," Ralph declared. "As a matter of fact, I have to leave town. My mother had a heart attack. I just came to tell Mrs. Stein good-bye. She's a nice lady. She's been real good to me."

Bob Wiley smiled. "Well then," he said. "You'll be happy to hear the good news. Dr. Wentworth just proposed."

"Yeah?" he questioned. "What was her answer?"

The policeman's retort sounded sarcastic. "What do you think?"

Noland began perspiring heavily. The heat in the hospital was oppressive. He wished he could remove his jacket. He had to think what to do. He realized he must look stupid. He tried to continue his conversation, all the while his mind was racing to concoct a plan.

"Are you married?" he inquired.

Wiley merely nodded. His facial expression remained stoic. Ralph took it as a positive response. "I bet me and you could give her a piece of advice before she says I do."

The man smirked. "Yeah, I'd tell her to say I don't!"

Ralph laughed along with the cop.

"Why don't you join the others next-door? Someone brought a bottle of champagne to toast the happy couple. It's pretty quiet up here. The nurses are sneaking a little drink. Even Dr. Ellis is there."

Ralph shook his head perhaps a bit too strongly. He hesitated, seemingly faltering.

"I don't want to bother them. Could you let me into her room for a minute? I'd like to write her a little note before I leave." Ralph pretended to glance at his watch. "I have to catch a plane soon."

Officer Wiley hesitated briefly. "I guess it's okay. But hurry up, pal. I don't want to get into trouble."

Ralph was permitted entry into Kathleen's room. He hoped the policeman would shut the door behind him while he thought what to do. He didn't. The door to Kathleen's suite remained open. He wished he had quick access into Philip's room. He didn't. He couldn't push past the two policemen and the staff to shoot her.

Dejected, he walked past her easel to the window. He glanced outside. The snow was falling heavily now but in the distance he could see the Plaza. He shuddered. In less than an hour, they'd all be dead. The little girl and her father. And countless others. Mothers, fathers, little children. All there to sing Christmas carols and watch the lights. Then there were the select few invited to the big party at the Winds. All dressed up in their finest regalia. Just like at Maggie Hall. In less than an hour, when the building exploded, they'd be killed as well.

Trembling violently now, Ralph turned away from the window. There on the small table near the sofa rested the evening paper. The headline read: *"1000 Expected to Attend the Dedication of the Winds."*

He picked up the paper and peered closer. To the right of the headline was a photograph of a beautiful little girl. She was all dressed up with a huge smile on her pretty face. Her name was Tanya Cole. The caption read: *"Kansas City's Sweetheart, Tanya Cole, to Light the Plaza. A Record Number 300,000 Expected to Attend."*

Ralph Noland began to weep. "Oh God!" he sobbed. "What have I done?"

He threw his glance back to the window. "I'd stop it if I could!" he cried.

What could he do? Who could he call? There were two policemen posted right outside the door. He could tell them to stop it. Who would believe him? He'd be locked up as a lunatic. Then when it happened, he'd be blamed. He'd spend the rest of his life in jail. And for what? Everyone would still be dead.

He glanced outside through the snow to the Plaza a final time.

"Tell me what to do, dear Lord. And I will!"

It was then his prayer was answered.

Turning his back on the window, he walked to Kathleen's easel. A black charcoal pencil rested near her sketch pad. He had used it so many times before to jot her a happy note when she was not around and he'd brought her coffee. He fingered the worn pencil a final time. He had one last note to write. He had to concentrate. He wanted his words to be clearly understood. He had to force his trembling hand to be calm.

"Michael Clay ordered me to kill you. I tried but I couldn't do it! I shot the doctor by mistake. The Iranian commander made me wire the Plaza. It will explode precisely at 8:00. So will the Winds. You must stop it!"

Ralph could hold back the tears no longer. The tears he'd held inside since Vietnam. His last words to Kathleen came from the depth of his heart.

"I'm so sorry for everything. Please forgive me. I truly wanted to be your friend."

The sound of happy laughter echoed down the hallway through the door. Then he heard her voice.

"Thank you! Thank you, everyone!"

Kathleen would be returning to her room soon. He couldn't let her come upon him. Not like this. And he couldn't shoot her. He couldn't let her be counted among the dead. She was too decent. She was one of the few people on the face of the earth who'd been kind to him.

Ralph Noland withdrew his revolver, then he glanced at his watch and noted the time. He wanted to remember the last minute he had inhabited the earth. The time was 7:15 pm.

He placed the gun by his right temple and closed his eyes.

"Father, forgive me," he prayed. Then he pulled the trigger.

The sound of a gunshot shattered the laughter on the sixth floor. Philip froze. Kathleen screamed. The nurses ran for cover. Both policemen drew their revolvers. Motioning everyone down, they entered the room, their eyes darting in all directions. Their guns were leveled, ready to fire.

"Oh my God!" Kathleen cried out. "What's happening?"

"Stay here with Philip!" Sam Ellis ordered. "I'll be right back!"

Sam slowly entered Kathleen's room. The two policemen, with their weapons now holstered, stood in front of the body. The cop named Bob Wiley was badly shaken.

"The guy said he knew her. He only wanted to leave her a note. That's why I let him into her room. I had no idea he had a gun."

"What guy?" Sam demanded.

"The janitor." Wiley turned to his fellow officer, Tim Mitchell, for confirmation. "You remember him. He's the guy who always brought us coffee."

Sam Ellis slowly approached the body and knelt down beside it. Instinctively, he reached for his wrist. There was, of course, no pulse. Neither was there a recognizable face.

"What was his name?" Sam asked. "Does anybody know his name?"

Neither policeman could remember the janitor's name.

Feeling bile rising in his throat, Officer Wiley had to walk away. The sight of Ralph Noland made him ill. As he looked around the room, his eyes came to rest upon the sketch pad and the last words Ralph Noland had written.

"Look at this!" he exclaimed, turning to the others.

Sam and the other officer hurried to the easel. At first, Sam could not comprehend what he was reading. Then slowly what little color remained on the doctor's face drained away. Sam did not visualize the Winds exploding. Neither did he see the Plaza. His thoughts were focused only on two people he cared very deeply about. One was his wife. The other was Tanya Cole.

"We have to stop it!" he cried.

"Stop what?" Wiley retorted.

"The bombing of the Plaza and the Winds!" Sam countered sharply.

The second policeman stepped forward.

"Sir, we have no way to confirm what this man has claimed. He's dead. How could we possibly determine where a bomb might be placed? The Plaza covers over a square mile. It could be anywhere!"

Sam wasn't listening. "My God!" he shouted. "What time is it?"

Mitchell glanced at his watch. "It's 7:25 pm."

"How in the name of God *can* we stop it?" Wiley asked.

"I'll call the captain," Mitchell declared. "Maybe he'll know what to do."

"We don't have time to wait!" Sam pleaded. "I have to get there! I have to warn them!"

Mitchell was busy trying to locate his captain. It was Wiley who had to answer. "There's no way, Dr. Ellis. Even if we get you a police escort, traffic will be backed up for miles. People go nuts when it comes to the lighting ceremony. They park all over the streets. I've seen cars abandoned on the sidewalks. There's no way even emergency vehicles can get through the Plaza."

Sam stared at the policeman incredulously. His own expression was nearly childlike when he stammered, "You don't understand. My wife is there."

Mitchell returned to Sam and to Wiley. He shook his head helplessly. "I located the captain. He's trying to mobilize the bomb squad now. Frankly, I don't know what we can do. There's no time to find the bomb and no time to evacuate all those people . . ."

Sam thought to call the television station. He'd forgotten it was a holiday. He got a recorded message. He tried Sydney's cellular phone. It wasn't on. He was getting frantic.

Suddenly he had an idea. "How long would it take to get to the Plaza by helicopter?"

The two policemen exchanged worried glances.

It was Wiley who responded. "Normally, just a few minutes. But there's a problem. The air space over the Plaza is congested with low-flying aircraft tonight. It's the only time small planes and choppers can hover overhead without restriction." The officer hesitated and then asked, "Who's got a chopper?"

"I do!" Sam exclaimed, bolting from the room.

Trying to steady his mind and his nerves, he struggled to think while the two policemen gazed upon him as a man gone mad. The chopper was on the roof. Life Flight had not been dispatched today. But where in the hell was the crew?

■

The lobby of the Michelangelo Hotel was packed. Most of the people in the lobby were dressed in cocktail attire. They were folks who had made their reservations a year in advance to be part of the festivities Thanksgiving night. Others, dressed more casually in jeans and heavy jackets, had merely sought refuge in the lobby from the cold and the snow.

There was no room to walk and barely enough air to breathe as seven men tried to push their way through the crowd towards the reception area. It was Joe Morrison, Tom Andrews and Jake Kahn who approached the front desk. The other men had been ordered to remain behind in hopes they could spot something that would help them locate a faceless, nameless victim who would be carved to pieces within minutes for the price of his viable organs. Morrison's men were looking for Farhad Rajid, a man they would recognize instantly. The detectives were looking for a prostitute—someone, anyone, who looked suspicious. No one fit the bill.

A young woman in her mid-twenties stood behind the ornate

mahogany desk. She was obviously frazzled by the demands of the boisterous crowd. She was not pleased to see three new faces.

"Yes, sir?" she said.

"Get me the manager!" Morrison demanded.

"Sir, I'm afraid that's not possible. He's terribly busy. Is there something I can help you with?"

Morrison threw his badge upon the desk. "Get me the manager! Damn it! Now!"

Seeing the FBI badge, the young woman nodded, then immediately disappeared through a door. In less than two minutes a man appeared—a fastidiously groomed gentleman in his late fifties. He had gray-blond hair, small rather cold eyes, and a mouth that turned down at the edges.

"I am Maurice Blumenthal, the general manager," he said in a British accent. "I understand you wish to see me."

Joe Morrison was edgy. The minutes were ticking away. "Is there somewhere we can talk in private?" he asked.

"Really, sir, as you can see, I'm quite busy. Can't this wait until tomorrow?"

This time Tom Andrews intervened. "I'm the Chief of Police. And no, sir, it can't. Now where can we talk?"

With a disgusted grunt, the general manager of the Michelangelo led the three men back to his private office. Blumenthal was also perspiring now. But it was from annoyance, not the heat.

"Can we make this fast? I have a big party upstairs. And the lights will be turned on shortly. What is this about?"

Morrison was rapidly getting angry. That wasn't good. His gut was killing him. "I understand there's an escort service that operates within the hotel. I need to know where."

The general manager of the Michelangelo Hotel feigned shock and surprise.

"We would never tolerate that kind of behavior here! This is a five-star, first-class hotel!"

"Cut the bullshit, Blumenthal," Morrison countered.

"I don't know what you're talking about," he repeated.

Now it was Andrews who was getting angry. He stepped forward and grabbed the haughty man by his silk tie.

"Look, you little prick, we don't have time for games. A hooker was arrested just a few days ago right outside your front door. A hooker everybody around here seemed to know well. My friend, Joe Morrison, asked you a question. I want a straight answer. On what floor and in what rooms do these people operate?"

Maurice Blumenthal was scared. Both his reputation and his job were at stake. If he answered incorrectly, he could lose it all. He tried to continue the charade.

Jake Kahn had remained silent. He saw an opening he couldn't pass up. He knew what the man was trying to do, but time was too precious to waste. He decided to call his bluff.

"This bastard isn't going to cooperate, Joe. Tom, call in every policeman in the area! Surround the hotel! My camera crew is set up outside, ready to film. My reporter is already on air covering the ceremony. I'll have her switch live to the Michelangelo. We'll evacuate the whole goddamn hotel, then we can search room by room. My God! What a story! An exclusive high-dollar prostitution ring busted right here at the Michelangelo Hotel on Thanksgiving night! That's better than the lighting ceremony anytime!"

"Wait just a minute!" Blumenthal stammered. "You can't do that!"

Jake Kahn headed for the door. It was in a deep commanding voice that he roared, "The hell I can't! Just watch me!"

"Stop!" Blumenthal pleaded. His starched, white shirt had begun to wilt from the sweat now exuding from his body.

"All I can tell you is that if such a thing were going on—and I can't say that it is—they would probably be operating from the fourth floor."

"Why?" Morrison countered.

"Those are our finest suites. Men who pay the price for a high-dollar hooker usually want the best."

Tom Andrews stepped forward. He took a softer approach with the trembling man. It was apparent Blumenthal was rapidly losing his composure. They had no time to risk his falling apart.

"Look, a man's life is at stake. If we don't locate him soon, he will be murdered. We think a number of men have already been murdered right here in your hotel. You have enough to answer for, Mr. Blumenthal. Don't add one more problem to your list. For the love of God, help us! Where would we find him?"

Maurice Blumenthal locked eyes with the Chief of Police. He was terrified. He was sincere when he answered. "I don't know."

In truth, he didn't know. For a price, he turned a blind eye on the illegal act of prostitution within his hotel. He sought not to know the details. Too much knowledge made him vulnerable.

Morrison glanced at his watch. The time was 7:35 pm.

"Come on!" he shouted. "We don't have time to waste on this bastard. Let's go!"

Jake Kahn had remained poised by the door to the office. As the others were wearing the man down, he was going over the facts in his mind. An idea struck him.

"There was a maid who was found dead in the river. She worked in your hotel. Her name was Anna-Marie Lopez. What do you know about her?"

"I don't know anything about her. Wasn't her death ruled a suicide?"

Jake Kahn ignored his answer. He was digging for something else. "She worked nights sometimes, right?"

Blumenthal shrugged. "I don't know. Perhaps the night supervisor could tell you. Her name is Loretta."

Morrison could wait no longer. They had to get to the fourth floor.

"Find this Loretta. Have her meet us up on the fourth floor immediately." Morrison paused momentarily. "One more thing, Blumenthal. Do you have a master key to the suites up on four?"

Blumenthal's haughty response was ludicrous. "Sir, this is a modern first-class hotel. We use electronic door cards."

"Well get me a fucking master key card or we'll kick every god-damn door down! You got that, Blumenthal?"

He got it. He picked up the phone immediately. He could hardly find his voice to talk.

The lobby was still packed; the elevators jammed. Motioning for the other men to join them, Morrison, Andrews and Kahn found the stairs and began running to the fourth floor. Each man was preoccupied with his own thoughts.

Morrison wondered just how many rooms they would have to search before they found the one? Andrews wondered how much time the unsuspecting victim had before he was simply another cadaver added to their already grisly list?

Wheezing, Jake Kahn was the only man not conditioned for the physical journey up the stairs. Briefly he wondered if he might have the *big one* before he made it. His thoughts turned to Anna-Marie Lopez. Could she have entered a room by mistake? What suite was it? What would she have encountered when she did so?

Susan M. Hoskins

49

Crouched just behind the pilot, Sam Ellis had to shout to be heard above the chopper's roar.

"Can you set it down near the building? Every minute counts."

Bolting from Kathleen's room, Sam had located his pilot in the hospital cafeteria, drinking coffee and chatting with the staff. The chopper was poised on the pad, fueled, and ready for takeoff. This flight would be unlike any other Mark Horner had ever made as he guided his chopper towards the Plaza. It was tricky. The closer he got, the more congested his air space. Never before had he shared the sky with so many other aircraft. He brought the chopper down as low as he could. There he hovered, beaming his floodlights in all directions as he studied the multimillion-dollar project called the Winds.

The twenty-five-story office building was aglow. Cars were packed in the parking lot. There was quite a crowd to celebrate the dedication of the Winds. The time was 7:42 pm.

The experienced Life Flight pilot was satisfied. The unbroken ground adjacent to the office building, where the next phase of construction was scheduled to begin, seemed solid. He decided to give it a try.

Glancing back to Sam, he shouted, "I'll get you as close as I can, Dr. Ellis."

Sam gripped the pilot's shoulder tightly. "Thanks, Mark. Once I'm out, I want you to move the chopper a safe distance away

315

from the building. Don't go near the Plaza. If I'm not successful, we're going to have a major disaster here. I don't want you hurt. We're going to need you."

Mark Horner landed his chopper without incident. Sam prepared to descend quickly.

"Radio in. I want St. Vincent's on full alert! Pray we're in time!"

Checking the perimeter of his building, the security guard at the Winds heard the commotion of the helicopter's roar. Choppers made him nervous, still reminded him of Vietnam. He approached the aircraft cautiously and he tried to wave the annoying chopper away. The sky above the Plaza was jammed with curious spectators anxious for a panoramic view of the lighting ceremony. He figured this was just one more curious spectator. No one had told Charles Cole that a guest would be arriving at Gary Atwell's party by helicopter.

As he neared the aircraft, he noticed that it bore the title *"LIFE FLIGHT."* Suddenly the intrusion made even less sense. Cole stood back as a man jumped from the idling chopper. Instantly Charles Cole recognized his face.

"What in the name of God are you doing here?" he yelled to Sam Ellis.

Frantically, as precious seconds ticked away, Sam grabbed Charles by the arm and urged him quickly towards the building.

"I don't have much time to explain, so listen carefully, Charles. A man committed suicide at the hospital a few minutes ago. He left a note."

Sam grabbed a piece of paper from his pants pocket. On the flight there, he had jotted the words contained in the message verbatim. He knew that the exact words might be important. He handed Charles the torn piece of paper.

Retrieving the flashlight he kept attached to his belt, Cole tried to make sense out of Sam's scribbling. He was aghast.

"The man claims he's wired the Winds to explode!" Charles cried. "That's not possible! Who is this man?"

"You wouldn't know him," Sam countered quickly. "He was a janitor at the hospital. His name was Ralph Noland."

Charles Cole felt his knees wobble. He remembered the man

who claimed to be an electrical contractor. He remembered their conversations. Ralph Noland had served in Vietnam just like himself. The man bore the scars of the war, that much Charles Cole had determined. He knew one thing to be true in this moment. If Ralph Noland claimed to have wired the Winds to explode, then that is precisely what he had done.

"Oh God!" he cried. "It must be true! We've got to find the bomb!"

With a sick sinking feeling in his gut, Charles Cole glanced to his watch. The time was nearly 7:47 pm.

Sam gripped Charles Cole tightly by the shoulders. "The lunatic claims he's wired the Plaza as well. I've got to try to stop it!"

For a moment the anguish in Cole's eyes was unbearable. His wife and baby daughter were there, not on the outskirts of the Plaza but centered in the place of honor. Sam held him tightly as the poor man began to tremble.

"You worked demolition in the Army just like this guy, right? Put yourself in his place. If you wanted the Plaza to explode precisely at 8:00 Thanksgiving night, how would you do it?"

Cole's mind focused quickly. His answer was instantaneous.

"I'd set the charges to go off when the main light switch was thrown."

"Exactly what I thought!" Sam exclaimed. "I've got to stop the lighting ceremony!"

"Oh my God . . . Tanya . . . !"

"Get a hold of yourself, Charles. You're the only one who can find the bomb in *this* building! You've got to do it!"

Charles Cole was a man of honor. There were a thousand people trapped inside his building. With less than ten minutes to go, there was no time for a safe evacuation. He was their only hope. He bolted inside his building as Sam began running to the Plaza.

■

Tom Andrews positioned his two men at the west corner of the fourth floor. Morrison stationed his back-up, George Massoud and Ned Powell, at the end of the opposite hallway. Andrews,

Morrison and Kahn remained poised by the elevators waiting for Blumenthal and the night supervisor to arrive. It was quiet except for occasional laughter and bits of inebriated chatter that wafted into the hallway. These were the best suites in the hotel—facing directly north—offering guests the choicest view of the lighting ceremony. Most guests reserved these suites a year in advance to accommodate their lavish Thanksgiving night parties. All but one man was enjoying the festivities. That was the one they had to find.

Suddenly the sound of a cellular phone intruded upon the edgy stillness.

Police Chief Andrews fumbled in his jacket pocket and pulled out the phone, quickly extending the antenna. This was a phone to be used only in emergencies. This was the phone that meant trouble. He listened intently as the message was relayed. Then he uttered only one word: "fuck."

He kept his voice as low as possible when he spoke. "Let me get this straight. You're telling me that some crackpot, who just blew his brains out, claims some Iranian commander made him wire the Plaza to explode at 8:00. And you want me to take this seriously? You've got to be kidding! Look, I've got my hands full up here. You've done the right thing, Mitchell. Have the bomb squad check things out, but you won't be able to get near the Plaza buildings until the crowd thins."

Andrews shook his head with pure disgust, all the while thinking that the nut cakes were getting fruitier every year. "No, I can't stop the lighting ceremony. Not based on this. We've had bomb scares before."

There was one man who had a look of horror plastered on his face. He had overheard the entire conversation. Nothing struck him as odd until he heard the words "some Iranian commander." It was then he remembered the gnawing feeling that had troubled him all day, and he knew his worst fears were hovering on the brink of reality.

"Hold it!" he cried.

The sense of urgency in Joe Morrison's voice caught Chief Andrews off-guard.

Morrison glanced at his watch. It was twelve minutes before 8:00.

"Holy mother of God!" he swore.

Grabbing the Police Chief by the sleeve of his jacket, he barked, "Take it seriously, Tom! I don't have time to explain! I just know it's true!"

Luckily, Tom Andrews had not broken the connection.

"Mitchell, call in every cop in the city, on-duty, off-duty, everybody! I need every available unit to converge on the Plaza now! Put the fire department, rescue squads and hospitals on full alert! We've got the potential for a major disaster here! I'll set up an immediate command post in the lobby of the Michelangelo! Got that? I'll try to call the mayor!"

Andrews signaled for his men. Then he confronted Joe Morrison a final time.

"Looks like you've got jurisdiction here, pal! I got a bigger mess on my hands!"

Andrews together with his men fled the stairs leaving Joe with only George Massoud and Ned Powell. The door to the service elevator opened. Maurice Blumenthal had located Loretta, the night supervisor.

Time had become more than of the essence. Time had become the enemy. Morrison had none to spare. He had this crisis to settle. Then he had yet another one close at hand.

He jerked the hotel manager and the night supervisor roughly aside. He ignored Blumenthal. His eyes were riveted upon Loretta.

"You remember the maid?"

"Yes," the mature black woman answered. "She was a friend of mine."

"Were you working the night she disappeared?"

"Yes, sir. I am the last one who saw her alive."

"Do you remember the assignment you gave her?"

The woman's soft eyes filled with tears. "I remember it well. I asked her to deliver towels and clean a suite on this floor. These particular guests stay here quite often. They're very demanding."

Morrison held his breath as his eyes scanned the hallway. "Did they have a favorite room?" he dared to ask.

The supervisor of housekeeping nodded. "Yes, sir. It was Suite 415."

"That's it!" he told his men.

"But sir," Loretta countered. "Anna-Marie never made it to their room. That's why I remember. They called at midnight. They were angry that the maid had not cleaned their suite or delivered clean towels. We started searching for Anna-Marie. I never knew what happened until they found her body in the river."

Joe Morrison sagged. "I'll have to do a room by room search. Did you get me a card?"

Maurice Blumenthal handed Morrison the master key card. With a curt nod, Joe dismissed the hotel manager and the night supervisor. He told them to get the hell out of the way.

Morrison had a problem. With only three of them, they had neither time or back-up for a room by room search. He had to gather his wits. A thought crossed his mind. Start where the maid was supposed to go. Assume she made an error.

"Jake, stay here by the elevator. Don't let anyone off. George, Ned, follow me."

The men took out their guns and readied the chambers. Following Joe's lead, they moved quickly but quietly to the far end of the east hallway.

With no time Morrison had only his raw gut instinct to rely on. "Come on, come on," he told himself. "Don't let me down."

Nearing the end of the hallway, the hair on his neck stood on edge. There were three suites clustered together—415, 413, and 411. Briefly he turned toward each one, hoping for some sound to alert him. Suite 415. Nothing. Suite 411. Nothing. Pivoting to 413, his gut lurched.

Signaling his men to take their positions, Joe grasped the door knob to Suite 413. It wouldn't turn. With his gun poised and ready to fire in his right hand, he slipped the control card into the electronic lock with his left. He waited for the blinking green light. Then as quietly as possible he pulled the card out. He nodded to his men. He turned the knob. He threw open the door and yelled, "Freeze, FBI!"

All but one man did. Instinctively the ex-cop named Thomas drew out his own revolver and fired. He missed. Joe Morrison didn't. He killed the man instantly with a single, precise shot to the heart.

"Whose next?" Morrison shouted.

Nathan, the owner of the escort service, had dismissed his prostitute an hour ago. He had remained behind simply to collect the last of his money. He looked for a means of escape. There was none.

Farhad Rajid remained defiantly mute. He said nothing. He did nothing. He was intelligent enough to recognize that it was over. His operation was finished. Yet, it didn't matter. He had served the New Savak well. He had funded the Cause. Being caught was simply the price he had to pay. His brother would carry on without him.

Poised over a body on a bloodied rubber sheet, William Scofield cowered like a stricken animal. Then, he held up his hands in surrender.

"Oh fuck!" Morrison swore.

In his bloodied gloves, he dangled a human organ.

■

Gary Atwell was furious. Someone had informed him a helicopter was trying to land on his property. He had excused himself from the party in the penthouse and taken the express elevator directly to the lobby. He wanted to make sure the security guard had everything under control. He had to hurry. He only had a few minutes before he'd be needed center stage. In just a few minutes the building would go dark. Then just after the Plaza lights and the Winds were illuminated, the coverage would switch to the party in the Penthouse for the official dedication of the Winds. There was no time to waste on the nuisance of an intruder.

Seeing Cole running into the building, he demanded an explanation. "What's going on here?"

Charles Cole spoke quickly. Every word he wasted was a second lost. "There's a bomb in this building. I need your help to find it."

Like Cole, Gary Atwell's first reaction was one of disbelief. But glancing into Cole's eyes, he saw the truth. He saw the terror.

"I'll call the police . . . . "

"There's no time."

For perhaps the first time in Gary Atwell's privileged life, he had to relinquish power. "What do you want me to do?"

Cole said nothing. Rather he had to force his legs to remain still while his eyes quickly scanned the lobby.

"Where would he place it?" he asked. Then remembering Sam's words, he chided himself. "Where would *I* place it?"

Not here, he quickly determined. Not in the lobby. The lobby of the Winds was terribly ornate. It was the first part of the building a visitor would see. No expense had been spared. It had a marble floor and a high ceiling. Too high for easy access. It had huge decorative columns. And while the bomb could have been placed at the rear of any of the columns, it would be far too risky to hide the bomb here. There were too many interested parties— from the construction engineers to the high priced interior designers—whose job it was to make sure the lobby looked good. No, Noland wouldn't have risked placing the explosives here.

A huge winding staircase led up to the mezzanine. Cole flew up the flight of stairs with Atwell close behind. The mezzanine, while certainly attractive, represented an entirely different look. Here is where reason began to prevail and economics became a factor. Here is where conservative measures were employed to begin saving dollars.

Instead of a marble floor, there was durable carpet. The decorative columns and high ceiling were absent. There was a low grid ceiling with removable panels designed for easy access.

Cole's eyes immediately scanned the ceiling. A few yards from the elevator he saw two of the panels askew. It was a long shot but it was all he had. He had no ladder. He had no time to find one. He searched for something, anything, to boost him.

"Help me!" he shouted.

Together he and Atwell inched a ceramic flower urn directly below the ceiling panels. He fumbled for the flashlight in his hip pocket. It was the one item he, as a security guard, never forgot to carry. Balancing himself on the urn, he slid the panels aside. Then he hoisted himself up through the hole for a closer look. He was a thin, agile man. Even so, it was a terribly tight squeeze. He beamed the flashlight in all directions. Then he saw it about three feet away. Several charges of dynamite bound together. He couldn't reach it from where he was.

His first impulse was to try. His second thought was to wait and think. What would Noland have done?

Sweat began dripping from his forehead.

"Pretend you're Noland. What would you do? What did he do?"

He directed his flashlight yet again on the explosives. This would do damage to be certain. But it was not sufficient to level the building. There had to be more than one charge. Yes, Noland would have set more than one charge. That Cole quickly determined. He had no time to find it. Dismantling this one, even if he could, would be useless if there were others.

Something very quickly struck him as odd. He beamed his flashlight in every direction around the explosives. There was no timing device. Where was the detonator? Ralph Noland didn't have it. He was dead. Yet in his suicide note, he asked that the bombing be stopped. He didn't name anyone else except the Iranian. If Ralph Noland didn't possess the detonator, who did?

Charles wiped the sweat away which was clouding his vision. There had to be more than one charge of explosives. Somehow they were tied together. The detonating device had to be internal, somewhere within the building. But where?

Suddenly the entire building went dark. The time was 7:55 pm.

■

Unlike Charles Cole, Sam didn't dare think. He focused only on running as fast as his body would permit. The first two blocks were not the problem. It was when he neared the periphery of the Plaza that the crowd thickened. He tried to elbow his way through. People, thinking he was jockeying for better position, knocked him back.

He began shouting, "There's an emergency! Let me through!"

In the distance, he heard first the song of the Christmas carolers and then he heard the sirens. He yelled even louder. Why couldn't anyone hear him?

■

What's happening?" Charles cried, inching his way back through the hole. Everything was dark. His flashlight was the only source of light.

Gary Atwell's voice quivered. "The building's gone dark. The computer has shut everything down. The lights won't come back on until eight o'clock."

Suddenly like the rush of lights that would soon illuminate the building, Charles Cole had his answer.

"Oh my God!" he exclaimed. "He's tied it into the computer! But how?"

Scrambling back down the stairs, he and Atwell ran for the control room. Unlocking the door, they stared at the awesome equipment.

"How do we shut the computer down?" he asked.

"I have no idea," Atwell countered. "Roger takes care of all that. We could call him."

Charles Cole wanted to cry at the sheer absurdity of the situation. They had no electrical power. More than likely the phone lines were dead. They had no time. And Gary Atwell, the developer of the Winds, was useless. Charles Cole was on his own.

Cole focused his light and all his attention on the computer. He studied the setup carefully. He called upon his training in the Army for guidance. He tried to calm his nerves. He dared not think about the time. He had to remember the logic of computers. Every cable had a purpose. The computer sat on a large desk. To the side of the computers were the television monitors used for security. The monitors were tied into every floor and into the parking levels of the garage. In this situation, they were useless. For an instant his eyes found the monitor located on the Penthouse floor. There were a thousand people trapped upstairs unaware that their deaths were imminent.

He forced his attention to the computer. Directly behind the computer were three panel boxes.

"Which one?" he questioned. "Which one?"

"They're marked," Atwell offered. "Look closer."

Cole pointed the flashlight. The box on the right nearest the television monitors was marked *Security*. To the far left was the one that controlled *Heating and Air*. It was the one in the center that Charles needed. It was marked *Electrical*.

"That's it!" he cried. "Somehow the explosives are tied into the electrical system of the building. The computer has shut the lights down. When the flow of current was shut off, the explosives were armed. At eight o'clock, the computer orders the electrical system on all over the building. That's when the bombs go off! Sweet Jesus! How much time do we have?"

Atwell grabbed Cole's flashlight. His Rolex watch kept perfect time. It was 7:59 pm.

Holy Mother of God! What was Cole to do? He couldn't search the wiring. That would take too much time. He had to cut the cable. But with what? Trying to remember every detail of the control room, Charles fumbled his way to the closet where emergency tools were located. Using his flashlight he searched for what he needed. He found a pair of bolt cutters.

He returned to the computer. He located the cable running directly from the motherboard into the panel. With tears streaming down his face, he placed the bolt cutters in position. Then he uttered a prayer. He begged God for help and for mercy. There was one thing Charles Cole knew for certain. There was live current in the 480 volt cable. If he made the cut he would die. If he didn't, there were a thousand others who surely would. There was no choice. Taking his last deep breath of life, he threw the full force of his being into his arms and cut the cable. There was a tremendous arc as the cable parted; molten metal showered the room. His hands remained clenched on the bolt cutters as the uniform he wore melted into his skin. Only the undamaged shadow of the man remained on the wall behind him with the stench of burning flesh.

■

Like a man devoid of all sanity, Sam fought his way through the crowd. Finally he could see them. Tanya stood high on the platform in the center of the stage. Sydney was crouched just below her, holding the microphone in place. The cameras were focused on the pretty child. Her hand rested upon the light switch.

"No!" Sam shrieked, waving his arms frantically. "Stop her!"

People glared at him with fury. Who was this madman? The sound of sirens could be heard wailing in the distance . . . getting closer and closer . . . but not close enough.

The final countdown began. The crowd roared the familiar chant.

10 . . . 9 . . . 8 . . .

Sam was barely three feet from the platform. He could see the mayor. He cried out. "Stop it!"

The mayor was flanked on either side by plainclothes detectives. They saw Sam running towards the platform. They heard his words but his words meant nothing. Sam was wildly flailing his arms. They had to wonder if he were armed.

7 . . . 6 . . . 5 . . .

They ordered Sam to halt but he kept coming. The mayor's cellular phone rang, but before he could answer it, the detectives shoved him to the ground out of any line of fire. They drew their weapons.

Positioned directly below the platform, Sydney had a direct view of Tanya. She could even see the mayor. She watched in disbelief as she saw his guards shove him aside and draw their weapons. Her eyes immediately flew to Stage Left. It was then she knew the danger. "SAM!"

4 . . . 3 . . . 2 . . .

He saw the guns. He knew they'd probably fire. He saw his wife's eyes. With a bounding leap, Sam hurled himself upon the platform. With the full force of his weight, he threw himself towards Tanya.

1 . . .

The child screamed from the startle of the impact as Sam threw her to the ground before she could throw the switch. A stunned crowd waited for the thrill of the colored bulbs. A thousand people stood in darkness at the Winds. The two armed detectives surrounded Sam, thrusting their guns to the back of his head. The Plaza remained dark. It was then they heard the explosion at Tripoli's.

Joe Morrison had to fight the urge to vomit. He'd seen plenty of blood in his day. But he'd never seen a human being carved up for profit.

"Get up!" he ordered the doctor. William Scofield was helpless to move. Cowering on his knees, he still cradled the human organ. Gingerly, Joe Morrison helped him to his feet. Not knowing what the doctor possessed, he asked, "What is it?"

"Say nothing!" Farhad Rajid warned.

"Shut the fuck up or I'll blow your goddamn brains out!" Morrison shouted. Training his revolver on the Iranian, he left no doubt he was sincere.

"What the fuck is it?" he repeated.

"It's his right kidney," the doctor quivered.

Joe Morrison and his men had certainly accomplished that which they had set out to do. They had caught Farhad Rajid and his cohorts in the act of stealing a human organ. He now had the evidence to crack their organization and bring these bastards to justice. Yet seeing the hapless victim slit open—with the doctor cradling his live organ—made capturing these animals in the act a meager consolation.

Morrison knelt down beside the unconscious victim. He was a Caucasian probably in his early forties. Joe wondered if he had a family. He placed two fingers on the man's neck and felt for a pulse. It was weak and very thready.

"He's still alive! Get an ambulance!" he ordered. George Massoud immediately picked up the phone to comply.

Joe felt helpless. The victim was bleeding heavily. He knew he couldn't trust the butcher's ability to safely reattach the organ. He glanced quickly around the hotel suite. He spotted the ice chest marked *"Human Organs."*

"What's that?"

"It's a container used for the preservation of organs."

"Put the kidney in there!" he ordered. The doctor quickly obeyed. After placing the organ on ice, Scofield returned to his comatose victim. He didn't know what to say or what to do. He began trembling violently. There were still bits of flesh clinging in between the fingers of his sterile gloves.

Staring at him in disbelief, Morrison roared, "My God! What have you done?"

Ned Powell trained his revolver on Nathan, the owner of the escort service. The man urinated in his pants.

"Down on your knees!" Powell ordered. Adeptly, he drove the man's face into the carpet while he cuffed his hands behind his back.

Just then an explosion rocked the Michelangelo. Morrison ran to the north window. It was the biggest window in the suite. It gave the best view of the Plaza. But the Plaza remained dark. Not a single Christmas light illuminated the Plaza, only smoke and a billowing fire.

Morrison struggled to get his bearings in the dark. It didn't take him long to determine where the explosion had taken place. It would take him a bit longer to figure out why.

"Get Rajid over here!"

Farhad Rajid, with his hands twisted painfully behind his back, was shoved to Joe Morrison's side by Ned Powell. Morrison drove his gun into Rajid's cheek.

"What has your brother done?" he demanded.

"Go to hell!" was the Iranian's only answer.

With the butt of his gun, Morrison knocked the smaller man to the ground. "You son of a bitch!" was his reply.

Morrison turned to his subordinate. "What's near Hassan's?" he asked.

"The jewelry store," Powell quickly answered. "Tripoli's!"

"That's it!" Morrison exclaimed. "He planned a jewelry heist. That's why he got the maniac to wire the Plaza to explode. He wanted to create a diversion so he could steal the jewels. That son of a bitch doesn't give a shit how many people he murders! We've got to stop him!"

Massoud cradled the phone. "We got a problem, Joe! There have been a number of casualties reported with the explosion. People are panicking. The police fear that a significant number of bystanders will be trampled as they try to get out of the Plaza. Every available unit has been dispatched to the area. The police are having a hell of a time getting any emergency vehicles through!"

Morrison stared at him in disbelief.

"It'll take a few minutes for our guys to get here. I can't even get an ambulance for this poor bastard. We can try to get a chopper in, but that's it!"

"Well then get me a chopper!" Morrison roared. "Let's go! George will come with me! Ned, you stay here and wait for back-up! If any of these fuckers give you trouble, shoot them. Don't kill them. Just fuck them up real good!"

The Michelangelo was a hotel designed to capture an old-world European flavor. That's why it was decorated with antique furniture. That's why old-fashioned radiators still graced every room. Joe Morrison took great pleasure in cuffing Farhad Rajid to the radiator.

"I wouldn't move if I were you," he warned. "Otherwise you're going to get burnt real bad!"

Morrison turned back to the unconscious victim. He knew there was no way he was going to make it. Not without immediate help. Slowly his eyes came to rest on the so-called surgeon who still wore his bloody gloves.

"What's your name?"

"William Scofield," the quaking man replied.

"You're a doctor, huh?"

Scofield nodded. "I'm a surgeon."

"Well I got to go, asshole. And you're the only son of a bitch who can keep this guy alive until help arrives. I have no idea when that will be. I'd do whatever it takes to try to stop the bleeding and save his life. Otherwise, you're going down for capital murder. Got that, motherfucker?"

■

Hidden in the alley directly behind his store, neither Hassan nor his men were injured in the blast. At eight o'clock, Ali Hassan had anticipated hearing the massive explosions he had planned with the bombing of the Winds and the Plaza. He was disappointed; but at the moment he was far more interested in the accuracy of the secondary charge Ralph Noland had set. After the blast, the men carefully entered the basement and made their way through the rubble towards what had once been the inner wall separating Hassan's and Tripoli's. Only a pile of rubble remained. Snapping his fingers, he ordered his men into the vault. True to his promise, Ralph Noland had set the perfect charge, blowing the door to the vault without damaging its precious contents.

Barking orders in his native tongue, Hassan urged his men onward. Time was critical. Seconds were vital. One by one, his trusted soldiers returned carrying bags of precious gems.

"We've got it all, sir!"

Quickly Hassan led his men out of the basement to the alley behind the store. He paused to savor the chaos he had created on the Plaza. The devastation was not nearly what he had hoped. Yet it gave him pleasure to hear the agonizing screams of those who had been injured and the wailing sirens of those trying to reach them.

It would be hours before anyone would be able to sift through the rubble and discover the robbery, but Ali Hassan was a man who took no chances. With cool precision, the group of soldiers crept in the dark to the undamaged building directly to the north. There they were met and let in by another of Hassan's men dressed in the uniform and carrying the keys of the security guard he had just murdered. The three-story office building was empty. Seeking the stairs, Hassan and his men climbed to the roof. There his helicopter was waiting.

■

It took fifteen minutes for Morrison's chopper to arrive. Out of airborne confusion, a single helicopter emerged hovering in front of the Michelangelo Hotel. It was plainly marked *"FBI."* The pilot studied the conditions carefully. He needed a safe place to set down, but the area was congested with abandoned cars and emergency vehicles. The police quickly directed him across the street to the creek. The city had been renovating Brush Creek for a year. The water had long ago been drained, the creek bed remained dry. The pilot landed the helicopter without incident.

Morrison issued his final orders to Massoud. "I'm leaving you in charge here. We can't do anything until we know for sure if Hassan is responsible for this. Mobilize our men and have them stand by. Call Bill Hoffman for reinforcements."

Morrison sprinted across the street to the helicopter. The sound of wailing sirens was deafening. He climbed on board and shook hands with the pilot. His name was Frank McGrade. Morrison quickly took his seat as McGrade lifted off.

"Where to?" he asked.

"Can you hover over the site of the explosion? I'll tell you then what I'm looking for."

Nodding, the pilot guided the chopper to the north. Observing the chaos below, he shouted above the engine's roar. "What a mess!"

Joe Morrison had to agree. There had been casualties from the explosion and the resulting stampede of the crowd. Luckily, the casualties were limited, the devastation contained in a single city block.

"Shine your light," Morrison ordered.

Avoiding power lines, the pilot brought his chopper as low as he safely could. Beaming his floodlight in all directions, Joe scanned the block carefully. There was chaos, confusion and damage, as he expected. Something further to the north caught his eye.

"Over there!" he shouted, pointing.

On a nearby rooftop behind Hassan's store, he spotted a group of men scrambling on board another helicopter.

Extinguishing his spotlight, McGrade approached the rooftop slowly. It was dark. Morrison couldn't be sure what he was seeing.

"Is it Life Flight?" he asked.

The pilot strained for a better look.

"I don't think so. It's bigger than a Life Flight craft. It's built to carry more people. I'd say it's an old Army chopper. I don't see any markings."

"That's what I thought. Follow him but be discreet. I don't want to tip our hand too soon."

Both helicopters proceeded north, some distance apart, flying high above power lines and houses, but below the path of approaching aircraft. Nearing downtown, the first helicopter slowed.

"He's approaching Municipal Airport. What do you want me to do?"

Morrison hesitated. Two airports serviced Kansas City, Municipal Airport and Kansas City International. The main international airport, KCI, was built to accommodate large commercial traffic. After it was built, the old Municipal Airport was maintained to service smaller, private planes.

It didn't take a genius to determine that Hassan was making his departure by private plane.

Morrison cursed. "Get the dispatcher!" he ordered. "Then patch me through to Massoud!"

Morrison had a dilemma. All available police units had been dispatched to the Plaza. The local police could be of no assistance. He had only his own small band of men to call upon. He knew from the start he was in trouble. Massoud would quickly confirm his worst fears.

■

Hassan's pilot landed their helicopter on a deserted strip of ground a short distance from the main runway. It was quiet at the downtown airport. It was Thanksgiving night after all. The snow had tapered to a soft mist. Still, most private planes were grounded. Hassan's own aircraft stood fueled and ready nearby. Everything had gone smoothly. The jewelry heist had been a success. Yet there were two things troubling the New Savak commander. One was the daughter he was forced to leave behind. The other was his brother. It was now well past their appointed hour. Farhad Rajid was nowhere in sight.

As the men loaded the jewels on board, Hassan turned to his trusted major-domo.

"Something has gone wrong, Mansur. Farhad should be here by now."

Mansur checked the time. It was fifteen minutes past nine.

"How long can we wait, sir?" Mansur inquired.

Ali Hassan sighed deeply. "Five more minutes," he replied. "That's all."

■

"Joe, we've got serious problems." It was Massoud's voice over the headset. "Back-up finally arrived and the prisoners are being transported to headquarters. The ambulance came but they were too late. The poor bastard bled to death. I left men at both the mansion and the hospital in case Hassan shows up either place. I've got three men with me. We're halfway downtown now."

Morrison had ordered his pilot to land a safe distance away from Hassan. In tense silence, they watched as Hassan's men prepared to depart. Morrison checked his Beretta. He wondered how heavily Hassan's men were armed.

The sound of sirens wailing in the distance startled Joe. It couldn't be his men. They had been ordered to come in quietly. He had no way of knowing it was the police, dispatched from north of the river to aid with the evacuation of the Plaza. It didn't matter. The sound of the approaching sirens made Ali Hassan's most difficult decision easier.

Hassan glanced at his watch a final time. His brother was not coming. The time had come to sacrifice both his daughter and his brother for the Cause.

He turned to Mansur. "We must go!"

Likewise, Morrison scanned the airfield for any sign of his own men. There was none. Leaving the helicopter pilot behind, with only his 9mm Beretta, he bolted for the plane. Too late. Cursing, he watched as Hassan's private plane taxied down the deserted runway and took off, veering into the darkness, heading southwest.

The force of the plane's take-off buffeted Joe with a swirling blanket of snow as he stood alone with his gun poised. It wouldn't do any good. He couldn't take on a plane—filled with armed men—lifting off into the dark night sky. He didn't have a make on the plane and Hassan wouldn't have filed a flight plan.

Shivering in the deathly stillness, Morrison realized that for now it was over. He had cracked the case, but the ultimate prize had just gotten away.

A thousand people, now safely evacuated from the Winds, had Charles Cole to thank for their lives, while Sam had averted a massive disaster on the Plaza. Charles Cole was dead and Sam in serious trouble. The Plaza would remain in darkness until the bomb squad had located and dismantled all explosives.

Sam had been handcuffed and transported downtown to Police Headquarters for interrogation. Sydney had followed. Her explanations made no sense to the detectives who'd not witnessed the near disaster. Only when Chief Andrews heard what happened was Sam finally released.

Sydney wanted to take her husband straight home. Sam wouldn't hear of it. There were at least thirty injuries resulting from the blast at Tripoli's that required medical attention. Sam's place was at his hospital. They were taken by squad car to St. Vincent's. It was there that Sydney located a badly shaken Tanya Cole. It was there they all heard the news about Charles. Sydney, Belva and Tanya put their arms around one another and wept.

It was well past midnight when Sydney found Sam just outside the Emergency Room.

"Sam, I only have a few minutes," said Sydney. "I have to meet Jake. We'll be working all night broadcasting the story for CNN and we're the lead-off story tomorrow morning on *Good Morning America, CBS This Morning* and the *Today* show."

Sydney allowed herself the satisfaction of only a brief smile.

She understood that this national exposure could be a turning point in her career. But there was another matter weighing on her mind.

"Could we check on Lydia? If Hassan is truly gone, then she's all alone."

Sam kissed his wife briefly. "Afraid I can't, Sydney. I'm scheduled in the OR. Luckily most of the casualties from the blast at Tripoli's are not life threatening, but I'll be in surgery for the next several hours. You go. Give Lydia my love. I'll stop in to see her later."

Although the hospital was filling rapidly, the Heart Unit remained quiet. The child slept peacefully, unaware of what had happened that night. Sydney sat down on the bed and gently woke her. Opening her eyes, Lydia smiled.

"Sydney, is that you?"

"I'm here, honey," she replied.

"Where's my father?"

There was a catch in her voice when she said, "I don't know."

Lydia's question seemed so innocent. "Is Thanksgiving over yet?"

Sydney sighed. She'd never been happier to see a particular holiday end.

"Yes, Lydia. Thanksgiving is over."

Now fully awake, Lydia sat up in bed. "My father told me to give you something as soon as Thanksgiving was over."

Holding something tightly in her right hand, Lydia reached with her left hand for a sealed envelope which she had been told to keep hidden beneath her sheet. Sydney took it. She turned on the light by the child's bed. She read the single handwritten page carefully. Tears clouded her vision. She struggled to find her voice.

"Your father says that he loves you very much, Lydia. For reasons he cannot explain, he must leave you. He wants you to be with someone who loves you as much as he does. He wants you to be with Sam and me."

At first Lydia looked startled. Then she smiled. Slowly she unclenched her right hand. There was the mustard seed necklace Sydney had given her.

"I remembered what you told me about the necklace. I believed everything would be okay. It is."

Sydney took her new daughter in her arms and held her. The curtains in Lydia's room were open. The lights on the Plaza remained darkened. But the joy in two people's hearts burned bright.

■

The Kansas City story ran continuously the next morning on all three major networks and CNN. Details of the Iranian plot, as well as the suicide at St. Vincent's Hospital were broadcast throughout the country and abroad. Because of the coverage and a frantic phone call from Kentucky, a woman found herself in a cab outside St. Vincent's Hospital at eleven o'clock Friday morning. She was accompanied by a small boy.

"Wait here," she told the cab driver. The stately woman took the child firmly by the hand and led him inside the main entrance of the hospital. The child carried a small suitcase. The woman's luggage remained in the cab.

The silver-haired woman, whose features were sharp and body taut, sat down in a chair in the lobby. She positioned the child directly in front of her and fussed with his denim shirt.

"All right now, Daniel. What did your nana tell you?" *Nana* was the child's special name for his grandmother.

"I get to see my mommy now."

"That's right, Daniel. See that elevator?"

The child nodded.

"Push the button to six. Then ask them to take you to Mrs. Stein."

"But my mommy's name is Kathleen Clay."

"Yes," Margaret said, "I know. Mommy is playing pretend. Now who are you to ask for?"

"Mrs. STEIN," Daniel repeated.

Margaret opened her large purse and took out a Manila envelope. "This is very important, Daniel. Give it to your mommy."

Daniel took the envelope and held it tightly in his right hand. Inside were three items of importance: a check to the hospital for Kathleen's expenses, her final divorce decree, and legal documents establishing a trust fund for Daniel. The contents of the envelope represented the satisfaction of Margaret's perceived debt to a woman who'd been brutalized and nearly killed by her son . . . to a child who belonged with his mother . . . to a grandson she loved who was not her own.

When the story broke, it became clear to Margaret that Michael was behind the plot to murder Kathleen. She had called her son then. He told her that Solomon Bucy would delay his arrest as long as possible, but he was desperate. It was then Margaret understood that a bond between a mother and son could not—should not—be broken. That's why she'd brought Kathleen's child here.

"I must go now, Daniel." Tears misted her eyes. "I'll miss you."

"When will I see you again?"

"Soon," she promised. "Real soon." She lied.

For a moment she held the boy tightly. Then she walked him to the elevator and watched him march inside.

As the door slowly closed she heard a man say, "What floor do you want, son?"

"Six, please. I'm going to see my mommy. Her name is Mrs. Stein."

Standing erect, Margaret Clay glanced at her watch, then quickly left the hospital. Her cab was waiting.

"To the airport," she said. "Hurry."

Margaret Clay had a plane to catch. She prayed she was in time.

■

4:00 pm

Solomon Bucy rode in the back of a Kentucky State Trooper's car. They were on their way to the site where once Maggie Hall had stood. He'd been alone at the mansion when the police arrived. Henry, the butler, and Max, the driver, had been dismissed. Tony Baxter, Michael's personal care assistant, had vanished.

The police accompanied Solomon Bucy to a bridge overlooking the Ohio River. Michael Clay was nowhere to be found. His wheelchair teetered precariously on the bridge's edge. There were ice chunks dotting the water.

"He told me that he'd rather die than go to prison," Bucy reported.

The police looked on in bewilderment. There were questions that needed answers.

Where was the body, for one? And how could a man who was paralyzed find the strength to hurl himself off the bridge?

It would be months before they could dredge the river with the spring thaw. It might be years before they had their answers.

It was Christmas Eve in Kansas City. After several weeks, the lights had been repaired. The Plaza was once again—as in years past—brilliantly lit. A north wind was blowing, and fresh snow drifted outside the front door of the Colonial house on Verona Circle. Inside, a fire burned brightly in the hearth. Sam and Sydney were not alone. They were hosting a party to celebrate life and healing.

Philip and Kathleen were the guests of honor. Kathleen's son, Daniel, was there. Belva and Tanya Cole had been invited, along with Jake Kahn. Even Joe Morrison had decided to remain in Kansas City for Christmas so he could be present at this unique gathering.

The adults congregated in the living room to sip champagne while the children played in the rest of the house. Jake Kahn took Belva Cole aside. "I know how lonely you must be," he said simply.

"I have Tanya," she replied quietly.

"Your husband was a true hero. A thousand people owe their lives to him."

"He was a man of honor. He could do no less."

"What do you mean?"

"The people of this city cared enough to give my baby life. It was Charles's turn to give back."

"How are you doing?"

"Gary Atwell had a trust fund established for us. So many people have donated that Tanya and I will be well taken care of. But of course no amount of money can take my husband's place."

Holding hands, Kathleen and Philip warmed themselves by the fire. "You've never looked prettier," Philip whispered.

"Are you getting tired?" Kathleen asked, concerned as always about his health.

"Not yet," Philip replied. "It's good to get out."

Kathleen glanced fondly at her son. Then she studied her ring with pride. Finally her wistful sapphire eyes found Philip's. She dared to ask the question that plagued her.

"Do you think it's safe to be happy yet?"

Philip took his time answering. He flashed back to his own shooting. He recalled Ralph Noland's suicide. Then his thoughts, like Kathleen's, focused upon a wheelchair teetering over a bridge and a body that had not yet been discovered. He searched his gut for the truth. He never wanted to lie to Kathleen.

"I hope so, honey. I think it's our turn."

Joe Morrison came up to them. "When are you two getting married?"

Philip and Kathleen gazed at one another in their special way. Even the ultimate cynic thought them kind of cute. "Valentine's Day," Philip answered.

"Where?"

"Have you heard of St. John's?" Kathleen asked.

"Sure," Joe replied. "It's an island in the Virgin Islands. You could get married at sunset on the beach."

Sydney came up to stand beside Joe. "That sounds romantic."

Just then Sam came over to join them. "How much longer will you be in Kansas City, Joe?"

"It'll take a few more days to wrap things up. You wouldn't believe the network Rajid had created. He had contacts all over the country. He brokered thousands of human organs over the past few years. He funneled his brother millions of dollars."

Sam was sickened at the mention of Farhad Rajid. He blamed himself for not realizing his hospital was being so wrongly used. Joe seemed to read his mind.

"St. Vincent's played only a small part in his operation. Rajid had doctors from everywhere on his payroll. One is a famous heart surgeon in St. Louis. Greed corrupts even good people, Sam.

Speaking of good people," he said, shifting the subject, "what is fame doing for you, Sydney?"

Now it was Sydney's turn to blush. Thanks to her mentor, Jake Kahn, Sydney had gained national recognition as the investigative reporter who broke the story. She had received offers from all over the country to work for other stations, even one of the major networks. She had turned them all down.

Overhearing their conversation, Jake Kahn raised his glass of champagne to his hostess. "To the best damned investigative reporter I've ever seen! You've made me proud, little lady!"

The others raised their glasses in salute.

"I had to scramble to beat other offers. I kept my word and offered her the anchor's chair. She wanted more."

"What we've started here is too important to end. I want to anchor the nightly news and host a weekly program to air in-depth investigative stories."

"What choice do I have?" Kahn said. "I don't intend to let her go."

Sam watched his wife walk away. The look on his face was one of sheer pride.

"You've got yourself one hell of a fine lady!" Joe conceded. "You're a lucky man."

"Thank you, Joe."

"I want to thank you, Sam, for all your help these past few weeks. You and Sydney are fine people."

Sam shook Morrison's hand warmly.

"So how's the kid doing?" Morrison asked.

Sam's gentle eyes searched for Lydia. She was happily playing Nintendo with Tanya and Daniel. Knowing she had never been permitted friends, this warmed his heart.

"She's doing pretty well," he replied. "She seems to be adjusting."

"Does she miss her father?" Morrison asked.

"At first she did. Now we've become a family. I think she's really quite happy."

Sam hesitated. He had a question of his own to ask. "Do you have any word on Hassan?"

Morrison shook his head no. "He was spotted in London

briefly. He disappeared after that. I want the bastard, Sam. I want him real bad."

Sam laid his hand gently upon Joe's shoulder. "We'll all rest easier when you get him."

"Yeah, you got that right."

"Say, Joe," said Sam, "let me get you another drink."

The FBI agent leaned back against the hearth and studied the happy faces all around him. Philip and Kathleen. Sam, Sydney, Jake Kahn. It was Christmas Eve. This was one holiday Joe Morrison didn't mind celebrating. He would cherish these memories. He had so few friends.

Fumbling in his pocket, he desperately needed a smoke. He hoped nobody would mind. He rolled the butt between his thumb and index finger. Then he turned his back on the happy crowd. If there was a serpent in this Eden, it was the thought of Ali Hassan. He was still free. That left Sam and Sydney vulnerable. It didn't matter that legally they would adopt the child or that Lydia loved them. She was still Hassan's possession.

And so while the lilt of happy chatter filled the room and the celebration of Christmas continued, Joe Morrison lit his cigarette. Leaning against the mantle of the fireplace, he watched the dancing flames. He pondered the question that had plagued him for days.

"When in hell will the monster return?"

To order additional copies of

Twisted Lights

or

to arrange speaking engagements with Susan M. Hoskins

contact:

Integrity Press, Ltd.
P.O. Box 8277
Prairie Village, KS 66208
Phone (913) 384-1199

e-mail: integritypress@sprintmail.com

Be looking For *Twisted Secrets*,
the sequel, to be released Spring 1998.